PR

SH

"A brilliant debut."

—Steve Cavanagh

"An excellent crime novel, full of humor and pathos as well as utterly realistic action. A stunning debut."

—Elly Griffiths

"A thrilling debut…If you are a fan of police procedurals, this one set in the mean streets of Liverpool is for you."

—Mari Hannah

"A superb debut…Gritty, well-paced and packed with vividly drawn characters. T. M. Payne has hit the ground running with *Long Time Dead.*"

—M. W. Craven

"T. M. Payne is one of the most talented storytellers of our time. The gripping and authentic storytelling, clever and deeply satisfying plot and superb characters makes *This Ends Now* my standout novel of the year and puts Payne at the top table of crime writers."

—Graham Bartlett

"Make way for the brilliant Detective Sheridan Holler! True fans of Val McDermid will love Payne's writing."

—A. J. West

"A twisty, compelling, page-turning cracker of a debut. Full of great characters, T.M. Payne's *Long Time Dead* is so absorbing you'll miss your bus stop AND stay up past your bedtime. Perfect for fans of Val McDermid and Michael Connelly."

—Chris Merritt

"Dark and gripping, expertly plotted, and full of warmth and humour—you won't want this book to end."

—Mel Sherratt

"A propulsive and character driven mystery woven with authenticity and aplomb."

—Victoria Selman

"A brilliant and compassionate new detective joins the scene."

—Claire McGowan

"Such a great series. DI Sheridan Holler is one of my all-time favourite detectives. Written with warmth and humour, as well as a dark and twisty tale."

—Jo Callaghan

"TM Payne's 18-year career in the criminal justice system brings authenticity to every page of *This Ends Now*. An expertly woven plot combined with the warmth and wit of the main character, DI Sheridan Holler, make this second book in the series a must read for all crime fiction fans. A cracking police procedural. Don't miss this one!"

—D. S. Butler

"A gripping and gritty start to what promises to be an excellent new police procedural series."

—David Fennell

"T. M. Payne is one of the most exciting new voices in crime fiction. In *Long Time Dead*, she crafts a richly-textured thriller that brims with authentic detail. I loved the humor, the poignancy and the intricate rendering of Liverpool in all its heart and grit. The comparisons to Val McDermid are well earned indeed."

—Kia Abdullah

"Good twists, and plenty of red herrings, and the book builds to a very tense and unexpected conclusion, with some neat stings in the tale...a really quick and engaging read."

—*Deadly Pleasures Mystery Magazine*

"Worth every interminable minute it takes to wind down."

—Kirkus Reviews

PLAY WITH FIRE

ALSO BY T. M. PAYNE

Long Time Dead

This Ends Now

PLAY WITH FIRE

A DETECTIVE SHERIDAN HOLLER THRILLER

T. M. PAYNE

This is a work of fiction. Names, characters, organizations, places, events, and incidents are either products of the author's imagination or are used fictitiously. Any resemblance to actual persons, living or dead, or actual events is purely coincidental.

Published by Thomas & Mercer, Seattle

www.apub.com

ISBN-13: 9781662511318
eISBN: 9781662511325

Cover design by Dan Mogford
Cover image: ©GidioiDiana ©Addictive Creative / Shutterstock; ©Rekha Garton / ArcAngel

Printed in the United States of America

For Susie

There but for the grace of you, go I.

The storms are coming, so hold your breath
For one brings rage, and one brings death.
While Satan watches from the wings, awaiting
what will be
He will pretend that he's your friend.
Four souls. Two blind. Two see.
He's found you now, too late to run
And now the stakes are higher –
It's the sacrifice of men and mice
And those who play with fire.

PROLOGUE

Saturday 10 August 1974
Liverpool

Melissa Sinclair glanced into the pram and smiled, adjusting the blanket slightly around the little face that stared back at her.

'Can I push Molly now, Mummy?' Melissa's five-year-old daughter, April, asked excitedly as she held her mother's free hand.

'Maybe later, eh?' Melissa gripped April's hand tighter as they crossed the road.

'Is she asleep?' April asked, jumping up and down, trying to peek into the pram.

'Yes, she's asleep and we don't want to wake her, do we?' Melissa whispered.

'Where are we going?' April scratched her head, causing the little red bow that was weaved through her hair to come undone.

Melissa stopped and knelt down, deftly fixing the bow. 'We're taking a present to a friend. And then we're going to Woolworths to buy you a new dress because you've been such a good girl.' She held April's face in her hands for a moment. Melissa Sinclair had been eighteen when she'd fallen pregnant with April. She'd kept the pregnancy a secret for as long as she could, wanting to avoid the judging gossip that would inevitably erupt once the truth was out.

She had her own little flat and although money was always tight, she managed. Fiercely independent, Melissa struggled through, doing whatever it took to survive. But when she was twenty-two, she had fallen pregnant again. She rode the gossip, the pointing fingers, and the verbal abuse from her neighbours – but at night while she sat alone in her flat, with her two children sleeping in the bedroom they shared, she thought about how her life could have been so different. She'd watch out of her window as girls the same age as her would walk off into town for a drink with their mates, squealing with excitement when smartly dressed young men with cigarettes balanced on their bottom lips would whistle at them from across the street.

The sun was high in the sky by the time Melissa turned the corner on to Church Street. The place was full of shoppers dressed for the blistering heat of the day.

'Shall we get an ice cream later, April?' Melissa smiled down at her daughter, who was frantically nodding her head.

'Can we get one *now,* Mummy?' April tugged on her mother's arm.

'We just need to drop this present off and then we'll get one, I promise.' Melissa approached The Mason's Arms pub door and turned the pram around, opening the door with her backside and lifting the pram wheels over the step.

'Here, love.' A voice made her look up. An older gentleman with a slick black tie and slicker hair flicked his cigarette away and lifted the front of the pram for her, slowly easing it through the door before patting April on the head. 'Aren't you the pretty one, eh?' He winked.

'Thank you,' Melissa called out as he carried on walking down the road, immediately lighting up another cigarette.

The Mason's Arms was one of several pubs in Liverpool that turned a blind eye to children coming in. The place was thick with smoke hanging in the air like London smog. A row of men in dark suits lined the bar, resting their elbows on the counter as they sipped on froth-headed beers. An older, glamorous woman with perfect hair whipped up on top of her head like candyfloss stood behind the bar, drying glasses with a tea towel.

In the corner was a group of young men, deep in conversation, sharing a bottle of Scotch as they huddled together.

Melissa pushed the pram towards the bar, holding April's hand while she looked around the place.

'Yes, love? What can I get you?' The glamorous woman set her cigarette in the ashtray in front of her, its tip smeared with thick red lipstick.

'I'll have a Coke, please.' Melissa reached into her handbag for some change and after paying for her drink, she took a sip before holding the glass to April's lips. Setting the glass down on the bar, Melissa reached into the pram and pulled the blanket back. Revealing the little face. The little hands.

The little white face of the clock, the little hands of the clock.

And then she pressed the button.

The deafening explosion tore through the pub, glass boomed out and shattered on to the street. Splinters of wood and metal shot in all directions. Those who weren't killed instantly scrabbled out on their hands and knees, desperate to escape the fireball before it engulfed them.

CHAPTER 1

Present day
Friday 6 March 2009
Hale Street Police Station, Liverpool

Detective Inspector Sheridan Holler rubbed her temples and squinted at the clock just as Detective Chief Inspector Hill Knowles stomped into her office.

'Who do I need to bloody shout at about the constant drilling noise in the backyard? What buffoon decided to organise building work during the week and not at the weekend?' Hill was clearly in her usual bad mood.

Sheridan rested her hands behind her head and leaned back in her chair. 'I'm surprised you haven't been down there to yell at them,' she replied, knowing full well that Hill had already done that, the whole nick having heard it.

'I've already tried that.' Hill walked over to the window and scowled down at the men working below.

'And what did they say?'

'They said they couldn't hear me over the noise of their drills.'

Sheridan sucked in a smile. 'They'll be finished by Monday and you're off until then, so try not to let it get to you. Anyway, what have you got planned for the weekend?'

'Absolutely fuck-all.' Hill turned to walk out as Detective Sergeant Anna Markinson appeared in the doorway.

'You've got a visitor in reception,' she said, nodding at Sheridan.

Sheridan sat forward. 'Nice visitor or shit visitor?'

'Gabriel Howard.'

Hill Knowles looked at Sheridan and Anna, crossing her arms tightly across her chest.

'I didn't know he was out.' Sheridan frowned. 'What does he want?'

'Who's Gabriel Howard?' Hill snapped.

Anna continued, still addressing Sheridan. 'I've just spoken to Probation, he was released on licence two days ago. His only licence condition is an exclusion zone. Plus, there's the usual stuff – like reporting to his probation officer and keeping out of trouble.' Anna perched on the edge of Sheridan's desk.

Hill impatiently repeated her question. 'Hello? Who's Gabriel Howard?'

'I dealt with him briefly in October last year. It was just after the Parks case. You were on leave, but I did tell you about it,' Sheridan responded.

'Well, remind me,' Hill said. 'I can't keep every single case of yours in my head.'

Sheridan went on to inform Hill that Gabriel Howard had been locked up in October 2008, after being caught leaving the scene of a burglary. As someone with only a history of violence, breaking into properties was a new one for him. And he wasn't very good at it. The property he'd selected belonged to a male called Oliver Elliot, who was out at the time Gabriel broke in. It transpired that Oliver Elliot stayed at his girlfriend's flat every Wednesday night and would return the next day. It was assumed, although never proven during the investigation, that Gabriel Howard had been watching the property for some time and had very carefully chosen his moment to break in.

What Gabriel didn't know was that a few days earlier, Oliver had brought his eighty-seven-year-old mother, Edith, to stay with him. And the elderly woman was upstairs in bed when Gabriel gained entry.

By the time Gabriel reached Edith's bedroom, she had already dialled 999 from the phone beside her bed. The 999 call-handler stated that Edith didn't speak during the call, but her address was obtained from the landline number and officers were dispatched. Unfortunately for Gabriel Howard, there was a patrol vehicle around the corner and officers arrived seconds later – just in time to catch Gabriel leaving.

When officers entered the house, they found Edith sat up in bed, the phone still in her hand and the call still live. Edith Elliot had died while making that 999 call. Initially it was suspected that Gabriel had killed her, but the post-mortem concluded she had died from a heart attack. Edith Elliot had many ailments, including late-stage heart failure. Her medical records showed that her life expectancy was severely limited, and she might not have lived much more than a few weeks in any event. Oliver had moved her in temporarily and she was due to go into a hospice the following week to receive end-of-life care.

'If the patrol car hadn't been so close, Gabriel would have got away with it. There was literally nothing to link him to the break-in. He didn't leave any forensic evidence, and no one saw or heard anything. It looked like he'd entered the property through an open downstairs window, although Oliver Elliot swore it was closed when he left the house. Nothing was taken, but he didn't get the chance to steal anything. Once he saw Edith on the phone, he legged it.'

‘Didn’t we seek a more serious offence, seeing as Edith died as a result of Gabriel being in the house?’ Hill asked.

Sheridan nodded once. ‘We did, but CPS wouldn’t run it, the general consensus being that Edith was extremely poorly with literally weeks to live, if that. CPS were adamant that we didn’t have enough evidence and a jury would never convict him. I challenged it but they wouldn’t budge.’

‘And he’d been watching the house?’ Hill asked.

‘We assumed he had, because he knew that Oliver Elliot wouldn’t be there. In his interview he denied that he’d been checking the place out – said he just picked the house at random. He admitted he was in there looking for stuff to steal. That’s the only reason he was charged with burglary.’

‘His solicitor didn’t give him very good legal advice then?’ Hill Knowles replied.

‘He didn’t have a solicitor. He declined one.’

‘Now that he’s out, do I need to worry that our burglary rate will go up?’ Hill asked.

‘No, he’s not prolific,’ Sheridan said. ‘He’s got a couple of convictions for violence – mostly against other men. One of his victims was a guy in a pub who slapped his own girlfriend. Gabriel saw what happened and punched the guy in the face. Broke his jaw.’

Hill raised an eyebrow. ‘Fair enough.’

‘If you meet him, he doesn’t come across as your usual thug though. He’s actually very intelligent. A fitness fanatic who doesn’t drink, doesn’t smoke and hates druggies.’

Anna interjected. ‘Didn’t he swallow some drugs just before he was arrested?’

Sheridan shook her head. ‘He swallowed something, but it wasn’t drugs.’

‘What was it then?’ Hill asked.

‘We don’t know.’ Sheridan shrugged.

'I take it he's living on our patch. Is he married? Kids?'

Anna answered. 'He's staying with his sister, Denise – she's divorced. He's not married and neither of them have kids.'

'Why do you think he wants to see you?' Hill asked, turning her attention to Sheridan.

'I'm about to find out.' Sheridan left the room and made her way downstairs with Anna in tow. As they reached the bottom, Sheridan turned to Anna.

'Does Oliver Elliot know that Gabriel's out?'

'Yeah, Probation told him . . . and he knows about the exclusion zone.'

'Any concerns that Oliver might be looking for revenge?'

'Apparently not. When Probation spoke to him, he didn't give any indication of that. He was talking more about forgiveness, not revenge.'

Gabriel Howard was in reception, staring out of the door. He turned his head when Sheridan and Anna stepped into the foyer.

'What do you want, Gabriel?' Sheridan asked bluntly.

Gabriel shiftily glanced at Anna before whispering to Sheridan, 'Can we talk somewhere private?'

'We can talk *here*. What do you want?'

Gabriel looked around. There was one person sitting in the corner looking like he had crawled out of a skip, and another at the counter demanding to see the 'chief superintendent inspector', much to the veiled amusement of the public enquiry officer behind the screen. No such rank existed and even if it did, the chief superintendent inspector probably wouldn't deal with the neighbour whose dog had shit on your herbaceous border six times in the last two weeks.

Gabriel kept his voice low. 'I just wanted you to know that I'm out on licence and I want to ask that you lot leave me alone. I'm living at my sister's. She works long hours, and doesn't need the bizzies turning up in the middle of the night banging on the door and checking up on me.'

Sheridan crossed her arms. 'Why would we do that? You're not on a curfew. Trust me, I wish you were.'

Gabriel slowly shook his head. 'I'm sorry about the old lady. I really am.' Sincerity crept into his words, and he dropped his head for a moment.

Sheridan stepped forward. She kept her voice low, her face inches from Gabriel's. 'Can you imagine how terrified she would have been? Imagine that was your mother or your grandmother, how would you feel? If you hadn't broken into her house, she would have died in peace, not out of fear of you being there – I hope you realise that.'

'I made a mistake. I've done my time. I just want to be left alone now, make a fresh start. I said I'm sorry about the old lady.'

Sheridan took a step back. 'Goodbye, Gabriel.' She turned on her heel and made her way to the door leading into the station.

As she waited for the public enquiry officer to buzz her and Anna in, she turned to Gabriel. 'Oh, and that old lady had a name. But you've probably forgotten that, haven't you?' The buzzer sounded and Sheridan held the door for Anna, while Gabriel watched as they walked off down the corridor.

'Edith Elliot,' he said under his breath, his hands balled into fists. 'Her name was Edith Elliot.'

CHAPTER 2

As they sat at the kitchen table, situated by a large window at the front of the house, looking out on to their long drive, Adrian Crow watched as his wife, Caroline, put her knife and fork down.

'I fixed that bird box earlier, while you were in the bath. Hopefully we'll get some interest soon. Be nice to see birds using it, eh?'

Caroline wiped her mouth with a napkin. 'Yes. That would be lovely.'

'I meant to ask you yesterday, how was swimming club?'

'It was fine. Same as usual.'

'You seem a bit quiet, love. Are you okay?' He pushed his plate to one side and rested his elbows on the table.

'I'm fine, darling. I just feel a bit tired. Might get an early night.' Caroline smiled at him as she stood up to clear the dishes away.

'I'll do that. Why don't you pour a nice glass of wine and go and sit down?'

Walking around the table, she gently held his face in her hands, and looking into his eyes, she kissed him on the lips. 'I love you,' she whispered.

'I love you too.' He smiled sheepishly. 'Don't be mad at me but I've got to go into work tomorrow.'

Caroline walked across the open-plan kitchen and opened the fridge. 'Really? Why?' She pulled out a bottle of wine and reached into the cupboard above her head for two glasses.

'I've got a meeting in Manchester at nine.'

'So, you'll be home after the meeting?'

'No. I'm then off to Birmingham to meet a client.'

'What time will you be home then?' Caroline poured the wine.

'Late, I'm afraid, probably not before seven.'

'Bloody hell, love, you're going to burn yourself out, working weekends. Please think about taking some time off.'

'I will.' He stood up and started clearing away the dinner plates. 'Have you got any ideas about what I can get you for your birthday?'

'Not really. I wouldn't make too much fuss, it's not a special one.'

'You'll be fifty-nine, so I'll get you something cheap and nasty and then buy you an expensive present for your sixtieth next year.' He grinned cheekily.

Caroline felt her jaw tense as she sipped her wine. 'You don't have to spoil me.'

'I think I'll take you away somewhere. Yes, that's it, I'll whisk you off on a romantic trip for two.'

Her throat suddenly felt like it was closing up and she began to cough so hard she felt like she was choking.

'Are you alright, love?' Adrian touched her shoulder.

Caroline put her hand up. 'I'm fine. The wine went down the wrong way.' She quickly made her way upstairs to the bathroom, before lifting the toilet seat and vomiting into the pan. Taking deep breaths, she rinsed her mouth out, splashed water on her face and quickly patted it dry with a towel before rejoining Adrian in the kitchen.

She listened as he talked excitedly about her birthday. The more he talked, the more she could feel the bile rising once again and the guilt bearing down on her.

CHAPTER 3

Saturday 7 March

Caroline Crow waved as Adrian pulled away. She pulled her cardigan tighter around her as a chilly March breeze blew across the driveway. She continued watching until his car disappeared before turning back into the house. Quickly checking out of the window that he wasn't returning for something he'd forgotten, she made her way upstairs to grab the bag that was hidden secretly at the back of her wardrobe.

Flipping the phone open and turning it on, she dialled his number.

'Hi.' He sounded out of breath.

'Hi, are you okay to speak?'

'Yes, I'm fine, just out for a run.'

'Are you free to come round? It's safe, Adrian's at work all day.'

'I'll be there shortly. Do you need me to bring the usual?'

'Yes, please. See you soon.'

Thirty minutes later, Caroline was standing at the front door, her heart pounding so hard that she felt light-headed.

Smiling as his Mercedes pulled on to the gravel drive in front of the house, she stepped back inside as he got out and walked towards her.

Closing the front door behind him, they wrapped their arms around each other. 'I'm so glad you could come. How long have you got?'

He checked his watch. 'Couple of hours.'

Ten minutes later, he emerged from the bedroom, glancing back to see Caroline buttoning up her blouse before running her fingers through her hair.

'Would you like a coffee?' she called as he stood in the kitchen, staring out of the window.

'Yes, please. Are you alright?'

'Well, no.' She appeared behind him, smiling.

'Sorry. You know what I mean.' He inhaled deeply as he held her tightly, letting his lips touch her hair.

'I'll be fine.'

He stepped back and with his hands on his hips, he quickly asked, 'Adrian still doesn't suspect anything, does he?'

'No. Definitely not. I've been super-careful. He can't find out what we're doing. I can't tell him – it would destroy him. I do need you to do something for me though, if you've got some spare time today.'

After finishing his coffee, he got back into his car and started the engine, waving at her as he turned the steering wheel. His stomach heaved and he thought for a moment that he was going to be sick. Reaching for a bottle of water in the door, his hands shook while he unscrewed the lid and took a sip.

He knew it would all be over soon. He had been careful so far. Careful not to leave any evidence.

Anything that could link him to her.

CHAPTER 4

Gabriel Howard glanced up at the sky and felt snowflakes fall on to his face. Holding out his gloved hand, he watched as they landed in his palm and he allowed himself a smile. Buttoning up his coat, he walked around the corner and heard the 'ding' above the door when he stepped into his sister Denise's shop Fairweather Flowers. Taking advantage of her being on the phone, he slipped behind the counter and flicked the kettle on in the back room, checking the cupboard for biscuits.

Denise's face suddenly appeared around the door.

He looked up. 'I need to borrow your car, sis.'

'That works for me – because I need you to do me a favour and I'll tell you where the biscuits are if you say yes.'

Gabriel was on his knees, reaching into the back of the cupboard, emerging victoriously with a pack of bourbons. 'Ha-ha. Too late. Found them.'

Denise playfully slapped him across the back of his head. 'Don't you dare open them, Gabe – I mean it.' She grinned as she snatched the packet from his hand. 'Too slow.'

'Okay, you win. What's the favour?' He pulled himself up and readjusted the back of his coat.

'I need you to do a couple of deliveries for me.' She handed him a slip of paper.

Gabriel looked at his watch. 'Okay. But I can't be running around all day, I've got places to be. Can't Donny do them?'

'He's out on three jobs already. It won't take you long. Please, Gabe? Business is starting to pick up again and I really need these orders to go out as soon as.'

Gabriel felt an instant pang of guilt. After his arrest for the Edith Elliot burglary, the local gossip was that he had strangled her in her bed. Denise's business had suffered in the months following his sentence, but she had slowly built it back up, even after a bouquet was left on the doorstep one morning with a card attached that read, '*Rest in peace, Edith Elliot.*'

Before Gabriel's arrest, Denise Fairweather had been a popular figure in the area, known for her bubbly personality and generosity, often giving discounts to her regular customers, charging less when flowers were bought for Mother's Day, or special occasions. And when her neighbour's seven-year-old son died suddenly, Denise had supplied the flowers for his funeral at no cost to the grieving family.

When Gabriel first went to prison, Denise found herself sitting alone in the shop, surrounded by flowers that no one seemed to want any more. Locals would walk past, glance in and carry on without popping in for their usual friendly chat. She could see the years and money she had invested in the place slowly disappearing down the drain. Then, one morning as she was setting up, one of her regulars stopped outside to talk to her. Denise had explained that although the local papers had practically branded Gabriel a murderer, he had shown genuine remorse for entering that property and for Edith Elliot's subsequent death, which had been an accident.

After that day, gradually, the local community came round and, in solidarity, they stopped walking past the shop. Now, they pushed the door open and came inside. Denise's past generosity and friendliness preceded her and, slowly but surely, her business began to flourish again.

Gabriel knew that his actions and what had happened to Edith Elliot could have destroyed Denise's business and he carried the darkness of his guilt with him every day. And so, when she had asked him to help her out with these deliveries, he knew he had to do it.

He glanced at the addresses on the piece of paper that Denise had handed him, and was about to slip it into his pocket when his eyes fixed on one address. He looked up at Denise, who had turned her back to him and was busying herself with a flower display, before staring at the slip of paper.

He bit down hard on his bottom lip and forced a smile. 'Okay, I'll do the deliveries. What's it worth?'

Denise turned around to face him. 'It's worth me letting you use my car until you get your own one.' She pursed her lips and flicked his nose with her middle finger. 'And two biscuits.'

'Fair enough.' He folded the note and slipped it into his coat pocket.

'Make sure you get to the Julie Jones delivery before half three – she wants them within the hour.'

'The first job's closer; I'll do that one before I do Julie Jones. But don't worry, I'll get to her in time.'

Denise opened the packet and handed him two bourbons. 'There's a good boy.' She smiled and kissed him on the cheek.

An hour later, Gabriel pulled up outside Julie Jones' address and carefully lifted the bouquet that was resting on the passenger seat.

He was about to knock on the door when it was opened by a cheery-looking woman enveloped in a thick white dressing gown, a pale blue towel wrapped around her head.

'Julie Jones?' Gabriel asked.

'Yes. Thank you so much for getting them here so quickly.'

'No problem.' Gabriel nodded.

'While you're here, I need a tiny favour. Can you pop in for two minutes?'

Gabriel pulled his coat sleeve back and checked his watch. 'Sure.'

She took the bouquet from him. 'Can you just give me a sec to make myself look decent?'

'Of course.' Gabriel waited on the doorstep.

Two minutes later, she reopened the door. 'Please come in.'

Gabriel wiped his feet and stepped inside. The house was roasting hot. Gabriel Howard automatically undid his coat, feeling his cheeks flush with the sudden shift in temperature.

Twenty minutes later, he emerged and quickly got back into his car. As he pulled away, he checked his wing mirror to see if she was still standing there, but she'd already gone back inside. He called Denise.

She answered. 'Everything alright?'

'Yeah, fine. Deliveries all done.' He pulled out on to the main road and stopped at the red light.

'Cheers, Gabe. See you later. Love ya.'

'Love ya too, sis.'

Gabriel was about to pull away, as the lights turned green, when he felt a bump from behind, nudging his car slightly forward.

Checking his mirror, he spotted the driver behind put his hand up apologetically.

'Bollocks.' Gabriel pulled away from the lights and into a layby just up the road. The other driver parked behind him and got out, adjusting his bobble hat and shifting his bottle-bottom glasses further up his nose.

'I'm so sorry, mate.' He put his hands up in surrender as he inspected the back of Gabriel's car.

Gabriel did his own inspection. His sister's battered old BMW was covered in bumps and scratches; one more wasn't going to make a difference.

'It's fine. Don't worry about it.' Gabriel checked his watch.

The other driver reached into his own glove compartment to grab a pad and pen. 'Better exchange details. What's your name?'

Gabriel shook his head. 'Look, mate, that dent was already there. I'm not going make a claim – have you seen the state of my car?'

'I still think we should exchange details. This has happened to me before. The woman said I hadn't damaged her car, and she later tried to sting me for smashing her bumper to pieces. Who are you insured with?'

'But there's no damage,' Gabriel insisted.

The driver looked up from his notepad. 'You're very honest, mate. Wish there were more people like you in the world.' He leaned down to inspect the front of his own car. 'Looks like no damage to mine either.' He arched his head to look up at Gabriel who was checking his watch again. 'Are you sure you don't want to exchange details just to be on the safe side?'

'Honestly, there's no need.'

'Well, if you're absolutely sure,' the driver replied.

Gabriel nodded, got back into his car and pulled away, checking the time on the dashboard: 4.10 p.m. He'd be where he needed to be in time, traffic permitting.

CHAPTER 5

Adrian Crow turned into his drive just as a silver Mercedes was pulling away from it. He parked in front of his house and watched the Mercedes turn on to the main road. Opening his front door, he smiled as Caroline walked into the kitchen.

'You had visitors?' he asked cheerily, setting his briefcase down on the table.

'What do you mean?' she asked, her face red and her breathing laboured.

'The Mercedes,' he replied, kissing her on the cheek. 'You looked flushed, are you alright?'

'I'm fine. I was upstairs when the doorbell rang. It was just some guy who took a wrong turning.'

'Ah. Satnav problem, eh?' He waved a piece of paper at her.

'What's this?' She frowned, her heartbeat slowly returning to normal.

'It's our reservation to stay at the Hampshire Hotel, Llandudno, from tomorrow until next Wednesday.' He smiled broadly as he spoke.

'Oh.' She unfolded the piece of paper.

'I couldn't swing any more time off work,' he said. 'But will this do for now?'

'It's fine and of course it will do – it's wonderful. I don't know what to say.'

'You can buy me an ice cream in Llandudno.' He grinned. 'Talking of which, we'd better get packing.'

'I might need to ask you for some cash. I can't find my bank card anywhere. Lord knows what I've done with it.'

Adrian put his arms around her waist. 'Don't worry about it. This break is on me. I don't expect my wife to pay for anything when it's her birthday treat. Do you want me to cancel your card just in case?'

'No, it'll be in the house somewhere, don't worry.' Caroline made her way upstairs, opening her wardrobe to pick out what she was going to take with her. She swallowed as tears formed in her eyes, and she quickly wiped them away before Adrian joined her.

CHAPTER 6

DS Anna Markinson flew into DI Sheridan Holler's office. 'Have you spoken to Hill today?' she asked, catching her breath.

'No. She's off this weekend.'

'Shit.'

'Why, what's up?'

Anna peeked out of the door and down the corridor. 'The new assistant chief constable's here – apparently Hill was supposed to meet him at one o'clock to give him a tour of the nick.' She spoke quickly. 'The public enquiry officer has told him Hill's not here, and he's blowing his fucking stack downstairs.'

'Have you tried calling Hill?'

'Yeah, like a million times. But her phone's switched off.'

Sheridan grinned. Picking up her phone, she called the PEO. 'Hi, it's DI Holler, can you tell the ACC that DCI Knowles *is* here. She's in her office. Apologies for the confusion.'

'Yes, ma'am. Thanks, I'll send him up.'

Anna glared at Sheridan in horror. 'What the hell was that? Hill's not—'

'Trust me.' Sheridan got up and, grabbing Anna's arm, she ushered her down the corridor to Hill's office, sitting herself behind the desk.

Anna shook her head. 'Oh Christ. Please tell me you're not going to pretend to be Hill.'

'Oh yes, I am. For two reasons. One: Hill has clearly forgotten about the meeting – and even though she can be a pain in the arse, I don't want her to get in the shit.'

'And two?'

'And two: it'll be a bit of fun.' Sheridan pointed to the chair next to Anna. 'You sit and we'll pretend we're deep in conversation about a job.'

'Who am I?' Anna asked, suddenly excited as she sat, crossing her legs and placing her hands on her knees.

'What do you mean, who are you?'

'Well, you get to be Hill, who do I get to be?'

'It's not a bloody TV programme – you're *you*.' Sheridan blew out her cheeks.

'That's boring, can't I pretend to be *you*?' she asked just as there was a knock on the door.

'No.' Sheridan whispered. 'Just be yourself.'

Anna opened the door and standing behind it was the ACC. All six foot seven of him. His buttoned-up tunic stretched painfully across his enormous stomach. 'DCI Knowles?' he asked, his booming voice so loud it made Anna jump slightly.

'No, sir, I'm DS Anna Markinson. This is DCI Knowles.' She stepped back and indicated Sheridan.

Sheridan stood up and extended her hand, which the ACC took, practically dislocating her fingers as he shook it. Anna stood behind him and swiped her finger across her neck, which Sheridan saw and bit down on her lip.

The ACC sat down so heavily that the office chair groaned under his sheer weight. 'Can I call you Hill?'

Sheridan nodded. 'Absolutely, sir.' She made herself comfortable behind Hill's desk. 'So, how are you settling in?'

The ACC got straight to the point. 'Fine, thanks. Now, tell me about your team.'

Anna sat down, feeling a mixture of childish excitement and absolute and total fucking panic.

'Well, I have DI Sheridan Holler.' Sheridan then nodded at Anna. 'And DS Markinson here.'

'I've heard good things about DI Holler,' the ACC replied. 'I'd like to meet her.'

'I'm afraid she's just had to pop out on an enquiry. She'll be disappointed that she missed you,' Sheridan replied. 'So . . . what good things have you heard about her?' As she asked the question, Sheridan flicked a look at Anna who was surreptitiously shaking her head.

'That she's a good leader and a bloody good detective.'

Sheridan smiled broadly.

They spent the next ten minutes discussing how the CID team worked together, before Sheridan assigned Anna to show the ACC around the station.

Half an hour later, Sheridan could hear the ACC's voice still booming as she passed the stairs. But what she didn't expect to see was Hill walking towards her.

'Ah, Sheridan. I'm glad you're here. I've got a meeting with the new ACC at two. I want you to meet him, show him around the nick.' Hill opened the door to her office.

Sheridan peered over the banister and could see the ACC and Anna coming up the stairs. She followed Hill into her office, but quickly tried to usher her out again. 'You have to go – hide in the toilet or something.'

'What are you doing?' Hill pulled her arm free. 'Why have I got to hide?'

'The ACC is already here. Your meeting was at one, not two . . . and so I had to be *you*.'

'What *are* you talking about?' Hill snapped. She still hadn't budged from her office and that was when the ACC appeared, with Anna in tow and wide-eyed.

'So, how was the tour?' Sheridan asked cheerily, while swallowing down hard on the sudden nausea rising in her throat.

'Very good. And this is?' The ACC nodded at Hill.

Sheridan jumped in. 'This is . . . Detective Constable Trudy Higginbottom, she's new to the team.' Sheridan turned to Hill, who was looking very confused. And a little bit angry. 'So, Trudy, if you could get that file to me as soon as, that would be great.'

Sheridan flicked her head at Hill in a motion to suggest that she left, sharpish.

Hill glared at her for a moment. 'Excuse me?'

Although she was slowly dying inside, Sheridan smiled and turned to Anna. 'Could you show the ACC out for me? I think Trudy and I need to have a little chat.'

Anna obliged and once she and the ACC had left, Sheridan puffed out her cheeks and turned to Hill. 'You're welcome.' She flopped herself down on to Hill's chair.

Hill stared at the empty doorway. 'What the actual fuck just happened?'

CHAPTER 7

Friday 13 March

Adrian Crow stood at the window and dialled 999.

'Emergency,' said the handler on the other end. 'Which service?'

'Police, please.' He could feel his voice shaking as much as his hands were as his call was connected.

'Police, what's the nature of the emergency?'

'My wife is missing. I've been away on business, and I've come home . . . and she's not here. I tried calling her last night and this morning, but she wasn't answering. This isn't like her, it really isn't. I'm so worried. I don't know what to do.'

'Alright, sir, let me take some details first.'

An hour later, Adrian Crow was sitting at his kitchen table answering questions being put to him by the uniformed officer, PC Jack Staples. The officer had confirmed with Adrian that the property was secure when he'd returned home that day and there was no sign of a break-in.

'Is that your car outside?'

'Yes.'

'Does your wife drive or have access to another vehicle?'

'No, only mine. But she rarely drives. I do most of the driving. She has a pushbike, but that's still in the shed.'

'Is she on any medication?'

'No.'

'Has she ever talked about harming herself?'

'Good God, no. Caroline's the happiest person you could ever meet.'

'Has she taken anything with her that you know of? Her purse? Phone?'

'Her mobile is still here. She told me the night before we left for Llandudno that she'd lost her bank card. Her handbag is missing and her purse . . . and . . .'

'And what, sir?' PC Jack Staples looked up from his notes.

'Her suitcase has gone.' Adrian suffocated on his words as he stood up. 'And most of her clothes.'

Adrian went on to explain that he and Caroline had been away for a few days, staying at the Hampshire Hotel in Llandudno, north Wales. They'd left home on the morning of Sunday 8 March and returned home at around 11.30 a.m. on Wednesday the eleventh. Adrian had unpacked his case but Caroline had said she was tired and would unpack hers the next day.

That evening, Adrian had received a call from a potential client in Norfolk asking if he could meet them at their shop in Norwich this morning, Friday the thirteenth. Adrian had booked into the Kingsley Court Hotel in Norwich for one night on the Thursday. He'd called Caroline when he arrived at the hotel but there was no reply. This in itself wasn't unusual, as she often went to bed early, or she may even have been out with her friends from the swimming club she attended every Thursday. He tried her again before he went to bed but there was still no reply, so he left a message.

That morning, he had arrived at the shop where he had arranged to meet his potential client, but the staff in the shop knew nothing about the meeting – and had never heard of the client's name. Adrian called the number that the client had rung him from, but the phone was switched off. Then he tried calling Caroline again, but there was still no reply, so he left yet another message asking her to call back. By this time, he was getting really worried about her. He then headed home, stopping once on the way to re-fuel and buy a sandwich. During this stop, he called her again. Still no answer.

He arrived home at 2.30 p.m. The house was locked, and nothing appeared out of place. Adrian checked around the grounds of the property in case she'd fallen in the garden. He then checked around the house and found that practically all of Caroline's clothes, her handbag and purse were missing. Her mobile phone was on the bed. He went for a drive around the area where she often liked to walk but with no sign of her, he returned home.

'You said you were meeting a client. What exactly is your job?' Jack Staples asked.

'I'm a rep for a pet food supplier.'

'Does Caroline work?'

'She's a housewife.'

Jack Staples glanced down at the missing persons form. 'Do you know what Caroline might be wearing?'

'No.'

'So, the last time you saw her was in the morning when you left to go to Norfolk?'

'Yes.'

'And how did she seem?'

'She was fine. I was about to go, but we always kiss before I leave the house. She was in bed but insisted on getting up and waving me off. She seemed absolutely fine.'

'Do you have any security cameras?'

'No.'

'Have you spoken to family and friends?'

'No. She doesn't have any family and neither do I. I didn't want to panic her friends. I tried looking through her phone, but she has so few contacts on there. She has a couple of friends at swimming club. We're quite private people and we're not unsociable but we love our own company. I can't think of anyone that Caroline would go to.'

'May I have a look through her phone?' PC Staples nodded at Caroline's mobile on the table.

'Of course.' Adrian slid it towards him.

Jack Staples noticed that the phone was an older, basic model – one that didn't require a passcode. He took his time, checking the text messages and call logs. It appeared that she hardly used it at all. He went through her missed calls and voicemails, listening to the ones that Adrian had left while he was away in Norfolk. He noted down the time and date of the messages, which matched Adrian's account. When he finished, he handed the phone back.

'Please don't delete anything, we might need to look at her phone again.' Staples studied his notes before asking, 'Have you checked if her passport is missing?'

'No. I'm not even sure where she keeps it or if it's even in date. We haven't been abroad for years.'

'Would you be able to have a look around and let me know if you find it?'

'Yes. But why would she take her passport? None of this makes any sense.'

'Does Caroline have any children?'

'No. Neither of us do and her parents died when she was young. We only have each other.'

'How long have you been married?'

'Ten years. We met eleven years ago. It all happened very quickly. I proposed after a few months, and she said yes.' A momentary smile drifted across Adrian's face before he swallowed, feeling tears tumbling down his cheeks.

'Have either of you been married before?'

'No.'

'Difficult question, I'm afraid, but as she's taken her suitcase with her, could it be that she needed to get away for a while? I'm not suggesting you have any marital problems, but maybe she felt she needed some time away for some reason?'

'We've just *been* away. We had a wonderful few days together. Besides, we've hardly had a cross word since the day we met. It really doesn't make any sense. I can't tell you how completely out of character this is for her. She's my whole life. We adore each other.' Adrian sat back down and dropped his head into his hands.

Staples stood up. 'Is it okay if I take a look around?'

'Of course.' Adrian pulled himself up and followed the officer as he checked the house.

Staples made his way from room to room, opening doors and cupboards as he went. He didn't expect to find Caroline, but perhaps something would seem out of place and give him a clue as to what might have happened to her.

He reached the main bedroom and opened the large wardrobe that stood by the window. It was empty, except for a woman's top that was folded on the shelf. On the other side of the large room was another wardrobe, filled with pressed shirts. A collection of suits hung neatly at one end with jeans and tracksuit bottoms at the other. A half-drunk bottle of water sat on a coaster on the bedside table. There were two en-suite bathrooms, his and hers, and Jack Staples noticed a hairbrush lying next to the sink. There was also an electric toothbrush, beside a can of deodorant with the lid off and a lipstick.

Staples pointed to a suitcase that stood by the bedroom door. 'Is that your suitcase?'

'Yes.'

'Is it similar to Caroline's?'

'It's identical.'

'Is it okay if I take a picture of it?'

'Of course.'

'You have separate bathrooms?'

'Yes.'

'I need Caroline's hairbrush and toothbrush. Have you touched them since you discovered that she was missing?'

'No. I haven't. Why do you need to take them?'

'It's purely routine, we can get DNA from them . . . It's just so that . . .' *Just so that if your wife is found dead we can identify her*, Jack thought.

'Why do you need her DNA?' Adrian interrupted, feeling his legs give way as the reality of the situation set in. 'Is it in case something terrible has happened?' He put a hand on top of his head and burst into tears.

Jack Staples tried to reassure him. 'In the majority of cases, the missing person returns or is found safe and well within a few days. Please don't think the worst. I'm sure she's just taken herself off for a little while. She's taken a lot of things and her suitcase and that's a good sign. If you know what I mean.'

Adrian put a hand on the bed and sat down. 'She'd never leave me. I just know she wouldn't,' he said brokenly.

'I'm going to take a look around outside – it's just routine.'

Adrian nodded and showed the officer to the back door.

Staples stepped outside and flicked on his Maglite torch, walking slowly through the garden in his size nines, the torch light creating eerie shadows as it lit up the trees and bushes. Terracotta pots were dotted around the patio and an unreeled hosepipe lay outstretched across the lawn.

He walked over to the shed at the side of the house. 'Can you open this for me?'

'Of course.' Adrian went back into the house to retrieve the key, undid the padlock and opened the door.

Leaning against the tool cabinet was a pushbike. 'Is that your wife's bike?' Jack Staples asked.

'Yes,' Adrian replied.

Staples was looking around at the various pots of paint, tools and a stepladder. A huge spider's web stretched out in the corner and Jack tried not to shudder. He was terrified of spiders. 'It all seems in order here,' he said, slowly backing out, goosebumps prickling his arms.

To the side of the house was also a small coal shed. Staples pulled the door open and peered in. He had to duck down to step inside, his torch lighting up the place. There was nothing but a small pile of coal and an untidy stack of wood, some logs and a pile of broken planks. And more spiders.

He moved towards the door. 'I'll need to pop back tomorrow when it's light. I'm on duty at 8 a.m., so I'll come over about 8.30. If I get called to another job, I'll get a colleague to attend in my place. Is that okay?'

'Yes, of course. But can I ask what you're looking for?' Adrian said as they walked back to the house.

'Just checking that everything seems secure,' he replied. *And checking that your wife's body isn't here*, he thought.

'I see . . .'

Staples wiped his feet on the coir doormat.

'One final question – what was the name of the client you went to meet in Norfolk – the one who doesn't appear to exist?'

Adrian rubbed his temples, thinking. 'Henry Blanchflower.'

CHAPTER 8

Saturday 14 March

Gabriel Howard's lungs were burning as he slowed down from his run. The months he'd spent in prison had provided little opportunity to keep up with his fitness regime and he felt completely out of shape. The Saturday morning traffic was building up, with shoppers heading into Liverpool city centre, and he could taste the flood of car fumes. Crossing the road, he headed over to the Albert Dock for a jog along the waterfront. After a few minutes, he slowed to a walk before sitting on a vacant bench to stretch out his calf muscles, leaning his head back and closing his eyes.

As his breathing returned to normal, his mobile rang. Recognising the number, he sat up straight and answered. 'Hello?'

'Hi, it's me. You okay to speak?'

'Yeah. How you doing?' Gabriel wiped a bead of sweat that was trickling down his cheek.

'I'm fine. I was wondering if you wanted to meet up? It would be good to see you.'

'I'd like that. We'll have to be careful though . . . How about Princes Park?'

'Perfect. Do you know the monument – just inside the sunburst gates?'

'Yeah.'

'Okay. I'll meet you there at three o'clock?'

'Sounds good.' Gabriel swallowed, feeling a field of butterflies dancing in his stomach. 'We'll have to be really careful; I don't want anyone to overhear us.'

'Of course not.' There was a silence before he continued, 'How's it going with the plan?'

'I'm working on it. Obviously, I had to put it on hold when I was in prison, but I'm back on track now.'

'I need to ask you something, Gabriel . . . I know what you're planning to do and the reason why, but if you end up back inside . . .'

'I won't end up back inside.' There was a long pause before Gabriel spoke again. 'I need to do this. You understand, don't you? I need to get them both.'

'I know you do.' Another silence. 'Are you going to kill them?'

'No.' Gabriel rested his head back and squinted at the sky. 'I'm going to do much worse than that.'

CHAPTER 9

Sunday 15 March

Sheridan pulled on to her drive and melted when she saw her cat, Maud, who was sitting at the window. As Sheridan opened the front door, the familiar smell of burning was wafting through the house.

'Don't come into the kitchen!' her girlfriend, Sam, called out as Maud appeared in the doorway. Sheridan picked her up and pushed her nose into the cat's fur.

'Do I need to call the fire brigade?' Sheridan kissed Maud's head and carried her through the living room into the kitchen, ignoring Sam's plea.

Sam spun round holding a blow torch, the blue flame sparking out of it like a rocket's engine. 'It's an experiment. It's gone really, really bloody wrong – and now I can't turn this thing off.' She held the blow torch at arm's length.

Sheridan chuckled and, gently placing Maud down, she took the blow torch and turned the nozzle, extinguishing the flame. 'What's the experiment?'

Sam kissed her on the lips and opened the fridge, pulling out a bottle of wine. 'Crème brûlée.' She filled two large glasses and took a huge swig, handing one to Sheridan.

'It was going really well until the last bit when you have to burn the sugar on top to caramelise it.' Sam took another swig of wine. 'That's when it went very tits up.'

Sheridan stepped closer to the ramekins filled with a black charcoal-like substance, which were smoking like little volcanoes. 'What happened?' She swallowed a laugh rising in her throat.

'Well, the recipe thing said to use a culinary blow torch, which we don't have.' Sam tilted her head slightly. 'So, to save time arsing around trying to find a kitchen supply shop open on a Sunday, I popped to B&Q and bought a normal blow torch.' Another sip of wine. 'I think now, with hindsight, that the blow torch was a bit too powerful and as soon as I tried browning the tops of them, the flame was too hot . . . and they caught fire and exploded.'

Sheridan choked on her drink.

◆ ◆ ◆

Later that evening they sat top and tail on the sofa, heady from the wine.

They had met just over four years earlier, while Sheridan was investigating a case where an off-duty police officer had been shot dead. Sheridan was visiting a nursing home where one of the residents had been caught by a stray bullet while walking next to the officer, suffering a significant and unrecoverable head injury. The morning that Sheridan had arrived to interview the woman was the same morning that Sam was there, visiting her best friend, Joni, then a carer at the home. The attraction between Sheridan and Sam was instant and obvious, and Sam had moved in a few months later with her beloved cat Maud.

Sam and Joni had met when they were seven years old. Joni was being beaten up in the school playground when Sam had jumped in, apparently saving her life. That was Sam's account of what had happened – and she reminded Joni of her heroics whenever the opportunity arose. Joni had spent the last thirty-two years trying to shut her up about it.

'How's work?' Sam asked, running her fingers around Sheridan's toes. Sam was used to Sheridan's job and nothing fazed her. Being a schoolteacher, she'd told Sheridan that when you've dealt with thirty out of control children who stick stones up their noses and eat plasticine, you're pretty much set up for anything. Sam wasn't squeamish, never had been, and so when Sheridan went into detail about the cases she was working on, Sam didn't bat an eyelid.

'I don't want to tempt fate, but I'll just say it's Q.'

Sam grinned. Her four years with Sheridan had taught her to never say the word 'quiet'. Because if you did, all fucking hell was probably about to break loose.

CHAPTER 10

Monday 16 March

Sheridan was glaring at the vending machine when Anna Markinson and DC Rob Wills came up behind her.

'Oh dear. Has it eaten your money again?' Anna grinned.

Sheridan put both hands against the glass. 'No, but it will. I swear to God . . . one day I'm going to smash this stupid machine to pieces.'

'Think positively, boss. Maybe today's the day that it takes your money and you finally get your chocolate bar.' Rob smiled. That cheeky smile he knew he'd get away with.

'How much do you want to bet that it isn't?' Sheridan replied.

Rob jumped back in with, 'I think if you get your chocolate this time you should buy the whole team something. I'll have a KitKat.' He winked at Anna.

'Rob, I've been arguing with this machine for years and only twice have I not had to shake the thing, to get out of it what I've paid for. It only works for about a day after the guy comes to service it and I haven't seen him for ages. So, if you're wrong, *you* have to buy chocolate for everyone.'

'You're on.' Rob extended his hand and Sheridan shook it.

'Right, you little bastard.' Sheridan dropped coins into the slot and made her selection. The mechanism inside whirled around and her Twix dropped into the tray below.

'How many detectives does it take to work a bloody vending machine?' DCI Hill Knowles' voice boomed from behind them. 'Sheridan, Anna, I need to see you both right now. We've got a job come in and it's a fucking weird one,' she barked, marching down the corridor back to her office.

'Shall I tell the team that you're buying them all chocolate, or will you?' Rob puckered his lips at Sheridan, who put her hands on his shoulders and turned him around.

'Off you feck.' Sheridan gave him a nudge in the back before turning to join Hill, mumbling to herself something about robbing-bastard-vending machines.

Anna smiled at Rob. 'Nice one. We all get chocolate.'

Rob whispered, 'Don't tell Sheridan but I saw the maintenance guy fixing the machine this morning.' He raised his hand and Anna high-fived him.

◆ ◆ ◆

When Sheridan and Anna walked into Hill's office, Hill was in the middle of the room, her hands snapped on to her hips.

'We've just had a 999 call from a Simon Banks, who lives at Maple View, Crosby. He's been away at a conference and got home this morning to find a package on his doorstep.'

'What kind of package?' Sheridan asked.

Hill raised her eyebrows. 'A human left hand. Looks like it's been in a fire. Uniform and CSI are on their way to his house now.'

Sheridan glanced at Anna. 'Me and Anna will go out there.'

Hill nodded and put her thumb up. 'Okay. We'll brief the team when you get back.' And with that she picked up her phone, prompting Sheridan and Anna to leave and make their way to Simon Banks' house.

◆ ◆ ◆

Twenty minutes later, Sheridan and Anna pulled up behind the CSI van that was parked outside the property. Marked police cars lined the road and residents watched out of their windows, curious as to what was happening in the usually quiet area.

Once inside, Sheridan and Anna quickly spoke to the crime scene investigator, eager to see the package before it was taken away for forensic examination.

'Hi, Charlie, what do you think? Male or female?' Sheridan asked.

'Too hard to tell. It's pretty badly burnt and not in great condition, as you can see for yourselves.'

They all looked down at the macabre package. 'Was it addressed to him by name?'

Charlie turned the packaging over. 'No. No name or address.'

Sheridan replied, 'Okay.'

She and Anna made their way into the living room to introduce themselves to Simon Banks. He was tall and slim, with short greying hair. A crumpled linen suit hung awkwardly across his broad shoulders and his blue eyes were so wide he looked like someone was pointing a gun at him.

Sheridan focused on the man before her. 'Is it okay if I call you Simon?'

'Yes. Of course. Sorry, I'm in a bit of shock.' He breathed in slowly and ran a hand through his hair.

'I'm not surprised. Shall we sit down?' Sheridan asked, taking out her pocket notebook.

Simon Banks pulled out three chairs from the dining table that stood at one end of the living room. The table's surface was almost completely covered with textbooks and piles of paperwork. Sheridan noticed most of the books were medical related, as were the ones that stood shoulder to shoulder on the bookcase on the other side of the room.

'So, Simon, I understand you've been away and came back to find the package this morning?'

'Yes. I've been at a conference since Thursday.'

Simon Banks went on to explain that on Thursday 12 March he'd attended a conference in Oxford. He had stayed at a hotel near the conference centre and had left at 7 a.m. to return home that morning. He had parked his car on the drive and at first hadn't noticed the package as he walked up to the front door. As he put his key in the door, he saw it out of the corner of his eye, the end of it poking out from under the thick layer of ivy that had spent the last few years crawling up the side of the house.

'Any idea when it could have been left there?'

'No. It wasn't there when I left for the conference, or if it was, I didn't spot it. I only noticed it when I got home this morning.' He swallowed and anxiously ran his tongue along his lip.

'Have you had any other post delivered while you were away at your conference?'

'No.'

'Do you live alone?'

'Yes.'

'This might sound like an odd question, but do the contents of the package mean anything to you at all?'

He shook his head. 'No. It makes absolutely no sense.'

'Do you have any family?'

'I have a son who lives in Australia. I'm actually flying out this evening to visit him. I go once a year.'

'How long will you be away for?'

'A couple of weeks. He's just moved into a new house.'

'Do you have the address?'

'No. I could call him – but I don't know if he'll answer at this time and I don't want to worry him.' Simon checked his watch.

'Silly question, but how are you visiting him if you don't know his address?'

'He never gave it to me. He's picking me up from the airport. I'll call you when I'm there if you want and let you know the address. Can I ask why you need it?'

'Just being cautious. I want to know where you are and if, for some reason, I can't get hold of you, I can get the local police to visit you at your son's house. Whereabouts in Australia does he live?'

'Perth.'

'Okay. Can I ask, are you in a relationship?'

'No. My wife and I separated seven years ago.' He hesitated. 'We're not in contact.' His eyes suddenly widened. 'Oh God, do you know whose hand it is?'

'No,' Sheridan replied immediately. 'Do you have your ex-wife's contact details?'

Simon Banks nervously rubbed his forehead, pulling his mobile out of his pocket. 'I have an old number for her, but I don't know if she still uses it.'

Anna wrote the details down and stepped outside.

Sheridan continued with her questions. 'Do you have any security cameras?'

'No. I've thought about it in the past, but we don't really get any problems here. I've never had any issues. Until now.'

'Is there anyone you can think of that would send this kind of package to you? Someone you've fallen out with, maybe someone who's threatened you?'

'It's all I've thought about since I opened it. I genuinely can't think of anyone. I don't have enemies, I've never been in trouble with the law . . . or with anyone, really. I've never even been in a bloody fight.' He shook his head slightly. 'Do you have any suspicions about what sort of person could have done this?'

Sheridan looked up from her notes. 'We'll make enquiries and I'll have a team of detectives working on it.'

Simon Banks sat back in his chair. 'Is this a murder enquiry?'

Sheridan cleared her throat. 'We don't know yet. I see you have lot of medical books. Are you in the field?'

'Yes. I'm a doctor. I work at the Cranmire private hospital in Liverpool.'

'What kind of doctor?'

'I'm an orthopaedic surgeon. I specialise in sports injuries.'

'Any problems with your colleagues or patients? Any kind of threats?'

'No.'

'Do you have a secretary?'

'Yes. Janet.'

'Maybe she's taken a message from someone, maybe something odd that she hasn't passed on to you?'

'I doubt it, but I can call her if you like. Or do you need to speak to her?'

'Yes, I'd like to speak to her. Can you give me her name and contact number?'

'Of course.' Simon Banks wrote the details down and handed them to Sheridan, who in turn gave Simon her card.

'Can I just get your full name and date of birth, Simon?'

'Yes, it's Simon Aubrey Banks – 12/02/49.'

Anna came back into the room. 'Your ex-wife is safe and well,' she reassured Simon before again stepping outside, this time to make a call to the control room. They confirmed that Simon Banks was no trace on PNC.

Sheridan looked around the room. 'Simon, we'd like to consider a few things. I'd like to put a marker on your address in case there's any further incidents. We can arrange for an alarm to be fitted and I'd really like our technical team to put cameras up in case whoever left this on your doorstep comes back.'

'I don't think I need an alarm. I'm not going to be here. The marker thing is fine though. And the cameras, too.'

'Thank you. We also need to get a statement from you, a DNA sample and take your fingerprints, just for elimination purposes on the package. Has anyone else touched it?'

'No. Just me. How long is this going to take? I'm more than happy to help of course but I've got to get to Heathrow. My flight's at 6 p.m.'

Sheridan checked her watch. 'If we take you to the police station now, we can get everything done and have you back in plenty of time.'

Simon Banks' shoulders dropped. 'Fine.'

CHAPTER 11

After he gave his statement, provided his fingerprints and DNA sample, Sheridan and Anna took Simon Banks home. The cameras had been fitted and he glanced up at them as he got out of Sheridan's car. They walked him to his door. As he stepped inside, Sheridan thanked him, before confirming she would call him if there were any developments. He agreed to let her know when he was back in the country so that he could reconsider the alarm if he felt vulnerable. He'd planned to stay with his son for two weeks but said that he might extend his visit. He would let them know what he decided.

As Simon closed the front door behind them, Sheridan and Anna walked down the pathway, heading back to their car. On reaching the pavement, Sheridan stopped and checked up and down the road.

'What's up?' Anna asked, rummaging in her pocket for the car keys.

'I won't be a minute,' Sheridan replied and crossed the road, standing for a moment to inspect Simon's house. She crossed back over and walked down the road, stopped, turned and walked past the house in the opposite direction. Banks lived in a detached house at the end of a cul-de-sac with no houses directly opposite. To the left of his house was a field, with a narrow river carving through it. Sheridan could see cars on the other side, through the trees.

When she returned, Anna unlocked the car and they got in. 'What are you thinking?' she asked.

'I'm wondering something about the package, how it was found.'

Anna put the key in the ignition but stopped short of switching it on. 'Go on.'

'Well, if I didn't know any different, I would have thought that this being a rather nice area that most people living here would have security cameras. There are no houses opposite Simon Banks' house and nothing to the left, just a field. So, if I'm going to leave a parcel on his doorstep and don't want to risk security cameras seeing me, how do I avoid them?'

Anna turned her head to look at the house. 'Come across the field.'

'Yes . . . but I've still got to avoid cameras when I leave the parcel on the doorstep.'

'Maybe whoever delivered the package knows the house and knows there's no cameras.'

'So, it could be someone he knows.' She rested her head back and turned her face to Anna. 'Or someone who lives in this street.'

'It's a very strange thing to leave on someone's doorstep. Like proper fucking threatening.'

Sheridan nodded slowly. 'Play with fire.' She let the words hang in the air for a moment.

'What do you mean?' Anna asked.

'That's the saying, isn't it? Play with fire and you'll get your hands burnt. Maybe whoever this hand belongs to has either played with fire and got them burnt, or Simon Banks is the one playing with fire and is about to get burned.'

'That's quite a good theory. Where do you get these ideas from?'

'I'm a genius.' Sheridan grinned and put her seat belt on.

CHAPTER 12

The midday sun was gently streaming in the window as Adrian Crow pushed Caroline's pillow into his face, sobbing. 'Why have you done this to me?' He inhaled deeply. 'Caroline, Caroline, Caroline.' He rocked back and forth, the pillow clenched between his arms. Placing it back on the bed he wiped a hand down his face, rubbing tears off his hand on to his shirt sleeve.

He stood motionless in the middle of the bedroom for a moment, before turning and closing the door quietly behind him. He went downstairs to the kitchen and stared at the empty whisky bottle that had been his friend in the dark for the last three nights. The ticking of the clock on the wall sounded like a train ploughing through his head and he grabbed the bottle and launched it at the wall, sending broken glass in every direction, tinkling across the kitchen floor.

Just then, he looked up to see a post van parked on the drive and heard the letterbox flap shut. Ignoring the glass crunching under his feet, he strode across it to the front door, pulling it open and startling the postman.

'Made me jump.' The postman theatrically clamped a hand against his own chest.

'Have you seen my wife?' Adrian blurted out.

'Sorry?' The postman stopped and turned around.

'You're our regular postman, aren't you?'

'Yeah.'

'My wife, Caroline . . . do you know her?'

'I've spoken to her a few times . . .'

'She's missing.'

'Missing?'

'Yes, since Friday. She's gone somewhere and I don't know where. I had to call the police. When did you last speak to her?'

The postman blew out his cheeks. 'Blimey, that's awful. I'm so sorry. Do they know what might have happened to her?'

'No. Not yet. When did you last see her? Can you remember?' Adrian's questions came thick and fast.

The postman shook his head. 'I'm trying to think. Probably a couple of weeks ago now. I didn't speak to her, but I saw her through the kitchen window – she waves sometimes. I can't remember when I last spoke to her though. Will the police want to talk to me?'

'I don't know. Can I take your name and a contact number, just in case?'

'Yeah, of course.' The postman returned to his van and reached inside for a pen and small notebook. After quickly writing his details down, he handed them to Adrian.

'Thank you.' Adrian looked at the note. 'Paul.'

'I hope she's alright. Your wife.' And he added, 'I'm sure she'll turn up okay.' He got back into his van and Adrian watched as he drove back out on to the main road.

Adrian stood there for a moment, staring at the tree in his front garden, before going back inside.

CHAPTER 13

The CID team were congregated as Sheridan updated them with the details of her and Anna's visit to Simon Banks. Hill Knowles was sitting in her usual place at the back of the room, chair tilted back, arms folded. Looking pissed off. Not that she *was* actually pissed off, she just had that kind of tangible aura around her. Like insect repellent.

Sheridan tucked a pen behind her ear and pointed towards the whiteboard behind her. 'Right,' she said, loudly enough to quieten any remaining chatter in the room. 'This morning, Dr Simon Banks returned home from a conference in Oxford to find this human hand on his doorstep. It was delivered by hand, pardon the pun, and as you can see it's been in a fire and is not in great condition. The hand was well packaged but not addressed to Simon by name.' She paused, noting that her team were paying attention. 'It could be that it wasn't meant for him, but we have to assume for now that it was. He can't give us anything that would indicate who's behind this. He's travelling to Australia this evening to visit his son for a couple of weeks.'

Sheridan hesitated, searching the photographs stuck up on the whiteboard behind her.

'I'm going to task your jobs out in a bit. I've fast-tracked the DNA and forensics on the hand and the package it came in, so hopefully we'll get the results back quickly. House-to-house is being done and I want CCTV checked around the area and let's look into missing persons. I also want intel checked to see if any other body parts have turned up anywhere else. We need to act fast on this one. I don't want you to lose focus on the fact that the victim could still be alive.'

◆ ◆ ◆

At the end of the day, Sheridan was packing her things up ready to head home when Anna appeared.

'Dipesh has been looking at mispers and the only active one at the moment is a woman called Caroline Crow, reported missing by her husband, Adrian, last Friday. Jack Staples is dealing with it.'

'Anything that could link her to the burnt hand?'

Anna was about to answer when Sheridan's phone rang. Hill's extension number flashed on the screen. 'Yes, Hill?'

'Do you know a PC Jack Staples?'

Sheridan looked at Anna. 'Yeah, why?'

'He's standing in my office, wants to talk to us about a misper he's dealing with.'

'Caroline Crow?' Sheridan asked, already knowing the answer.

'Yeah. How did you know that?'

Sheridan smiled at Anna and winked. 'Psychic powers, Hill. Psychic powers.'

Hill put the phone down.

CHAPTER 14

PC Jack Staples looked very awkward as he stood in the middle of Hill's office. And he had good reason – Hill wasn't known for doing small talk. She had a reputation for being somewhat blunt. All the time.

Sheridan and Anna felt sorry for him as they walked into the office. Hill was sitting at her desk with her shoulders back, stretching her legs out.

'Hello, Jack.' Sheridan smiled. Trying to put him at ease.

'Hi, Sheridan. You doing okay?'

'Yeah, you know, busy but—'

'Shall we spend the next ten minutes talking bollocks or have you got something you need to talk to us about?' Hill chipped in impatiently.

Jack Staples cleared his throat. 'I know this doesn't fall into the remit of CID, but I'm dealing with a fella called Adrian Crow. He reported his wife, Caroline, missing last Friday evening. They'd been away for a few days in Llandudno, came back on Wednesday. That evening, he got a call from some guy called Henry Blanchflower who set up a meeting in Norfolk. Adrian's business is in pet supplies, and this guy claimed to be a potential client with a strong proposal. But when Adrian got there this bloke didn't exist. Adrian tried to contact Caroline to let her know he was coming home, but there was no reply, and when he got back on the Friday, she wasn't there. Almost all of her clothes and her suitcase were missing. They have matching cases – I've taken a picture of Adrian's. Her bank card was last used on Saturday the seventh of March at 10.50 a.m. at a Tesco's ATM on Church Street in Liverpool. Four hundred pounds was withdrawn. But then her husband Adrian says that she told him she'd lost her bank card a few days earlier. Anyway, I checked the house and grounds, and went back the following morning to look around the garden in daylight. Everything seemed fairly normal – except I found a pair of gloves hidden in a bush next to the lounge window. Adrian said he'd never seen them before, so I sent them off for forensics. I also requested the CCTV from the ATM.'

'Have you checked out this Henry Blanchflower?' Sheridan asked, smiling to reassure Jack Staples that she was impressed by his diligence.

'Yeah, I found one on PNC, Henry James Blanchflower, born in Bootle in 1948. He's got one arrest back in 1999 for drink-driving. There's a couple more on PNC – none in Norfolk, though – but I'm still making enquiries.'

'Sounds like you're doing a cracking job.' Sheridan smiled again. 'What about an all ports alert on Caroline?'

'Yeah, that's been done, so we'll know if she uses her passport. Adrian doesn't know where it is, so unless he finds it, she's got it with her. The property is set back off the main road but house-to-house was done, CCTV was checked and nothing as yet. Local hospitals have come up blank. The area around the house has been searched. There's a field to the side and back and that's been searched, and I looked in the main shed and the small coal shed.'

'Does Caroline drive?' Sheridan asked.

'Not very often according to Adrian – and the only car they have access to is his. She's got a bike which she rides everywhere. But that was still in the shed when I checked.'

'Okay, so how did she leave the property? Taxi?'

Jack Staples shook his head slightly. 'Local taxi firms have been contacted and none of them picked her up from the home address.'

'She must have left the property somehow, maybe she got picked up by someone. What about a bus?'

'The closest bus stop is half a mile away and there's a CCTV camera which she would have to have walked past to get there. That's been checked and there's no sign of her.'

Sheridan fiddled with the pen that was still tucked behind her ear. 'What about her mobile?'

'She left that in the house.'

'Computer?'

'She doesn't have a computer. Her husband's got a laptop, but Caroline never uses it. He says she wouldn't even know how to turn it on.'

'Anything on the system for them? Any DV?'

'No, there's no domestic violence reported and they're both no trace on PNC. It was reported to the missing persons unit this morning. I seized Caroline's hairbrush and toothbrush. Adrian Crow is in a bit of a state, says it's totally out of character.'

'Good job,' Hill said abruptly. 'So, Caroline Crow has done a runner and left her husband. It happens. She packed her things, waited for him to be away from the house, withdrew some cash from her account and fucked off.'

Jack Staples raised the disc he'd been holding in his hand. 'Except, I've just got the CCTV back from when the money was taken out of her account.'

'And?' Hill asked impatiently.

'It wasn't her who made the withdrawal.'

Staples pushed the disc into Hill's computer, and they all watched as the screen flickered into life.

He pressed 'Play' and stood back with his arms crossed.

As the recording started, Sheridan and Anna leaned in closer.

'Pause it there,' Sheridan said, and Hill pressed pause.

'Fuck me.' Sheridan's shoulders dropped.

'Who's that?' Hill asked, staring at the image on the screen.

Anna and Sheridan replied in unison. 'That's Simon Banks.'

Hill looked up. 'The guy who had the severed hand delivered?'

'The very same.' Sheridan nodded.

'Where is he now?'

'Catching a flight to Australia.'

'What time's his flight?'

They all looked at the clock on Hill's wall.

Sheridan sighed. 'He took off ten minutes ago.'

CHAPTER 15

Dipesh confirmed that Simon Banks had boarded the plane at Heathrow. Airport CCTV was being checked to see if he was travelling alone. Sheridan also tasked Dipesh to place an all ports alert on Simon's passport, so that he'd be stopped when he landed in Perth.

As Anna drove them to Adrian Crow's house, Sheridan sent a text to Sam.

> *Hey beautiful. Sorry but I'm going to be at work until quite late. I'll see you at home later. Give Maud a kiss for me. x*

Sam texted back: *No worries hun. Just be careful out there. x*

Sheridan replied: *I love you. x*

Sam replied: *I love you too. And you have a nice bum. x*

Sheridan grinned and put her phone away, just as they arrived at Adrian's house.

Adrian Crow looked like he was about to collapse as Sheridan and Anna sat at his kitchen table. He hadn't stopped pacing the floor since they'd arrived.

'Can I call you Adrian?' Sheridan asked, glancing around the kitchen, suddenly feeling a crunch under her shoe. She looked down and noticed the light glimmering off a shard of glass.

'Yes.' Adrian Crow answered as though he hadn't even heard the question.

'There's glass on the floor. Did something get broken?' Sheridan knew immediately that her question was drenched in suspicion. *His wife is missing, cut him some slack, Sheridan*, she consciously checked herself.

Adrian went to the sink and filled a mug full of water. 'I got a bit upset earlier and threw a whisky bottle at the wall.' He took a sip of water and set the mug down on the draining board, his hands shaking like a junkie in withdrawal.

'That's understandable.' Sheridan cleared her throat. *So, you have violent tendencies?* she thought. 'Adrian, tell me about Caroline, what sort of person she is.'

Adrian leant back against the kitchen worktop, his eyes raw and bloodshot. 'She's perfect. In every way.' He burst into tears.

'We know this must be agony for you, but I'm trying to build a picture of Caroline. Her life and what she's like. Anything can help.'

Adrian went on to describe how they'd met eleven years before when he saw her standing in the rain one night, a broken umbrella flapping in her hand as the wind whipped around her. He'd offered her a lift home and they got talking. Months later, he proposed.

He talked about their relationship and how he couldn't remember them ever arguing. Caroline was quiet and unassuming – she didn't like confrontation, and neither did Adrian. They lived a simple life, blissfully happy in their own company, enjoying long walks together and meals out. Adrian felt guilty that he spent so much time away from home, but Caroline never complained, she was just always happy when he got home safely. His work as a rep for a pet food company took him around the country and although he loved his job, he'd recently contemplated retiring.

'I'm sixty-one this year. We're financially very secure. I should have given up work before now.' His face crumpled and Sheridan and Anna waited patiently for him to continue. But he remained silent, as though he had no more words inside him.

Sheridan broke the silence. 'Where are you based? Your job, I mean. Do you have an office somewhere?'

'The main office is in Manchester, but I hardly go in. They send me details of potential clients who might be interested in our range of pet foods, and I travel the country visiting them. So, I'm either at home working on the laptop or on the phone, or I'm visiting clients.' His head went down. 'I spend too much time away from home.'

'So you use a company car?'

'No. The car's mine, but the company pays all my expenses.'

Anna spoke next. 'Adrian, we've read the missing persons report. We understand that you took Caroline away to Llandudno for a few days and got back on her birthday, Wednesday eleventh March. You then got a call from a potential client that evening asking you to visit their shop in Norfolk, and while you were away overnight you tried calling Caroline but there was no reply. Is that unusual? Would she normally answer the phone?'

'Not always. She often goes to bed early or goes out to her swimming club on Thursday afternoons, and she and her friends might go out afterwards for a drink or a meal. She often doesn't answer the phone, so I didn't worry too much. But then when she didn't answer on the Friday morning, I got a bit concerned and as soon as I'd been to the shop, which turned out to be a wild-goose chase, I tried calling her again, and when there was no answer, I drove home as quickly as I could.'

'Did you call any of her friends?'

'No. The only friends she has are from her swimming club, and I don't really know them. I didn't want to panic anyone. I was panicking enough myself, which was why I called the police. I didn't know what else to do. As soon as I realised she wasn't here and her suitcase had gone, I . . .' His jaw tensed, and tears formed in his eyes.

'Is Caroline on social media? Is she on Facebook?'

'No, neither of us are.'

'The officer, Jack Staples, said that you were going to look for her passport. Did you find it?'

'No.' He peeled off a sheet of kitchen roll and blew his nose, before joining them at the table. 'I can't believe what's happening. She just wouldn't leave me.' He suddenly began gasping for breath, his chest heaving as he clasped his hands together to stop them shaking.

Sheridan and Anna waited patiently, stealing a look at each other. Both thinking exactly the same thing. Was this a genuine reaction? Or was Adrian Crow putting on a very convincing performance?

'I'm sorry.' He put his elbows on the table and rested his face in his palms.

When Adrian had regained his composure, Sheridan showed him the still from the ATM CCTV. 'Adrian, do you know this man?'

Adrian stared at the picture but didn't answer her. His eyes appeared glazed as if he was somewhere else completely.

'Adrian?'

'He looks vaguely familiar, but I can't place him. Who is he?'

'We know that Caroline's bank card was last used at an ATM on Church Street in Liverpool on Saturday seventh March. Does anyone else have access to her card?'

'Just me, but I never touch her account. Why?'

‘This man was captured on CCTV at the ATM, where he withdrew four hundred pounds from Caroline’s account.’

‘How did he know her PIN number?’

‘We don’t know.’

‘Do you know who he is?’

‘His name is Simon Banks. Does the name mean anything to you?’

‘No.’ Adrian stood up sharply.

‘Caroline’s never mentioned him?’

‘No. How has he got hold of her bank card?’ Adrian bit his lip. ‘She told me she’d lost it but thought it was in the house somewhere.’

‘We’ll be speaking to him.’

Adrian’s face flushed red. ‘Arresting him you mean? He’s stolen money from her.’ His words were tinged with anger. ‘What if he’s taken Caroline?’

‘We’re going to—’

Adrian interrupted. ‘So, this Simon Banks is known to the police, right? He has to be, because you know who he is.’

‘Not in that way—’

‘Then how do you know him?’ Adrian pressed.

‘He had a package delivered to his house, which he reported to us,’ Sheridan replied.

‘What kind of package?’

‘We can’t say at the moment, it’s an ongoing enquiry.’

‘Did the package have something to do with Caroline?’

‘As soon as we have more details, I’ll let you know, but it’s too early to assume anything.’

‘So, is he going to at least be arrested for stealing money out of Caroline’s account?’ Adrian stared at Sheridan. ‘Then you can question him about her disappearance . . .’

‘Like I said, we’ll be speaking to him.’

'When?'

'As soon as we can. He's out of the country at the moment.'

'He's done a runner, you mean.' Adrian spat out his words.

Sheridan didn't give Adrian the chance to ask any more questions before she pressed on. 'Tell us about the call you had from this Henry Blanchflower – the potential client who asked you to meet him in Norfolk?'

'He just called me out of the blue and it sounded like a promising meeting but then when I got there, no one had heard of him. I tried calling the number he'd left me, but it was switched off.'

'Did you think that was odd?'

'Too bloody right I did. I was going to call the number again when I got back home, but then I found Caroline was missing and I didn't give it another thought. I can't think straight about anything.'

'Does she have a lot of friends who visit her?'

'Not really, I don't think anyone comes. Actually, I saw the postman today. I asked him when he last saw Caroline and he said he thinks it was a couple of weeks ago. He said he can't remember when he actually last spoke to her.' Adrian went over to the kitchen dresser and picked up the piece of paper that the postman had given him with his details on. 'I took his name and number in case you needed to speak to him.'

'That's helpful. Thank you. I understand that Caroline doesn't have any family?'

'No. She's an only child and her parents died when she was young. She doesn't have children and neither do I.'

'What about your parents?'

'Long gone.'

'How does Caroline get around? Does she use taxis? Buses?' Sheridan asked, watching every expression that crossed Adrian's face, looking for any signs that might give her an indication that he was involved in his wife's disappearance. He seemed genuine, but Sheridan inwardly reserved her opinion. For now.

'When we're not together in the car, she goes everywhere on her bike,' Adrian replied.

'Have you tried calling any of her friends since you reported her missing?'

'Yes, a couple of them, but they didn't answer the phone and I didn't want to leave a message. Like I said, the only friends she has are from her swimming club and I don't know them.'

'We'll need to speak to them.'

'Of course.'

Sheridan wrote everything down in her pocketbook.

Before they left for Hale Street, Sheridan and Anna looked around the house while Adrian remained in the kitchen. Sheridan stood in Caroline's en-suite bathroom, taking in every detail. There was a wooden stacking unit in the corner and with gloved hands she opened it, finding each drawer was allocated for a different type of toiletry. One for hair products, shampoo, conditioner and an unopened box of hair dye. The second was for shower gel, body and face creams. The third contained toothpaste, a pack of toothbrushes, dental floss and mouthwash. She noted that Caroline's wardrobe was practically empty, as was her bedside cabinet.

As they rejoined Adrian in the kitchen, Sheridan asked him, 'Did Caroline own a lot of clothes?'

'Not really, she's quite minimalistic.' Adrian leant back against the kitchen worktop, looking frail and broken.

'I understand you had matching suitcases – can we see yours?'

'Of course.' Adrian fetched his suitcase from upstairs and returned to the kitchen with it. 'I haven't unpacked it yet.'

It was made of a soft material, dark blue with a single white stripe around the middle. Not particularly large and certainly not big enough to hold too much. More like the size you take on an aircraft as hand luggage.

Sheridan responded. 'It's quite small. I'm surprised if Caroline could fit much stuff in there. Does she have another suitcase?'

'No. Just the one. Like I said, she didn't have many clothes.'

'What about any other type of bag? Are there any others missing?'

'No. I don't think so.' Adrian looked at the case. 'So, what happens now?'

'We'll keep you posted. Are you happy for PC Staples to stay in touch with you?'

'Of course I am. Sorry, can I just ask, are you actually out looking for Caroline?'

'We have a team working on it. I promise you we're doing everything we can, Adrian.'

'Can I say something?'

'Of course.'

'This is totally out of character for Caroline. I know you're probably thinking that she's taken herself off somewhere, but I'm literally begging you to believe me when I say that she wouldn't do that. Please don't treat this as just another missing person case. Something is wrong and I mean, really wrong.'

Sheridan stopped short of saying that there was no such thing as '*just another missing person case*'. After assuring Adrian that they would do everything they could to locate Caroline, Sheridan and Anna left and got back into the car.

'So, what do you think? Do you reckon the hand belongs to Caroline?' Anna asked, looking up at the house.

'Possibly. But I'm more inclined to think she's done a runner. I know Adrian thinks otherwise, but all the signs are there that she's left of her own accord.'

'I agree.'

'We need to find the link between Caroline and Simon Banks. They've had contact somehow, because the CCTV footage shows he clearly knows her PIN number.'

'And now he's pissed off to Australia. Maybe Caroline's with him?'

'Her passport hasn't been picked up on the all ports alert, so she's not with him. Maybe she's going to join him though.'

Anna nodded. 'I'll get Dipesh to do some checks on Simon's mobile – let's see if we can track his steps before Caroline disappeared.'

'And while we're at it, let's check out Adrian's too.'

CHAPTER 16

Tuesday 17 March

Sheridan poured herself a cup of water from the machine at the back of the CID office.

DCI Hill Knowles walked in and scanned the room before she perched on the corner of Rob Wills' desk.

Anna Markinson was sitting at the front of the room, notepad and pen poised.

'Right – good morning, everyone.' Sheridan made her way to the whiteboard and squinted at it. 'Let's see what we've got.' She turned to face her team. 'You've all read the statements from Simon Banks and the misper report on Caroline Crow, so let me summarise and then I'll go through what we need to focus on. As we know, Simon Banks is on his way to Perth and there's an all ports alert on his passport, so when he lands this afternoon, he'll be stopped.'

She updated the team on their visit to speak to Adrian Crow. 'Now, as to how Caroline actually left the house, I think she was picked up by someone. This would be the only method that fits the facts we currently have, so let's bear that in mind.' She paused. 'Right, let's have a catch-up before I task out some more jobs. Rob, what's the update on house-to-house at Simon Banks' road? Have we got any CCTV?'

'House-to-house is done, no one saw anyone looking suspicious, no one actually saw anyone deliver anything to the property. Two residents down the road have cameras and again, I'm going through the downloads.'

She turned to Anna. 'Anything on intel?'

'Nothing, we've got no other cases where a body part, burnt or otherwise, has been delivered.'

'Okay, what about Henry Blanchflower? Have we found anything more about the one born in Bootle?' She directed her question at Rob Wills.

'Yeah, he was killed in 2001, hit-and-run incident. He was knocked off his motorbike and found in a ditch, no one was ever arrested. There are other Henry Blanchflowers, but none that stand out at the moment. And it's probably an alias.'

'True. But keep going with it.'

Dipesh raised his hand. 'We've been through the CCTV at Heathrow, and it shows Simon Banks alone. He didn't travel with anyone else.'

'Okay, thanks, Dipesh. We need to check out Adrian Crow's account of the trip that him and Caroline made to Llandudno, and we need to speak to the hotel staff. I want details of everyone who was staying at the hotel at the same time as them, see if anyone remembers them. I also want it checked that he actually did go on the trip to Norfolk.'

Dipesh piped up. 'Is Adrian a suspect in Caroline's disappearance?'

'I think until we get an ID on the hand, the evidence points to her leaving of her own accord. She's taken most of her things, Adrian can't find her passport and she's left her mobile in the house, so maybe she knows that we can trace her from it.' Sheridan paused.

'Maybe she doesn't *want* to be traced. But yes, he's a person of interest until we can discount him. What's the saying?' She raised her eyebrows.

The whole room replied in unison. 'It's always the husband.'

She turned to Rob Wills. 'House-to-house is being done with Adrian Crow's neighbours. Rob, can you look at any CCTV around Adrian's home address? We really need to know how she left the house.'

Rob Wills nodded. 'No problem.'

Sheridan continued, 'I want Simon Banks checked out. Let's make sure he did go to the conference in Oxford. I've seized Caroline's mobile phone and it's being looked at now. The landline is also being checked for incoming and outgoing calls. We need to speak to Caroline's GP. And I want financial checks done on her bank account – see what that brings up. Adrian told us that Caroline had lost her bank card, so let's assume that's just what she told him. We know that Simon Banks used her card on the seventh of March. So we don't know where it is now.'

She turned to Dipesh. 'Can you do some work around Simon Banks' mobile – find out his movements before Caroline disappeared? And also . . . Adrian's mobile – let's see where he's been.'

'Will do.'

Sheridan took a sip of water. 'I'll give Simon Banks' secretary a call. I'll just ask if Simon's ever treated Caroline or Adrian, see if there's a link there, even though Adrian says he's never heard of him – he did say he looked vaguely familiar.'

Hill put her thumb up. This was a habit of Hill's that when they'd first started working together had irritated the shit out of Sheridan. But she and the team were used to it now. Even if it still irritated Sheridan. Just a little bit.

Sheridan looked around the room and picked out Dipesh again. 'Dipesh, can you contact a Valerie Moss – she runs the swimming club that Caroline Crow goes to on Thursdays. See if she said anything to her friends that raised any suspicions with them.'

Dipesh nodded. 'Will do.'

Sheridan addressed the whole team. 'Let's not assume that Caroline has decided to disappear. Let's keep an open mind. Until we can prove that she planned this, then it's still possible that something has happened to her. The hand might be hers, remember.' She glanced at the clock. 'Simon Banks is due to land in a couple of hours, so he'll be picked up. Until then, let's crack on. Keep me and Hill posted.'

CHAPTER 17

Sheridan looked up as Hill stormed into her office. 'Simon fucking Banks wasn't stopped at the airport.'

Sheridan's jaw dropped. 'What? Why not?'

'I don't know, but he's landed and gone.'

Sheridan looked to the ceiling. 'Fuck. How the hell did he get through without being stopped?' She thought for a moment. 'Bollocks. I bet he's got two passports. He's flown out on his English one and used an Australian one when he landed. I should have realised that when he said he had a son living there and he visited him regularly.' She looked at Hill. 'I'm sorry. That's my cock-up.'

Hill put her hand up. 'We all missed it, it's not just you. Have we got his son's contact number?'

Sheridan sighed. 'No.'

'Okay, well, we'll just have to see if the Australian police can trace his son's address and I'll ask them to ping Simon's phone. Get yourself off home, I'll update the team.' She put her thumb up and left.

Sheridan picked up the phone and dialled Simon Banks' number. Switched off.

At that moment Anna walked in and Sheridan updated her. 'I am so pissed off with myself. We could have had him.' She sighed. 'Anyway, you might as well go home, mate.'

'It wasn't just you, Sheridan. We all missed it. We're a team, remember, and so we're all just as responsible.'

Sheridan shook her head and sent a text to Sam.

Hey gorgeous. I'm just leaving work. x

Sam replied: *I thought you were on a late one? No worries, I'll throw something together for dinner. x*

Sheridan took a deep breath and texted back: *Great. See you soon. x*

Sheridan looked up at Anna, who was still hovering in her office. 'You off home or what?'

'Yeah. You?'

'Yeah. Sam's throwing something together for dinner.' She pulled her jacket from the back of her chair. 'You look fed up – you okay?'

'I'm fine. Just sometimes hate going home to an empty house.'

'Come to ours, we've got wine. You can stay over.'

'Are you sure?' Anna perked up.

'Well, I figured that your pathetic "I hate going home to an empty house" comment was a hint.'

'It was a bit lame, wasn't it?' Anna smiled.

'You can leave your car here. We'll go in mine.' Sheridan ushered Anna out of her office.

'I've just got to grab something.' Anna scurried off down the corridor, returning a minute later.

'What's that?' Sheridan pointed to the brown leather suitcase that Anna had wheeled out of her office.

'My overnight case. Well, my "staying at Sheridan and Sam's case". It's just a few clothes . . . don't look at me like that.'

Sheridan shook her head. 'Move in, why don't you?' she said sarcastically, grinning. 'I got hold of Simon Banks' secretary earlier.

I just asked her if either Adrian or Caroline have ever been a patient of his and neither of them have. I want to know how he knows Caroline.'

As Sheridan drove home, the conversation turned to Anna. It had been ten months since she had thrown her partner, Steve, out of her house. They'd been together for over ten years and everything was perfect on the surface, but they argued like any other couple. Sheridan was aware there were problems, she had seen bruises on Anna's arm and had asked her outright if Steve was hitting her. Anna swore to Sheridan that he hadn't once put a hand on her. He hadn't *once*. He'd hit her several times and on one occasion had punched her so hard in the face that she lost a tooth. She kept it a secret from everyone, including Sheridan. She'd also kept it a secret from Steve that she'd fallen pregnant and had a termination. Sheridan had taken her to the hospital for the procedure and again made Anna promise that he hadn't been violent. And again, Anna had lied to her best friend. She had to lie, because she knew that if Sheridan knew the truth, she'd rip his balls off and throw them in the River Mersey.

After Steve had gone, she started to rebuild her life on her own. And then he turned up one day and told her he'd found work in Glasgow and was moving away. But Steve also told lies. He wasn't going anywhere. And unbeknown to Anna, he'd been watching her house at night.

'Why don't you get a lodger?' Sheridan asked as they emerged on the Wirral side of the Kingsway tunnel.

'I could do I suppose. But then I couldn't walk around naked eating cornflakes.' Anna grinned.

'Oh my God, do you really?'

'Do I really what?'

'Eat cornflakes. They're bloody rank.'

As they drove up Bidston Hill and turned into Sheridan's road, her mobile rang. She let Anna answer.

'Hello?'

'Is that you, Sheridan?' DC Dipesh Mois asked.

Anna recognised his voice. 'Hi Dipesh, it's Anna – Sheridan's driving, let me put you on loudspeaker.'

'Can you hear me okay?' Dipesh asked.

'Yeah, go for it.'

'I spoke to Valerie Moss, the woman who runs the swimming club that Caroline Crow goes to.'

'Okay and what did she say?'

'Caroline stopped going three months ago. She told them she was going away.'

'Really?'

'Yeah, and I spoke to her friends at the club, too – they all said the same thing. Apparently, she'd become more and more distant and was going to the club less and less. They all said that the last time they saw her, she said she was going away and wasn't coming back, but when they asked her where she was going, she was really vague and just said that her and Adrian were looking to settle abroad.'

'Okay, cheers, Dipesh.' Anna ended the call and turned to Sheridan. 'What the fuck is going on in Caroline's life?'

CHAPTER 18

Sheridan opened the front door and bent down to pick up Maud, who appeared to have a lump of Bolognese sauce stuck to her head.

Anna closed the front door behind her, leaving her suitcase in the hallway before following Sheridan into the kitchen, taking off her coat and laying it over a kitchen chair.

'Hi, Anna. This is a nice surprise. You staying for dinner?' Sam quickly kissed Sheridan, then whipped a tea towel over her shoulder before giving Anna a hug.

'Only if you've actually managed to cook something that won't give me the galloping shits.'

'Very funny. Wine?' Sam opened the fridge.

'I'd love a glass.' Anna cocked her head at Sheridan as a thought struck her. 'If Caroline told her swimming club that her and Adrian were planning to go away, maybe they're in it together somehow?'

Sam put out two wine glasses and filled them to the top, opting for a beer herself. 'Is this the missing woman case?' she asked.

'Yeah,' Sheridan replied.

'So, you think it's a set-up?' Sam opened the oven door, prompting Maud to wriggle out of Sheridan's arms and jump on to the floor, sniffing the blackened garlic bread.

'Bollocks.' Sam waved the tea towel over the cremated remains, before dramatically putting one hand in the air. 'Before either of you say anything, the spag bol is perfect and so the fact that I have slightly overdone the garlic bread doesn't count.' She peered at them over her beer bottle. 'Now get out of my kitchen.'

Sheridan and Anna settled down on the living-room sofa. Maud followed them a moment later, with crispy garlic bread resembling a flattened piece of coal clenched between her teeth.

Anna pulled her boots off and sipped her wine. 'So, come on, Sherlock, what do you think about Caroline Crow?'

They talked through the case over dinner, bouncing ideas and theories off each other, and as always, Sam had her own suggestions.

Later, as they cleared the dishes away, Sam was wiping the worktops down as she spoke. 'Maybe it's an insurance job. Caroline and Adrian have planned it together. She disappears, and after a while she's declared dead. Then they grab the insurance money and bugger off to some remote island and live out their days in the sun.' She dramatically threw a tea towel into the washing machine, turned and took a bow. 'Case solved. I am a genius.'

'Not bad,' Sheridan replied as she and Anna gave Sam a round of applause.

'So, what about the burnt hand?' Anna asked, putting the last of the cutlery back in the drawer.

Sam shook her head. 'Jesus. I can't solve the *whole* case for you . . .'

'You have no idea, do you?' Anna grinned.

Sam looked to the ceiling, thinking. 'Okay. So, Adrian and Caroline hang out at a crematorium and when no one is looking . . .'

'Stop there.' Sheridan put her hand up and threw a look at Anna, just as they both burst out laughing.

CHAPTER 19

Dipesh Mois was sitting at his desk, spinning himself around on his chair. Counting the number of revolutions out loud. 'Forty-seven, forty-eight . . .'

Rob Wills turned off his computer, ready to head home. 'Are you done?' he asked, shaking his head.

'Nope. I'm about to break my personal record. Fifty-one . . .'

'You're an idiot,' Rob replied, just as the phone on Dipesh's desk rang. 'Now what are you going to do?' he asked, grinning.

Dipesh said, 'You could answer it for me, if you were a true friend. I think this is going in the Guinness Book of Records . . . fifty-three . . .'

'I'm not answering your phone.' Rob grabbed his coat from the back of his chair. 'It's probably your wife telling you to grow up and get home.'

Dipesh conceded and answered, grasping the side of his desk and blinking away the little white spots that danced in front of his eyes. 'DC Mois, Hale Street CID.'

'Oh, good evening, can I speak to DS Anna Markinson, please?'

'I'm afraid DS Markinson's off duty. Can I take a message, or can I help?' Dipesh spoke slowly, feeling suddenly seasick.

'Oh, don't worry, it's nothing important. I'll catch up with her tomorrow. Is she back on duty in the morning?'

'She should be, yes . . .' The line then went dead. 'Bollocks.' Dipesh stood up.

'What?' Rob asked.

'I wasted a potential record-breaking opportunity for a call I didn't need to answer.'

Rob sighed. 'I worry about you sometimes.' He stepped over to Dipesh and put his hand on his shoulder, smiling. 'Go home and practise there.'

'No chance, mate, my wife would kill me if I did this at home.' He chuckled and together they headed out of the office, Dipesh a little unsteadily.

◆ ◆ ◆

Anna's ex-partner, Steve, stared at his phone after hanging up on Dipesh. Then he looked up at Anna's house. He'd been parked up the road for nearly an hour in the darkness. *So, you're not at work and you're not at home,* he thought, glaring at the empty drive. He felt his knuckles stiffen as he gripped the steering wheel and closed his eyes, squeezing out tears of rage.

'Let's see if you're staying with your mate, shall we?' He started the engine and headed towards the Kingsway tunnel, to Sheridan Holler's house.

Twenty minutes later he drove slowly past, heart thumping in his chest. Anna's car wasn't there. He turned at the top of the road and drove past again, scouring the cars parked on either side. None of them were Anna's. *She's not here. She's met someone else.*

He sat there for an hour. His mind filled with images of Anna sharing a bed with another man. His throat felt like it was closing up, and his mouth was dry.

In the last ten months, he'd driven down Anna's road so many times. When her car wasn't on the drive, he knew he would find it always parked outside Sheridan's. But tonight was different. She was somewhere else. With *someone* else.

He started the engine and made his way back to the Kingsway tunnel to sit outside Anna's house, where he'd sit parked in the shadows. Planning what he was going to do next.

If he couldn't have her then no one else was going to.

CHAPTER 20

Wednesday 18 March

Rob Wills quickly closed his desk drawer as Hill Knowles stomped into CID, looking like she was about to punch someone. When she had first joined the team almost eighteen months before, a betting pool had been set up to guess her real name, with everyone assuming that 'Hill' was shortened from something. Various suggestions were put forward, including Hillary, Hillman and Hill Billy. Unbeknown to the whole of CID, Hill had discovered the envelope marked *Guess Boss's Real Name* tucked in Rob's drawer and the money that had been collected. As someone normally lacking in the sense of humour department, Hill had found the whole thing very amusing and periodically checked the envelope, making a mental note to herself that if and when – mainly *if* – her real name was ever guessed, she would disclose that she was aware of the bet, confiscate the money and give it to charity.

'Morning, Rob,' she said as she strode past his desk. Biting down on a smile.

'Morning, ma'am.' He raised an eyebrow at Dipesh as he pushed his knee against his drawer, ensuring it was fully closed.

'Where's Sheridan and Anna?' Hill put her palms in the air. 'Anyone?'

'I think they're in the loo, ma'am.'

'Jesus Christ. Those two spend more time in the ladies' toilet than Cagney and fucking Lacey.'

'Morning, Hill,' Sheridan said as she breezed through the door, with Anna in tow, carrying a mug of coffee. 'Can I be Cagney? She was ballsy.' Sheridan joined Hill at the whiteboard. 'Anna can be Lacey. Wasn't she the frumpy one?' Sheridan turned to Rob, the trivia king, for the answer.

Rob tilted his head. 'She wasn't really frumpy. She was probably always knackered – holding down a full-time job, married with two boys. But there *was* something quite sexy about her.'

Silent nods of agreement from the older ones in the room. Male and female.

'Wasn't her husband called Harry?' Sheridan set her coffee mug down.

'Harvey. And her sons were Michael and Harvey Junior. Did you know that Sharon Gless, who played Cagney, wasn't the original one? The original one was actually Loretta Swit from—'

'Let's talk shit all day, shall we?' Hill barked, shaking her head. 'Okay, before we go round the room, Dipesh spoke to Valerie Moss yesterday, the woman who runs the swimming club that Caroline was attending. I say "was", because, apparently, she hasn't been there for three months. She told her friends at the club that she was going away – that her and Adrian were moving abroad.'

Sheridan added, 'The strange thing is, unless he's lying, Adrian doesn't appear to know anything about this alleged plan.'

Hill pointed at Rob, who abruptly sat upright. 'Rob, what's happening with the CCTV?'

'We're still going through the footage we got from Simon's neighbours. None of it's brilliant. So far, we've just got a few dog walkers, postmen, a couple of delivery vans, and some kids on bikes. But we can't tell if any of them actually stop outside his house or go down his path. We'll keep going through what we've got. Nothing obvious from the CCTV near Adrian's either, but we've got more to look through.'

Hill folded her arms. 'Okay. Dipesh? What have we got from Caroline's mobile and the landline?'

'The landline has thrown up a few numbers, but it doesn't look like it's used very often. The last call made from it was on Saturday seventh March at 14.32 and lasted seven minutes. Then the same number was called again at 17.13. This time the call lasted one minute.' He paused. 'She hardly used her mobile by the looks of it. The only number she seems to call is Adrian's and that's not very often. He calls her most days and there's quite a few missed calls from him going back a few months. I've got the voicemails that Adrian left her when he was in Norfolk.'

Dipesh played the voice messages to the team, who all listened in silence.

Thursday 12 March 2.22 p.m.: *Hi darling – well, I made it to Norfolk, just checked in. The hotel's basic but seems okay. I'm just going to grab something to eat, and I'll call you later. Hope you're enjoying swimming club. Love you.*

Thursday 12 March 9.14 p.m.: *Hello darling, I'm off to bed. I expect you're in bed or out with your swimming club friends. Hope you're okay. I miss you. Goodnight, sweetheart.*

Friday 13 March 7.45 a.m.: *Are you there? Caroline? Can you pick up, darling? Are you still in bed? I expect you are. Anyway, I'm off to see my client in a bit. I'll call you later. Text or call me when you get this. I love you.*

Friday 13 March 9.35 a.m.: *Hi, well, that was a waste of time. I've been to the shop and apparently no one has heard of Henry Blanchflower. I've just tried ringing his number but the phone's switched off. Sorry if I sound pissed off but I've come all this way and . . . anyway, please call me if you get this, I'm a bit worried about you now.*

I'm on my way home so I'll see you in a few hours. Please call me. I love you, darling.

Sheridan pinched her mouth between her thumb and forefinger. 'Anyone pick up anything a bit off from those messages?'

Anna twisted round in her chair. 'Well, as worried as he appears to be about Caroline not answering, the first thing he talks about on the Friday morning is the fact that the client isn't there, and then ends the message by saying he's worried about her. I would have thought it would be the other way around.'

'Me too,' Sheridan agreed, turning to Dipesh. 'What about the mobile that called Adrian's phone? This Henry Blanchflower character?'

'I've tried calling,' Dipesh said, 'but it's permanently switched off. It's a pay-as-you-go, unregistered. There have been no incoming calls, just outgoing. And apart from that call to Adrian's phone, it has only ever called one other number. I've checked that one out and it's also an unregistered pay-as-you-go. And that phone only ever receives calls, doesn't make any outgoing. The phone that does make calls, the one Henry Blanchflower used to call Adrian, wasn't far from Adrian's house when he made the call either. It pinged off a mast just up the road.'

Sheridan replied, 'That's interesting. There was a pair of gloves found in a bush outside Adrian's lounge window. Could the person who made the call to get him away from the property be linked to those gloves? When do we expect the forensics back on them?'

'Anytime now. And I'm waiting on data to see what area both phones have covered over the last few months.'

Anna spoke up. 'We've spoken to Caroline's GP. She hasn't been to the doctors' for two years. She's not on any medication. Her history shows the usual stuff – the odd chest infection, an eye infection, smear tests. No mental health issues and no indication that she's ever been depressed or suicidal. No evidence that she's ever reported domestic violence or anything like that.'

Sheridan nodded. 'Okay, thanks, Anna. Moving on . . . Bridie, what about Adrian and Caroline's visit to the Hampshire Hotel in Llandudno?'

DC Bridie Sexton picked up her notes and read them out to the room. 'They checked in together on the Sunday and the staff said that Adrian had called ahead and asked for champagne to be left in the room. He told them that it was his wife's birthday treat and when they arrived, he seemed very happy and excited. They said that Caroline was quiet, didn't say too much but she seemed fine. They left the room a few times, had breakfast and dinner in the hotel restaurant. Nothing out of the ordinary.'

'And she was with him when they checked out?'

'Yeah, I've asked for the CCTV from reception just to make sure. I'm also going through the list of people who stayed at the hotel at the same time as Adrian and Caroline. I've spoken to a few, but they don't remember them.'

'Okay. And what about the Kingsley Hotel in Norfolk that Adrian went to?'

'Yep, that all checks out too. Adrian checked in just after 2 p.m. on the Thursday. The reception staff remember seeing him go out around 3.30 p.m., and saw him return an hour or so later. As far as they know he was in his room all evening and they didn't see him again until breakfast. He checked out at 8.15 a.m. Again, I've asked for the CCTV to confirm all of this.'

'What about the pet shop Adrian went to in Norfolk to meet this Henry Blanchflower person?'

'I spoke to the manager. He confirmed that Adrian turned up on the Friday morning and asked for Henry Blanchflower, who they've never heard of. Adrian was there for around twenty minutes or so and then left. They've already sent me the CCTV. You can clearly see Adrian, and the timing matches his story.'

'Good work. And, finally, what about Simon Banks' visit to the conference in Oxford?'

'That all checks out as well. He booked into the Porchester Hotel in the city, about a five-minute walk from the conference centre. He checked in at 3 p.m. on Thursday twelfth March and checked out at 7 a.m. on Monday the sixteenth . . .' Bridie Sexton paused as the phone on Rob Wills' desk rang.

'DC Wills.' He looked up. 'I'll put her on.' He held the phone up for Hill Knowles. 'It's for you. Forensics have got a result on the burnt hand.'

CHAPTER 21

Hill Knowles kept the phone pressed to her ear. No one moved. Was this it? Was this when they found out that someone had cut off Caroline Crow's hand and delivered it to Simon Banks? If the hand did belong to Caroline, then where was she? Was she still alive? If it was her hand, then she certainly hadn't set up her own disappearance.

Hill finally ended the call. She took off her glasses before addressing the room. 'Well, it's not Caroline Crow. The DNA doesn't match. We know it's a female, hard to age her exactly but possibly between thirty and sixty years old. Her hand was sawn off, and that was done before it was set on fire. There's no other fingerprints or DNA on the package, except Simon Banks', but that's no surprise seeing as it was delivered to him.'

Anna put her hand up. 'We're in the process of getting DNA and fingerprints from the postmen and women who deliver to Simon's house. I think we should still get them, in case any other packages are delivered.'

'I agree.' Sheridan nodded, as Hill thumbed up; her usual mode of approval.

Hill went on to tell the team that whoever the hand belonged to, they already knew she wasn't on the DNA database, so there was no forensic evidence that could provide her identity.

Unless the rest of her body was located.

CHAPTER 22

Sheridan and Anna pulled up outside Adrian Crow's house. They had called ahead to let him know that they were on their way to discuss a development in the case.

He was at the door before they even got out of the car.

They walked up to the front door. 'Hello, Adrian.' Sheridan and Anna wiped their feet on the doormat before following him into the kitchen.

Sheridan noticed that Adrian appeared to have aged in the last two days, his skin now taking on a grey hue.

'How are you doing?' Sheridan asked as they all sat at the kitchen table.

'I feel lost, if I'm honest. I can't get used to Caroline not being here.' Adrian leaned forward in his seat as he spoke. Both Sheridan and Anna could smell stale alcohol on his breath. 'So, you said there was a development?'

Anna clasped her hands together, hesitating for a moment before dropping the bomb at Adrian's feet. 'Adrian, we spoke to Valerie Moss at Caroline's swimming club. I'm afraid that Caroline stopped going there three months ago. She told Valerie that she was going away.'

Adrian abruptly stood up. 'What?' He put his hands on his head and marched across to the other side of the room. 'That's not possible. She must have made a mistake. Caroline *has* been going, she goes every Thursday.' He turned on his heel and walked back to the table. Leaning forward, he placed his palms flat down on the tabletop. 'Caroline would never lie to me. This Valerie must be mistaken. Maybe she's thinking of someone else?'

'She's not mistaken, Adrian. She was definitely talking about Caroline. Apparently, Caroline told her friends at the swimming club that you were planning to move abroad.'

'That's ridiculous. Something's not right.' Adrian sat back down. 'Why would she say that? We had no plans to go *anywhere*.'

'Adrian,' Anna said, 'we want to talk to you about the phone call from Henry Blanchflower, when he asked you to meet him in Norfolk. It appears that whoever made that call to you was fairly near the house at the time.'

'Near my house?'

'Yes. Is there anyone locally you think that Caroline may have been in contact with?'

'No,' he answered immediately, clenching his teeth together.

'Are you sure?'

'I'm sure.'

'Who has your mobile number?'

'Caroline obviously, everyone I work with, clients, loads of people.'

Anna nodded, but kept pressing. 'It's just that the mobile number for this Henry Blanchflower – if that really is his name – has only ever called one other number apart from yours.'

'What number?'

'It's another unregistered phone, so we don't know who it belongs to.'

Sheridan's mobile rang and she looked at the screen. 'Sorry, I have to take this.' She stepped outside. 'Yes, Dipesh.'

'Are you free to speak?'

'Yes, mate. Go ahead.'

'Do you remember a case you dealt with last year? That burglary where the elderly woman – Edith Elliot – died in her bed . . .'

'Yeah, of course I do. Gabriel Howard went down for it. He got released a couple of weeks ago.'

'Well, we've got a DNA hit on the gloves found in Adrian's garden. The ones hidden in the bush.'

'Don't tell me it's Gabriel fucking Howard.'

'It is.'

CHAPTER 23

Sheridan pulled out on to the main road. 'That little shit.'

'What do you think he was doing there?' Anna clicked her seat belt in.

'My guess? He was going to burgle the place. He's got previous for it. Nice big house, nice area . . . He's probably been watching the house like he did with Oliver Elliot's.'

'Bit sloppy leaving his gloves there,' Anna said. 'Why take them off?'

'I don't know,' Sheridan replied, her mind working overtime. Recalling the details of the Edith Elliot case. 'Bastard.'

'Why do you hate him so much?'

'Because, in my eyes, he literally scared that poor woman to death, and I don't think he regrets it no matter what he says.'

'In fairness, Edith Elliot was very poorly anyway and . . .' Anna hesitated as she noticed Sheridan's jaw tense. 'I know she should have died in peace, as you always say, but Gabriel didn't kill her.'

'No. In the eyes of the law he didn't, but I can't bear to think of how scared she would have been in her last moments.'

Anna frowned, changing the subject. 'Bit of a coincidence that Simon and Gabriel are both linked to Caroline.'

Sheridan chewed her bottom lip. 'I'm going to get his phone checked out, see what the little fucker's been up to. Hopefully it'll show he's been to the house.'

◆ ◆ ◆

As soon as they arrived back at Hale Street nick, Sheridan and Anna made their way straight to Hill's office.

'I take it you've heard about the DNA hit?' Hill was sitting behind her desk. As they walked in, she tipped the remains of a packet of crisps into her mouth, scrunched up the packet and dropped it in the bin.

'Yeah. I think Gabriel has been watching Adrian Crow's place.' Sheridan bit her lip again. 'I want the forensics team to check Adrian's house. Now that we know that Gabriel Howard has been there and left his gloves outside, I want to see if he's been *inside*.'

Anna suddenly clicked her fingers. 'I'll be back in a minute.'

Hill raised her hands. 'Where's she going?' she asked, impatiently.

Sheridan shrugged. 'No idea. So, how about this forensic search on Adrian's place?'

'I agree. But not just to see if Gabriel's been inside, we can't justify that. We can however ask Adrian if he'll consent due to our concerns that Caroline may have come to harm.'

'What if he says no?'

'Then he's got something to hide.'

'Exactly. Anyway, Gabriel doesn't own a car, but he's probably using his sister's car. So, I'll get Rob to check CCTV, see if we can place the car near Adrian's house and I'll have a marker put on it to see where he goes. I'll also get his phone checked out.'

Hill ripped open the miserable pre-packed sandwich that had sat on her desk for the last two days and bit into it.

Suddenly, Anna charged back in. 'If Gabriel Howard *has* been to Adrian's house, then he's never going to admit it.' She shoved a sheet of paper under Sheridan's nose.

Sheridan smiled as she read the paper. Then she passed it over to Hill, who didn't read it but waited for an explanation.

'He's got an exclusion zone on his licence conditions not to go within the area marked in red,' Sheridan said. 'Basically, to keep him away from Oliver Elliot's place. And what do you know? Adrian's house is within that area too. If we can place Gabriel there, we can report him for breaching his licence. And maybe get the fucker locked up while we're at it.'

CHAPTER 24

It was gone 7 p.m. by the time Sheridan pulled up outside her house. Anna had accepted the offer to stay over again, and as Sheridan switched off the engine, they agreed that they wouldn't discuss the case all evening.

'So, we're agreed? No talking shop. We'll ask Sam how *her* day was and switch off from work, okay?' Sheridan got out of the car.

'Agreed.'

Sam was upstairs, emerging from the toilet as they came through the front door. Maud was sitting in the hallway and stretched her back legs, purring loudly.

'Hey, you two. I've ordered a takeout. Thought I'd take a night off from cooking.'

Anna and Sheridan flicked a look at each other, their thoughts mirrored but unspoken. *A night off for us enduring your cooking, more like.*

Sam reached the bottom of the stairs, and kissed Sheridan on the cheek. 'You look knackered. Go and sit down. I'll pour you both a drink.'

'You're an angel.' Anna clasped Sam's cheeks between her hands and kissed her on the forehead.

'How was your day?' Sheridan asked, keeping the promise not to talk about work.

'Same old, same old. How's the case going?' Sam asked, almost tripping over as Maud raced past her and into the kitchen.

'Fine. So, anything exciting happen at school?' Sheridan pulled off her boots.

'Nope. Anyway, what's the latest? Have you found out anything more about the hand?' Sam forged on.

Anna stood in the kitchen doorway and threw a look at Sheridan, who dropped her shoulders. 'We tried.'

Sheridan went on to tell Sam about the forensic results on the hand and the fact that the gloves found hidden in the bush at Adrian Crow's house belonged to Gabriel Howard.

'He's the burglar, right?' Sam poured out three glasses of wine.

'Yeah.'

Three hours later, they were still discussing the case when Sheridan's mobile rang. It was Hill.

'Hi, boss, what's up?'

'We've found Caroline Crow's suitcase.'

'Shit.' Sheridan looked at Anna. 'Where?'

'Stuck in reeds in a river at the back of Maple View in Crosby. Member of the public called it in, thought it looked suspicious.'

'That's where Simon Banks lives – there's a little river at the back of his garden.'

'I know.'

'Are we sure it's hers?'

'Yeah, it's identical to Adrian's and it's got her passport in it.'

'Anything else?'

'Nope. Just her passport. I've organised a search team to cover the area around and along the river.'

'Any news from the Australian police about pinging Simon's phone?'

'They've put a marker on it, but nothing yet. It's probably switched off. They'll keep me posted.'

‘Okay. Is it alright if I don’t speak to Adrian tonight?’ Sheridan asked. ‘I’d rather go straight round there first thing in the morning.’

Hill replied, ‘Yes, I agree. I’m speaking to the super again in the morning, when he’ll organise a press conference. The press are going crazy over this case. I’m also authorising a forensic search of Simon Banks’ house and car. Uniform have done a drive-by and his car’s not there. I take it he drove to Heathrow?’

‘Yeah, he was planning to.’

There was a momentary silence before Hill spoke again. ‘Are you okay?’

‘I’m fine, bit tired but—’

‘I meant about tomorrow.’

‘Seeing Adrian Crow?’

‘No. Matthew’s anniversary.’

Sheridan was stunned at the question and even more stunned that Hill had remembered the date.

The nineteenth of March.

‘Oh. Yes, thank you,’ Sheridan stuttered her reply.

‘Good. Right, see you tomorrow.’ Hill abruptly ended the call, leaving Sheridan staring at her phone.

‘What’s wrong?’ Anna asked.

Sheridan put her mobile on the coffee table and told Anna about the suitcase. ‘She also remembered it’s the anniversary of Matthew’s death tomorrow.’

CHAPTER 25

Thursday 19 March

Before heading out to Adrian Crow's house with Anna, Sheridan called her parents. She spoke to them every few days and often visited them, their house being only a few miles away in New Brighton.

It had been thirty-two years since Sheridan's twelve-year-old brother, Matthew, went out to play football with friends in Birkenhead Park. And never came back.

After his friend, Chris Hoe, had headed off home, Matthew carried on playing with his best mate – fourteen-year-old Andrew Longford. They had spotted a man watching them nearby. Later, when interviewed by the police, Andrew described the man as white, medium build, with a beard, wearing blue jeans and a brown coat. He told police that he and Matthew decided to go home, and they walked via the pathway that crossed a small bridge before going their separate ways.

Sheridan's parents reported Matthew missing later that evening. His naked body was found the next day. The cause of death was a single blow to the forehead which had fractured his skull. There was no evidence of sexual assault.

Chris Hoe told the police that he hadn't noticed anyone hanging around the park. Matthew's murder had been reopened by the cold-case team after Sheridan herself had made contact with Andrew Longford. While sat in his cluttered living room, she had noticed a collage of photographs in a frame on the wall. As she'd studied the pictures, she spotted a man in the background in one of the photographs and when she pointed him out, Andrew had remarked that he hadn't noticed the man before. After sifting through boxes of other old photographs taken by Andrew's father in Birkenhead Park, he'd spotted the same man again, standing in the background. In two of the pictures, the man was clean-shaven, but in the third, he had a beard and was wearing a brown coat. Sheridan had handed the photos to the cold-case team who made enquiries to try to identify the male.

A name was put forward, Stephen Tubby, who had been arrested in 1989 for indecent assault on a twelve-year-old female. He was never convicted. When spoken to by the cold-case team, he admitted to being the man in the picture but stated he was working away at the time of Matthew's murder. He remained a person of interest until his alibi was confirmed.

Andrew Longford lived alone, wracked with guilt. Having lost his own father to cancer several years before, Andrew himself was in remission with his own health issues.

Sheridan was fourteen when Matthew had died and since that day, she had only one goal. To join the police force, become a detective and solve his case.

CHAPTER 26

Sheridan and Anna pulled away from Adrian Crow's house, having told him that Caroline's suitcase had been found and that the gloves found hidden in a bush in his garden belonged to a locally known burglar. Adrian had agreed to have cameras installed on his property. They left him with PC Jack Staples, who had been appointed as family liaison officer. It made sense as he had been the first officer Adrian had talked to, and had training as an FLO.

Adrian also agreed to a forensic search of his house and garden. He questioned what the police were looking for and it was explained to him that they wanted to be satisfied that Caroline hadn't come to any harm inside the house, and to check for signs of forced or attempted entry into the property.

By the time Sheridan and Anna arrived back at Hale Street nick, Hill was in the CID office and waved them over.

'Caroline's suitcase has been sent off for forensics. We've got some pictures of it, and her passport.'

Sheridan dropped her coat on to the desk. She parked herself on the edge of the desk and flicked through the images on the computer screen. 'Her passport's nearly out of date. It's only got a month left.'

Anna frowned. 'But if she did pack to leave of her own accord, then why would she dump her suitcase?'

Sheridan bit the inside of her cheek. 'Unless it wasn't *her* that dumped it.'

CHAPTER 27

Adrian Crow sat at his kitchen table, staring at the empty bottle of whisky. He'd searched the cupboards, trying to find anything alcoholic – anything to numb his mind. There was usually at least a bottle or two of wine in the fridge, but he'd finished them several days earlier. There was nothing left for him to drink. Or eat. That second part was fine. His appetite had disappeared, and what food he tried to eat just made his stomach turn. But he *did* want a drink.

He stood up, and as he grabbed his jacket from the hook by the front door, he heard the gravel crunching outside. He checked from the window and, seeing it was the postman, he put his jacket on and opened the door.

'Hi there.' The postman, Paul Copperfield, gave Adrian a sympathetic look. 'How are you? Any news on your wife?'

'No,' Adrian replied.

And then he saw the package.

Bending down, he picked it up. 'You just delivered this?'

'No, mate. It was already there.' Paul Copperfield went to hand Adrian two letters, which he ignored, leaving Paul holding them out in front of him.

Adrian turned the package over, examining it closely. 'There's no address.'

'Maybe it's a present from someone.'

Adrian didn't reply; instead he proceeded to undo the tape around the package.

Paul Copperfield stood there, watching. Intrigued. Adrian seemed to forget he was there and as he pulled the cardboard lid open and looked inside, he let out a cry.

'Oh God.' He dropped the package on the ground, and snapped his hand to his mouth.

'Jesus,' was all Paul Copperfield could say as he stared in disbelief at the blackened hand that had fallen out of the package and now lay on the gravel at his feet.

CHAPTER 28

It was mid-afternoon. Detectives were working tirelessly to patch together Caroline Crow's last movements. Hours of CCTV were being scrutinised, and a search and forensics team was being organised to start work on both Adrian and Simon's houses. The technical support team had arranged to meet their colleagues at Adrian's house and install the cameras. A specialist team was searching the river behind Simon Banks' house and Hill had spent the morning attending a press conference. She loathed this part of her role as a DCI. Sheridan tried again to contact Simon Banks, but his phone was switched off.

She called the crime scene office to speak to one of the lead investigators. 'Hi Charlie, it's Sheridan Holler. Can you do me a favour when you go out to the Crow job? Can you grab me a few more items belonging to Caroline? I just want some other things checked for her DNA.'

'Sure. No problem.'

'Thanks, Charlie.'

As she put the phone down, Anna walked into her office. Sheridan knew that Anna was still struggling with being home alone and invited her to stay over again.

'No, I should go home really. I can't stay at yours all the time. But thanks anyway, mate.'

'Well, the offer's open, anytime.'

'I need to go home tonight. I'm running out of clothes at your place – and I need to get my toothbrush charger.'

At that moment, Hill walked in. 'Simon Banks' car isn't parked at Heathrow.'

Sheridan put her hands on her hips. 'Bollocks.'

'We've got him on ANPRs in Birmingham and Oxford. But then . . . nothing. So Christ knows where he left it.'

'Well, he was definitely heading in the right direction. And we know he got on the plane,' Anna replied.

Hill leant against the doorframe. 'And he was alone in the car. So, he's either parked it up somewhere or . . .'

Sheridan pre-empted her. 'Or someone else is driving it.'

'And whoever it is has managed to avoid any ANPR cameras.'

Sheridan's mobile rang and she quickly answered it. 'DI Holler.' Her eyes widened as she listened. 'Jesus Christ. Okay, thanks, Jack. Where are you now?' She threw a look at Anna and Hill, shaking her head slightly. 'Okay, we'll head out there.'

She ended the call.

'What now?' Hill asked.

'That was Jack Staples. He's just taken a call from Adrian Crow. He's had a package delivered. Another burnt hand. The right hand this time.'

'Are the cameras up yet?' Hill asked.

Sheridan shook her head. 'No. They're going in later today.'

'Shit,' Hill replied.

Sheridan continued, 'The package wasn't there when we left Adrian's house this morning and Jack Staples was still there. It also wasn't there when he left. Adrian spotted it when he was heading out to the shops. He thought the postman had delivered it but apparently it was already there when the postie arrived.'

'So, we have a window of time to work with,' Anna interjected.

Sheridan replied, 'Yeah. But I bet whoever delivered that package is watching the house.'

CHAPTER 29

Sheridan and Anna spent the afternoon – and most of the evening – at Adrian Crow's house. The package and hand were photographed before being sent off to Forensics. The search team and forensic officers were working their way through the house, while the technical support officers installed the cameras. Everyone worked slowly, methodically, quietly.

Jack Staples remained with Adrian in the kitchen, while he gave his statement and provided his fingerprints along with a DNA sample. The postman, Paul Copperfield, had been taken to the police station for the same process to take place.

Sheridan organised house-to-house while Rob Wills and Dipesh scrutinised the CCTV in the area, trying to find any clue to who may have delivered the package.

Adrian Crow was slowly disappearing before their eyes. He looked like an empty shell, and was barely able to move from his seat at the kitchen table. He answered questions in a whisper.

Sheridan sat opposite him and gently explained that an identical package had been delivered to Simon Banks, a burnt human left hand. That first hand had been forensically examined, the results of which confirmed it wasn't Caroline's. As Adrian had received a right hand, Sheridan was inclined to think that this was likely from the same victim. The reaction from Adrian was a mixture of horror and relief.

'Are you absolutely sure?' he asked, tears rolling down his cheeks.

'As sure as I can be at the moment. We need you to stay positive, Adrian. I know this is a terrible time for you, but please know we're doing everything we can to find Caroline and work out who sent these packages.'

'Do you know whose hands they are?' he asked, choking on his words.

'No. Not yet.'

Sheridan felt strangely guilty as she silently prayed that the hand was from the same victim. The unknown woman. Someone else's wife. Someone else's daughter, sister, friend.

'It doesn't make sense. This Simon Banks stole money from Caroline's account . . . But then we both get these awful packages.'

'I know,' Sheridan said. 'Are you absolutely positive you don't know Simon Banks?'

'I'm pretty positive. I can't place his face, and the name means nothing to me. You said he's a doctor. Has he been asked if *he* knows *me*?'

'He's an orthopaedic surgeon. It's a bit difficult trying to get hold of him at the moment. Like I said before, he's out of the country, but we've asked his secretary if he's ever treated you or Caroline, and he hasn't.' Sheridan was cautious not to divulge too much to Adrian. The press were giving the chief constable and Hill enough of a hard time, desperately trying to get information on the case.

'And her suitcase was found near his house?'

'Well, it was in a river that runs at the back of a lot of houses in the area, so we can't be sure if it was left where it was found, or it just ended up there. We don't want to speculate at the moment.'

'But you said earlier that none of her clothes were in it. So where are they?'

'We're searching the area.'

'What if she's in the river?' Adrian swallowed and blinked hard down on his tears.

'Wherever she is, we'll find her,' Sheridan emphatically replied.

It was late into the evening by the time she and Anna headed off, leaving Adrian in the capable hands of Jack Staples.

As they stood out on the gravel drive by the car, Anna turned to Sheridan. 'You okay to drop me back at the nick to get my car?'

Sheridan didn't answer. She was looking across the field that was visible from the side of Adrian's garden.

'Sheridan?'

'Sorry.' She'd heard the question. 'Yeah, of course,' she said, distractedly.

'What's up?'

'Nothing. I'm just trying to figure out where someone would hide up if they were watching this place.'

'Well, if they're watching now, then they'll probably know that we've got cameras in.'

As Sheridan and Anna got into the car, Gabriel Howard kept his head down, hiding in the tall grass. Watching silently as the two police officers drove away.

CHAPTER 30

DCI Hill Knowles reversed on to her drive and switched the engine off. She tried to muster up the energy to get out of the car. Resting her head back she glanced over at her neighbour Gloria's house and noticed a vehicle on the drive. Gloria didn't drive and rarely had visitors. Hill dragged herself out of the driver's seat, walked across the road, and used her spare key to let herself in.

'Only me, Gloria!' she called as Gloria's dog, Barney, met her at the front door, his tail wagging in a circle like a rotor blade. Hill bent down to tap him on the head before pushing the living-room door open.

Gloria was sat in the armchair, and perched on the sofa opposite her was a young spotty lad, drowning in what appeared to be his father's suit.

'Hello, Hill,' Gloria acknowledged her before turning her attention back to the lad.

'Who's this?' Hill pointed at him accusingly, prompting him to reach into his pocket and offer her his card, which she snatched out of his hand and squinted at.

Gloria tutted loudly. 'Please excuse my friend. She's a police officer and thinks that every man who comes to my house is going to bludgeon me to death.'

The lad's eyes bulged at Gloria's comment, and he looked Hill up and down. 'Pleased to meet you,' he said nervously, his enormous Adam's apple sliding up and down as he spoke.

Hill read the card out loud. 'AAA Will Writing Services.' She eyed Gloria. 'You're making a will?'

'Not that it's any of your business, but yes I am.' Gloria clasped her hands together and rested them on her lap.

Hill looked at the card again. 'Elvis Donkley.' She looked at him. 'Your name is *Elvis*?'

He readjusted his position on the sofa. 'Yes, my mum was a big fan.' He smiled.

Hill didn't smile back. 'Where did you find *him*?' she asked Gloria, pointing a thumb at Elvis.

'A leaflet came through the door – and I thought at my age I should think about making a will in case I pop my clogs. But I repeat: not that it's any of your business.'

'How much are you charging her?' Hill continued with the interrogation and Elvis looked like he was about to shit himself.

'Four hundred and ninety-nine pounds, but you get a free hamper,' Gloria answered for him before pulling herself up from the armchair and grabbing her walking frame. 'I was about to make me and Elvis a cuppa. Do you want one?'

'How much?' Hill frowned. 'That's ridiculous. Has she signed anything yet?'

Elvis shook his head. 'No, I was just about to take some details.'

Gloria was in the kitchen and Hill stepped over to Elvis. Leaning down, she could smell his cheap aftershave and nervous sweat. 'You can leave now. She won't be using your services. Five hundred quid for a bloody will? That's robbery.' She pointed to the door. 'Off you trot.'

Elvis scrabbled his paperwork together and had hurriedly left just as Gloria re-emerged from the kitchen.

'Do you take sugar, Elvis?' She looked at the empty sofa. 'Where's he gone?'

'Elvis has left the building.' Hill shook her head.

'You threw him out?' She tutted and turned back into the kitchen. 'Meddling old cow,' she muttered.

Hill followed her and put two teabags into the pot. 'You should've asked me to find you a will writer, one that isn't going to charge you five hundred bloody quid.'

'I don't need a will writer. I've already got a will.' Gloria opened the bread bin and slid out a Battenberg.

'Then what was *he* doing here?' Hill nodded towards the door.

Gloria cut into the cake. 'The pamphlet said that even if you don't go ahead with the will, you still qualify for a free hamper – which I now won't get because you turned up and scared the living shite out of that poor young man. Do you want some cake?'

'No, thanks. I'm going home.' She leaned forward and kissed Gloria on the cheek before heading for the door.

'Hill?' Gloria called after her.

'Yes?' Hill hovered for a moment.

'You owe me a feckin' hamper.'

Hill smiled and quietly closed the door behind her.

CHAPTER 31

Friday 20 March

Hill was at the front of the room when Sheridan and Anna walked in for the morning briefing. When they were settled, she promptly kicked off proceedings. 'Right – we've got a lot of information coming in, so I need to go round everyone in a minute . . . but this is what's come in so far.' She turned to Sheridan, who took the lead and updated the team that the CCTV from Simon Banks' road had drawn a blank, as had the house-to-house enquiries. The search team had found nothing to link Banks to Caroline Crow. A small amount of blood had been found in his bathroom sink and sent for DNA testing. The river behind his house had been searched, but as yet nothing had been found. Simon Banks' phone had still not been traced by the police in Perth. It was also agreed that Banks could be anywhere in the country.

Due to the location of Adrian Crow's property, no CCTV or house-to-house had revealed anything of note. They were coming up blank at every junction.

Caroline had still not accessed her bank account and no irregularities had shown up on her account. A small private pension was paid in every month, along with a standing order set up by Adrian. Caroline had no savings and no other accounts.

DC Bridie Sexton had contacted most of the guests who had stayed at the Hampshire Hotel in Llandudno at the same time as the Crows, but no one remembered them.

Sheridan took a sip of her coffee before continuing. 'There is one thing though. We know that the passport we found in Caroline's suitcase expires in a month, but we've just found out that she applied for a new one three months ago and it was issued and sent to her home address. The FLO, Jack Staples, has asked Adrian if he knew about this and he said he didn't. Basically, she applied for a new passport at the same time as she stopped going to her swimming club. So, where is this passport? Unless it turns up at the house, then she must have it with her. We've also checked that she, unlike Simon Banks, does not have dual nationality.'

Sheridan looked down at her notes. 'I've been trying to contact Simon Banks, but his phone is switched off. He's due back around the thirtieth, so unless our colleagues in Australia can find him, we'll speak to him on his return to the UK. We've got markers on both of his passports now, so we'll be waiting for him when he lands. We know his car isn't parked at Heathrow, so we've got a marker on it in case someone else is driving it.'

Sheridan pointed to Rob Wills. 'So, what have you got for us, Rob?'

'We've got the CCTV from the Hampshire Hotel in Llandudno which covers the reception area, and it clearly shows Adrian and Caroline arriving before they go out a couple of times. We can also see when they checked out.'

'And they definitely have matching suitcases?'

'Yep. Identical.'

'I take it Caroline only has the one suitcase with her, no other large bag or case?'

'Nope.'

'Are they always together?'

'No. There's one time when Adrian leaves on his own – Tuesday tenth March. He leaves reception at 08.36 and returns at 09.14. It looks like he's got a card in his hand when he comes back into reception.'

'It was Caroline's birthday the following day, so this could be him going out to buy her a card,' Sheridan suggested.

Hill spoke. 'The search and forensics teams should be done at Caroline's house this morning, so we'll see what that brings up. We know that Gabriel Howard's gloves were found outside, so that potentially puts him there at some point. Fingers crossed we'll find evidence that he was *inside* the house as well.'

The phone on Rob's desk rang. 'DC Wills.' His expression grew serious and the room went quiet. After he finished the call, he looked at Sheridan. 'The search team at Caroline's house have found a mobile phone hidden in her wardrobe. The same phone that was used by Henry Blanchflower to make that bogus call to Adrian and get him to go to Norfolk.'

CHAPTER 32

Sheridan dialled Simon Banks' mobile number. Switched off. She slammed the phone down in frustration. 'Turn your phone on, you fucking prick.'

She closed her eyes for a moment and took a breather. She could so easily have laid her head on the desk. *Just five minutes*, she thought. Five minutes of silence before the phone rang or someone came knocking on her door.

And then Hill walked in, her face the colour of a baboon's backside. 'I'm going to start shouting at people if we don't get the results back on the phone enquiries soon.'

'Which phone enquiries? There's a lot of them.' Sheridan sighed.

'All of them. Why is it taking so bloody long?' She stepped over to the window and stared out as if she were waiting for the postman to deliver a parcel she'd been waiting for.

'The team are rammed, Hill. You know these things take time.' Sheridan was surreptitiously typing an email to Dipesh as she spoke.

How's it going with the phone enquiries? Hill is on the warpath in my office and she's turning a funny colour.

Dipesh immediately pinged back: *Good timing, I've just got some of it back. Gabriel Howard has been a very naughty boy.*

Sheridan replied: *I'm smiling.*

Dipesh responded*: I've also got the call log back on Caroline's landline as well. Very interesting.*

Sheridan quickly typed back: *Call me right now.*

Hill was rattling away about incompetence when Sheridan's desk phone rang.

'DI Holler.' She hid a grin behind the receiver. 'That's brilliant. Thanks, Dipesh,' she said, looking at Hill as she did so. 'We'll be right there.'

'Well?' Hill asked when Sheridan ended the call.

'Talk about great timing. Dipesh has got some of the phone stuff back and, apparently, it's thrown something up. Let's go and see what he's got, shall we?'

Hill turned and walked straight out of Sheridan's office, heading to CID. 'I'm still going to find someone to shout at by the end of today,' she mumbled to herself.

Dipesh glanced up as Hill and Sheridan approached. 'Are you ready for this?' he asked.

'Go for it,' Sheridan replied enthusiastically, having been joined by Anna.

'Gabriel Howard's mobile pinged off a mast near to Adrian's house on Saturday seventh March. It's close enough to just put him within his exclusion zone.'

'We've got him.' Sheridan put her hand up to Hill, encouraging a high five. Hill crossed her arms. She did not do high fives. Sheridan turned to Anna, but the moment had gone.

'Okay, so, we've got his phone in the area, but that doesn't prove *he* was there.' Hill merrily pissed all over Sheridan's parade.

'Does he make any calls to Caroline, Adrian or Simon Banks?' Sheridan asked.

Dipesh replied, 'No. And none received from them.'

'What about Caroline's landline?' Sheridan asked, momentarily putting aside her urge to immediately drive to Gabriel's house and confront him.

'Well, first I checked Adrian Crow's statement. He said that on Saturday seventh March he left home around 08.00 to go to work and didn't get back until just after 17.00. Now, at 14.32 a call was made from Adrian and Caroline's landline, which lasted seven minutes. The same number was called again at 17.13. This second call lasted one minute. The number that was called from Caroline's landline was Fairweather Flowers – the shop that belongs to Gabriel's sister.'

Sheridan locked eyes with Anna.

Dipesh continued, 'Both calls to the florist were deleted from the call log but of course they still show up on the record.'

Anna spoke. 'So, the first call was definitely from Caroline because Adrian was still at work. But the second call could have been made by him. He said he got home just after 5 p.m. – but why delete the call logs?'

'I need to go and speak to Denise. If Caroline called her, then I need to know why.' Sheridan put her hand on Dipesh's shoulder. 'Good work, mate.'

Hill interjected. 'Don't go off-piste with this, Sheridan. I don't want Gabriel Howard spooked. If he gets wind we're on to him, he'll completely shut down.'

Sheridan crossed her arms and just as quickly uncrossed them. 'We've finally got a link between all of these people. We've got Gabriel's gloves in the Crows' garden. We've got a call from Adrian and Caroline's landline to Gabriel's sister's florist shop. We know that Henry Blanchflower made a call to Adrian to get him to go to Norfolk. And that the phone he used was hidden by Caroline in her wardrobe. We've got CCTV of Simon Banks withdrawing four hundred quid from Caroline's account, and her suitcase is found in a river not too far from his house.' She allowed herself a wide smile. 'All we need to do now is fit it all together.'

Hill sighed heavily. 'I get it, but we need to make sure we don't go at this half-cocked.'

'I agree. But I want to know what Denise can tell us about the call to her shop from Caroline.'

Hill's phone rang on her desk. 'DCI Knowles.' She clicked her fingernails together as she listened. 'Thank you.' She put the phone down. 'That was the search team at Adrian's house. They've found letters from what appears to be Caroline's ex-partner. According to Adrian she hasn't got any children, right?'

'That's right.' Sheridan nodded.

'Well, these letters show that she has.'

Sheridan sighed. 'Bloody hell.'

'There's also letters that appear to indicate that Caroline was having an affair.'

CHAPTER 33

Sheridan heard the bell ding above the door as she stepped inside Fairweather Flowers. The smell of cut stems and perfume reminded her of lazy summer days. She clasped her mobile in her hand, waiting for it to ring with an update. Anna was at Adrian Crow's house, liaising with the search team.

The shop was empty of customers, and Denise Fairweather was behind the counter preparing a small bouquet.

'Detective Holler,' she said as she looked up and smiled. 'Nice to see you. How have you been keeping?'

'I'm fine thanks, Denise. How's business?'

'Crazy busy, but I'm not complaining. Are you here to place an order? You know I like to look after Liverpool's finest.' Denise grinned.

'No, ta. Is Gabriel about?'

'He's at home, I think. Why? Is he in trouble?' She put the bouquet down on the counter, giving Sheridan her full attention.

'Who does your deliveries for you?'

'Donny, mostly. Sometimes Gabriel and sometimes me. Why?'

'Who's Donny?'

'He's a guy who's been doing my deliveries for a couple of years. He's a bit slow, if you know what I mean, but he helps out when I need him.'

'Have you seen on the news about the woman who's gone missing from her house near Sefton Park – Caroline Crow?'

'Yeah, I saw it last night. It's bloody awful.'

'A phone call was made to your shop from Caroline Crow's house on Saturday seventh March, a week before she went missing. The first call was at half two in the afternoon and the other at just gone five. Do you remember speaking to her?'

'No. Are you sure she called *here*?'

'Positive.'

'I honestly don't remember. Do you know if she placed an order?'

'I was hoping you could tell *me*.'

'Hang on.' Denise bent down and lifted a heavy book from under the counter and flicked through the pages. 'Here we go, seventh of March.' She ran her finger down the page. 'There's no Caroline Crow.'

'May I?' Sheridan nodded at the book and spun it round, checking through the names and phone numbers. And then she spotted it.

Caroline Crow's landline number and address. Written next to it was:

> *Julie Jones. Bouquet of sweet pea, white roses, dahlia, lilies. £30 COD. W/I the hour.*

'This one.' Sheridan pointed to it.

Denise arched her neck and read it. 'Yes, I remember her – Julie Jones. She was adamant the flowers had to be delivered within the hour. Cash on delivery.'

'Who made the delivery?'

'I did.'

'What did she look like, the woman you delivered the flowers to?'

'She was probably in her fifties, very slim, longish hair, quite chatty.'

'What was the house like?'

'It's off the main drag. At the end of a long drive. Big place.'

'Did you go inside?'

'No. I waited on the doorstep while she took the bouquet inside and then she came back out with the cash. We chatted for a minute or so and then I left.'

'Why did you make the delivery and not Donny?'

'He was already out in the van on other jobs and so I had to go.'

'Why didn't Gabriel go?'

'He was going to, but the address is within his exclusion zone, so I had to do it.'

'And Gabriel stayed in the shop the whole time you were out?'

'Yeah. I remember it because when I got back in the car, Gabriel's mobile was in the footwell on the passenger side, so I used that to call him at the shop and tell him I was on my way back and that I had his phone, in case he was worried he'd lost it. I got back to the shop and then he used my car to run some errands.'

'Why didn't you use your own mobile?'

'The battery was dead. I'd left it charging in the shop.'

'Tell me about your conversation with this Julie Jones.'

Denise described the conversation as 'normal' – Julie Jones was polite and cheerful, and had told Denise she was treating herself to some flowers. She was alone in the house as her husband was at work. Denise couldn't remember anything else.

'Did she say why she wanted the flowers delivered within the hour?'

'No, I don't think so. I'm confused, what's this Julie Jones got to do with the woman who's gone missing?'

'Didn't you recognise her from the television last night?'

'No. I only caught a bit of the news. I'm still confused.'

Sheridan pulled out Caroline Crow's photograph and showed it to Denise. 'Is that the woman you delivered the flowers to?'

Denise took the picture from Sheridan and looked at it closely. 'Yeah, I think so.' She handed the picture back. 'So, Julie Jones is actually Caroline Crow?'

'Looks that way. And she called back later that day at just after 5 p.m., do you remember that conversation?'

Denise thought for a moment. 'Oh yes, I remember now. She rang to say I'd dropped my gloves on the doorstep, and that she'd post them back to me.'

'Why post them? Why not drop them off?'

'She said she was going away that day, and asked me not to go back for the gloves. She said she was literally about to leave the house.'

'Did she say where she was going?'

'No.'

'Did she say she was going away on her own or with someone?'

'I can't remember.'

'Did you get the gloves back, then?' Sheridan knew that Caroline couldn't have posted the gloves back because they were found outside, hidden in a bush, but she asked the question anyway.

'No. But it's okay. They were just an old pair of Gabriel's I was using.'

Sheridan nodded slowly. *You fucker. You're covering for him.*

'I need a statement detailing what you've just told me,' said Sheridan.

'Can I do it after work?'

'Sure.'

Sheridan left, and walking back to her car she dialled Anna's number.

'Hi, mate,' Anna said.

'You still at Adrian Crow's house?' Sheridan asked.

'Yeah.'

'I'm on my way.'

'How did it go with Denise?'

'She's lying. She's covering for Gabriel.'

◆ ◆ ◆

After Sheridan was gone, Denise Fairweather quickly called Gabriel.

'Hi, sis,' he answered.

'You were right. Your mate, Sheridan Holler, was just here asking questions about that Julie Jones delivery. I've got to give a statement later.'

'Did you stick to the story?'

'Yeah. I think I remembered it right. Let's just hope I can remember it exactly the same when I give my statement.'

'You'll be fine, sis. Did you mention the gloves?'

'Yeah, I told her that I was wearing them when I made the delivery, and I'd dropped them on the doorstep.'

'Perfect. Thanks, sis.'

Denise thought for a moment. 'The problem is, we'll both be in the shit when this Caroline Crow turns up because she'll tell the police that it was *you* who made the delivery and not me.'

There was a pause before Gabriel said, '*If* she turns up.'

CHAPTER 34

Sheridan pulled into Adrian Crow's drive and parked just behind Anna's car. Anna emerged from the property and Sheridan told her all about the conversation with Denise Fairweather.

'Why do you think Caroline used a different name when she ordered the flowers?' Anna asked.

'I don't know. I'm beginning to wonder how many secrets Caroline has. According to Denise, Caroline told her she was going away that day, that she was leaving straight away and that's why she didn't want Denise going back to get the gloves.'

'But Adrian didn't tell Caroline about their trip to Llandudno until he got home that night. And say if Caroline *was* planning to leave the house before Adrian got home, then why order flowers?'

'Exactly.'

'But you don't believe Denise's story that she made the delivery?'

'Not in the slightest. She's covering for her shit-bag brother. She even said they were *his* gloves so that cocks up our evidence that he was at the house. She's got it all covered.' Sheridan sighed. 'I still think Gabriel's been here.'

Sheridan put her hands on her hips and glanced towards the shed. 'Anyway, tell me about these letters that have been found.'

Anna went on to tell Sheridan that hidden behind a small panel in Caroline's wardrobe were two letters to Caroline from her ex-partner which had been placed in clear evidence bags. Anna handed them to Sheridan. 'There's no envelopes, and no dates on the letters themselves.'

Sheridan read the first letter.

Caroline,

I got your letter and I'll keep it simple. You lost your children years ago – you gave up on them because you couldn't kick your habit. You were never their mother, and you still aren't. They've forgotten about you – and I want to, as well.

Stop writing to me. The children aren't even in this country any more and you will never find them. I don't want you near them.

Do not write to me again.

W

She then read the second letter.

Caroline,

This is the last time I will write to you. Your letters are pathetic and so are you. How dare you threaten me. From the way you're talking, I can only assume you're back on the drugs.

You'll be wasting your time if you write to me again. I'm moving abroad. I leave tomorrow.

W

Anna then handed Sheridan a sheet of paper, also protected in an evidence bag. 'This was found behind another panel in her wardrobe. They're a bit random, but you get the gist.'

Sheridan read the words.

My darling, I know we can't be together and that breaks both our hearts. I lie in bed and think of you

I love you so much it hurts.

I just want to be with you

I've kept the earrings you gave me, I feel so bad that I can't wear them, but I look at them every now and then and I know they were given to me with love, with your love

I bought you this watch so that every time you look at it, you'll remember the wonderful times we spent together. If it's too difficult to wear it, then put it away somewhere and maybe just take it out when you can. Maybe you can say you bought it yourself rather than me, if that makes it easier. I'd love you to wear it but understand if you can't

I long to hold you

I'm so sorry that I kept so many secrets from you, please don't be angry with me. I love you. I hated going behind your back. But I did it because of love

You have been the one, but I can't hide this love any more

I hated all the lies I've told. You deserved a better wife than me

I've lied and lied and lied to you

'So Caroline Crow has – or had – a drug habit. And she has children. That's a huge fact that she didn't share with Adrian. Or if she did tell him, he's been lying to us.' Sheridan handed the notes back to Anna. 'We really need to find out who W is.'

CHAPTER 35

As the search team were finishing up, Sheridan and Anna sat in the living room with Adrian.

'Is it all done now? The search and everything?' he asked them. His voice was hoarse, his hair dishevelled, and heavy dark bags hung under his tired eyes.

'Yes, it's all done. Sorry it took so long.'

'So, what happens now?'

'Adrian, I need to ask you a couple of things. On Saturday seventh March, Caroline made a call to a local florist and ordered a bouquet of flowers which were delivered here. Did she say why she'd ordered them?'

Adrian sat rigid, his mouth moving slightly, but no words came out. He stared at the floor and then closed his eyes tight shut.

'I'm sorry, what day was this?' he finally asked, breathing slowly and deeply, his eyes blinking so fast it looked rather odd.

'Saturday seventh March,' Sheridan replied, taken aback by his bizarre reaction. His hesitancy piqued her suspicion. Was he stalling? Giving himself time to think?

'She didn't have any flowers delivered,' he finally responded, very slightly shaking his head.

'She did, we spoke to the florist who delivered them. Caroline paid cash and said she wanted them delivered within the hour.

There must have been a bouquet of flowers here when you got home that day from work.'

'No. There wasn't.' Adrian stood up. 'I'm sorry, who *actually* delivered them?'

'The florist that she ordered them from. Caroline never mentioned anything about a delivery to you?'

'No. And there were no flowers here when I got home.'

'Maybe they were for someone else? A friend, maybe?'

Adrian eventually replied, 'Maybe. But she would have said.' His response was distant, like he was talking to himself.

'She didn't mention that the florist left her gloves here?'

Adrian answered, 'No. She didn't mention anything about that. So, were they the gloves that were found in the back garden? You said they belonged to a local burglar.'

'There is a possible link. Apparently, Caroline rang the florist back and told her that she would post the gloves to her because she was going away that day.'

Adrian frowned and sat back down. 'But I didn't tell Caroline about the trip to Llandudno until I got home that day. So, what was she talking about?'

'We know, it doesn't add up. Does the name Julie Jones mean anything to you?'

It took an age for Adrian to reply. 'No. Is that the name of the florist she used?'

'It's the name Caroline gave when she ordered the flowers.'

Adrian slowly looked to the ceiling. 'What is going on? Why would she use a different name?' A hint of despair had seeped into his voice.

'We don't know.'

They sat in silence for a moment, Sheridan letting Adrian absorb everything she'd just told him. His house and his life had been turned upside down, and it was really starting to show. He hadn't shaved recently, and his clothes were creased as if he'd slept in them.

Sheridan hesitated. She was about to broach the subject of Caroline's children and the letters – a conversation that could go one way or the other. If Adrian knew about the letters, then he'd lied to the police and suspicion would hang over him. If he didn't, then Sheridan was about to drop a concrete block on his head.

She stole a glance at Anna who knew exactly where Sheridan was about to go with this. Anna gave the subtlest of nods and Sheridan took a deep breath.

'Adrian, we know that everything that's happened has been so hard for you to deal with, but we found some things in the house today that I need to talk to you about.'

He didn't answer, but kept his gaze intently focused on her face.

'You said before that Caroline doesn't have any children. Are you sure about that?'

'Of course I'm sure.'

'We found two letters from her ex-partner that mentioned children . . .'

Adrian suddenly took to his feet. 'This is not happening. She doesn't have children. She doesn't have any children.' His head dropped to his chest. 'What is going on?'

'You've only known her for – what – eleven years?'

'Yes. But she would have told me if she had bloody children. Why would she keep that from me?'

'I don't know. Did she ever mention drugs to you?'

'Drugs? What sort of drugs?' he replied, exasperated.

'The letters from her ex-partner indicate that she may have taken drugs in the past.'

'That's ridiculous. Absolutely ridiculous. Caroline would never take drugs. I don't know what's going on but none of this makes any sense.'

'Do you know her ex-partner's name?'

'No.'

'He signed the letters with his initial, W.'

'Caroline never talked about her exes, and I never asked.' Adrian crossed his arms. 'Seems like there's a lot of things she didn't talk to me about.'

Sheridan noted the shift in Adrian's demeanour. One moment despair, the next a hint of anger that appeared to creep in. She pressed on. 'There's a couple of other things, and I know this might upset you, but I need you to see these.' Sheridan handed him the random notes that Caroline had written.

As Adrian read them, his grief was palpable. His eyes filled with tears that he didn't bother trying to wipe away. 'This isn't happening,' he whispered as he read the words over and over. 'Caroline would never be unfaithful to me. This is all wrong. Something's very, very wrong.' He handed the notes back to Sheridan.

'Does it look like Caroline's handwriting?'

Adrian nodded, just as his mobile rang. 'Hello?'

Sheridan and Anna watched him as he wiped tears from his cheeks. 'Okay. I'll see you soon.' He dropped his phone on to the kitchen table. 'That was my family liaison officer, Jack Staples. He's on his way over.'

'How are you getting on with him?' Sheridan asked, wanting to bring Adrian back into a relatively normal conversation, before she told him about the phone found in Caroline's wardrobe.

'He's a good fella. It's a real help having him around. Someone to talk to, you know?' Adrian said, nodding. 'I actually don't think I'd get through this without him. I feel like I'm in a nightmare.

Everything I've known for the last eleven years, the life I had with Caroline, my job, my home – everything seems like it's not real. I feel like I'm slowly being destroyed and there's no end to it.' He looked at Sheridan. 'Does that make sense?'

'Yes, of course it does. And I'm conscious that you've had to try to process a lot of information. I'm sorry.'

'I just want Caroline home and I want everything back the way it was.'

'I know you do.' Sheridan waited for a moment before she said it. 'Adrian, there's one other thing. You remember we told you that the phone that Henry Blanchflower called you from was very close to the house?'

'Yes, I remember.' He scraped his hand through his hair.

'Well, we've found that phone today. It was hidden in Caroline's wardrobe.' Sheridan watched his reaction very closely.

Adrian closed his eyes tightly, taking in a lungful of oxygen, slowly letting it out. His voice suddenly broke and he opened his eyes, blinking. 'So, she knew about the call from Henry Blanchflower?'

'It looks that way.'

'But it can't have been Caroline who made the call, it was a man—' Adrian suddenly looked at the floor. 'Oh, God.'

'What?' Sheridan asked.

'The picture you showed me of the man who took the money out of Caroline's account . . . have you got it with you?'

'No. But I can get it.' Sheridan called Rob and he sent the picture to her phone.

Adrian stared at the image. 'That's him. That's where I've seen him before, I knew he looked familiar.'

'Where have you seen him before?'

Adrian gave a slight, almost invisible nod. 'Here. He was here a couple of weeks ago. I got home from work, and he was driving away from the house. I asked Caroline who he was, and she said it was just some guy who had got lost and taken a wrong turning. Knocked on the door, you know, asking for directions? She seemed flustered, almost panicky when I came through the door. It was the same day I told her about the trip to Llandudno.'

'Do you remember what kind of car he was driving?'

'Yes. A silver Mercedes, but I couldn't tell you the registration number or anything.' He stared at the floor as if trying to wrack his brains for more information. 'No. That's all I remember.'

At that moment, there was a knock on the door and Adrian slowly got up to open it, letting in PC Staples. Sheridan updated Jack with the conversation they'd just had before she and Anna left.

As they walked to their cars, Sheridan whispered to Anna, 'So, Simon Banks is Henry Blanchflower.'

It was gone 6 p.m. as Sheridan and Anna were wrapping up the team briefing. Rob Wills walked into CID.

'How did it go with Denise?' Sheridan asked, suddenly feeling dead on her feet.

Rob sat down. 'Her statement matches what she told you earlier.'

Sheridan shook her head. 'Gabriel's a sly little fuck.'

Hill walked in. 'Who's a sly little fuck?'

'Gabriel Howard, that's who.' Sheridan summarised Denise's statement, and Hill agreed that Gabriel Howard was indeed a sly little fuck.

Hill perched on the edge of a desk, clearly running over this new information in her mind. 'So, we've established that and the fact that Simon Banks is Henry Blanchflower. We've also established that Caroline has children and she's having an affair. We also know that she's involved in the call that got Adrian to go to Norfolk. Good work. Right, get yourselves off home everyone. We'll pick this up with fresh heads tomorrow.'

CHAPTER 36

Saturday 21 March

The day had been long, the whole team working doggedly to fit the pieces together. Little new information had come to light and every piece of evidence they already had was being checked and re-checked. The team was determined to solve this complex case. Sheridan switched off her computer and after checking in on Rob and Dipesh, who were on a late shift, she headed out of the door. As she pulled out of the backyard, her mind filled with the enquiry, her head felt as heavy as the dark clouds gathering slowly over the Liverpool skyline. She wondered about Caroline Crow. Was she dead? Was she hiding? Who was she with? She wasn't with Simon Banks, so was she waiting until she could join him in Australia? Or were they going to meet up when he returned to England? It appeared that Caroline had planned everything in detail, but why? From what they had learned about Caroline, she clearly had a past that Adrian was unaware of.

As she pulled up behind a queue of traffic, her mobile rang. 'DI Holler.'

'Sheridan, it's Jack Staples.'

'Hi, Jack. Everything okay?'

'Yeah, I just wanted to touch base with you about Adrian. Are you free to speak?'

'Yes, I'm driving but you're on loudspeaker.'

'I'm worried about him – his mental health, I mean. It's like he's losing control of his life. I don't think he's had a shower or changed his clothes for days. He's lost weight and I'm worried he's not eating.'

'Do you think he's suicidal?' Sheridan asked, nudging along the queue of traffic. Heavy rain battered the windscreen as it came down sideways.

'We've talked about his feelings, and he says not. I suggested he made an appointment to see his GP, but he doesn't want to. We've talked about him getting counselling and support, but he's not interested. I think that while there's a chance Caroline's alive, he won't do anything stupid, but if we find her dead, then I wouldn't be surprised if he tops himself. He's a mess. He's talked about this affair he thinks Caroline has had and it's destroying him.'

'Okay, look, thanks for the update, Jack. Keep me posted.'

As Sheridan ended the call, the traffic still hadn't moved. She sent a text to Sam.

> *Hey gorgeous, just popping out on a quick job and will then be home. Won't be long. x*

Sam replied: *No worries. Stay safe. Love you. x*

Sheridan texted back a single kiss and as the traffic inched forward, she indicated to turn left at the road up ahead, deciding to head to Adrian Crow's house.

She struggled to see as her wipers slapped across the windscreen, clearing a river of rain away. A darkness now shrouded the sodden streets and the cars in front of her had come to a halt.

It was then that she spotted a figure in her rearview mirror, running towards her. As he got closer, she recognised him.

Gabriel Howard.

CHAPTER 37

Sheridan watched as Gabriel slowed down. His hair was pasted to his head. His tracksuit bottoms hung heavy and awkward, and a white T-shirt clung to his chest. In his hand was what appeared to be a towel and as he reached her car, he stopped and looked to his right, waiting to cross the road. And then he spotted her.

Smiling, he raised a hand.

Sheridan thought quickly about her location and having previously memorised Gabriel's exclusion zone, she knew he wasn't in breach. *Fuck.*

Gabriel ran a hand down his face and stepped towards her car, signalling for her to wind her window down.

'What?' she asked bluntly, her window open half an inch to stop the hammering rain from soaking the inside of her car.

'Hi, Inspector Holler. How you doing?' Gabriel leaned down, squinting as horizontal rain spattered into his eyes.

'Nice and dry, thanks. You?'

Gabriel laughed. 'It wasn't raining when I left home.'

'Then why did you bring a towel with you?'

Gabriel didn't answer her. 'How's it going with that lady who went missing? Has she been found yet?'

'Not yet.' *You slimy fucking swamp toad*, Sheridan thought as she inched forward as the traffic began to snail-pace down the road.

'Is the husband a suspect? You find that, don't you? It's normally someone close to the victim? I take it you're watching him?'

Sheridan ignored the question. 'So, where are you off to?' she asked. *Checking out your next burglary?* she thought.

'Just out for a run.' Gabriel looked up as a siren suddenly wailed and he watched as a police car squeezed itself past the cars, all of which now sat completely stationary. 'What's going on?' Gabriel grinned. 'Anything interesting?' he asked, nodding towards the police car as it disappeared.

Sheridan ignored him again. 'How's Denise? Still making her own deliveries?' *I know you've been in Adrian Crow's house. You left your gloves there. You sloppy twat*, she thought.

Gabriel looked Sheridan in the eye. 'I know you hate me, but you've got me all wrong.'

'I'm usually a pretty good judge of character. So, I don't think I've got you wrong, Gabriel. Your convictions speak for themselves.'

'Two assaults and a burglary? You're judging me on *that*? I'm sure you've dealt with worse than me.'

'I've dealt with better burglars. I mean, you are the shittiest burglar in the history of burglars.'

'Am I?'

'Yes, you are. Not only are you shit at it – you also killed Edith Elliot.'

'I didn't kill her.' Gabriel's voice was almost inaudible now as the rain hammered down on the car roof.

'You being in that house literally scared her to death. She called 999, but died before anyone could get there. She was so frightened that she couldn't even speak to the operator.' Sheridan's voice rose as she spoke.

Gabriel shook his head. His clothes were stuck to his skin, and he looked like he was standing under a bathroom shower. He wrapped the towel around his neck as rain seeped into his eyes and he wiped them with his soaking-wet hand. He answered her but the noise of another siren drowned out his words.

'What?' Sheridan snapped.

'She didn't call 999.'

'What are you talking about?'

'Edith Elliot didn't call 999.' He sighed. 'I did.'

◆ ◆ ◆

Sheridan unlocked the car door and Gabriel went to get in. 'I'm soaked. I don't want to make your seat wet.'

'Just get in,' Sheridan snapped. 'And what are you talking about? You were the one who called 999? I hardly think so.' She shoved a wad of tissues into his hand.

Gabriel looked at her. 'I knew something was wrong with her. And I knew it was bad. Her head flopped to one side and that's when I called 999.'

'It was a silent 999 call, you didn't speak, you didn't ask for an ambulance. And why didn't you say all of this when you were arrested? I'll tell you why. Because you're bloody lying.'

There was a long silence before Gabriel answered. 'I put the phone in her hand before I left. I couldn't tell the police that I was the one who rang 999. Can you imagine the shit I would have got in prison? I would have been a laughing stock. Look, oh there's that Gabriel Howard, the idiot who calls the police on himself.' He tilted his head to one side. 'Do you see what I mean?'

Sheridan shook her head. 'I don't believe you.'

'It doesn't matter if you don't believe me. I just wanted you to know, that's all. I'm not the monster you think I am.' He looked straight ahead and sighed. 'I'm not a bad person. And of all the people, I really want *you* to know that.'

'Why?' Sheridan noticed his head drop slightly.

'It doesn't matter.' He turned to face her. 'Sorry I made your seat wet.'

And with that, he got out of the car and disappeared into the darkness.

Sheridan watched him in her rear-view mirror. 'What the hell was that all about?' she said under her breath and frowned as she realised the traffic was going nowhere. Deciding to abandon her plan to visit Adrian Crow, she did a U-turn and headed home.

CHAPTER 38

Sunday 22 March

CID was packed when Sheridan walked in. The whole team were busy, silently accepting the fact that Sunday was just a normal working day – weekends didn't exist when a job as complex as the Crow case came in. Hill was leaning over Dipesh Mois, studying his computer screen when she noticed Sheridan approaching.

'You're going to love this.' Hill straightened up and took Sheridan's arm, leading her to the front of the room. 'Okay, everyone, listen up.' She nodded at Dipesh. 'Go for it.'

Dipesh cleared his throat and stood up. 'We got the phone enquiries back last night and Rob and I have been going through them. I'll start with the mobile we found in Caroline's wardrobe. Basically, we know that this phone never leaves the area. It only ever pings off the same mast, so we can probably say that it's never left her house. Now, the phone number that it rings *does* move. A lot. On Saturday seventh March at 07.00 it pings off a mast near Crosby. At 08.30 it pings off the same mast as Caroline's phone, near to her house. At 10.50 it pings in Liverpool, near Church Street. Then we've got it near to the Cranmire Hospital later that day. And, finally back at the mast near to Caroline's house at 17.15.' Dipesh looked at Sheridan who was smiling broadly. And then he continued, 'We've got the same phone pinging off masts near to Simon Banks' house and in Oxford.'

Sheridan nodded. 'So, the phone that Caroline rings is definitely Simon Banks'.'

'Yep. And the beautiful thing is, the record shows that Simon Banks' *own* mobile phone pings off the same masts at the same times and dates.'

'That is bloody wonderful. Great work, you two.' Sheridan pointed at Dipesh and Rob. 'So, when was the last time that Simon Banks' phone pinged anywhere? Let's call it his burner phone.'

'Slough in Berkshire. But then it stops and nothing since.'

'Slough?'

'Yeah, about a fifteen-minute drive from Heathrow Airport.'

Sheridan looked up as she spoke. 'We know he didn't park his car at Heathrow, so, he's either binned the phone and someone else is driving his car, and somehow it hasn't been picked up on ANPR yet. Or the phone is still in the car, and he's parked it somewhere in Slough.' She turned her attention to Dipesh. 'What about his own actual phone?'

'That last activated at the airport.'

Sheridan looked up at Hill, who answered the question before it was asked. 'Nothing from Australia on his phone.'

Rob raised a finger. 'And there's more.'

Sheridan grinned. 'I'm loving this. Go on.'

'On Thursday twelfth March, Adrian left his house at 09.00 to travel to Norfolk. In Simon Banks' statement, he says he left home at 11.30 a.m. the same day to travel to his conference in Oxford. Then at 11.45, both of his phones ping off the mast near Adrian's house.'

Sheridan clasped her hands together. 'So, now we know how Caroline left the house the day she disappeared. Simon Banks picked her up.' She sat on the corner of Dipesh's desk. 'So, it had to be Simon Banks who called Adrian, pretending to be Henry Blanchflower.' She chewed her lip. 'But it still doesn't answer the question of why. Why would Simon need to use Caroline's phone to call Adrian? Why didn't he use his own?'

'That's where it gets a bit tricky,' Dipesh replied.

'What do you mean?'

'Well, the call to Adrian from Henry Blanchflower – or as we now know him, Simon Banks – was at 18.30 hours on Wednesday eleventh March. But Simon Banks' mobiles show him being near to the hospital where he works. He wasn't at Caroline's.'

Hill interjected, 'That doesn't mean that Simon didn't make the call. He could have left his phones at work. Maybe that's why he had to use Caroline's burner phone.'

'Possibly,' Dipesh agreed. 'But the phone's been examined and there're no fingerprints or DNA on it. So, either Simon or Caroline have wiped it clean.'

'Whoever made that call to Adrian had to be a man, a man whose voice he didn't recognise, and we know whoever that was, was near Adrian's house. With everything we have on Simon Banks, it *has* to be him,' Hill replied.

Dipesh continued, 'We also got the intel back on Adrian's mobile.' He looked down at the printout. 'Adrian told us that on Saturday seventh March, he had to go to Manchester and Birmingham.' He looked at Sheridan. 'He lied.'

Sheridan's jaw tensed. 'Go on.'

'Adrian's mobile was in the area of his house most of the day. He never went to Manchester *or* Birmingham.'

Sheridan turned to Hill. 'I'm going out to see him.'

Hill put her thumb up. 'Please do and we'll have another briefing when you get back.'

Before Sheridan left the office, she made her way over to Rob Wills and plonked herself down next to him. 'Can you do me a favour?'

Rob leaned back, grinning. 'Is it something dodgy? Because so far in this enquiry you haven't asked me for anything off the record and I'm getting worried.'

Sheridan winked at him. 'This time, it's not dodgy. Can you contact the hospital and get any info or CCTV to prove that Simon Banks was or wasn't there when Adrian got the call from Henry Blanchflower?'

'You're worried that we've got the wrong guy?'

'Just making sure, that's all.'

CHAPTER 39

As they drove to Adrian Crow's house, Sheridan told Anna about her encounter with Gabriel Howard the night before.

'I think he fancies you,' Anna replied, grinning at the disgusted look on Sheridan's face.

'What the fuck gives you that idea?' Sheridan pulled into Adrian's drive.

'I saw the way he looked at you when he turned up at the nick that time – and what he said last night about wanting you, of all people, to believe him. To believe he's not a monster. Why do you think he said that?'

'Because he's a slimy piece of shit.'

'You really hate him, don't you?'

'I just hate burglars. They ruin lives, and they don't care. And he's not just a burglar. He's a killer in my eyes.' Sheridan opened the car door. 'Anyway, let's see what Adrian has to say for himself.'

As they approached the front door it was opened by Adrian, whose appearance took Sheridan back a little. He looked grey and old, his hair limp and greasy. 'Have you found her?' he asked, his voice hoarse and crackly.

Sheridan answered, 'Not yet. We've come round because we need to check something with you.'

He stepped back and let them pass before they all sat at the kitchen table. He didn't offer them a drink, which Sheridan was thankful for as the kitchen smelt like a dustbin. Cups and plates were stacked in and around the sink and empty wine bottles were lined up along the worktop.

'Adrian, in your statement, you said that on Saturday seventh March you had to go to work because you had appointments in Manchester and Birmingham . . .'

'Yes.'

'Well, we have your phone records, and they show—'

'I lied.' Adrian weaved his fingers together. 'I didn't go anywhere.'

'Why did you lie?' Sheridan asked. *Because you clearly have something to hide. So, let's hear it*, she thought.

'I haven't been completely truthful with you, and I'm sorry.'

Adrian went on to tell Sheridan and Anna that in the last couple of months, Caroline had changed. She'd been distant and quiet, like something was on her mind. But every time he asked what was wrong, she told him that she was fine. He was genuinely unaware that she'd stopped going to her swimming club and had no idea that she had children from a previous relationship – that much was true. But he'd convinced himself that she might be seeing someone else – so he periodically came home unexpectedly, or else didn't go in to work at all. Sometimes he'd leave the house as normal and sit in his car up the road. Thinking. Worrying. He struggled to concentrate at work. He didn't like being away from home but had to force himself. On the day he told Caroline he was going to Manchester and Birmingham, he'd already cancelled the appointments.

He left home as usual and drove around the corner, parked up in a nearby street and just sat there, going over and over in his mind what he feared the most: that Caroline had met someone else, and they were visiting her when he was at work. But he also knew that every time he came home unexpectedly, Caroline was always alone. There was nothing to suggest that anyone else had been in the house. There was nothing to prove that Caroline was being unfaithful. But he still felt like he was missing something.

Then on Friday 6 March, when he told Caroline he was going to plan a trip away for her birthday, her reaction hadn't been what he expected. Again, she seemed vague, almost dismissive. Adrian got the impression that she didn't want him to book the trip. On the Saturday morning, he left the house. Caroline believed he was going to work.

He didn't. Instead, he drove to a nearby street, contacted the hotel in Llandudno and made the booking. Then, he just sat there for hours, going over everything in his head, eventually realising he was being ridiculous. Caroline would never have an affair. They adored each other. Their relationship was perfect. After a few hours, he went for a drive locally before heading home. And that was when he saw the Mercedes pull away from his house.

'I'm sorry I lied. I was just so worried that if the police thought I had suspicions that Caroline was being unfaithful, that you wouldn't take her disappearance seriously. You would have just assumed that she'd packed her bags and walked out on me.' He turned to Sheridan, his tired eyes hardly able to stay open. 'I still don't believe she'd leave me. Our relationship was perfect. But if she has gone off with someone, then I assume it's the guy who took the money out of her account. She must have given him her PIN number.' Adrian put his head down.

As Sheridan processed Adrian's reasons for lying to the police, she realised he'd pretty much convinced her. It made sense and his body language gave her no reason to doubt his explanation. But was he really genuine? Or, as she had previously thought, was he just putting on a very good performance?

She responded, 'Adrian, when you took the call from Henry Blanchflower, where was Caroline?'

'What do you mean?'

'Was she in the same room?'

'No. She was in the bedroom. I think she was having a lie-down. Why?'

'Where were *you*?'

'In the kitchen.'

'Did she come in at any time while you were on the phone?'

'No.'

'Can you describe Henry Blanchflower's voice?'

'Not really. He didn't have any particular accent.'

'And you definitely didn't recognise him?'

'No. I don't think so.'

Adrian started to talk about Caroline again – mostly memories, and justifications as to why she couldn't have been having an affair. Although Sheridan was keen to get back to her team, she listened, as did Anna. Every now and then, a faint smile would show on Adrian's face as he recalled happier times.

As they drove back to Hale Street nick, Anna asked Sheridan what she thought of Adrian's reason for lying to the police.

'It makes sense,' Sheridan said. 'And a bit of me believes him.'

'Why only a bit of you?'

'You know me, mate. I don't believe anyone.'

'He's falling apart, I wouldn't be surprised if he topped himself. If Caroline has been having an affair, which is looking highly likely, I don't think he'll ever get over it.'

'He's definitely not in a good place. He looks a complete mess, and the house stinks.'

'Yeah, what *was* that smell?' Anna screwed up her nose.

'Christ knows. But at least we've smelt enough dead bodies to know he hasn't buried her under the floorboards.'

'Smelt like cabbages.' Anna grinned. 'Maybe he farted before we got there.'

Sheridan bit down on a grin. 'That's not funny.'

'Yes – it is.'

CHAPTER 40

Monday 23 March

Hill was standing with her hands behind her back looking out of the window when Sheridan walked in.

'Sorry to bother you, Hill. I just need to go over some of the DCs' other cases – we're getting a bit behind with everything that's going on.'

'Fine,' Hill replied without turning round.

'You okay?' Sheridan asked, pulling up a chair.

Hill coughed slightly. 'Yes.'

Sheridan opened up her notepad. 'Okay, so, Rob has got a GBH and . . .' Sheridan looked up. 'Are you sure you're okay?'

'I said I was fine. Carry on.' Hill stayed facing the window.

Sheridan stood up and walked over to her. 'I know you can be a miserable old trout, but I also know when something's wrong. Are you going to tell me?' Sheridan noticed tears glistening on Hill's face. 'Hey. Come on, what is it?'

'It's my wedding anniversary today. Thirty-three years.' She didn't look at Sheridan. 'It just pisses me off. Now, tell me about these other cases.'

Sheridan knew that Hill never talked about her family and what had happened to them. As far as she was aware, Hill had told no one at work and the only reason she'd told Sheridan was because she'd seen Hill at the cemetery, fifteen months earlier, on Christmas Day. The same cemetery where Matthew was buried.

Hill had been visiting a grave, too. She hadn't seen Sheridan at her brother's grave with Sam and her parents. When Hill had gone, Sheridan and Sam – curious about Hill, who kept her life so private – went over to the headstone where she'd been standing and read the words engraved upon it.

Ralph Knowles Born 2nd March 1956 – Died August 17th 1983
Beloved husband and father
Alison Knowles Born 1st May 1977 – Died August 17th 1983
Abigail Knowles Born 1st May 1977 – Died August 19th 1983
Now both safe in Daddy's arms.

When Sheridan had told Hill that she'd seen her at the cemetery, Hill had confided that on her twenty-sixth birthday, her husband, Ralph, had taken their daughters out in the car to buy Hill's birthday cake. He'd swerved to miss a cat and had been hit by an oncoming vehicle. Ralph and Alison had died instantly, Abigail two days later. Hill had made it very clear to Sheridan at the time that she never talked about her family and she'd asked Sheridan to do the same. Sheridan had only told Anna, because she knew it would go no further.

Sheridan spoke softly. 'I'm sorry, Hill. I know today must be hard for you.'

Hill turned her head to look at Sheridan. 'It's the reason I can be a miserable old trout.' A hint of a smile crossed her face.

Sheridan grinned. 'Sorry.'

'Right. Well, anyway . . .' She looked up to see Anna walking in.

'Got the result on the hand delivered to Adrian Crow.' Anna looked at Sheridan and Hill in turn. 'Sorry, have I interrupted something?'

'No. What's the result?' Hill asked. The tears were now dry on her face.

'It's a match to the one delivered to Simon Banks. Same victim, so now we have both her hands.'

Hill pulled her chair back and sat at her desk. 'What about the package?'

'No DNA, and just Adrian's fingerprints.'

Hill looked at Sheridan. 'Well, I think we can safely say that whoever the hands belong to is dead.'

Sheridan nodded. 'And who better to know how to cut off someone's hands than an orthopaedic surgeon.'

Hill raised her eyebrows. 'Simon Banks.'

CHAPTER 41

Gabriel Howard's phone vibrated in his pocket. He answered it without taking his eyes off the house across the road.

'Hello?'

'It's me. How's it going?'

'Hi. It's going well. I'm actually watching him as we speak.'

'What's he doing?'

'He's watching television. He watches a lot of television at this time of night. If I'm right, he'll go to bed in about half an hour.'

'And what will you do then?'

'Stay and watch the house. See if his routine stays the same.'

'You going to watch all night?'

'Yeah. That's what I do, remember. I watch, and when I've got their routines down pat, that's when I make my move.'

'What's happening with the other guy? Any sign yet?'

'No. He hasn't been there the last couple of times I checked. So, I'm going to concentrate on this one instead for now.'

'How close do you think you are?'

'I probably need another week. I've only got one shot at this, so I need to get it right. It has to be perfect. Then hopefully I get to watch as they slowly get destroyed and wonder how their perfect little lives fell to pieces.'

'You okay, though? You know I worry about you.'

'You don't need to worry about me.'

'I can't help it. Anyway, let me know when you need more stuff to plant on them.'

'Just keep it coming. I'll let you know when I've got enough.'

Gabriel ended the call and rolled his shoulders, ready to settle in for the night. Watching.

CHAPTER 42

Tuesday 24 March

Sheridan held the receiver under her chin and tutted as she spilt her coffee down her shirt. 'Bollocks.'

She dialled Simon Banks' number, which she was surprised to hear ringing, but it went to voicemail. 'Hi, Simon, it's DI Sheridan Holler. I was wondering if you could give me a call. I've tried calling you a couple of times now. I just wanted to give you an update on the package you had delivered. Nothing to worry about, but I do need to speak to you. Please give me a call back when you get this. Thanks.'

She then dialled Simon Banks' secretary, who confirmed that she hadn't heard from him since he left for Australia.

Anna walked in just as she ended the call. 'That's got to be a personal record. You've managed to get to three in the afternoon before staining your top.' Anna pointed at Sheridan before she sat down.

'Simon Banks' phone is switched on. I've just left him a voicemail,' Sheridan replied, patting the coffee stain with a tissue, which only made it worse.

'What did you say on the message?'

'That I've got an update on the package. I'm hoping that will make him think that's all I'm ringing for. I don't want him to suspect we're on to him. He's due back in the country in six days.'

Hill appeared in the doorway. 'What the hell have you got down your shirt?'

Sheridan instinctively looked down. 'Coffee. Cappuccino, actually. Extra milk, no sugar, sprinkling of chocolate on the top,' she said, cheerfully. 'By the way, Simon Banks' phone is switched on. Can we let the police down there know?'

'Yeah. Leave that with me,' Hill replied, unaware that Rob Wills had appeared behind her.

'Got an update,' he said.

Hill jumped. 'Jesus Christ.' She turned to see Rob stifling a laugh.

'What's the update?' Hill asked impatiently.

'We've found Caroline Crow's ex-partner.'

Sheridan stopped trying to clean her shirt. 'What do we know about him?' she asked eagerly.

'Okay, well, first of all, Caroline had two children. Scott and Phoebe Collins. Scott lives at an address near to a male called William Collins. So, we're thinking that the letters found hidden in Caroline's wardrobe signed by W, is William.'

Sheridan nodded. 'Where are they?'

'Stonehaven, Scotland. It's just south of Aberdeen. We haven't found Phoebe yet. William Collins owns a couple of pubs in the area, which he runs with Scott.'

Sheridan looked at Hill, pursing her lips. 'I've never been to Scotland.'

Hill shook her head. 'And you're not going now. Rob and Dipesh can go.' She looked at Rob. 'Get yourselves home. You've got an early start in the morning.'

CHAPTER 43

Wednesday 25 March

Rob and Dipesh walked into The Thistle pub in Stonehaven. The place was practically empty, and they were welcomed by a tall, strapping man in his fifties, with a thick, perfectly trimmed moustache. 'Good afternoon, gentlemen, what can I get you?'

Rob discreetly showed his warrant card and the man squinted at it. 'What can I do for you?'

'We're looking for a gentleman called William Collins.'

'Well, you've found him. How can I help?'

'Is there somewhere we can talk privately?'

William Collins called for a member of his bar staff to keep an eye on things, and invited Rob and Dipesh into a small back office. William pulled two tattered chairs together for Rob and Dipesh, and tucked himself behind a small desk.

Rob opened up the conversation. 'William, we're here to talk to you about your ex-partner, Caroline Crow.'

William sat back slightly. 'Caroline Crow?' He frowned. 'My ex *was* called Caroline, but not Crow. Unless she got married? Do you mean Caroline Lewis?'

'Sorry, yes, Caroline Crow is her married name.'

'So, she did get married?'

'Yes. When was the last time you saw her or heard from her?'

'I can't remember exactly . . . When the kids were small. Why?'

'Caroline was reported missing by her husband on Friday thirteenth March.'

'Missing?' William looked down and wiped a hand across his mouth. 'Blimey.'

'We found a couple of letters from you to her – there's no dates on them, but you told her that the children weren't in the country any more and that you were moving abroad.'

'I deliberately said that so she would stop looking for them.'

'Why?'

'Because Caroline was a danger to our children.'

William Collins went on to tell Rob and Dipesh that after Phoebe was born, Caroline started drinking heavily. William would come home from work and find her unconscious on the sofa and Phoebe wet and screaming in her cot. As the months went on, Caroline grew increasingly unpredictable, often leaving Phoebe in the house alone. She hung out at the pub, mixing with local drug addicts and eventually succumbing to the draw of heroin.

She smoked it, injected it and stole money out of William's pockets to pay for it. William was working long hours for a construction firm, and while he wanted to help her, he simply wasn't able to. Caroline's addiction took hold of her, so William moved himself and Phoebe out of the house. It was a wake-up call for Caroline, who – not wanting to lose touch with her daughter – got herself clean. William eventually agreed to move back in, bringing Phoebe with him. For the next year, things seemed to be moving along well and then Caroline fell pregnant with Scott. Two months after giving birth, she was back on the drink and the drugs, and back on the path to hell.

William was working seven days a week and Caroline was neglecting the children, leaving them alone in the house, while she met her supplier on street corners and down alleyways littered with rubbish and rats. Her life was spiralling out of control. This time, William took time off work to look after the children, while Caroline disappeared for days on end. William was terrified that he'd lose his job, or that the children would be taken away.

And so, one day, while Caroline was out, he packed her things and waited for her to come home. When she rolled in at three in the morning, high and drunk, he told her to leave. She initially refused until he threatened to report her to social services. And that was enough. She moved out, and stayed with a heroin-addict friend who was squatting in a rundown flat in Liverpool.

William changed his job so he could be at home more with the children.

Caroline would turn up every now and then, demanding or begging to see her children. But William wouldn't allow her in – not unless she was sober. And when she was allowed in, he wouldn't take his eyes off her, ever protective of the children that he adored.

He told Rob and Dipesh that the last time Caroline had seen the children was just after Christmas, 1987. Phoebe was twelve and Scott nine. She hadn't made contact over the Christmas period, but then turned up one morning in her usual state. She had argued with William, saying that she wanted to move back in, clean herself up and be the mother she should have always been. But William had heard it all before. He couldn't break the children's hearts again. He told her to leave.

She wrote to him incessantly, the same words, the same empty promises. And that was when he knew he had to get away.

He found a job running a pub in Scotland. He made the initial journey up to Glasgow alone, while the children stayed with a friend. The pub's owner was a young woman called Rebecca and they instantly hit it off. Rebecca was divorced with no children of her own, but she and William soon became a couple. He introduced her to Phoebe and Scott, and they immediately clicked. It was perfect. The children settled into their new school and routine. They were bright kids who thrived in their new, stable and safe life, while Rebecca became the mother they never had before.

William put the house in Liverpool up for sale. He regularly made the journey down to check on the place while the sale went through. That was when he had found more letters that Caroline had written, still being sent to their old address. He wrote back, telling her that the children weren't in the country any more. In his mind – technically, at least – Scotland was another country. He told her he was moving abroad with them, and that he wasn't willing to share where they were going. Anything to stop her writing and trying to look for them. That letter had been the last time he'd heard from her.

'So, are you and Rebecca still together?' Rob asked.

'Yes – and very happily married, actually.'

'And what about Scott and Phoebe? How are they doing?'

William's jaw tightened. 'Scott runs another pub that Rebecca and I own. He's doing well. He's been with his girlfriend for a few years now. We're all very close.'

'And Phoebe?'

William's head dropped slightly. He swallowed. 'Phoebe met a guy from the States. They fell in love and she moved over there, got a job working for Morgan Stanley. She loved it. She was so happy there, but she always kept in touch with her old dad.' A brief smile drifted across William's face and a moment of silence hung in the room.

William continued, 'She applied for a promotion and got the job. I remember her ringing me to say she was starting her new job the next day. That was the Monday, September the tenth, 2001.' He looked up for a moment and Rob nodded slowly, realising where this was going.

'She got to work early to make a good impression.' Tears filled William's eyes and he blinked down on them. 'She was in the North Tower of the World Trade Center when the first plane hit.'

'I'm so sorry,' Rob replied, his voice at a whisper.

'We never got her back. I like to think she died instantly and didn't suffer.' William clasped his hands together. 'You never get over losing a child.' He swallowed again.

'We're so sorry for your loss.' Rob waited, thinking he should leave a polite gap before he continued. 'So, if Caroline hasn't had contact with the children since 1987, I'm guessing she doesn't know about Phoebe?'

'No. If she has found out somehow, it didn't come from me.' William wiped a hand up and down his thigh. 'Did Caroline leave a note or anything to say where she was going?'

'No note. She has just disappeared. We thought perhaps she might have headed here.'

'Well, she hasn't. If I hear from her, I'll let you know of course.'

'Would she have made contact with Scott?' Rob asked.

'No. If she had, he'd have told me. We don't keep anything from each other.'

'We'd like to speak to him anyway.'

'Of course. But can I ask that you come back tomorrow? I just want some time to talk to him. He never speaks about Caroline and if she's ever mentioned he gets really upset. I'd rather just warn him that you want to talk about her. Is that okay?' William's voice broke slightly as he spoke. It was evident that talking about Phoebe had evoked strong emotions – bringing back the pain of losing his daughter.

'Of course. What's a good time?' asked Rob.

'Say 10 a.m.?' William replied.

'Okay.'

They talked for another half an hour before Rob and Dipesh left. They called Sheridan to update her on what they'd learnt, before heading off to find another pub where they could down a pint or three. Resisting the temptation to visit the pub that Scott ran, both wanting to move on with the enquiry and a little frustrated that they had to wait until the following day. They found one near to their B&B and their frustration was eased a little as they sat supping into the evening.

CHAPTER 44

William Collins watched as Rob and Dipesh pulled away, before returning to the office. He opened the top drawer of the filing cabinet and reached back to the last hanging folder and pulled out the letter.

The letter was dated two and a half weeks earlier.

Saturday 7th March

William,

I know it's been a long time since we had any contact, but I hope you are keeping well. I was going to ring, but I was worried that you might hang up on me. And I can say what I need to in a letter much more easily than over the phone.

When I was young, I made some terrible mistakes, as you know, and I have always regretted them. I can't change any of it. I can't change the fact that I was a terrible mother to our children. I can't even blame the drugs I took because it was my choice to take that path in life.

But many years have passed since I turned myself and my life around. I'm a completely different person to the one I was back then.

I got married to a wonderful man who is so kind and generous that I'm not sure I deserve him. He's my soulmate, and I am thankful every day that we met. He knows nothing of my past, or the person I was back when you knew me. He loves me for who I am now. I'm so lucky to have found him.

I know what I put you through and I can never say sorry enough. I also want to say sorry to Scott and Phoebe. I know why they haven't been a part of my life and I accept that.

But I really would love to see them. They are my children, and I have never forgotten about them – and I have never stopped loving them.

I'm making plans to come to Scotland. I thought I would let you know rather than simply turning up. I would be so grateful if you could let Scott and Phoebe know. I know Scott works in the pub business with you, and I'm guessing Phoebe is still in touch with you both. You three were always very close and I have an image in my head that you spend a lot of time together.

I know I can't make up for everything that happened, and I don't intend to even begin to try. But everyone deserves a second chance, don't they?

Anyway, I'll let you know when I make it to Scotland, shouldn't be too long now. I found a number for the pub, so will call you and not just turn up out of the blue.

Until then, take care,

Caroline

After reading the letter twice, William screwed it up and, clasping it in his hand, he made his way out of the back door of the pub.

The embers from the firepit were fading now, but tiny flames licked around its edges as he threw the letter on top.

CHAPTER 45

Anna pushed her shopping trolley into the alcohol aisle of the supermarket, scanning the wine shelves. She picked one for herself and then another for Sheridan and Sam, ready to take with her next time she stayed over. As she made her way to the checkout, she spotted Steve at the end of an aisle and stopped. At that moment he looked up and raised his eyebrows.

'Hello, you,' he said cheerfully, and Anna smiled back at him.

'I thought you were in Glasgow.' She parked her trolley next to his.

'I was. But the job finished, and there wasn't much else going on. So I came back a couple of months ago.'

'Where are you living?'

'Crashing at a mate's. But I'm looking at a couple of flats.' He tilted his head to one side. 'You look great.'

'Thanks. You look well.'

'I feel good. Life's good.'

There was an awkward silence before he looked into her shopping trolley. 'Two bottles of wine?' He grinned. 'Thought I was the one who had a drink problem.'

'Only one of them's for me.' Anna peered into Steve's trolley. 'I take it you haven't been down the booze aisle yet?'

'I don't drink any more. Haven't touched the stuff since you chucked me out.' He gave her a cheeky wink and Anna couldn't help remembering how he used to make her feel. How that cheeky wink once melted her. She had loved him deeply for seven years and then suddenly she was alone; even though it had been her choice to throw him out, there was still love there. She felt it and by the look in his eyes, she knew he felt it too.

They chatted for a while before making their way to the check-out, Anna clocking what Steve had bought: a typical single guy's shop. Four microwave meals for one, milk, teabags, tins of beans and a box of cereal. For a moment, she felt a pang of sadness for him. After paying for his shopping, he helped Anna pack her things away, making her chuckle as he commented on every item.

'Sure deodorant – cos your pits smell like cat wee,' he quipped as he dropped the can into one of the bags.

Anna slapped his arm. 'Cheeky twat,' she said under her breath, but loud enough for him to hear.

They walked to the car park together and after loading her boot, she turned to him. 'I'm glad you're doing okay, Steve.'

'Thanks. I'm glad you're okay too.' He smiled, and after touching her momentarily on the arm, he turned his trolley and walked off slowly towards his own car.

Anna got in and started the engine, watching him for a moment in her rear-view mirror, before pulling away.

She immediately felt the steering was heavy, so, after cutting the engine, she got out and saw the flat tyre.

'Shit,' she said under her breath, spotting the telltale end of a nail embedded in her tyre. As she knelt down, she noticed several nails on the ground around her car and the car next to hers, which she picked up, not wanting anyone else to suffer the inconvenience of having to change a tyre.

CHAPTER 46

William Collins' hands wouldn't stop shaking as he dialled Scott's number.

'Hi,' Scott answered.

'Hi, son. You busy?'

'Not really. Pub's quiet. You?'

'Yeah, quiet.' He hesitated. 'Can you pop over and see me? I need to talk to you about something.'

'Sure. Everything okay?'

'Yeah, it's fine. I just need a quick chat.'

'Can't you tell me now?'

'No. Rather do it face to face. It's nothing to worry about.'

An hour later, Scott was sitting in the back room, watching his dad making coffee. After handing Scott a mug, William sat down opposite him, smoothing his fingers across his moustache.

'You're acting weird, Dad. What's going on?' Scott set his mug down and sat back, crossing his legs.

'I've got something to tell you, but before I do, I want you to know that I love you.'

Scott uncrossed his legs and sat bolt upright. 'Jesus, Dad – you're scaring the shit out of me. Are you ill?'

'No. I'm fine. And Rebecca's fine. It's nothing like that.'

'Is it the business? Are we struggling?'

'No. It's nothing like that either. Please just listen to me.'

Scott remained silent. His face had paled slightly, and he was shifting awkwardly in his seat.

'I love you very much and everything I've ever done since you were born has been to protect you. You and Phoebe. You know that, don't you?'

'Of course, but . . .'

'Please, just let me talk.' William went to take a sip of coffee but his stomach churned, the smell of caffeine making him feel nauseous. He set the mug down. 'It's about your mum.'

'What about her?'

William looked Scott straight in the eye. 'I've done something unforgivable.'

CHAPTER 47

Sheridan rested her head in Sam's lap before wearily closing her eyes. Maud was sitting on the arm of the sofa, licking her paw and swiping it over her ear.

Sam was reading a book on first aid, having earlier practised the recovery position on Sheridan, inadvertently turning her over too heavy-handedly and bashing her head on the leg of the coffee table. Sam had enrolled on the course after a suggestion from Joni, who had advised Sam that as her cooking was so hideous the least she could do was to be prepared if anyone ever choked on it. Sam had initially enrolled in a cookery class – but being the worst student the tutor had ever experienced, she had been tentatively asked to leave.

'That's interesting,' Sam suddenly piped up.

'What is?' Sheridan opened her eyes.

'The Resusci Annie doll was invented by a Norwegian toy maker. He used a woman's face for the mannequin because he thought men would be reluctant to put their lips on another man's face.'

'That *is* interesting.' Sheridan grinned. 'What does it say about banging your partner's head on the coffee table while putting her in the recovery position?'

'Shit. Don't. I'm so sorry.' Sam instinctively brushed her hand over Sheridan's forehead. 'Does it still hurt?'

'No. I'm just messing with you. I'm fine. And if I have got concussion, then at least you'll know what to do.'

'You can't get concussion. I haven't got to that page yet.'

Sheridan's work mobile rang. She reluctantly sat up, grabbing it from the coffee table, noticing the number was withheld. 'DI Holler.'

'Hello. It's Simon Banks.'

Sheridan's eyes widened. 'Hello, Simon. How are you?' she asked, her mind racing with how to play this conversation. Each time she'd called him it was always when she was at work, at her desk, prepared and ready for if and when he answered. Now, in her living room, she felt taken by surprise.

'I'm fine. Sorry I missed your call, the signal here is terrible and my phone's been playing up. I've had to use my son's old one. You said that you had an update on the package that was delivered to my house?'

'Yes. Yes, that's right.'

'Have you managed to identify the victim?'

'No. We know the hand belonged to a female, but we don't know who she is.'

'I see.'

'Simon – what's your son's name? What's the address you're staying at? Just in case I can't get hold of you and need to get in touch? And an up-to-date phone number – you've come up as withheld.'

There was a long silence before he answered. 'I'd rather not say at this point. I had a phone call from my secretary. She said you were asking if I knew a Caroline or Adrian Crow. I was wondering why you asked?'

Sheridan got straight to the point. 'Caroline Crow is missing and we're extremely worried about her.'

'Missing?'

'Yes, her husband reported her missing on Friday the thirteenth. We understand that you know her.'

'Did she leave a note?'

'No.'

'Look, I'm back in the country on Monday. I'll come and see you.'

'Simon, we need to know everything we can about where Caroline might be—'

'She's not missing.'

Sheridan frowned. 'What do you mean?'

'She's safe.'

'Is she with you?'

'No. Look, I have to go. I'll be in touch when I get back to the UK.'

And then the line went dead.

'Bollocks.' Sheridan stared at her mobile and then quickly dialled Simon Banks' number. Switched off. And then she rang Anna.

'Hello?' Anna answered.

'Hi, mate. Guess who just called me?'

'Go on.'

'Simon bloody Banks.'

Sheridan told Anna about their brief conversation.

'Bit weird him not telling you his son's address.' Anna paused. 'So, he could know *everything*.'

'Exactly, but we're going to have to wait until he gets back. Anyway, I'll see you tomorrow, yeah? I'll give Hill a quick call and update her.'

'Okay. See you tomorrow.'

◆ ◆ ◆

Anna ended the call and put her mobile back on the bedside table. Then she felt Steve's hand on her back. She turned to face him, and he kissed her gently on the lips.

'I think you should go, Steve,' she said quietly.

'Really?'

'Yeah, really.'

'You don't regret sleeping with me, do you?' He pushed himself up on one elbow.

'No. But I'm not ready to start anything either. This was lovely, and you're a star for sorting my tyre out, but . . .'

'It's fine.' He threw the duvet back and swung his legs out of the bed. 'Honestly, it's fine.' He picked his clothes up off the floor and proceeded to get dressed. 'You're checking out my bum, aren't you?' He grinned.

'No.' Anna couldn't help smiling. 'It's not your most endearing feature.' She raised an eyebrow.

Five minutes later, she was standing at her front door, watching him pull away.

He waved at her, smiling.

And then he reached into the driver's door and pulled out the bradawl. The one he'd used to puncture her tyre before scattering nails near her car and the car parked next to hers, and finally pushing one of them into the hole he'd made himself.

CHAPTER 48

Thursday 26 March

Rob and Dipesh parked in the car park of The Thistle pub. They were a few minutes early for their 10 a.m. meeting with Scott Collins.

'I always wanted to run a pub,' Rob said as he switched off the engine.

'Why didn't you?'

'My dad was in the job and wanted me to follow in his footsteps. He did his thirty years, ended up as a DS in CID at Hale Street actually. He always wanted me to join the job.' He turned to Dipesh. 'I'm probably a better copper than I would have been a landlord.'

'What are you talking about? You're a shit copper,' Dipesh replied.

'You're a shit copper,' Rob said, in a high-pitched childish voice.

'You're shittier.' Dipesh looked up as William Collins opened the pub door and waved them over.

'Shittiest shit shitty copper,' Rob whispered to Dipesh as they walked across the car park and followed William into the back office, where Scott Collins was sitting, arms crossed.

'Hi, Scott,' Rob said, then introduced himself and Dipesh before turning to William. 'Is it okay if we speak to Scott alone?'

'Of course.' William nodded at Scott and left, making his way through the bar to set up for the day.

'So, Scott, we understand that your dad has told you that your mother is missing?'

'Yes,' Scott answered abruptly. Stoically.

'And you haven't had any contact with her since you were little.'

'No.'

'So, you haven't had any contact recently?'

'No.'

Dipesh watched Scott very closely as Rob continued to ask him questions. Every answer either a blunt 'yes', 'no' or 'don't know'.

Rob tried a different tack. 'Scott, we know that your mum had issues when she was younger and that you struggle to talk about her, but anything you can tell us could help find her.'

Scott's jaw tightened. 'I don't know anything. She hasn't been in contact, and I have no idea where she is.'

'Would you like us to let you know if and when she's found?'

Scott shrugged his shoulders. 'If you want.'

Half an hour later, Rob and Dipesh thanked Scott for his time. He showed them out, not even waiting until they'd pulled away before closing the door.

As he turned around, William was standing in the middle of the empty pub.

'How did it go?' William asked.

'I lied for you like you asked me to,' Scott replied through gritted teeth.

'Thank you, son.'

'Don't thank me. I don't want your thanks. I can't even begin to comprehend what you've done.' Scott's face flushed with anger.

'I did it for you . . .'

'Was she that much of a fucking risk? For God's sake, Dad, *was* she?' He raised his voice. 'I don't know you. I thought I did, but I really don't know you.'

William Collins' head dropped. 'I had to do it. I had to protect you.'

CHAPTER 49

Sheridan was sitting at her desk when her phone rang. 'DI Holler.'

'Sheridan, it's Rob.'

'Hi, mate. How's it going?'

'We're heading back now. Just wanted to give you an update on our meeting with Scott Collins.'

'Okay.'

'He's fucking weird.' Rob went on to tell Sheridan about the stilted and difficult conversation they'd had.

'Do you think he was lying?' Sheridan asked.

'I think he's hiding something.'

Hill walked in with Anna at her side, and after closing the door, they both sat down.

'Okay. How long will it take you to get back to the nick?' Sheridan flicked a look at the clock on the wall. 11.02 a.m.

'About six hours or so.'

'Okay. I'll still be here. Safe journey.'

'Cheers, boss. Me and Dipesh are going to pick ourselves up a kilt each and a sporran – give you lot a nice thrill when we get back.'

Sheridan grinned. 'Do they do sporrans that small?' Without giving Rob a chance to reply, she ended the call and relayed Rob's comments about Scott Collins to Hill and Anna.

Hill crossed her arms. 'We've got the blood results from the spots that were found in Simon Banks' bathroom. It belongs to Simon, I'm afraid.'

Sheridan sat back. 'This is so frustrating. Simon Banks is the key to all of this. He clearly knows where Caroline is, and he says she's safe. But where the hell is she?'

Hill replied, 'I'm getting my arse kicked by the super and if it wasn't for the hands that were delivered to Simon and Adrian, this would be punted to the missing persons unit. The severed hands enquiry has so far drawn a blank, we're no closer to identifying the victim, and I'm not sure how long I can keep full resources on the case.'

Sheridan jumped in. 'We're keeping it for now though, aren't we? We've still got enquiries ongoing with the hands case, we're reaching out to a shitload of other forces and intel units – something will come up. And we're going to find out where Caroline is when Simon Banks gets back from Australia on Monday. The police over there didn't get a hit on his phone when I left the voicemail the other day.'

'Yes. But let's face it, Sheridan – Caroline has clearly planned her own disappearance. There's nothing at this stage to suggest that she's come to any harm. The hands don't belong to her, that's been confirmed. She wanted to get away and has been planning it for months. It's fairly clear that her and Simon are in some sort of relationship. It's evident that he was the one who called Adrian, to get him away from the house so that he could pick Caroline up the next day. We know that Simon Banks is Henry Blanchflower.'

'She hasn't used her bank account since she went missing,' Sheridan said.

'Maybe Simon gave her money? He's a doctor so he's probably not short of cash.'

Sheridan sighed. 'We're missing something here. Why did someone send those burnt hands to Simon and Adrian? What does it mean? Was it a warning? Because it feels like a bloody warning to me.'

After discussing their theories about the hands, Hill checked her watch and stood up to leave. Being the DCI involved wearing several hats. Keeping the press at bay and overseeing other cases meant she often had to stretch herself thinly. Once Hill had left, Anna frowned at Sheridan.

'You okay?' she asked Sheridan, who was leaning back in her seat, staring at the ceiling. 'You're doing that thing, aren't you?'

'What thing?' Sheridan asked.

'That thing where your eyes glaze over and your mind goes off on one.'

Sheridan replied, 'It's about seeing, not just looking.'

'What do you mean?'

'I remember a tutor I had when I first joined the job. He said it's not what you're looking at, it's what you *see*. You can look at something all day long, but it's how you see it that makes the difference. We've looked at all the evidence in this case . . . but what is it we're not seeing?'

Anna shrugged her shoulders.

'Anyway. What's on *your* mind?' Sheridan asked, raising an eyebrow.

'How do you know something's on my mind?'

'Because I know you. Come on, spit it out.'

Anna took a breath. 'I saw Steve yesterday.'

Anna told Sheridan about her encounter with her ex.

'So, are you seeing him again?'

'I don't know. We haven't made any plans. It was just nice to have someone there, you know? I hate living on my own. I'm so shit at it.'

'We're on lates tomorrow. Do you want to stay at ours tonight?' Sheridan hoped her suggestion didn't sound like an attempt to keep Anna close. Close and away from Steve. Anna had always denied that Steve had ever hit her, but Sheridan's instinct told her that he had.

'That would be cool,' Anna replied.

'Have you got your overnight bag?'

'Always.' Anna grinned.

◆ ◆ ◆

It was half five by the time Rob and Dipesh got back from Scotland. Anna was sat in Sheridan's office when they both walked in.

They went over their conversations with William and Scott again and Sheridan agreed that something was off. 'We know Caroline applied for a new passport and received it. So, what if she *did* know that Phoebe lived in the States, but didn't know that Phoebe had died? What if she was actually planning to visit her?'

'Maybe she planned to go to Scotland first and then the States?' Anna added.

Sheridan nodded. 'Maybe. And maybe she's driving Simon's car. He said she was safe. Maybe that's what he meant.' She paused. 'His car hasn't shown up on any ANPR cameras. I wonder, if she *is* driving it, how she's managed to evade them.'

Rob stretched out his legs, tired from the journey. 'Well, if she did head to Scotland, then according to William and Scott, she never arrived.'

CHAPTER 50

Anna unpacked her overnight bag in Sheridan's spare bedroom – a room that she felt had become hers over the last few months. She knew that she was spending too much time away from her own house, but she struggled alone. She had been so used to having Steve there that, after he left, she found herself rattling around the place, talking to herself and hating the silence she got in return. Anna adored Sheridan and Sam's company. She could only dream of having a relationship as solid as theirs. One day, she promised herself, she'd meet the perfect guy and be as happy as her best mate was. Steve came into her head. Had he really changed? She mentally stripped away his bad side – the side of him that was violent and angry – and what was left was the Steve she'd loved. Could it work with him again if she took it slowly? She closed her eyes and shook her head slightly. Doubts suddenly overtook the positive thoughts – she couldn't forget the times he'd hit her.

She switched the light on in the en-suite bathroom and placed her toothpaste next to the sink before rifling through her case to find her electric toothbrush charger.

'Bollocks.' She flipped the case shut and made her way downstairs where Sheridan and Sam were chatting in the kitchen. Maud was under the table bashing her paw at a Jaffa Cake.

'Have you got a spare toothbrush? I've forgotten my charger again.' Anna quickly lifted her foot up as Maud suddenly launched the Jaffa Cake across the floor. 'You do know that chocolate is poisonous for cats, don't you?' She opened the fridge and took out the bottle of wine she'd picked up at the supermarket the day before.

'Yeah, I know. But to be fair, she doesn't actually eat the chocolate,' Sam said, leaning around Anna and grabbing a beer. 'There's a pack of new toothbrushes in the main bathroom under the sink. Just don't pick an orange one – that's Sheridan's favourite colour.'

'It's not just orange – it's vermilion, to be exact,' Sheridan clarified.

'Thanks.' Anna poured out two glasses of wine and handed one to Sheridan, who was sitting at the table.

'Have you always used an electric toothbrush?' Sheridan asked, absent-mindedly twisting her wine glass around by the stem.

'Only since I lost my tooth that time. The dentist recommended I go electric. I never looked back.' Anna sipped her wine and grabbed a handful of crisps from the bowl on the worktop.

'Do you use normal toothbrushes as well?' Sheridan asked, staring at her wine glass.

'No. Jesus. Are we going to talk about my dental hygiene all night?'

'So, you just have an electric one? You don't keep normal ones in the house?'

'Seriously?' Anna sat opposite Sheridan. 'No, your honour, I don't keep normal toothbrushes in the house. I have one electric toothbrush and when the head starts to look sorry for itself, I change it. Case closed. Can we talk about something more interesting?'

Sheridan stood up. 'I need to make a phone call.' She swiped her mobile from the table and went into the living room.

Ten minutes later, she returned. 'We're going to Llandudno tomorrow morning.'

CHAPTER 51

Friday 27 March

Sheridan and Anna walked into the reception of the Hampshire Hotel, Llandudno. The old building stood proudly on the seafront, a stone's throw from the pier.

The young woman behind the reception desk didn't look up from her phone as they approached. The only other person present was an elderly lady sitting in a wing-back chair, her suitcase by her feet and her weathered brown leather handbag balanced on her lap.

The receptionist put the phone down. 'Your taxi will be here in ten minutes, Mrs Hamilton.'

The old lady was staring at Sheridan and Anna and didn't answer.

'Mrs Hamilton?' The receptionist raised her voice. 'Your taxi will be here in ten minutes.'

Mrs Hamilton still didn't respond, her milky eyes fixed on Sheridan, who stepped over to her and bent down. 'Your taxi will be here in ten minutes.'

'Oh. Thank you, dear.' Mrs Hamilton smiled and started unwrapping a boiled sweet.

The receptionist smiled. 'Thank you for that. How can I help?'

Sheridan pulled out her warrant card. 'I'm Detective Inspector Holler and this is my colleague Detective Sergeant Markinson . . .'

The phone rang again, and the receptionist quickly answered, mouthing 'Sorry' as she did so.

When she finished the call, her attention came back to Sheridan. 'I'm sorry about that. I'm on my own this morning. There's normally three of us.'

'It's fine. I called last night and spoke to someone about a couple who stayed in room 314 from the eighth to the eleventh of March, Mr and Mrs Crow. We'd like to see the room. I was told last night that it's available.'

'Of course, let me just double-check.' She tapped her keyboard. 'Has something happened?'

'We've got concerns about Mrs Crow. She's gone missing.'

'Oh yes, I heard. That's awful.'

'Were you here when they stayed? Do you remember them?'

'I was on leave. My colleague told me that the police had been in touch asking about them. I think they wanted some CCTV and they asked a few questions about Mr and Mrs Crow.'

'Did they ask if Mr and Mrs Crow left anything in the room – anything that was found after they checked out?'

'I'm not sure. You'd be better off speaking to the manager, she'll be in shortly. And room 314 *is* unoccupied.'

'Has it been used since they checked out?'

'Yes, twice by the looks of it.'

The phone rang again.

'I can't leave reception until my colleague gets here at nine. If I give you a swipe card, are you okay to go up and see the room? It's on the third floor.'

'Yes, that's perfect, thanks.'

Sheridan took the card. She and Anna made their way to the lift.

'Has my taxi been called?' Mrs Hamilton asked as Sheridan passed her.

'Yes, it'll be here in eight minutes, Mrs Hamilton,' Sheridan replied, with a smile.

As they stepped out of the lift on the third floor, Anna nodded a good morning to the housekeeper who was carrying an armful of towels into one of the rooms. They walked down the corridor to room 314 and let themselves in using the keycard.

The room was large and airy, the whitewashed walls adorned with tasteful pictures of Llandudno hanging in silver frames. A deep clawfoot bathtub stood at the back of the bathroom, with a walk-in shower situated to the right.

In the main room, Sheridan got on her knees and looked under the bed while Anna opened drawers and checked on top of the wardrobe. They lifted the mattress, then checked down the side of the two wing-back chairs by the window. They didn't find what they were looking for.

'Right, let's go,' Sheridan said, heading back out to the corridor. 'I'm going to try out my theory.'

Anna curiously followed her down the corridor to one of the housekeeper's trollies. Indicating for Anna to stay where she was, Sheridan peered around the door of the room being cleaned before walking in.

The housekeeper was making the bed, sweeping her hand across the duvet cover to smooth out any creases. She looked up from her task as Sheridan appeared. 'Hi,' Sheridan said. 'Just grabbing something from the bathroom – thanks for cleaning my room.'

She emerged a moment later with a small bottle of complimentary shampoo and a huge grin on her face. 'How easy was that?'

'Too easy.' Anna raised an eyebrow.

'I think Caroline did the same thing. She walked into someone else's room and took a hairbrush and toothbrush.' Sheridan pressed the lift button for the ground floor.

'Yeah, but what for? And how would she know that there wasn't a bloke on his own staying in the room? How would she know there would be a woman's hairbrush in there?' Anna asked.

'I don't know.' They stepped into the lift, rode it down to the ground floor and went back to the reception desk.

'Everything okay?' the receptionist asked, looking up from the computer screen, phone tucked under her chin, which she placed back on the desk.

'Do you know if any guests had anything taken from their room while Mr and Mrs Crow were staying here?' Sheridan asked.

'Can I help you?' said a voice from behind them. They turned to see a tall, painfully thin woman dressed in a dark grey suit. 'I'm the manager.'

Sheridan introduced herself and Anna and explained their reason for being there. 'Can I ask if after Mr and Mrs Crow checked out, was anything left in their room?'

'No. Definitely not.'

'Did any of the guests that were staying here at the same time as the Crows report anything missing from their room?' Sheridan asked.

'There was one report of a theft. The guest blamed my housekeeping staff, but I assured her that my staff are fully vetted. In the twelve years I've been in charge here, nothing has ever gone missing,' the manager replied defensively.

'What did she say was stolen?'

The manager crossed her arms. 'Money, perfume, a gold necklace, an expensive jumper and a pair of boots worth several hundred pounds. I told her to report it to the police if she wished. But I haven't heard anything yet.'

'Do you have her contact details?'

'I've already given all the contact details of everyone who was here at the same time as Mr and Mrs Crow to a DC Sexton.' She stepped behind the reception counter and punched her password into the computer. A moment later, she was writing down a name on a compliment slip which she handed to Sheridan, who made a mental note to check in with DC Bridie Sexton when they got back to the nick.

'Jacqueline Blackstone,' Sheridan read out loud. 'Do you remember what Jacqueline looks like?'

'About fifty – quite short, medium-length brown hair, quite smart looking.'

'Do your housekeeping staff clean the rooms at the same time every day?'

'Yes.'

'What room was Jacqueline Blackstone in?'

'325.'

'Is that near to Mr and Mrs Crow's room?' *Please say yes*, Sheridan thought.

'Yes. It's just along the corridor on the opposite side.'

Sheridan and Anna sat in Hill's office, going through the details of their trip to Llandudno that morning. Sheridan described how easy it had been for her to enter another guest's room and potentially take a hairbrush and toothbrush. Hill asked the same question as Anna: how would Caroline know that a woman was staying in that particular room? Sheridan resignedly admitted that she hadn't worked that out. Yet.

'Where's your head at with this, Sheridan? What would be the reason that Caroline took someone else's things and planted them in her own bathroom? If they *were* planted, maybe it was Adrian who did it?'

'Possibly. But Caroline didn't unpack her case when they got home. I think it was because Adrian might have seen what was in it.'

'But this Jacqueline Blackstone reported her jewellery and money missing, not her fucking toothbrush,' Hill replied.

'I know. But Bridie hasn't managed to get hold of her – so I'm going to keep trying and hopefully I'll have more luck and I can ask her exactly what went missing.'

Hill sighed. 'Again, where are you going with this, Sheridan? I'm not following you.'

Sheridan inhaled. 'The toothbrush that Jack Staples seized from Caroline's bathroom was electric, but I noticed that in Caroline's bathroom there was a cabinet where the toothbrushes – normal ones – were kept, but I couldn't see a charger for an electric toothbrush. I also didn't see any spare electric toothbrush heads. So, my guess is that Caroline doesn't use an electric toothbrush. So, on the way back from Llandudno today, I called Jack Staples, who confirmed that Adrian wasn't present when he seized Caroline's hairbrush and toothbrush – he was downstairs. Which means that Adrian wouldn't have seen Jack seize an electric toothbrush. Anyway, I asked Jack to check with Adrian if Caroline ever uses an electric toothbrush and Adrian said she didn't.'

'Okay. But there seems to be a few things that Adrian doesn't know about Caroline and maybe her charger was in her suitcase that she took with her when she left,' Hill replied.

'Why take her toothbrush and not the charger?' Sheridan asked.

'I'd question more why she *planted* a toothbrush,' was Hill's response.

The early morning start was catching up with Sheridan, who yawned before answering. 'I've asked CSI to take some more samples from the house, so we'll soon know if I'm right about Caroline making the swap. She's up to something, and for some reason she doesn't want us to have her DNA.'

CHAPTER 52

Sheridan sat at her desk and dialled Jacqueline Blackstone's number. Bridie Sexton had already confirmed that she was still working through the list of guests and hadn't heard from three of them, including Blackstone.

The first calls went to voicemail and Sheridan hung up. The third call was answered.

'Hello?'

'Hello, is that Jacqueline Blackstone?' Sheridan tapped her pen on the notepad in front of her.

'Speaking. Who's this?'

'My name is Sheridan Holler, I'm a detective inspector—'

'Is this about the stuff that was nicked from my hotel room?'

'It is actually, yes.'

'But I haven't reported it to the police. Did the hotel ask you to call me?'

'No. Why haven't you reported it to the police?'

'I was hoping I wouldn't have to take it that far. I just want the manager to pay me compensation for the things that were nicked.'

'I see. Well, can I ask you something? Apart from the things you already reported stolen, was there anything else taken?'

'Like what?'

'Like a hairbrush or toothbrush?'

Laughter down the phone. 'You're joking, right?'

'No. I'm not.'

'No, they didn't steal my hairbrush or my toothbrush – they were too busy robbing my money and jewellery. Is the hotel going to pay up?'

'I don't know, that's between you and the manager. Of course, if you wanted to report it to the police then you can. Whereabouts do you live?'

'Shrewsbury.'

'Jacqueline, I'm investigating the disappearance of a woman who was staying at the Hampshire Hotel the same time as you and I really need to be certain that nothing else was taken from your hotel room.'

'I've already given the manager a list of the items. Look, I'm sorry that someone is missing, and I hope you find her – but I just want the hotel to pay up so I can forget the whole thing. I'm sorry but I'm going to have to go. I'm at work, and my boss is staring at me.'

She took Sheridan's number and hung up.

'Shit,' Sheridan said as she put the phone down.

Rob Wills stuck his head around the door. 'You okay, boss?'

'Yeah. Except my theory just went into the big box of shit theories.'

Just then, her phone rang. 'DI Holler.'

'Sheridan, it's Charlie from CSI.'

'Hi, Charlie – please tell me something wonderful because right now this investigation is going down the toilet.'

'Ah. Then maybe my timing isn't good.'

'It's okay, mate. What have you got?'

'Well, firstly, I'm sorry it's taken so long to get back to you, but you asked for further samples to be taken in relation to the forensic search at Caroline Crow's house.'

'Yeah.'

'Well, I seized a lipstick, her pillowcase, a top from her wardrobe and a bottle of water from her bedside table. The results show that they belonged to Caroline. The samples match the DNA from her hairbrush and toothbrush.'

Sheridan's shoulders dropped. 'Okay. Cheers, Charlie.' She ended the call and looked at Rob. 'I can't figure it out. I was so sure Caroline had planted those things.'

CHAPTER 53

Gabriel Howard kept his head low, camouflaged by the tall grass. He dialled the number, which was answered immediately.

'Hi, Gabe. How's it going?' he asked.

'All good. I'm almost there. You're positive none of this stuff can be traced back to you?'

'Absolutely positive.'

'And I suppose I don't need to know where you're getting these things from?'

'Correct.'

'Fair enough. Well, once I've finished the job, we can sit back and wait for the shit to hit the fan.' Gabriel smiled to himself. 'Thanks for all you're doing. I couldn't have done it without you.'

'You're welcome. So, that'll be one down and one to go.'

'Yeah, still no sign of the other guy, but I'm in no rush. Just gonna enjoy this bit.'

'Good. You okay though?'

'Yeah.' Gabriel paused. 'Does it sound weird when I say I'm enjoying it? I don't forget why I'm doing this – it's always there. Sometimes I close my eyes and all I can think about is what they did.'

'Gabe, just think about what's happening now. You need to stay focused. You're almost there.'

'You're right. Anyway, I'll keep you posted.' Gabriel ended the call and looked up.

He could see Adrian Crow in the kitchen – and watched as he put his coat on.

CHAPTER 54

Monday 30 March

Sheridan pulled into the car park at Heathrow Airport. 'We're a bit early.'

Anna handed her half a sandwich. 'Cheese and pickle?'

Sheridan pulled a face of disgust. 'No, thanks. It's eight in the morning. Is that your normal breakfast?'

'No, normally cornies and coffee.' Anna took a bite. 'Do you reckon Simon Banks will kick off when he sees us?'

Sheridan pulled her shoulders back. 'I doubt it. I think he's expecting us. I can't wait to hear what he's got to say. We're finally going to find out where Caroline is and hopefully put this job to bed.' She stretched out her legs and leant her head back. 'Except, we still have to figure out who the hands belong to . . . and who sent them.'

Anna nodded. 'True.' She took another bite of her sandwich. 'Shall we go in? I need crisps with my butty.'

Sheridan shook her head and undid her seat belt. 'I need a coffee.'

They made their way to the arrivals lounge and checked the board. Simon Banks' flight was on time and due to land in an hour.

They sat in a café and while Anna stacked crisps into her sandwich, Sheridan people-watched.

Businessmen and women on their phones, families dragging bulging suitcases while their children cried and looked totally pissed off. A woman standing by the arrivals gate, looking expectant – waiting for her lover maybe?

As the board showed that Simon Banks' plane had landed, Sheridan felt a slight pang in her stomach. Did Banks hold the key to where Caroline Crow was? Were they so close to the truth now? Would he admit and explain why he had called himself Henry Blanchflower and made the call to Adrian, getting him away from the house? She stared at the board. And then her mobile rang.

'DI Holler.'

'Sheridan, it's Rob. You at the airport yet?'

'Yeah. Just waiting for Simon Banks to come through arrivals.'

'We got it wrong, Sheridan. Simon Banks *isn't* Henry Blanchflower.'

Sheridan looked at Anna. 'Shit.'

Rob continued, 'I checked the hospital CCTV like you asked, and on the day and time that Henry Blanchflower made the call to Adrian Crow, Simon Banks was at the hospital.'

'Is it definitely him on the CCTV?'

'Yeah. But I dug a bit deeper. Not only was he at the hospital at the time – he was in theatre, performing surgery.'

'Fuck,' said Sheridan as she looked up to see Simon Banks emerging from arrivals.

CHAPTER 55

Sheridan approached Simon Banks with Anna at her side. He stopped and waited for her to reach him.

'Hello, Simon.'

'Am I under arrest?' He looked calm and composed and didn't appear surprised at the sight of Sheridan and Anna.

'Why would you be under arrest?'

'It was a joke,' he replied, tiredly.

'We just need to speak to you about Caroline Crow.'

'And you couldn't wait until I got home?' He tilted his head to one side.

'No. We need to know where she is,' Sheridan replied.

They walked to a coffee bar and sat in the corner, away from other travellers.

'Where's Caroline?' Sheridan asked, getting straight to the point.

'I don't know,' Simon Banks replied.

'You said she wasn't missing, and that she was safe. So, if you don't know where she is, how do you know she's safe?'

'Caroline had issues. She's taken herself off to sort herself out. She wouldn't tell me where she was going, but I assure you, she's not missing. Not in the sense of how the police would see it.'

'What issues?'

Simon took a deep breath and rested his hands on the table. 'I don't know how much you know about her, but she was a drug addict. I say "was" because she'd managed to kick the habit some years ago, but recently, certainly in the last few months, she was back on the drugs and decided that she was going to take herself off and get clean. Once and for all.'

'Where was she getting the drugs from?'

'I don't know. She just told me that she knew some people and she could get any drugs she wanted. I didn't want to get involved.'

'How was she paying for these drugs?'

'I don't know. Like I said, I didn't want to get involved, so I didn't ask.'

'Do you know her husband, Adrian?'

'No. Caroline always spoke of him fondly, but we've never met.'

'How do you know Caroline?'

Simon Banks explained that when he was an A & E doctor, many years ago, Caroline was brought in. She had slipped in the street and banged her head. They got talking as he examined her, and that was when she'd told him how her life had spiralled. She was painfully thin, cold, tired and hungry. After she was released from hospital, he took her to a local café and they sat for hours, just talking. He'd taken pity on her and arranged to meet her at the café the following week and again, they talked.

There was never anything sexual between them. Simon was happily married, with a son, but knew his wife wouldn't understand his relationship with Caroline and so he never told her about it, even though there was nothing to hide.

'Did you ever supply her with drugs?'

'Good God, no. Of course not. I gave her information about local support groups and bought her the odd meal or cup of coffee. I wanted to help her, she seemed so lost. But as the months went on, she slowly got off the drugs and things were looking up for her. She even started visiting the red-light area of Liverpool, talking to the young prostitutes about drugs, handing them leaflets. It was like she wanted to protect them, get them off the drugs and the streets. She's a good person. Even after my wife and I separated, I stayed in touch with Caroline.'

'You and Caroline have secret mobile phones. Why is that?' Sheridan asked.

'After Caroline and Adrian met, we stayed in contact and sometimes used to meet up. She didn't want Adrian to know about her past addiction and as a result, she didn't want him to know that we were in contact. Whenever we wanted to meet up, she had to find a phone box. More often than not, I couldn't answer her calls because I was at work, so I asked her if she wanted a cheap mobile phone. She loved the idea, so I bought us one each, and the agreement was that I would never call her in case Adrian found the phone and came to the completely wrong conclusion. So, she always called *me,* but I never called *her*.'

Sheridan waited for the café worker to finish cleaning the table next to them before she continued with her questions. 'On Wednesday eleventh March, Adrian received a call from someone called Henry Blanchflower, a potential client, asking him to meet him in Norfolk on Friday the thirteenth. Adrian drove to Norfolk the next day but when he got to the meeting place on the Friday, this Henry Blanchflower didn't exist. Someone made that call to Adrian, seemingly to get him out of the house. When Adrian returned home on the Friday afternoon, Caroline had gone. And she hasn't been seen since.'

Simon sighed heavily. 'All Caroline told me was that she was planning to leave when Adrian was at work. He spent a lot of time away, so she knew she'd have plenty of opportunities to leave.'

'But this call was set up by someone, and we don't know who.'

'Maybe it was one of Caroline's friends, or someone she was getting drugs from.'

'The only thing is, the call to Adrian was made from the secret phone *you* bought Caroline, and whoever made the call was very close to the house.'

'I don't know what to say. I have no idea who that could have been. But like I said, she knew a lot of shady characters and maybe one of *them* made the call.'

'With *her* mobile?' Sheridan asked.

Simon scooped a hand through his hair. 'Maybe she gave it to someone to make the call. I really don't know the answer.'

'You were at Caroline's house on Saturday the seventh of March, twice. What were you doing there?'

'She called me in the morning after Adrian had gone to work and said she needed a favour. Adrian wasn't due home until the evening, so I went over. She asked me to take her bank card and withdraw some cash – four hundred pounds. So, I went into Liverpool and withdrew the money. I was supposed to take the cash and her bank card back, but I got called into work and didn't get back to Caroline's until about 5 p.m. As I drove up to the house, I saw Adrian come home, so I just left.'

'Why did Caroline ask you to withdraw the money? Why not get it herself?'

'She said she had things to do . . . and I was popping into Liverpool anyway.'

'So, when you drove away from the house, you still had Caroline's bank card and the four hundred pounds?'

'Yes.'

'What did you do with it?' Sheridan asked.

'I was waiting for Caroline to text or call me to say it was safe to go back and drop it off, but I never heard from her. She'd mentioned that Adrian was planning to take her away for her birthday, so I assumed that's what had happened and that's why she couldn't call, because she was with him. Then, on the Thursday, I still hadn't heard from her. I had to get to my conference in Oxford, so I drove to the house and when I saw Adrian's car wasn't there, I left the card and cash in the coal shed.'

Sheridan sipped her now cold coffee. 'Why the coal shed?'

'Because that's where Caroline told me to leave it if she wasn't there.' Simon shifted in his seat. 'On the Saturday when I took the money out, she said that Adrian had mentioned taking her away for her birthday, but she didn't know the details of where or when, so she said that if I couldn't get the card and cash back to her, I was to leave it in the coal shed, so I did. It won't be there now, because she will have taken it with her.'

'Caroline hasn't used her bank card since she went missing.'

Simon sat back slightly. 'She's probably using cash.'

'But you only withdrew four hundred pounds for her. What was the money for?'

'She was buying a train ticket.'

'To where?'

'I don't know.'

'Did *you* give her any cash, any of your own money?'

'No.'

Sheridan watched Simon's face very closely as she revealed the next piece of the story. 'Caroline's suitcase was found near your house.'

Simon frowned. 'My house? Are you sure?'

'Positive. It was in the river that runs along your back garden.'

Simon sat in silence for a moment, the colour draining slightly from his tired face. 'So, all her things were in it?'

'No. Just her passport. It was old, almost out of date.'

'That's *very* odd.'

'Has Caroline ever been to your house?'

'No.'

'Does she know where you live?'

'Yes, but she's never been there,' he replied defensively.

'Knowing what you now know about her suitcase, do you still think Caroline is safe?' Sheridan tilted her head.

'Yes. I can't explain why her suitcase was in the river, but there must be a reason. I just know that she planned all of this, and so I still don't think she's in danger.' He hesitated. 'Maybe she came to my house for some reason, thought I might be there and decided to dump the case and put her things in another bag. I don't know.' He shook his head, rubbing his temples.

'How did she plan to leave her own house the day she disappeared?'

'I don't know.'

'Where's your car?'

'It's parked in a friend's garage. Why?'

'Whereabouts? And why didn't you park it at the airport?'

'It's in Slough and I don't like to leave it at the airport, so I get the train. Why do you ask?'

'Would anyone else have driven it while you were in Australia?'

'No.'

'Have you heard from Caroline since you saw her on the seventh of March?'

'No.'

'Don't you think that's odd?'

'Not really. Like I said, it wasn't always easy to have contact, and like I've told you, she *planned* to go away.'

'Where's the mobile that you use for your secret calls?'

'In my car. I told Caroline I was leaving it in there. There was no reason for us to have contact while I was in Australia.' He sighed. 'Look, I'm extremely tired and I'd really like to go home.'

'We'll drive you to your car,' Sheridan replied.

'That won't be necessary, I can catch the train.'

'It's no trouble. Anyway, we have some other things we need to talk to you about.'

◆ ◆ ◆

Simon climbed into the back of the car and Sheridan drove out of the car park. As Anna carried on talking to him, Sheridan tried to concentrate on the road, but her eyes flicked to the interior mirror, trying to gauge his response to Anna's line of questioning.

Anna had turned in her seat to speak to him. 'The hand that was delivered to you . . . Adrian Crow had one delivered to him as well.'

'Really?' Simon seemed genuinely shocked by this. 'So, do you know whose it is? The victim, I mean?'

'No. But it's the same victim as the hand that *you* had delivered and in the same condition.'

'And does Adrian have any idea who would have sent it?'

'No.'

He stared out of the window. 'That's really strange. I don't know what to think.'

'Did Caroline ever tell you if she had children?'

'No. As far as I'm aware, she doesn't have kids.'

'Yes, she does. She has a son and daughter from a previous relationship.'

'Really? She never said. So, where are they?'

'Her son lives in Scotland. Her daughter died in 2001.'

Simon turned his head to look at Anna. 'God, that's awful, she must have been young. What happened to her?'

'She was working in the North Tower of the World Trade Center. She died on 9/11.'

'Christ.' Simon shook his head.

'So, in all the years that you knew Caroline, she never once mentioned her children?'

'No. But then, she's a woman who likes to keep secrets, so I'm not surprised.'

'How long ago did she start planning to get away?'

'A few months now.'

'Do you know she used to go to a swimming club?'

'I think she might have mentioned it, yes.'

'She stopped going three months ago. She told her swimming club friends that she was moving away – that her and Adrian were heading abroad.'

'That's not right. She planned to leave on her own, to get clean. I don't know why she'd say that.'

'We don't know either . . . and nor does Adrian.'

It appeared that Simon felt a yawn rising in his throat and tried to swallow it before he responded. 'Caroline will come back when she's clean. She just wants to sort herself out.'

'Simon, we had to search your house.'

Simon suddenly looked very awake. 'My house? What the hell for?'

'We had to be certain that there was nothing linking you to Caroline's disappearance. We did try to contact you to let you know.'

'Jesus. How did you get in? Please tell me you didn't smash my door in.' He raised his hands, palms up.

'We made good any damage. The house is secure.'

'For God's sake. So, I take it that you now know that I'm just an innocent party in all of this?'

'Yes. But can I ask why you use two passports?' Anna asked.

'No particular reason. Just because I can.'

Simon directed them to his friend's house, where he opened the garage and unlocked his car.

'Do you mind if I take a look?' Sheridan asked.

'Be my guest.' Simon stepped back and waited while Anna and Sheridan searched the car. Finding Simon's secret phone in the glove compartment, she turned it on and waited for it to come to life. 'I need to check that Caroline hasn't been in touch.'

'Of course,' Simon replied.

Sheridan checked for any missed calls, messages or voicemails and there were none. 'I need to take this phone.'

'But what if Caroline tries to contact me?' He lifted his suitcase into the boot. 'I'd really rather keep it with me.'

Sheridan dropped the mobile into her pocket. 'It's better that *we* have contact with her.'

'Fine,' he snapped, tiredness and impatience now creeping back into his voice. 'Is it alright if I go now? I'd really like to get home and get some sleep.'

'Of course. Are you alright to drive?'

'I'll be fine.'

'We'll be in touch and, obviously, do let us know if Caroline makes any contact with you.'

Simon nodded and hauled himself into the driver's seat. Sheridan and Anna watched as he reversed out of the drive and pulled away at speed.

Once he was gone, Sheridan took her mobile out of her pocket and rang Hill to update her on their conversation with Simon Banks.

Hill responded, 'I'll get someone over to Adrian's and check the coal shed. If her card and the cash are gone, like Simon said they would be, then I think we're done on this. We'll send it over to the misper unit and let them take it on.'

'What about the hands that were delivered?' Sheridan asked.

'We'll keep going with that side of it, but so far, we've come up blank. Caroline Crow has clearly taken herself off, Sheridan. She's getting clean and then she'll be back. Either that or she's gone on a bender. But either way, she's planned all this.'

Sheridan climbed into the passenger seat. 'You know I'm going to fight you on this one, Hill. I know it seems likely that she's gone of her own accord, but—'

'I'll tell you what, let's save this and we can shout at each other when you get back to the nick.' Hill abruptly ended the call.

CHAPTER 56

Sheridan and Anna pulled into the backyard of Hale Street nick. Anna hurriedly emptied the car of crisp packets and sandwich crumbs before they made their way upstairs to Hill's office. Hill was busy talking to two officers from the missing persons unit and she quickly introduced them to Sheridan and Anna.

Sheridan threw a look at Hill. 'That was quick,' she said sarcastically.

'What was quick?' Hill asked, defensively.

'This job being handed over to the misper unit.' Sheridan eyed the two officers sitting in front of Hill's desk. Hill stood up and walked to the door. 'Your office.' She marched down the corridor, followed by Sheridan and Anna.

As they stood in Sheridan's office, Hill crossed her arms. 'Before you start, this is not my decision. I'm with you, not against you. I fought the boss over this, and I lost. I know things don't add up and for all we know Caroline Crow is lying in a ditch somewhere. But he won't budge, Sheridan.'

'Could we at least wait until the coal shed is checked—'

'It *has* been checked. There's no bank card and no cash in there. So, Simon Banks was right – Caroline did take herself off.'

Sheridan stared at the floor. 'What is she living on?'

'I don't know. Look, I need you to go through the handover to the misper unit with me. Our work is piling up and the sooner they've got what they need, the sooner we can concentrate on our other cases.'

Sheridan reluctantly agreed and they spent the afternoon briefing the misper officers on the Caroline Crow case.

Once they had left, Sheridan texted Sam: *On my way home soon. I need a drink. Do we have wine?*

Sam texted back: *About six bottles. Is that enough?*

Sheridan responded: *That will have to do. I love you. See you soon. x*

As Sheridan drove towards Adrian Crow's house, all she could think about was Caroline. She had spoken to Jack Staples and arranged to meet him at Adrian's house, so they could explain in person that the case was now being handled by the misper unit.

As Sheridan pulled up, she could see Jack Staples and Adrian sitting at the kitchen table through the window. She waved and Jack went to let her in through the front door.

Adrian Crow raised his head as she walked in, his dark eyes looking blankly at her.

'Hello, Adrian.'

'Inspector Holler.' He gave a slight nod of his head.

Sheridan sat down and carefully explained the situation to him, delicately conveying the account that Simon Banks had given. Adrian initially refused to believe that Caroline had ever taken drugs and had succumbed to her old drug habit, but as Sheridan spoke, he eventually accepted that the wife he had known and loved for eleven years had a secret past. And was still keeping secrets now. He was grateful that specialist officers would continue to try to locate her, but the truth was, Caroline Crow wasn't a high-risk missing person. She had carefully and meticulously planned her own disappearance. Taken herself off to beat the drug habit that had dominated much of her life. The demons were back and she wanted to chase them away before she could return to the husband and the life she knew. Adrian told Sheridan that he would be there, waiting for Caroline, whenever she decided to come home.

Sheridan shifted in her seat. 'Did you notice any change in Caroline? Physical or otherwise?'

'Only how distant she'd become. Why do you ask?'

'Well, if she was taking drugs again, then I'd expect her to not only behave differently, but there'd be a change in her physically – maybe she lost weight or stopped taking care of herself?'

Adrian slowly shook his head. 'No, not really. I mean, every now and then she might put on a few pounds – but then she'd diet and lose it all. She likes to look nice, and keeps herself smart and tidy.' He sighed heavily, before continuing.

'If she was on drugs, I just wish she'd felt that she could talk to me. I would have supported her, got her specialist help. I've got the money.'

'Sometimes people feel that they don't want to burden their partner or family,' Jack Staples tried to explain. 'They need to do it themselves.'

Adrian sighed again. 'Everything you're saying makes sense – except where her suitcase was found. Do you know why she might have left it there?'

Sheridan admitted that this was a piece of the puzzle that didn't add up.

'I guess she'll tell me when she comes home, eh?' Adrian rubbed his face with the palm of his hand. Sheridan noticed a change in his demeanour as he talked. For the first time, she saw a man with hope in his eyes, hope that his wife would come home. A glimmer of something to hold on to – a hope that once she had cleaned herself up, she would walk back through the door and they would start to rebuild their lives. With no more secrets.

As Sheridan got up to leave, Adrian shook her hand. 'Thank you for everything you've done. I know you've all worked so hard to try to find her.'

'Just look after yourself. We'll keep you posted on anything we find out about the package you received.' She looked at Jack Staples who agreed with a quick nod of his head.

As she drove home, Sheridan's head was swimming. There were just too many questions without answers, and that bugged the living shit out of her. Most of what had happened made sense. But there were enough parts of the case that didn't, and that rested heavily on her shoulders.

By the time she reached home, her head was thumping. She was looking forward to wrapping herself around Sam. And Maud.

Sam was in the kitchen when she walked in. A glass of wine was sitting on the worktop, and Sheridan could smell pizza warming in the oven.

Sam put her arms around Sheridan's waist and kissed her gently. 'Tell me all about your day.'

Sheridan rested her head on Sam's shoulder. 'My day was a little bit shit.'

CHAPTER 57

Tuesday 31 March

Anna came out of the ladies' toilet and spotted Sheridan glaring at the vending machine.

'Morning,' Anna said cheerfully.

'Morning. Do you want some chocolate?' Sheridan fed the machine and pressed her selection into the keypad.

'Is it working?'

'Yeah. But keep your voice down, it'll hear you.' Sheridan smiled in triumph as her Twix dropped into the tray and she quickly opened the drawer to retrieve it. Six bars of chocolate later, they made their way to CID where Sheridan handed out treats to her team. Hill, standing at the front of the room waiting to start the briefing, declined the offer.

Hill explained to the team that the Caroline Crow case had been handed to the misper unit. All heads turned to Sheridan, who raised her eyes to the ceiling.

Hill knew Sheridan well enough to be aware of her reaction without turning around. 'I know you've all worked so hard on the case, and I want to thank you. It wasn't my decision to hand it over – and I'm sure Sheridan is making faces behind my back. Right, let's go around the room and see what everyone's working on. Anna is keeping the burnt hands job, so she'll be linking in with the misper team if that throws anything up.'

One by one, the DCs updated her on the cases that had been placed on the back burner while they'd worked on the Crow enquiry.

Finally, Hill turned to Rob Wills. 'I know you've got a couple of GBHs but there was one particular job that came in last night. I've read the handover and I think everyone needs a good laugh.'

Rob grinned. 'This guy, Kenneth Blake, comes home and finds his house trashed, so he calls it in on three nines, saying he's been burgled. When uniform turn up to check around the place, they find scales, bags, cling film and a shitload of drugs. So, he gets himself nicked for possession with intent.'

Laughter erupted around the room and even Hill allowed herself a grin. 'Okay,' she finally said, 'let's crack on.' And with that, she headed back to her office. Still grinning.

Sheridan looked around the room as everyone turned back to their computers or picked up their phone. There was a mixed atmosphere in the office – partly disappointment that they hadn't got to the bottom of the Caroline Crow case and partly a sense of work returning to normal. Everyone had a caseload that they had tried to keep on top of and now they could turn their attention back to it.

Sheridan went to her office and stood at the window for a moment, taking in her view of the Albert Dock. For a moment, she was sitting in one of the restaurants there, sharing a meal with Sam. Then, as quickly as the image came into her head, it was gone, and she was back in her office – the questions about the Crow case nagging at her again.

Everything that Simon Banks had told them made sense. It fitted. The contact he'd had with Caroline and how they'd met. The visits to her house matched the data they had from his mobile phones. The cash he took out of her account and how he drove away from her house when Adrian came home early. It also matched Adrian's account of seeing Simon there. The letters that her ex-partner, William, had written, stating that she had taken drugs in the past. The same drug habit that Simon was aware of. The fact that Caroline had told her swimming club friends that she was going away. The same thing she'd told Denise Fairweather. Then there was Simon's account of Caroline wanting to get away and get clean. It all added up.

But there were still things that made no sense at all. And it was these things that Sheridan couldn't let go of.

Caroline Crow had, according to Simon Banks, started taking drugs again. But how was she paying for them and who was she getting them from? What kind of drugs were they? According to Adrian, there was nothing to suggest she'd succumbed to her old habit.

Why was her suitcase found abandoned and empty, apart from an old passport, near to Simon Banks' house?

Why had Caroline ordered a bouquet of flowers? Where were they now? Who were they for?

How had she left the house the day she disappeared?

Who was Henry Blanchflower, and how and why did Caroline give him her phone to call Adrian?

Why did someone send Simon Banks and Adrian Crow a burnt hand? Who had delivered them and why? Who did they belong to? They had made extensive enquiries to try to identify the victim, followed up on missing women, in and around the area and beyond. Linked in with other forces. And nothing. Yet.

Sheridan squeezed her eyes tightly shut as if doing so would make the answers pop into her head.

And then her phone rang and brought her back to the here and now.

'DI Holler.'

'My office,' Hill said as abruptly as Hill always did. Yes, things were getting back to normal.

CHAPTER 58

Sunday 12 April

Sheridan turned over and looked at the clock. 8.57 a.m. She could hear Sam singing downstairs and for a moment she lay there, trying to make out the song. Remembering that Sam had an atrocious singing voice, she gave up trying to figure out the tune and swung her legs out of bed. As she came down the stairs, the smell of something cooking made her stomach rumble. Maud was sitting in front of the oven, staring longingly through the glass.

'Smells good. What is it?' Sheridan asked, yawning loudly.

'Slow-cooked beef. Thought we'd have a proper Sunday dinner.' Sam turned and kissed her. 'I've texted Joni and Anna and invited them over, is that okay?'

'Yeah, of course. The four of us haven't got together for ages. Have they got back to you yet?'

'No. They're probably thinking up excuses not to come, so they don't have to chance my cooking.'

Sam flicked the kettle on, pulled on a pair of oven gloves and took the beef out of the oven, checking on its welfare. Every move she made was being closely monitored by Maud, who appeared to be in a state of delirium at the smell of meat juices filling the kitchen.

Sheridan scooped Maud up in her arms, then sat at the kitchen table, nuzzling her face into the cat's fur. 'Is it driving you crazy, Maud, the smell of food?' she asked, feeling Maud's purring rumble through her body.

Sam's mobile rang and Sheridan found it highly amusing as she watched Sam clumsily try to pick it up off the counter, still wearing her oven gloves.

'Bollocks. That was Joni, I've cut her off.' Sam removed the gloves and dialled Joni's number.

Sheridan shook her head. 'You could have just taken the oven gloves off first. I do worry about you sometimes.' She gave Maud a final kiss on the head, before making her way upstairs to shower.

◆ ◆ ◆

Joni and Anna arrived at the same time and gave each other a knowing look as they got out of their cars.

'How brave are we?' Anna said as she locked her car door before hugging Joni rather clumsily, Joni holding the carrier containing her cat, Newman.

'Hi, Newman.' Anna peered in at Joni's cat and he meowed loudly back at her.

'He's excited about seeing Maud.' Joni rang the doorbell. Sheridan answered quickly, ushering them both into the hallway.

As soon as Joni released Newman from his carrier, he darted off to join Maud in a front-row seat, both now gazing lovingly at the oven door.

'Go through to the kitchen,' Sheridan said, after accepting the bottles of wine that Anna and Joni had brought.

Joni and Sam hugged. 'So, how long has the beef been in?' Joni started her interrogation.

'Three hours,' Sam replied.

Joni screwed her face up. 'Jesus, it'll be cremated. What are you cooking it in?'

'The oven.'

'I meant have you basted it in anything, you dickhead.'

'No. It's cooking perfectly in its own juices. I'm slow-cooking it. I've actually read the instructions.'

'It'll be like a lump of rock. What veg are you doing?'

'Roasties, carrots and cauliflower. Any other questions, your honour?'

Joni helped Sam chop the carrots and Sheridan poured them all a glass of wine. As she chatted to Anna, she watched Sam carefully lifting the beef out of the oven.

And then it hit her.

'Fuck,' she said under her breath.

'What?' Anna asked as they all turned to look at her.

'I know who Henry Blanchflower is.'

CHAPTER 59

'Shouldn't we be passing this to the misper unit?' Anna asked as she clicked her seat belt in place.

'No. I want to go to his house and speak to him myself.' Sheridan started the engine and pulled off her drive. They'd left early, having apologised to Sam and Joni that she and Anna would have to skip dinner. Sam promised to save some of the beef, even after Sheridan insisted that she really, really didn't have to.

'What are we going to tell Hill?' Anna asked.

'Nothing yet. I'll speak to her later. She's in today, so we'll go and see her afterwards.'

'What are you going to say to him?'

'I'll just say we're checking something out.'

Twenty minutes later, they pulled up outside the house. Sheridan was first out of the car, and rang the doorbell.

When the door opened, she stepped back.

'Hello, Adrian.'

'Inspector Holler. Has something happened?' he asked.

'No, not exactly, we just wanted to check something.'

He opened the door wider and stepped back to let them in. The kitchen was as untidy as when they'd last visited and a woody, unpleasant odour hung in the air. The sink was full of dishes and empty microwave food cartons were still stacked up in a heap by the sink.

'Sorry about the mess. I'm due to give the place a clean later.'

'Don't worry about it.' Sheridan smiled. 'Adrian, can I take a look outside? I know the missing persons unit are dealing with the case now, but I wanted to clarify something from our enquiry. Just so I've got all the facts.'

'Yeah, sure,' Adrian said. 'Can I ask what you're looking for?'

'Are you able to show me exactly where Jack Staples found the gloves?'

'Yes, follow me.'

Anna and Sheridan let Adrian lead the way, where he pointed to a forsythia bush. 'Just there.'

'Were they hidden in the bush or lying on top of it?'

'They were kind of on top. Not really hidden.'

Sheridan stood back and took it all in. She walked down the side of the house, looked across the field and then to the upstairs window. Taking her time, as she always did.

'Okay, that's great. Thanks, Adrian.'

As they got back into the car, Anna turned to her. 'Well, you still think it's him?'

Sheridan started the engine. 'Definitely. Gabriel Howard is Henry Blanchflower.'

CHAPTER 60

Anna hovered outside Hill's office, trying to listen to the conversation Sheridan was about to have with her.

She heard Sheridan speak first. 'Okay, you're not allowed to shout at me.'

'Then don't give me a reason to.'

'I think Gabriel Howard is Henry Blanchflower.'

Hill's voice suddenly rose. 'I'm sorry, have we suddenly gone back in fucking time?'

Sheridan remained calm and controlled. 'Look, I know this is now the misper unit's case, but we did a lot of work on this job, so please just hear me out.'

'Why do you always do this?' Hill snapped.

'Do what?'

'You just love charging at walls, don't you? How many times do you and I need to have this conversation? How many times have I had to say "case closed" or "it's not our case any more", but you just keep going? My hands are tied, Sheridan. I'd love for you to keep the Crow case in its entirety, but Anna can pass this info on to the misper team, seeing as she's dealing with the burnt hands case. We have jobs coming out of our arses that I need the team to concentrate on.'

'I know. But at least hear me out.'

Hill crossed her arms, in an all too familiar sign. Hill was clearly in an unbudgeable state of mind, and Sheridan braced herself before continuing.

'Caroline and Gabriel are in contact somehow. He goes to the house, and she gives him her mobile. He's outside and takes his gloves off to make the call to Adrian. Then, rather sloppily, he leaves his gloves on the bush, and that's where they're found. It makes sense.'

'How did you come up with *that* theory?'

'Sam's oven gloves.'

'Excuse me?'

'Sam was cooking dinner earlier and tried to answer her mobile. But she hadn't taken her oven gloves off . . . that's when I realised that Gabriel must have taken his gloves off before he dialled Adrian's number. Then just wiped his prints off.'

'What's the link between Gabriel and Caroline?'

'I don't know. But we know that Gabriel's been to the house. It was him who delivered the flowers.'

'Denise delivered the flowers,' Hill said impatiently.

'She's lying.'

'Can you prove that?'

'No,' Sheridan replied.

Hill continued, exasperated. 'She's already explained how Gabriel's gloves were at the scene. She dropped them there.'

'Not in the fucking back garden she didn't. She said *she* made the delivery, to explain how his gloves ended up where they did. She's in on it and she's covering for him.'

'Can you prove that?'

'If I'm given more time I can.'

Hill put her hand up. 'We're done.'

'We're done . . . as in I can at least look into this further, or we're done as in get out of my office and don't discuss it any more.'

'The latter.'

Sheridan turned on her heel and left, bumping into Anna who was standing outside. 'Well?' Anna whispered.

Sheridan whispered back, 'I'm going to nail that little shit-bag.'

Anna frowned. 'But Hill said—'

'Hill said, "get out of my office and don't discuss it any more". She didn't say, "don't follow up on your theory".'

'You don't think she meant for you to let it go and pass it to the misper team?'

'Did you hear her say that? Because I didn't.' Sheridan smiled.

CHAPTER 61

Monday 13 April

Gabriel Howard sat on a bench in Princes Park, waiting. He'd got there early, giving himself the chance to check out that it was a safe time and place for the pickup. He found himself strangely fascinated as he watched a dog walker trying to pick up his dog's enormous shit with a little plastic bag, while the dog sat, looking somewhat smug and proud of its achievement. The dog's owner didn't look at Gabriel. No one that had passed his way had looked at him. He liked that. He liked to be invisible. He'd learned how to blend in, like camouflage. He was there, but nobody saw him. Or if they did, they paid him little or no attention.

That was why he was so good at what he did. The reason his plan was working. He'd have his revenge on the two men for what they had done. Yes, they were older now and no longer connected to their past misdemeanours – just two men, going about their lives, unrepentant about the crime they'd committed. Everyone had forgotten about them now. Everyone except Gabriel. He wanted them to suffer. And he was going to enjoy watching their lives be obliterated.

One down, one to go. He'd ruin them. Bit by bit, one thing at a time.

He looked to his right and spotted who he had been waiting for, walking up the pathway. Gabriel nodded, the signal that the coast was clear. He sat next to him.

'How's it going?' he asked, setting the package gently down on the ground between them.

'All good.' Gabriel stretched his arms out and rested them on the back of the bench. 'Thanks for this.'

He kept his voice low. 'You're welcome. You need any more?'

Gabriel nodded. 'I think a few more should do it.' He glanced down at the package. 'How many more can you get?'

'As many as you need, but it'll take a bit of time.'

'That's fine.'

The sun was disappearing behind the trees and Gabriel stood, picked up the package and tucked it deep inside his jacket. 'I'll speak to you soon.'

'Okay. I'm here if you need anything else. Now, and when it's all over.'

Gabriel hesitated for a moment. 'You do know, this might *never* be over. What I'm doing is just the beginning. I told you I'm going to ruin them both. And so far, everything's falling into place. But they have no idea what's coming. They have no clue just how bad it's going to get for them.'

And with that, he walked away, back down the path towards the gate. As he reached it, he started running, feeling the evening breeze sweeping across his face.

He noticed how calm he felt.

What he didn't notice was Sheridan Holler, watching him from her car across the road. She'd followed him to the park gate, but couldn't risk going any further in case he saw her. So, she'd waited for him to reappear. All she knew was that he'd arrived alone and left alone. Through the same entrance, one of many that led into the park. 'I know you're up to something. And I'm going to catch you, Gabriel,' she said under her breath.

CHAPTER 62

Tuesday 14 April

Sheridan heard a 'Good morning' from behind her as she walked across the backyard of Hale Street nick. She turned around to see Superintendent Barry Hanson lifting a briefcase out of his boot.

'Good morning, sir,' she replied.

'How's things?' he asked. 'Still giving Hill as much shit as she gave me?'

'Sorry?' Sheridan frowned.

'The Crow case. Handing it to the misper unit.'

'Hill gave you shit?'

'Let's just say I thought she was going to put my balls through a mincer when I told her to hand it over.'

'Really?'

'She reminds me of you. You both scare me.' He opened the door for her. 'After you.'

Sheridan smiled. 'So, what exactly did she say to you?'

Superintendent Hanson stopped, puckered his lips and looked up. 'If I remember correctly, it was something like, "My team have worked their arses off trying to get to the bottom of Caroline Crow's disappearance and if Sheridan Holler thinks we should keep the case, then I agree. She's annoying but she's rarely wrong. And if Caroline Crow ends up dead and we missed something, then I swear I'll remind you of this conversation until the day you retire."' He looked at Sheridan. 'Or something like that.'

Sheridan started laughing. 'She said I was annoying?'

'You *are* annoying. You're like one of those little yappy dogs that bites your ankle and no matter how much you try to shake it off, its grip just gets tighter. You and Hill are quite alike in that way.' He turned to head down the corridor. 'But I will say this: she's got your back. I know she sometimes comes across like she's against you. One minute you feel like she's on your side and the next, she's like the enemy. But she has to make some really tough choices and that will inevitably piss someone off.' And with that, he walked away.

'I know,' Sheridan said under her breath, making her way to CID, just as her mobile rang. She answered it, grinning at the image of Hill yelling at the superintendent in her head. 'DI Holler.'

'Sheridan, it's Ruth Manning from the cold-case team. Are you free to speak?'

'Yes, mate, what's up?'

'Got an update for you on your brother's case.'

Sheridan felt the usual butterflies in her stomach as she made her way to her office. There had been so few leads in Matthew's murder until they'd found the photograph of local man Stephen Tubby watching her brother and his friends playing football in Birkenhead Park – the same park where Matthew's body had been found, stripped naked and hidden under a pile of wet leaves.

Thirty-two years had passed since that day. Thirty-two years of her and her parents not knowing who had killed her little brother. Stephen Tubby had been spoken to by the cold-case team in October 2008 when he admitted to being the man in the photograph, stating that he often watched lads playing football in Birkenhead Park. But he'd also told the police that he was working away in Wales when Matthew was murdered.

DC Ruth Manning had been working for months trying to confirm his alibi. Stephen Tubby was a plasterer and had worked all over the north-west and Wales. Had Matthew's murder happened more recently, the records for where Stephen Tubby had been, what sites he'd worked on, and who had paid him, might have been easier to find. But back in the 1970s, things had been very different. Records were rarely kept and if paper files *had* existed, they certainly didn't exist now.

Ruth Manning explained this to Sheridan. Stephen Tubby had said he'd been working on a new housing development in Newport, south Wales, at the time of Matthew's murder. He'd stayed in a nearby B & B and as far as he could remember, the job had taken around three weeks to complete. This fact placed Tubby almost two hundred miles away at the time of Matthew's death.

Sheridan gripped the phone tightly to her ear. 'So, there's no way we can verify that Tubby was definitely in Newport at the time?'

'That's why I've rung you. Stephen Tubby wasn't working on the site in Newport in March 1977.'

Sheridan took a deep but silent breath. Fearful of exactly where this was going, yet solidly determined that whatever was about to come would never deter her from finding the truth. Exhaling, she asked the question. 'So, where was he?'

'Working on a site on the Wirral. Just two miles from Birkenhead Park.'

CHAPTER 63

Sheridan listened intently as Ruth explained that Stephen Tubby had worked for a building firm that secured contracts across the north-west of England and most of Wales. Also working for the same firm was Gary Brookes – a plasterer, like Tubby. Gary's wife, Christine, had grown concerned that two of Gary's workmates had become seriously ill, both succumbing to cancer at a young age, with one of them dying from the disease. And so, Christine, who was in her early twenties at the time, began to keep detailed notes of the sites Gary worked at and the men who worked with him. The one thing linking the men to their illnesses was asbestos.

Christine wrote to the government, after the building firm refused to engage with her. And she kept on writing and rallying, contacting local newspapers and generally making her voice heard. She never gave up and when Gary himself became ill, some eight years later, she fought even harder to have the material banned.

While checking Stephen Tubby's alibi, Ruth came across the story of Christine's fight and tracked her down. Now aged fifty-six, Christine was more than happy to show Ruth her records – years and years of site details, what kind of building was being constructed or worked on and what materials were used. And who was working there.

And in March of 1977, Christine's records showed that Stephen Tubby had been working with Christine's husband on a block of flats on the Wirral.

Sheridan flopped back. 'So, Tubby lied.'

'That's what I'm going to put to him, but he'll probably just say that he got the dates wrong.'

'Even so, it still puts him near to Birkenhead Park around the time Matthew was murdered.'

'It certainly does.'

'What happened to Gary Brookes?'

'He died of cancer.'

'That's terrible.' Sheridan paused. 'But thank you, Ruth – that's a really great piece of work. If you ever want to come and work in CID . . .'

Ruth laughed. 'No, thanks. I like cold cases too much. But I appreciate the offer. I'll keep you posted. It's a step forward, Sheridan.'

Sheridan smiled. 'It is. It really is.' She ended the call and closed her eyes. Every time a piece of information came out about her brother's case, she always had a hard decision to make. *Whether* to, or *how* to tell her parents. It wasn't that she didn't want to keep them updated, but she did want to protect them from building their hopes up.

But this was a breakthrough. Stephen Tubby had been working a stone's throw away from where Matthew's body was found. Not two hundred miles away, like he'd told the police.

CHAPTER 64

Wednesday 15 April

Anna walked into Sheridan's office eating a packet of crisps. 'You all done?' she asked, licking the salt off her fingers.

Sheridan grabbed her coat from the back of her chair. 'Yep. Just heading out on a quick job, and then home.'

'What job?'

'Never you mind.' Sheridan tapped her own nose and turned off her computer.

'I hate it when you do this. Why don't you just tell me what you're up to?'

Sheridan walked over to the door and closed it. 'Okay. I'm following Gabriel Howard. That's all you need to know.'

'Why are you following him?'

'Because I want to find the connection between him and Caroline Crow. I know he's Henry Blanchflower. I just need to prove it.' She turned back to her desk.

'Hill will go mental if she finds out . . .' Anna blew into the empty crisp packet and banged it between her hands. The loud pop made Sheridan jump.

'You silly cow!' Sheridan spun around, clasping her hand to her chest. 'I actually think I've just shit myself.'

Anna burst out laughing. 'Sorry,' she apologised, quickly scrunching up the crisp packet and throwing it in the bin. 'Anyway, bollocks to Hill having a hissy fit – do you want me to come with you?'

'No. I'd rather get in the shit myself, and not drag you down with me.'

'I don't mind getting in the shit.' Anna grinned. 'Who needs an exemplary record anyway?'

Sheridan pointed at her. 'You do, for when you finally go for your promotion.'

Sheridan's phone rang. 'DI Holler.'

'Hi, Sheridan, it's Jack Staples. Sorry to bother you, but have you heard from Adrian Crow recently?'

'No. Why?' She looked at Anna.

'Because I haven't been able to get hold of him and I'm getting a bit worried. I'm at his house now. His car's here but he's not answering the door, or his phone.'

'Have you spoken to his employers?'

'Yeah. They told him to take as much time off as he needed after Caroline went missing. The last time they spoke to him was a couple of weeks ago, and he said he was okay but had no plans to return to work for the foreseeable.'

'Okay. Stay where you are. We're on our way.'

Jack Staples was standing outside Adrian Crow's house when Sheridan and Anna pulled up. They tried the front door, which was locked, before calling Adrian's mobile, which went to voicemail. There was no answer on the landline either.

'When was the last time you spoke to him?' Sheridan asked.

'About a week ago and he seemed fine,' Staples said. 'Then I popped round on my way home last night, and although his car was here, there was no answer at the door, and he still wasn't answering his phone. I tried calling him again today and that's when I got a bit worried. I've spoken to the misper unit. They made contact with him when the case was first handed to them, but they haven't called him since.'

'Have you checked around the outside of the property?'

'Yeah, nothing obvious.'

Anna looked at Sheridan. 'What do you think? Enough concern for safety to get the door put in?'

'Yeah, I think so.' Sheridan quickly called the control room and arranged for uniform to attend and gain entry.

Ten minutes later a marked car arrived, and the front door was put in. Sheridan was calling out Adrian's name when she spotted his mobile on the kitchen table. There was an unpleasant odour in the air and Sheridan recognised it as the same smell as before. The kitchen was a mess, but that had become the norm for Adrian lately, according to Jack Staples. She lifted the lid on the kitchen bin and was immediately hit with the smell of discarded food.

Sheridan walked through the house, trying to slow down her racing heart. When she was a uniformed officer, entering a house where it was suspected the occupant was deceased inside had been part of the job she'd always struggled with. The elderly woman, whose neighbours had reported not seeing her for a few days. The alcoholic divorcee who had drunk himself to death and was found lying on the sofa, bottles and broken dreams all around him. The all-too-familiar smell, and the humming of bluebottle flies that were often present when police turned up. The emptiness of the house. The silence before you opened the door and found them.

Sheridan felt a wave of relief when her search finally established that Adrian Crow wasn't there. She arranged for the door to be boarded up and made secure. She waited with Anna at the house, the uniformed officers having been called out to a road traffic accident two miles away. Jack Staples had been sent back to the nick to hand over Adrian's mobile phone to Rob Wills, who'd been tasked with getting it checked, along with the landline, for any incoming or outgoing calls that might give them an idea as to where he'd gone.

Sheridan stood in the middle of the kitchen, looking at the mouldy plates in the sink.

And then she noticed the window.

CHAPTER 65

Sheridan called Hill to tell her that Adrian Crow was AWOL.

'Maybe he's taken himself off somewhere to get away from it all?' Hill suggested.

'But his car and mobile are still here. Something's off,' Sheridan replied.

'What's your thoughts?'

'Well, there's an unlocked window in the kitchen, which you just have to push to open and it's easily opened from outside. Rob and Dipesh are on lates, so I've asked them to start going through the footage from the cameras we've got set up at the house.'

'Do we need to worry that he's suicidal?' Hill asked.

'I think we need to worry in general.'

'Okay. Let's get a seal on the house,' Hill said. 'I'll meet you at the nick.'

Sheridan came off the phone and joined Anna, who was watching the crime scene officer pack his equipment away.

'You all done, Charlie?' Sheridan asked.

'Yeah, I'll get the results back to you as soon as I can. There's no sign that the window was forced, so maybe he just left it unlocked.'

'Okay. Thanks, mate.' Sheridan tapped Charlie's arm.

After uniformed officers arrived to maintain a seal at the house, Sheridan and Anna made their way back to Hale Street nick.

◆ ◆ ◆

Sheridan texted Sam: *I'm sorry, it's going to be a late one. Don't wait up. I love you. xx*

Sam replied: *No worries, just stay safe out there. xx*

Hill came into CID carrying coffees for Rob, Dipesh, Sheridan and Anna as they worked through the night, going through the camera footage from Adrian Crow's house.

By five in the morning, they had gone through all the camera footage. There was no sign of Adrian leaving the house.

'Well, he must have left somehow.' Hill rubbed her eyes. 'He's not still in the bloody house, is he?' She directed her question at Sheridan.

'No. He's not there, everywhere was searched, including the loft.'

'It's odd that we don't know how Caroline left the house and now we don't know how Adrian left either.' Anna yawned and got up to make some more coffee.

Hill piped up, 'The only way he could have got out of the house is by the unlocked window. But why not just walk out of the front door?'

Sheridan stared at her. 'That's it.'

'What?' Hill asked.

'It's Gabriel Howard. It's practically identical to the Edith Elliot case. We never figured out how he got into her house, and he never said. But we know he got out through the downstairs window, which Oliver said was shut when he left the house. This looks exactly the same.' She looked around at the tired faces gawping back at her.

Hill nodded. 'So, if Gabriel's been in Adrian's house, then where is Adrian now?'

Sheridan kneaded her thumb and forefinger across her temples. 'What if Gabriel's taken him?'

'Why would he do that?'

'I don't know.'

Hill tapped her fingers on the desk. 'Okay. Let's pay him a visit.'

CHAPTER 66

Denise Fairweather opened the front door. She stepped back in surprise when she saw Sheridan standing there, flanked by uniformed officers.

'What's this?' she asked. 'What's going on?'

'I need to speak to Gabriel.' Sheridan took a step forward. 'Is he in?'

'No. He's not. What's this about?'

'Can we come in and look around?'

Denise shook her head. 'He's not here.'

'Denise, it's really important that I speak to him . . .'

'Fine. Come in. But I swear he's not here. You can see for yourselves.'

'Where is he?' Sheridan asked.

'I don't know. What's going on?' Denise watched as uniformed officers entered the house and began looking around; two made their way upstairs. Sheridan stayed with Denise while they searched.

'When was the last time you saw him, Denise?'

'Yesterday morning.'

'Have you spoken to him since?'

'I can't remember, I don't think so. He's a big boy, I'm not his mother.'

'Your car's not parked outside.'

'Gabe's using it.'

'To go where?' Sheridan asked, as her mobile rang in her pocket. 'DI Holler.' She stepped outside to take the call privately.

'Sheridan, it's Hill. We've found Adrian Crow.'

'Where is he?'

'In the Royal Liverpool hospital. He's been in a hit-and-run and he's in a bad way, but he's been asking for you.'

Anna drove into the hospital car park – and as soon as she found a space, Sheridan was out of the car before she could turn the engine off. Hill had updated her with the circumstances of the incident. Adrian had been spotted lying in the road by a couple in their car, two miles from Adrian's house. As the couple came round the corner, they saw a vehicle ahead which was reversing back towards Adrian. As the couple got nearer, the vehicle in front suddenly sped off.

'He regained consciousness about an hour ago. It was only momentary, but he kept saying your name – just repeating to "get Sheridan Holler".'

'Did the couple get a look at the car that drove off?' Sheridan asked.

'No. It was too dark and it's an unlit road.'

Sheridan's jaw tightened. 'It's Gabriel who sped off. He was using Denise's car, and he didn't come home last night. He's probably trying to get rid of any evidence from the hit-and-run. We need to find him.'

'I'll sort that out. I'll get his phone pinged and get a marker on the vehicle,' Hill replied.

'Did Adrian say anything about the accident?'

'No. He just kept repeating your name and his own. Apparently, he didn't answer any of their questions.'

'Okay, well, hopefully he can tell us more when we see him. I'll keep you posted.'

◆ ◆ ◆

Anna and Sheridan arrived at ICU and were buzzed in by a nurse.

'Hi,' Sheridan said when they got through the door. 'I'm Detective Inspector Holler and this is my colleague, DS Markinson. We're here to see Adrian Crow.'

'Ah, yes, the doctors are with him at the moment. Come through and I'll let them know you're here.'

The nurse disappeared behind a curtain while Sheridan and Anna waited, desperate to speak to Adrian and hear his account of what had happened. After a few minutes, a middle-aged, slightly overweight doctor appeared. 'Hello, I'm Dr Carter, sorry to keep you waiting. Shall we step into the office so I can give you an update?' They followed him to his office and got seated.

'How is he?' Sheridan asked.

'He's stable. He's got a hairline skull fracture, a fractured cheekbone, two broken ribs and some lacerations on his arm and leg. We're keeping an eye on him, but we probably won't keep him in ICU very long. Do we know who the next of kin is?'

'His wife, but she's missing.' Sheridan noticed the look of shock on the doctor's face. 'Nothing to do with the accident, it's a separate ongoing enquiry,' she explained.

'I see. Well, I'm happy for you to try to speak to him, but please keep it fairly brief. His speech is quite slurred and difficult to understand.'

'Has he said anything else this morning?'

'Not really. He just keeps saying his name and asking for *you.*' The doctor stood and opened the door. 'I'll take you to him.'

Sheridan and Anna followed Dr Carter as he made his way to the end of ICU. 'There you go.' He pulled the curtains back; leaning down, he gently touched Adrian's shoulder. 'Adrian, DI Holler and her colleague are here to see you.'

Sheridan and Anna approached the bed, taking a moment to absorb the scene before them. They snapped a look at each other.

And then they looked back at the bed where Gabriel Howard was lying.

CHAPTER 67

Sheridan was waiting outside the ward for Denise to arrive. She had sent a police car to pick her up after calling her with the news that her brother had been involved in an accident. The door at the end of the corridor suddenly flew open and Denise came running in. 'Where is he?' she called out, looking terrified.

'He's in here. I haven't managed to get anything out of him yet.'

'Do we know what happened? You said it was a hit-and-run. Was it you bizzies chasing him?' Denise asked, clearly angry and demanding answers.

'He wasn't in a car. He was on foot. And no, the police weren't chasing him.'

'Just let me see him.'

Sheridan escorted Denise to Gabriel's bed, where the doctor explained his injuries to her.

Anna and Sheridan waited outside in the corridor and used the opportunity to call Hill with an update.

'Christ,' was Hill's immediate response. Followed by, 'So, why did he give his name as Adrian Crow?'

'He didn't. I asked the doctor again to tell me *exactly* what he'd said and apparently it was "get Sheridan Holler, tell her it's Adrian

Crow". So they *assumed* he was telling them his name. He didn't have any ID on him.'

'So, he's saying that Adrian Crow ran him over? But it can't be him – his car's outside his house.'

'Gabriel's not saying anything at the moment. He's been out of it since we arrived, and Denise is here now at his bedside.'

'Alright. Well, let me know if you get any more out of Gabriel and we'll keep looking for Adrian.'

'So, we're having this job back off the misper unit?' Sheridan asked tentatively.

Hill replied, 'Too bloody right we are.'

CHAPTER 68

Anna made her way back to the nick, leaving Sheridan at the hospital. Denise had sat at Gabriel's bedside for the last three hours, gently stroking his hand and talking to him. He'd opened his eyes twice, but had immediately closed them again.

By lunchtime, Denise got up and met Sheridan in the canteen for a much needed caffeine fix.

'What do you think he was doing out there?' Sheridan gently asked. 'It's quite remote, and your car wasn't nearby. Do you know where he parked it?'

'I've got no idea,' Denise replied. 'Why were you looking for him this morning?'

'I just need to talk to him.'

'Is he going to be arrested?'

'Why do you ask that?'

'Well, you don't turn up mob-handed if you're not going to nick someone.'

'I thought he might have some information about Caroline Crow's husband.'

'What kind of information?'

'Adrian Crow's missing.'

'What's that got to do with Gabriel?'

'I thought Gabriel might know something. Has he said anything to you about Adrian?'

'No.' Denise cradled her coffee and closed her eyes for a second. 'I don't know what I'd do if I lost him.' Tears fell down her face.

'He's young and he's strong. He'll get through this, Denise.'

There was a long silence before Denise spoke. 'He likes you, you know.'

'What do you mean?'

'He likes you, and he hates the fact that you hate him.'

'I don't hate him . . .'

'He's not what you think he is. He's not a bad guy and he's the best brother anyone could ever have.'

Denise went on to tell Sheridan that when they were children, Gabriel had never let Denise out of his sight. He had looked out for her, always wanting to protect her, always telling her that although most people were inherently good, there were enough bad and dangerous ones out there to be wary of.

Being four years older than her, he was her big brother – strong and fearless. He was the one who read her stories during thunderstorms – she had been terrified of them as a child. When she hit her teens, he explained to her that boys would show an interest in her and as normal as that was, she should never let anyone control her, or make her do something she didn't want to do. She was in control of her life, and nobody could ever take that away from her.

When Gabriel was twenty-three and Denise was nineteen, their parents had drowned during a boating accident while on holiday in Turkey. The loss brought Gabriel and Denise even closer and made Gabriel ever more protective of her.

He respected women like no other man she had ever known. Always the one to give up his seat on the train, open doors for them, carry their shopping to the car. He held them in the highest esteem, listened to them, valued their opinions and looked out for them.

When he was working at a printing firm, a female colleague confided in him that her ex-boyfriend was following her. He'd be waiting outside when she finished work. He'd turn up in pubs when she was out enjoying an evening with friends, even appearing on her doorstep and demanding to be let in. She'd reported it to the police, but no action was ever taken. So, Gabriel decided to fix it himself. He knocked on the ex's door and when the guy answered it, Gabriel pushed his way in. Held him up against the wall and told him that if he went within a hundred metres of his ex-girlfriend, Gabriel would be back. And the next time, he wouldn't be so polite.

The following day, the girl told him that her ex had been waiting for her when she left for work and shouted across the street that he wasn't afraid of Gabriel, and if he ever came near him again, he'd kick his teeth in.

Gabriel went back that evening, and when the ex saw him through the spyhole, he refused to open the door. Gabriel walked away and waited around the corner. All night.

The following morning, the ex emerged from his house and was about to get into his car when Gabriel appeared and punched him in the face. Seven times. Knocking four of his teeth out.

That was the first time Gabriel was arrested.

The second time was when he was in a pub with some friends and standing at the bar was a mountain of a man arguing with his girlfriend. Gabriel watched as the man grabbed the girlfriend around the throat and slapped her face. Gabriel marched across the pub and punched the man, breaking his jaw.

The third time was when he broke into Oliver Elliot's house.

Denise turned to Sheridan. 'He was devasted when Edith Elliot died. He's never forgiven himself, you know. That's why he thinks you hate him, because you judge him for what happened to her.'

Sheridan felt a slight pang of guilt; seeing the fear in Denise's face at the thought of losing her brother made her soften in her response. 'I don't hate him. I just don't like burglars.'

'He's not a burglar.'

'He was *that* night.' Sheridan stared at her coffee. 'Did he ever tell you why he was in Edith's house that night?'

'No. If I'm totally honest, I thought you had the wrong man. Right up to the moment that he admitted it in court. It's not his style – he's not a thief and he certainly wouldn't want to frighten an old lady. I did ask him what he was doing there, but he just always said that it was a moment of madness – he saw an opportunity and took it.'

'But there wasn't an opportunity, the doors were locked. We don't know how he got in, but it certainly wasn't an opportunist burglary.'

'I don't know the answer, Sheridan. And you're probably thinking that even if I did, I wouldn't tell you.'

'Would you tell me?' Sheridan eyed Denise over her coffee cup.

Denise smiled. 'Probably not.'

Sheridan tapped her finger on the table. 'Anyway, look, the most important thing now is that he gets better. As soon as I can talk to him, I'll know what happened and we'll get whoever did this to him.'

'Will you though? Will you treat him like all your other victims?'

'Of course I will. Don't think for a moment that I won't.'

'He'll be okay, won't he?'

Sheridan reached her hand across the table and put it over Denise's. 'He'll be fine.'

'And you don't hate him?'

'And I don't hate him.'

'He came to see you.' A faint smile touched Denise's face. 'He came to the police station a couple of days after he got out of prison.'

Sheridan grinned. 'Yeah, I remember. He asked me to make sure that us bizzies didn't come banging on your door, checking up on him. He said you worked long hours and didn't need the hassle.'

'He didn't come to say that to you. He came to ask if you'd like to go out for a coffee with him. But when he got to the police station, there was another police officer with you and Gabriel didn't want to make a dick of himself in front of her. So he made up the excuse that he didn't want any shit from the bizzies.' Denise blew her nose with a tissue. 'I told him he was barking up the wrong tree.'

'Barking up the wrong tree?'

'You married?'

'I'm in a relationship.'

Denise took a last swig of her coffee, before asking, 'What's her name?'

Sheridan smiled. 'Sam.'

CHAPTER 69

By the time Sheridan got home that evening, the exhaustion had kicked in. She wanted to flop into bed and sleep for a week.

Sam was on her laptop when she came through the door. She got up from the sofa and wrapped her arms around Sheridan, kissing her gently on the lips. 'You look whacked. Dinner's done, but I think you need a glass of wine first. I missed you last night, did you get any sleep?'

'No. But it's okay, I'll have an early night tonight and make up for it. You okay? How's work?' Sheridan picked Maud up and kissed her head.

'Work's fine. How's the case going?' Sam poured two glasses of wine.

Sheridan put Maud on the floor and took a sip of her drink. 'Gabriel Howard's in hospital. Someone hit him with their car, then drove off.'

'Is that such a bad thing? You hate that guy, don't you?'

'Actually, I think I might have gotten him all wrong.'

Over dinner, Sheridan told Sam about the conversation she'd had with Denise. How she'd listened to Denise's description of how and why Gabriel had been arrested in the past. Protecting others. Protecting women. On the face of it, Gabriel appeared to be the good guy, the big brother who always looked out for his little sister.

Sheridan recalled the conversation she'd had with him in her car nearly four weeks earlier. She'd called him a shit burglar, and his response had been, 'Am I?' She remembered the look on his face as he'd said it. That wry smile. Was he a shit burglar? Or was he actually very good at it?

Sam took a sip of her wine. 'So, Gabriel Howard has now said that Adrian Crow ran him over?'

'Not exactly. But he did say to tell me "it's Adrian Crow".'

Sam raised her eyebrows. 'I'd have thought if anyone was going to run Gabriel over, it would be Edith Elliot's son, Oliver.'

CHAPTER 70

Friday 17 April

Without breaking her stride, Sheridan walked past the vending machine situated down the corridor that led to ICU. Having lost a pound to it the day before, she muttered 'Wanker' under her breath.

Arriving at the doors of ICU, she was buzzed in and spotted Denise talking to the doctor.

Denise turned as she approached. 'Hi.'

'Hi. How's he doing?'

'He's trying to talk,' Denise replied. 'They're probably going to move him to another ward today. He's doing okay and they're not too worried about him.'

They approached his bed, and the doctor pulled the curtain round to isolate them from the rest of the ward. Gabriel opened his eyes, blinking, before focusing on Sheridan. He lifted a finger and beckoned her towards him.

'Hello, Gabriel,' she said quietly, bending closer to him. 'I need to ask you some questions if you're up to it.'

Gabriel opened his mouth, staring at her. He said something that none of them could make out, and then slowly but deliberately placed his fingers in his ears.

'You're not going to listen to me?' Sheridan tilted her head and smiled.

He moved his head from side to side, and removing one finger from his ear, he pointed to the doctor and indicated for her to come closer. As she stepped forward, Gabriel pointed to the pen in her top pocket.

'He wants to write something down.' Sheridan turned to the doctor. 'Can we get some paper?'

'Of course.' The doctor disappeared behind the curtain and Sheridan crouched down, her face close to Gabriel's. 'We're getting some paper for you to write on.'

Denise spoke. 'The doctors have said that it might be a bit painful for him to talk.' She reached for his hand. 'Don't try to talk if it hurts, Gabe.'

The doctor emerged with a small pad and laid it by Gabriel's hand, placing the pen between his fingers and thumb. The three of them watched and waited as he very slowly wrote.

When he'd finished, he turned the pad around for them all to read the four words he'd scribbled on the page.

I CAN'T HEAR ANYTHING.

Before Gabriel was sent for another scan – and before Sheridan headed back to Hale Street nick to carry out a team briefing – she wrote a few questions for him to answer. One being why he had been in the road where he was hit. He replied saying he'd gone out for a run. She asked him where he'd parked Denise's car and he wrote down that he couldn't remember.

Once Gabriel was returned to the ward, he wrote a message on the pad for Denise.

> *YOUR CAR IS PARKED IN HARVARD ROAD. MY MOBILE IS INSIDE. PLEASE GET IT FOR ME AND BRING IT HERE WITH MY CHARGER. LEAVE YOUR CAR WHERE IT IS. IT'S NOTHING DODGY. JUST NEED MY PHONE. DON'T TELL POLICE. X*

Denise ordered a taxi home to pick up her spare car keys, not wanting to ask the hospital staff for the set that Gabriel had on him when he was found.

After retrieving his mobile, she arrived back at the hospital, just in time to be told that Gabriel's scan had showed no bleed on the brain and the likelihood was that his hearing loss was temporary. He was moved out of ICU and on to another ward.

After the nurses settled him, Denise slid his phone into his hand, and he wrote a message on the pad: *THANKS SIS. I LOVE YOU. X*

Denise wrote back: *PROMISE ME YOU'RE NOT IN TROUBLE.*

He replied: *I PROMISE. GO AND GET A CUP OF TEA, YOU LOOK SHATTERED.*

Denise kissed him on the forehead, and he watched as she left the ward.

Taking out his mobile, he sent a text: *Don't worry but I've been in accident. In hospital. Police will be around for a while as hit-and-run. Will let you know when I can carry on with plan.*

CHAPTER 71

It was mid-afternoon by the time Sheridan returned to the hospital. Denise had called to let her know that Gabriel had been moved, and she was sitting at his bedside when Sheridan arrived.

'How's he doing?' Sheridan asked.

Denise smiled at Gabriel. 'He's okay. They think the hearing loss is temporary.'

Sheridan took the pad and wrote a message to Gabriel: *I KNOW YOU'RE TIRED BUT ARE YOU UP FOR A FEW MORE QUESTIONS?*

He nodded. 'Can I have some water?' His voice was raspy, and he coughed, wincing at the pain in his side.

Sheridan wrote another message: *DON'T TRY TO TALK. JUST WRITE IT DOWN.*

She handed him a cup of water, before writing her question: *DO YOU KNOW WHO HIT YOU?*

Gabriel shook his head and wrote: *DO YOU KNOW WHERE ADRIAN CROW IS*

Sheridan wrote: *NO.*

Gabriel replied: *YOU NEED TO FIND HIM*

Sheridan responded: *WHY?*

Gabriel replied: *HIS WIFE MISSING I THINK HE INVOLVED*

Sheridan: *HOW?*

Gabriel closed his eyes momentarily and the pen dropped from his hand. Then he frowned and carried on: *SORRY. PAIN.*

Sheridan nodded at him and mouthed, 'It's okay.' Then she wrote: *WHY DO YOU THINK HE'S INVOLVED? I REALLY NEED TO KNOW.*

Gabriel looked at Denise, and noticing the confused expression on her face, he wrote: *DO YOU NEED ANOTHER CUP OF TEA?*

Denise read the message. Denise *got* the message. She took the pad and wrote a note for Gabriel's eyes only: *BE CAREFUL.*

Gabriel nodded and Denise tore off the page and shoved it into her pocket, before leaving the ward.

Gabriel turned to Sheridan and wrote: *I NEED TO TELL YOU SOMETHING BUT DON'T WANT DENISE INVOLVED. NO TROUBLE FOR HER. IF YOU BRING TROUBLE FOR HER I WON'T HELP YOU*

Sheridan replied: *I CAN'T MAKE ANY PROMISES.*

He read Sheridan's reply and laid the pen on top of the pad, resting his hand on his chest.

Sheridan persisted: *DON'T PLAY GAMES WITH ME. I NEED TO FIND ADRIAN CROW. DO YOU KNOW WHERE HE IS AND WHY DO YOU THINK HE'S INVOLVED WITH HIS WIFE'S DISAPPEARANCE?*

Gabriel read her message and pointed to the last note he had made.

Sheridan squinted at him and mouthed, 'You fucker.'

Gabriel grinned and picked up the pen: *I CAN'T HEAR YOU. DID YOU SAY THAT OUT LOUD?*

Sheridan couldn't help but smile, shaking her head she wrote: *YOU'RE ANNOYING BUT I NEED YOUR HELP.*

Gabriel took the pen and drew a circle around the previous message he'd written: *I NEED TO TELL YOU SOMETHING BUT*

DON'T WANT DENISE INVOLVED. NO TROUBLE FOR HER. IF YOU BRING TROUBLE FOR HER I WON'T HELP YOU

Sheridan sat back and looked at him, crossing her arms. It was a stand-off. Sheridan weighed up her options and realised that she only had two. Either – one: she waited and hoped Gabriel would eventually fold and tell her everything, or two: she'd fold and agree to his request.

She picked up the pen and pad: *I'M GOING HOME NOW. I HOPE YOU FEEL BETTER SOON. I'LL BE IN TOUCH AND WILL LET YOU KNOW IF WE FIND WHOEVER DID THIS. I'M SORRY BUT I CAN'T PLAY GAMES.* She held the pad up for him to read her message, before grabbing her coat from the back of the chair and heading for the door.

And that was when she felt something hit her on the back. She stopped, turned and picked up the pad that he'd thrown at her. She walked back over to the bed and handed him back the pad. She'd won.

Gabriel, defeated, wrote: *BRING ME A MAP OF LIVERPOOL*

She replied: *WHAT FOR?*

Gabriel responded: *SO I CAN HELP YOU*

Sheridan read the message and mouthed, 'Okay.' Silently congratulating herself that she'd thought of option three: call his bluff.

CHAPTER 72

Sheridan updated Hill and Anna with her visit to Gabriel Howard. They were in Hill's office, and Sheridan was showing them the areas that Gabriel had pointed out to her. She'd provided him with a map of Liverpool as he'd requested, and he'd marked up points of reference, starting at Adrian Crow's house. Then he'd drawn a large circle around the area where he'd been hit by the car, telling Sheridan that Adrian Crow was, or certainly had been, somewhere in that area in the last couple of days. He hadn't seen who was driving the car that hit him, as it had come from behind. But whoever it was had stopped up the road and then proceeded to reverse, heading straight for him.

He'd tried to move, but found that he couldn't. And then he became aware of another car approaching. That was when the first car – the one that had struck him – drove off. He couldn't tell the make or model, but thought it was old, possibly a truck of some sort. Regarding the area on the map he'd drawn, he'd stated that the police needed to look for Adrian Crow there. He'd refused to divulge how he knew this, but he assured Sheridan that he was telling the truth. The last note he'd written on the pad read: *IT'S ALWAYS THE HUSBAND REMEMBER*

'What a little prick,' Hill said, leaning back in her seat. 'He's playing games.'

Sheridan agreed. 'Possibly. But what would he have to gain by lying to us? We've got to check it out, we've got no choice.'

Anna jumped in. 'Do we think it was Adrian that hit Gabriel?'

Hill answered. 'We've checked and Adrian Crow doesn't have any other vehicle registered to him. We've spoken to his employer, and he only has access to one car. We've also checked the local hire car companies but that came up blank.'

'Why would Denise be in trouble?' Anna asked.

Sheridan answered. 'I think he's referring to when she gave her statement saying that she was the one who delivered the flowers. We've always thought it was *him* and he won't say that because he'd be in breach of his licence conditions and Denise would be in the shit for making a false statement.'

She turned to Hill. 'I've got a suggestion which I don't think you're going to like.'

Hill replied, 'Try me. I'm in a relatively good mood today. It might not last long, though, so hurry up.'

'Okay. I want to go back to Gabriel and tell him that whatever he says, Denise won't be in the shit. We need to find out where Adrian Crow is, and I think we should take the chance that Gabriel is just referring to the fact that he's been in the Crows' house and that Denise lied to us. If he does have information about Adrian being involved with Caroline's disappearance, then I think we should—'

Hill interjected, 'I agree.'

Sheridan raised her eyebrows and flicked a look at Anna, before replying, 'Shit. You serious?'

'Yes, I'm serious. This job is mashing my head up, so let's get it done, once and for all. And if Gabriel is playing games, we can sort him out later. We also need to bear in mind that if Gabriel's description of whoever drove into him is accurate, then it sounds like they might have been reversing to finish him off. Luckily for him, the other car came along.'

'I totally agree.' Sheridan took a breath. 'What if he tells me something that we can't ignore?'

'I'll worry about that if and when it happens.'

Hill's phone rang and she answered it. 'DCI Knowles.'

Sheridan was about to leave when Hill put her hand up. 'Okay, thanks.' She ended the call. 'Denise's car has been located in Harvard Road.'

'So, that's about half a mile from where Gabriel was hit,' Anna replied. 'I'll let Denise know and give her a lift out there.'

Sheridan nodded and quickly grabbed her coat, before Hill changed her mind about the new plan.

CHAPTER 73

Armed with two new notepads, Sheridan sat by Gabriel's bed. He looked tired but certainly better than when she'd first seen him. She worded the first note: *WHATEVER YOU TELL ME, DENISE WON'T GET INTO TROUBLE. YOU HAVE MY WORD.*

Gabriel replied, 'Thank you.'

Sheridan wrote: *DOES IT HURT WHEN YOU TALK? RATHER WRITE IT DOWN?*

Gabriel nodded.

Sheridan wrote: *TELL ME EVERYTHING YOU KNOW.*

Gabriel wrote slowly, stopping regularly to readjust the pen and rest his hand. Sheridan watched, without interrupting him. When he'd finished, he turned the pad around and showed her.

> *ADRIAN CROW TRYING TO AVOID CAMERAS AT FRONT OF HIS HOUSE. CLIMBS OUT OF SIDE WINDOW AND WALKS ACROSS THE FIELD. I'VE SEEN HIM, FOLLOWED HIM, CAN'T YET FIGURE OUT WHERE HE GOES, HARD TO FOLLOW ON FOOT AND HIM NOT SEE ME. YOU NEED TO CHECK OUT PLACES ON MAP.*

Sheridan stared at the pad before writing: *WHY DID YOU FOLLOW HIM?*

Gabriel replied: *HE SUS. VERY ODD. SOMETHING WRONG*

Sheridan responded: *YOU KNOW YOU'RE IN BREACH OF YOUR LICENCE CONDITIONS BY TELLING ME THIS. YOU SHOULDN'T BE NEAR HIS HOUSE.*

Gabriel smiled and wrote: *NOT WORRIED ABOUT THAT. PLEASE FIND ADRIAN CROW.*

Sheridan: *WHY ARE YOU TELLING ME THIS? WHY HELP ME?*

Gabriel: *I DON'T LIKE MEN WHO HURT WOMEN*

Sheridan: *YOU DON'T KNOW THAT CAROLINE IS HURT. OR DO YOU?*

Gabriel: *ADRIAN CROW IS SUS. WHO CLIMBS OUT OF WINDOW TO AVOID CAMERAS?*

Sheridan: *HAVE YOU EVER MET HIM? DO YOU KNOW HIM?*

Gabriel shook his head.

Sheridan: *HAVE YOU BEEN INSIDE THE HOUSE?*

Gabriel shook his head again.

Sheridan wrote: *I DON'T BELIEVE YOU.*

She raised an eyebrow at him and tapped on the words.

Gabriel grinned and said, 'It's okay if you don't believe that bit.' His voice was still raspy, and it clearly hurt to talk. He swallowed, took a sip of water, and continued, 'Please, Sheridan, please believe me. He's well dodgy. Do you believe me?'

Sheridan hesitated. Did she believe anything he was telling her? Why tell her and put himself in breach of his licence conditions? If she reported the breach, he'd likely get off with a warning from his probation officer. But the fact that Gabriel had mentioned Adrian climbing out of the window explained how Adrian had left the house and hadn't been seen on the cameras. But what if Gabriel was trying to lead her somewhere? What if he was spinning a clever tale to account for Adrian's disappearance? Had he really seen Adrian climb out of the window? Had he really tried to follow him? And were the markings he'd made on the map really going to lead them to Adrian, or was he sending the police on a wild-goose chase?

If Gabriel Howard *was* Henry Blanchflower, then it wouldn't be the first time he'd done that. So many questions and possibilities went through her head. How could she be sure that Gabriel was telling the truth? Because if he was, then maybe Adrian had something to do with Caroline's disappearance.

Hesitantly she wrote her answer: *I WANT TO BELIEVE YOU.*

He smiled and replied, his voice at a whisper, 'You'll see I'm right.' He held his side as a cough made him wince. 'Better stop talking now.'

Sheridan nodded and picked up the pads, just as Anna texted her to say she could pick her up when she was done. Sheridan texted back that she would meet her outside, before writing a last message for Gabriel: *GET SOME SLEEP. IS DENISE COMING TO SEE YOU LATER?*

He replied: *NO. TOLD HER TO GO HOME AFTER PICKING CAR UP. SHE LOOKS TIRED. SHE BE BACK TOMORROW. YOU HAVE NICE EVENING.*

Sheridan made her way out of the ward and downstairs to wait for Anna. While she waited, she rang Hill's number. 'Hill, it's me. I think Caroline Crow's alive.'

'Why?'

'Because if Gabriel Howard is telling me the truth, then he's seen Adrian climb out of that window more than once. So, I think Adrian could be holding her somewhere, and when he leaves the house to go wherever that is, he does so by the window to avoid anyone following him.'

◆ ◆ ◆

Anna pulled up outside the hospital's main entrance. Sheridan climbed in, dropping the notepads on to the back seat.

Anna undid her seat belt and opened the driver's door. 'I want to hear everything, but can you give me a sec? I'm literally busting for a wee.'

'Go for it, the loos are to the right as you go in.' Sheridan got out herself, walked around the front of the car and settled behind the wheel. She saw Anna disappearing through the doors and watched her turn left. She grinned to herself as Anna reappeared moments later, now heading in the right direction. 'Dickhead,' Sheridan muttered to herself. Resting her head back, she idly observed a woman on crutches gingerly making her way out of the main doors, a bright new white cast on her leg up to the knee. An elderly man pushing his wife in a wheelchair stopped to readjust the blanket that covered her legs and kissed her on the cheek, before pushing her towards their car parked in a disabled bay.

And then she saw him.

Walking towards the main doors. It took her a moment to realise who he was. He looked different.

But it was *definitely* him.

CHAPTER 74

Sheridan ran into the main entrance and turned to see the man disappearing from view as the lift doors closed.

'Shit,' she said under her breath as she raced to the door leading to the stairs. Taking two at a time, she felt her heart thundering in her chest.

She grabbed the handrail to give her more momentum as she flew up the stairs, heading as fast as she could to Gabriel's ward. She thought of ringing Anna's number to get her to call the control room and send back-up, but even that would have slowed her down and she couldn't afford to lose a second.

The moment she'd seen Oliver Elliot entering the hospital, she knew Gabriel was in danger, Sam's words from the night before ringing in her ears: '*I'd have thought if anyone was going to run Gabriel over, it would be Edith Elliot's son, Oliver.*'

Of course, it made sense. Oliver Elliot would have blamed Gabriel for the death of his mother, Edith. He had every reason to hurt Gabriel. And driving his car into him on an unlit road was perfect. Maybe he'd driven back to the scene and realised Gabriel was still alive when they put him in the ambulance. And here he was, on his way up to the ward where Gabriel was lying, vulnerable and defenceless.

Sheridan reached the top of the stairs, her lungs burning as she ran down the corridor and pushed the doors open to Gabriel's ward. Her eyes scanning the place, praying she wasn't too late. That Oliver hadn't got there first.

Her mind filled with images of him standing over Gabriel, the curtain pulled around them and Oliver with his hands around Gabriel's throat.

As she turned the corner, she stopped dead in her tracks.

The scene before her was nothing like she could ever have imagined.

Anna came out of the toilets and headed back to the car, which she found unlocked and empty. Looking around for Sheridan, she walked slowly back through the main entrance, checking left and right before ringing Sheridan's phone, which went to voicemail.

She left a message: 'It's me. Not sure where you've got to, but I'm heading up to the ward. Call me. You've left the car unlocked and you've got the keys.' She ended the call and stepped into the lift.

Reaching Gabriel's floor, she marched down the corridor towards the ward, peering through the glass and spotting Sheridan standing sideways against a pillar. She pushed the door open. Sheridan turned, putting her finger to her lips, before beckoning her forward. Anna walked slowly towards her, unable to see what she was looking at.

'What's going on?' Anna whispered.

Sheridan replied quietly. 'You're not going to believe this.'

What Sheridan saw did not make any sense. Oliver stepped back after gently embracing Gabriel, who was smiling up at him. As Oliver sat in the chair next to the bed, Gabriel wrote a note on his pad which he showed to Oliver. Oliver took the pad and wrote a reply. Sheridan was too far away to see the words.

She turned to Anna, who stood motionless, completely unaware of what was unfolding around the corner. 'Oliver Elliot's here, he's visiting Gabriel. They've just bloody hugged each other.'

Anna's eyes widened in shock. 'What the actual fuck?' she mouthed.

Five minutes passed before Oliver stood up, and taking Gabriel's hand in his own, he smiled before making a move to leave.

Sheridan stepped away from the pillar and ushered Anna to the adjacent side of the ward, putting her head down as Oliver walked past.

'Let's go.' Sheridan and Anna stayed far enough behind Oliver for him not to notice them, but close enough to keep him in sight. As he stood at the lift, they headed for the stairs, arriving at the main door before Oliver emerged. Sheridan turned to Anna.

'Wait over there. See where he goes after I've spoken to him.'

Anna walked out of the main door. Sheridan made to do the same, but hovered for a moment, waiting for Oliver Elliot to appear.

'Hello, Oliver,' she said brightly, feigning surprise at seeing him there.

'Hello,' he replied. 'How are you?'

'I'm fine, surprised you remember me.'

'Of course I do. Inspector Holler.' He smiled.

'How are you keeping?'

'Fine, thanks. And yourself?'

'The job keeps me busy but I'm fine. You visiting someone?' Sheridan nodded towards the door.

'Yeah, a friend. She's just had a baby.'

'Oh. I think the maternity ward is in the other building.' Sheridan turned and pointed to her left.

'Yeah, that's what they've just told me at reception. I always get lost when I come to this hospital. Anyway, it was nice to see you.' Oliver tucked his hands in his pockets.

'You too. Take care.' Sheridan smiled and walked over to the car. Checking in her rear-view mirror, she could see Oliver walking away. Driving to the far end of the car park, she pulled out on to the main road, before turning around and driving straight back in.

Twenty minutes later, Anna called. 'You okay?' Sheridan asked.

'Yeah. He's just driven off. I'm out the front. I'll come round to you.'

When Anna got into the car, they just stared at each other for a few moments.

'What the fuck was that all about?' Anna asked.

'I don't know. Where did he go after I drove away?'

'He walked into A & E, and just hung around for about fifteen minutes, then came out and went to his car, I've got the index number. What did he say to you?'

'He said he was visiting a friend in the maternity ward.'

Anna frowned. 'I didn't know there was a maternity ward . . .'

'There isn't.' Sheridan puffed out her cheeks. 'I'm so confused. Gabriel Howard breaks into Oliver Elliot's house, Oliver's mother dies in her bed and yet they're bezzie fucking mates. I just don't get it.'

'We need to update Hill,' Anna said.

'I need to go back in first.' Sheridan got out of the car and headed up to the ward. Gabriel was asleep and she quietly and carefully lifted the pad and walked off down the ward, flicking through it to see what Gabriel and Oliver had written to each other. She was disappointed but not overly surprised to find the pages had been torn out. In fact, most of the pages had been removed, so there was no chance Sheridan could even send it off to obtain any evidence of indented writing. Gabriel was still asleep. She replaced the pad before making her way back downstairs.

Once she'd left, Gabriel opened his eyes, took out his mobile and sent a text to Oliver: *Police saw you here I think. Be careful. Will call you when I get out of here.*

CHAPTER 75

Back at the nick, Sheridan and Anna bumped into Rob Wills.

'We've got the stuff back on Adrian's mobile and landline. No recent incoming or outgoing calls, except for the cold-case team and Jack Staples. And a couple from your phone when you went to the house.'

'No other calls at all?'

'Nope.'

They made their way to Hill's office and updated her with Gabriel's account, and the fact that he'd been visited by Oliver Elliot.

'What's Gabriel up to, having contact with his victim's son? And being all chummy?' Hill stood up, logging off her computer.

Sheridan shook her head. 'I have no idea. It looked very cosy though, like they were bezzies.'

'What do you want to do?' Hill pulled her coat from the back of the chair.

'Well, putting Oliver aside for a minute, I think Gabriel's telling the truth about Adrian. And trust me, it hurts me to say that. But I think we should check out what he said about the area Adrian could be in.' Sheridan put her hand up before Hill could reply. 'I know, it's a huge area to cover and it'll take forever. But we can at least start at his house, walk across the field, and get to where Gabriel was run over. Maybe we'll get lucky. I don't want to lose sight of the fact that Caroline could be being held somewhere nearby.'

Hill picked up her briefcase. 'I get that. But you don't even know what you're looking for.'

'I know, but if we don't try—'

'Fine. I'll see what I can organise. You're on a rest day tomorrow, you've been working flat out and I need you sharp, so take your day off. Brief the team before you go home. I've got a meeting to go to now.' And with that, in typical Hill style, she left without another word.

Sheridan turned to Anna. 'Fancy a walk across a field?'

Anna grinned. 'How did I know you were going to say that?'

Sheridan raised her eyebrows. 'Well, do you want to?'

'Absolutely.'

As they made their way to CID, Rob Wills came out of the office. 'Sheridan. Guess who just rocked up at the front counter.'

'Tell me.'

'Adrian Crow.'

CHAPTER 76

Sheridan and Anna showed Adrian to a disused office in the downstairs corridor. His clothes were filthy, and his shoes were caked in mud. He clearly hadn't washed for a few days and smelt like a tip.

Sheridan handed him a coffee, and he gratefully took a sip.

'We've been worried about you. We had to get into your house and—'

'I know. I've been there and saw the notice on the door from the police. I'm sorry I worried you.'

'Where have you been?' Sheridan asked. *Where's Caroline?* she thought.

'I had to get away. I'm not coping very well, if I'm being honest. My life is ruined. I miss Caroline so much.' He wiped a hand down his face and stared blankly at the coffee cup. He went to pick it up but changed his mind. 'I actually thought about killing myself.'

Sheridan was desperate to confront him about her suspicions but decided to tread carefully, to keep him on side. 'Adrian, we can get you help if you need it.'

'It's okay. I've done a lot of walking and thinking over the last few days, and I've come to the decision that maybe Caroline *has* actually gone away to sort herself out, and if I did something stupid then I wouldn't be around when she comes home.' He looked up. 'I'm not going to kill myself. I need to sort myself out and carry on as best I can. Until she comes home.'

'So, you've just been walking?' Sheridan asked. *Or have you been visiting her?* she thought.

'Caroline and I used to love going on long walks, we'd go for miles.' A smile flickered across Adrian's face. 'We never cared where we ended up, we'd just walk and chat, put the world to rights.' He puffed out his cheeks. 'So, the other day I just decided to go, to keep walking and see where I ended up. Do you know Formby?'

'Yes,' Sheridan answered. *Is that where you're holding her?* she wondered.

'It's beautiful there. That's where I ended up. Slept on a bench.' He slowly shook his head. 'I actually wondered if I was going mad the day I left the house. I thought about throwing myself in the Mersey, just so I could be out of it all. As I was about to leave the house, I couldn't find my keys to get out. I looked everywhere and when I couldn't find them, I started to feel this weird panic take me over, like I was trapped somehow. I kept trying to force the front door, but I couldn't get out, and then I started to feel sick.' He picked up the coffee cup and took a sip. 'I don't know what's happened to me. I used to be so rational. But I don't recognise what I've become.'

'Did you find your keys?' Sheridan asked.

'No.'

'So, how did you get out of the house?'

'I did the most ridiculous thing. I climbed out of the window.' He looked at her. 'How crazy is that?'

Sheridan sat back. *So, this explains what Gabriel Howard saw*, she considered. 'It's not crazy, Adrian.' She chewed her bottom lip. 'So, we need to sort out getting you back into your house.'

'It's okay. I remembered that Caroline used to leave a spare back-door key under a pot in the garden. It was still there, so I grabbed my spare car keys and drove here.'

'You could have just called us, saved yourself the journey.'

'I *wanted* to come. I realised when I was lying on that bench, that I'm desperate for company. I need to be around people. It makes me feel safe in some weird way.' He picked at the polystyrene cup. 'And don't worry that I'm going to do something stupid, I've had time to clear my head. I'm going to go shopping for some food, go home, clean the house and sort myself out.' He smiled. 'Thanks for listening.' He stood up.

'I'll get Jack Staples to give you a call – maybe pop round and see you?'

'That would be nice, thank you.'

'We'll sort your front door out . . .'

'Oh, don't worry, I'll get it fixed. It'll take my mind off things, having something to do.'

'So you still haven't found your front-door keys?'

'No. They'll be in the house somewhere, I'm sure.'

Sheridan escorted him out and watched as he walked down the road. His shoulders were hunched like a man twenty years older. Anna met her in the corridor. 'What do you think?'

'Well, that explains why he climbed out of the window. Gabriel said he saw him climb out and now he thinks Adrian's dodgy.' Sheridan sighed.

'What do you think Gabriel was doing at Adrian's house?'

'I don't know. There's something about Gabriel that I can't put my finger on. The way Denise talked about him, the reasons behind his previous for violence. She painted this picture of him like he's some sort of bloody saint. But he's up to something. And now we know he's in touch with Oliver Elliot.'

'What do you want to do?' Anna asked.

'I want to go and see Gabriel in the morning.'

'I could go if you want, you're on a rest day.'

'No, it's okay. I want to see him myself.'

'You still think he could be Henry Blanchflower?'

'I don't know. I really don't know.'

CHAPTER 77

Henry Blanchflower opened the front door and craned his neck, listening in the darkness. Silence. He stepped into the kitchen and flicked the light on. Switching on the kettle, he pulled a mug from the cupboard before making his way down the hallway, floorboards creaking and groaning beneath his feet as he went.

'You'd better be exactly where I left you,' he called out, slowly turning the doorknob and peering in, before walking over to the corner of the room. His eyes narrowed as he opened the door and looked down at her.

'Hello, Caroline.' He reached in and touched her face, smirking at the fear in her eyes; the terror staring back at him.

'I said "hello", Caroline.' He touched her lips with his forefinger and closed his eyes. 'Aren't you going to say "hello" back?'

He waited for her to respond. And then her voice echoed around the room.

'Hello, Henry.'

'That's better.' He leaned down, his face an inch away from hers. 'Everyone's looking for you, Caroline.'

Her wide eyes were fixed on him.

He stood upright, reaching down momentarily to touch her hair. 'They're looking, but they'll never find you.' He smiled. 'My plan's too good. I'm way too smart for them. They'll never find you.'

And then he closed the door.

As he left the room, he could hear Caroline calling him from behind the door, her voice muffled and strange. He abruptly stopped, his face burning with rage. He'd told her enough times to only speak when he told her to and never at any other time. Breathing in and out slowly, he waited until the calmness returned and he again felt in control. Henry Blanchflower was in total control.

CHAPTER 78

Saturday 18 April

Sheridan was back at the Royal Liverpool Hospital – and as she reached Gabriel's bed, she stopped. Whoever was in the bed wasn't Gabriel Howard. She went over to the nurses' station.

'Hi, sorry to bother you. Has Gabriel Howard been moved?'

The nurse replied, 'No. He discharged himself last night.'

Shit, thought Sheridan. 'Okay. Thanks.' She called Anna as she made her way back to her car.

'Hi, mate,' Anna said when she answered the call. 'How you getting on?'

'Gabriel Howard discharged himself last night.'

'Christ's sake.'

'I'm going round to his house.'

'Pick me up first and we'll go together.'

Gabriel Howard was at the dining table sipping a coffee when Denise came in from the kitchen.

She mouthed to him, 'There's soup – have it later.'

He nodded. 'Thanks, sis.'

She put her hand on his shoulder and her face close to his, shouted, 'I still think you're an idiot by the way.'

He frowned, handing her a pad and pen.

She wrote: *YOU'RE AN IDIOT. YOU SHOULD HAVE STAYED IN HOSPITAL. I'LL BE BACK IN A COUPLE OF HOURS, JUST POPPING TO SORT SOME THINGS OUT AT THE SHOP. DO NOT LEAVE THE HOUSE AND TEXT ME IF YOU NEED ME. LOVE YOU, YOU DICKHEAD.*

He smiled. 'Okay.'

He watched her get into her car and pull away before sending a text to Oliver Elliot: *I'm home. Discharged myself. Still can't hear much but feel ok.*

Oliver replied: *You should have stayed in hospital. Please take it easy. Can I do anything?*

Gabriel replied: *No. Plan still going ahead.*

Oliver replied: *You need to concentrate on getting better.*

Gabriel responded: *Will do. Not long now and hopefully our man will get himself nicked.*

Oliver: *Definitely, we'll give the police enough to have him in. Text me when you're ok to meet up.*

Gabriel replied: *Will do. Have to be careful though. Don't want police to see us together. I think DI Holler saw you at the hospital. She might be keeping tabs on me.*

Oliver responded: *No worries.*

Gabriel stood up slowly, holding his side. Picking up his coffee cup he turned to go into the kitchen when he spotted Sheridan and Anna walking up the path.

'Hi,' Gabriel said as he opened the front door. 'You found me.'

'You still deaf?' Sheridan said loudly, her voice drenched in sarcasm. She ignored the grin on Gabriel's face, gestured towards herself and Anna, then pointed inside the house.

Gabriel stepped back, and they followed him in.

Sheridan shouted again. 'So? Are you still deaf?' Pointing to her own ear.

He nodded. 'It's still really muffled. Can you write stuff down?'

Sheridan pulled a pad out of her pocket and wrote out her question – why had he discharged himself? He replied that he hated hospitals and felt well enough to be at home, going against the advice from the doctor.

Then she wrote: *DON'T GO NEAR ADRIAN CROW'S HOUSE AGAIN.*

Gabriel read the message, and looked at her and Anna. 'Are you following him?'

Sheridan wrote: *NOTHING TO DO WITH YOU. IT'S A POLICE MATTER. JUST STAY AWAY OR I WILL REPORT YOU FOR BREACH OF LICENCE CONDITIONS.*

Gabriel responded to her, 'You can't prove I was ever there, it's only my word that I've been near his house. I'm not being difficult, but you have no proof. Look, none of that matters anyway, but you're making a mistake if you don't believe me about him.'

Sheridan wrote: *YOU SAW HIM CLIMB OUT OF A WINDOW ONE TIME. WE KNOW WHY HE DID THIS. YOU HAVE NO PROOF THAT HE'S DODGY.*

Gabriel shook his head. 'You're making a mistake.'

Sheridan wrote one last note: *STAY AWAY FROM HIM AND HIS HOUSE OR I WILL ARREST YOU MYSELF. GOT IT?*

She turned to leave and he followed her and Anna to the front door. As he leant past them to open it, he looked Sheridan straight in the eye. 'Don't take your eyes off him.'

They left without another word being said and Gabriel watched them getting back into their car.

'Fuck,' he said under his breath.

Taking out his phone he sent a text to Oliver Elliot: *Got to sort something. I'll be in touch soon.*

CHAPTER 79

Saturday 9 May

The next three weeks brought nothing but frustration for Sheridan and her team. The investigation into Caroline's disappearance hit brick wall after brick wall. Adrian Crow continued to be supported by Jack Staples, who reported back to Sheridan that Adrian was trying to stay positive. Extensive work was carried out to identify the victim who had had her hands sawn off, but it began to feel like she didn't exist.

And then two days before Sheridan's birthday, the call came.

The call that changed everything.

Sam was in the kitchen. She quickly put her hands behind her back as Sheridan walked in.

'Is that my birthday card?' Sheridan grinned as she opened the fridge, lifting out a bottle of wine.

'You'll find out in two days.' Sam slid the card under her T-shirt before making her way upstairs, mumbling to herself about having no secrets living with a bloody detective.

Maud stood at Sheridan's feet, looking up at her expectantly. Sheridan leant down and tickled the top of her head. 'You want a piece of ham?'

Maud meowed frantically, as though her life was in danger.

'Here you go.' Sheridan rolled up a slice and Maud took it from her fingers, hurrying into the front room to devour it under the coffee table. Why eat it on the hard wooden kitchen floor when she could leave a mess on the carpet?

The doorbell rang and Sheridan answered it. Anna was standing there, smiling as she shoved a bottle of champagne towards her. 'It was bloody extortionate, but you're worth it.' She kissed Sheridan on the cheek. 'Happy birthday in two days.'

Sam came down the stairs and hugged Anna and they went into the kitchen, where Sheridan put the bubbly in the fridge. 'We'll wait for Joni before we open it. Unless you want me to save it for when the Queen comes.'

Sam looked at the bottle. 'Blimey, you *have* splashed out.' She turned to Sheridan. 'Am I supposed to spend loads of money on you as well?'

The doorbell rang again. Sam let Joni in. Newman was rocking his cat carrier back and forth, desperate to get out and join Maud.

As they all stood in the kitchen, Sam made a toast. 'Dear friends, we are gathered here this evening to celebrate Sheridan's birthday in two days. Please raise your glasses and join me in toasting the best woman on the planet.'

They all raised a glass, just as Sheridan's mobile rang. 'Bollocks, that's bloody work.' She picked up her phone, took a sip of champagne and answered, 'DI Holler.'

There was a silence at the other end of the phone.

Sheridan spoke again. 'Hello?'

'Hello. Sorry, is that Detective Holler?'

'That's correct, who am I speaking to?'

'I don't know if you remember me? You called me a while back about some things I had stolen from my hotel room . . .'

'Jacqueline? Yes, I remember you. What can I do for you?' Sheridan put her glass down and took the call into the living room.

'I see the lady who went missing hasn't been found yet.'

'That's right.'

'You asked me about the things I had stolen.' There was a pause. 'I made a mistake.'

'What do you mean?' Sheridan looked up to see Anna emerge from the kitchen.

'You asked about my hairbrush and toothbrush. Well, they *were* taken from my room.'

Sheridan signalled for Anna to close the door leading into the kitchen before she put Jacqueline Blackstone on loudspeaker. 'Are you sure?'

'Absolutely sure. I'm sorry I didn't say anything before. Will I be in trouble with the police now?'

'No. So, tell me *exactly* what was taken. I know you mentioned your boots, some money and jewellery . . .'

'Look, I was pissed off at the hotel staff. Once I realised that some of my things had been taken, I thought I could get some compensation or something, so I just said that the money and jewellery were nicked.'

'So, they weren't?'

'No. I never reported it to the police though and I'm not going to take it any further.'

'Jacqueline, this is really important – tell me *exactly* what was taken.'

'Okay, well, my hairbrush, toothbrush, a lipstick, and one of my tops.'

Sheridan punched the air. 'What kind of toothbrush?' She grabbed Anna's arm.

'An electric one.'

Sheridan felt her pulse quicken. 'What about the charger?'

'No, that was in my case.'

Sheridan tried to keep her voice from breaking as the adrenaline rushed through her body. 'Okay, anything else? Anything at all?'

'Just a bottle of water that was by my bed, but it was half empty, so I think the cleaners probably chucked it. I didn't even want them to clean my room, I'd left my "Do Not Disturb" sign on the door.'

Sheridan's mind was racing. 'Do you have any idea who could have got into your room and taken the items?'

'No.'

'No one else went into your room or . . .' Sheridan hesitated. 'Don't take this the wrong way, but did you have company at all?'

'No. I was alone the whole time.'

Sheridan stared at Anna. 'Okay, look, we need to get a statement from you – remind me where you live?'

'Shrewsbury.'

'Are you free tomorrow if I arrange to meet you at a local police station?'

'Am I going to be arrested?' There was a glint of panic in Jacqueline's voice.

'No, absolutely not,' Sheridan said, 'but I need to get a statement and a DNA sample.'

'DNA? What for?'

'I'll explain everything when I see you. Are you free tomorrow?'

'Yes. So where do I have to go?'

'I'll make the arrangements and call you back with the details.'

'Okay.'

'Thank you, Jacqueline. Thank you for calling me.' Sheridan ended the call and puffed out her cheeks. 'Fucking hell.'

'You were right.' Anna grinned. 'You were bloody right.'

Sheridan smiled. 'Fancy a trip to Shrewsbury tomorrow?'

'On my day off? When I've got a load of washing to do? Absolutely.'

CHAPTER 80

Sunday 10 May

Sheridan checked the clock on the wall. They had been waiting for Jacqueline Blackstone to turn up and she was fifteen minutes late. As Sheridan was about to call her, she received a text from CSI which included photos of the items seized from Caroline's bedroom and bathroom.

The interview room door opened, and a young police officer peered in at them. 'Your lady is here. Shall I bring her through?'

'Yes, please.' Sheridan took a breath.

Jacqueline Blackstone didn't look how Sheridan had imagined her. She was petite and unassuming, dressed in jeans and a bright yellow jumper that almost reached her knees. Her brown shoulder-length hair was tinged with flecks of grey and her face was tired and drawn. Sheridan shook her hand and thanked her for coming, introducing Anna.

'Can I get you a coffee? Tea?' Sheridan asked, as Jacqueline sat down opposite them.

'No, thanks.'

'Okay. Can you start from the beginning and tell us about your stay at the Hampshire Hotel.'

Jacqueline Blackstone sat forward, watching Sheridan's pen move across the paper as she took notes. She explained that she had been visiting an elderly aunt who was in a care home in Llandudno. They had had little contact in the last few years, so Jacqueline had decided to visit her for a few days as she was receiving end-of-life care. With no other family around, Jacqueline felt it was her duty to prepare the necessary for when her aunt passed away, commenting that she had good intentions and wasn't interested in her aunt's small fortune – she was simply visiting her out of love.

The morning of the reported theft – Tuesday 10 March – she had showered and dressed, then placed the 'Do Not Disturb' sign on the door before making her way downstairs to breakfast.

When she returned to her room, she went into the bathroom to put her make-up on before the planned trip to the care home. And that was when she noticed her hairbrush was missing. And her toothbrush. After checking her case and looking around the room, she realised a top she had worn the day before was gone, along with a lipstick that she had left by the sink and the half-drunk bottle of water that had sat on her bedside table.

She left her room and walked down the corridor and found a cleaner. She asked if she had been in her room, to which the cleaner said that she had. Jacqueline challenged her about the missing items, but the cleaner became defensive and contacted the hotel manager. It was while Jacqueline was waiting in her room for the manager to appear that she came up with the idea for making a claim. Which was why she'd said jewellery, cash and other items had also been taken.

'I don't know why I said it. I just thought they'd give me some compensation and that would be the end of it. But they dug their heels in and told me that I should report it to the police. The manager was a right stroppy cow, banging on about how all her staff were vetted and the hotel had a good reputation.'

'So the items you said were stolen didn't exist?'

'No. It was such a stupid thing to do. I'm not a liar and I've never been in trouble with the police. I honestly feel ashamed.' She instinctively put her head down for a moment. 'I've been really worried about it since that police officer – DC Sexton – left me a voicemail asking me to call. I kept avoiding her. I'm sorry.'

Having run Jacqueline's details through PNC before the meeting, Sheridan was aware that Jacqueline had never been previously arrested.

Sheridan showed Jacqueline the photos of the toothbrush, hairbrush, top and lipstick and she confirmed they were the items taken from her room.

Sheridan asked her if she had seen Caroline and Adrian Crow at any time.

'When you first asked me about the theft, I actually hadn't seen anything on the news, so I didn't know what Caroline Crow looked like. It wasn't until a few days ago that I checked online and saw that she was still missing that I called a good mate of mine to ask her what I should do.'

'So you recognised Caroline from the internet images?'

'Yeah. That's what I told my mate, and she said I should come clean and call you. Her neighbour's son's a copper. She asked him about the connection with my hairbrush and toothbrush going missing and why the police might be interested. That's when I found out that people can be identified from them. You know, like when they find a body. So, I panicked and called *you*.'

Sheridan took Caroline's photo out of her folder and showed it to Jacqueline, who nodded. 'Yes, that's her. Definitely.'

Sheridan continued, 'So, now that you've seen what Caroline Crow looks like, do you remember seeing her at the hotel?'

'Yeah. Her and her husband came out of their room about the same time as I did the morning my stuff was taken. We all went to get into the lift together, then she said she'd forgotten something and would meet him downstairs for breakfast.'

Sheridan's eyes widened. 'She got out of the lift alone?'

'Yeah.'

So, that's when Caroline got into your room and took your belongings, thought Sheridan.

'Were the cleaners around when you got into the lift?' she asked.

'No. I don't think so. I didn't see anyone.'

'Did you speak to Adrian at all?'

'No.'

Sheridan took out a photograph of a still from the security cameras outside Adrian's house. 'Is this the man you saw with Caroline?'

'Yeah, that's him.'

'Okay, then what happened?'

'We got out of the lift and went into the restaurant for breakfast. She came down to join him a couple of minutes later.' Jacqueline shifted in her seat. 'Sorry, can I use the loo quickly?'

Anna stood up. 'Of course. I'll take you.'

After they'd left the room, Sheridan wrote herself a note.

> *While Jacqueline and Adrian were in the lift, Caroline gets into Jacqueline's room and takes the items, puts them in her own suitcase and, as previously thought, that's why she doesn't unpack when they get home. She doesn't want Adrian to see what's in her case.*

She sat back for a moment. Something didn't add up. She wrote another note.

Jacqueline's 'Do Not Disturb' sign was on the door. How did Caroline have time to flip the sign so that the cleaners saw it and went in to clean Jacqueline's room? Maybe she left the restaurant at breakfast time? This would make more sense. This would give her enough time.

She was tapping her pen on the notes when Anna and Jacqueline returned.

'Jacqueline, I have a couple more questions.'

Jacqueline sat upright and placed her hands on her lap. 'Okay.'

'When you were in the restaurant having breakfast, could you see Caroline and Adrian Crow?'

'Yeah, they were, like, two tables away.'

Sheridan focused intently on Jacqueline, before she asked the final question. The one that would seal her theory and set it in stone. That Caroline had left the restaurant for long enough to take the things from Jacqueline's room.

'Did Caroline leave at any time during breakfast? Did she leave Adrian there alone at any time?'

Jacqueline answered, 'No.'

Sheridan sat back, trying to hide her disappointment. *Shit*, she thought. 'Are you absolutely positive?'

Jacqueline Blackstone put her hand to her mouth and coughed. 'I'm positive. She *definitely* didn't leave the restaurant. But her husband did.'

CHAPTER 81

Hill answered her mobile. 'DCI Knowles.'

'It's Sheridan,' said the voice on the other end. 'You free to speak?'

'Yes, what's up?'

'It's Adrian Crow.'

'What about him? Oh shit, don't tell me he's topped himself . . .'

'No. It's *him*, he's the one who took the toothbrush and hairbrush from the hotel . . .'

'How do you know that?'

'Me and Anna are in Shrewsbury with Jacqueline Blackstone, she's given a statement and—'

'You're on a rest day. What the fuck are you doing in Shrewsbury?'

Sheridan went through the statement that Jacqueline Blackstone had given. She had provided a DNA sample and Sheridan and Anna were on their way back to Liverpool.

'I'll meet you at the nick.' Hill ended the call.

It was just after 3 p.m. when Sheridan and Anna met Hill at Hale Street. After grabbing a coffee, they all sat in CID, where Rob and Dipesh were absorbed as Sheridan explained the latest revelation.

'The CCTV from the hotel reception shows Adrian Crow leaving the hotel at 08.36 on the Tuesday morning. He returns at 09.14 with a card in his hand – which I'm assuming is Caroline's birthday card. So, looking at the timings and from what Jacqueline Blackstone told us, she was having breakfast from around 08.00 and got back up to her room at around 08.45. And that's when she discovered her things missing. Adrian left the restaurant around 08.20. I think he went up to Jacqueline's room while the cleaners were there, got in and took her things. He then leaves the hotel at 08.36 and returns at 09.14. It all fits.' Sheridan raised her eyebrows and smiled, turning to Hill. 'Can we nick him today?'

Hill responded, 'I want to wait until we confirm that the DNA from Jacqueline Blackstone matches the items from Caroline's house – then we'll have him in. The sample has been fast-tracked as a priority. The results will be back first thing in the morning at the latest.'

Sheridan jumped in. 'Of course it'll match. Jacqueline has already identified the items as belonging to her. And we need to start thinking now that if Adrian has planted DNA, then Caroline is probably dead. And if she's not, then we need to find her . . . now.'

Hill rubbed her temples. 'I still want to get the DNA back. I don't want to be nicking him and then having to bail him out. If we nick him too soon, and if he *has* got Caroline held somewhere, then he might not tell us where she is. We need to get it right, first time.'

◆ ◆ ◆

Sheridan left the nick thinking about what Hill had said. Hill's reaction was probably right, but Sheridan's sudden impatience to arrest Adrian Crow had irritated her. She would have bet her house that the DNA was going to match and sitting around waiting for the results was going to be torture. If Caroline was dead, they had nothing to lose, except to find her body. But if she was alive, then time could be running out. She thought about Gabriel Howard and what he'd said to her about not taking their eyes off Adrian Crow. His words echoed in her ears.

As she got into her car, she remembered what he'd written down when she went to see him at the hospital.

> *I NEED TO TELL YOU SOMETHING BUT DON'T WANT DENISE INVOLVED. NO TROUBLE FOR HER. IF YOU BRING TROUBLE FOR HER I WON'T HELP YOU*

She recalled their conversation and realised he hadn't elaborated on it. He hadn't elaborated because she hadn't pressed the point enough. Resting her head back, she closed her eyes. They had got so far and yet so many questions remained unanswered. Could she trust anything Gabriel Howard had told her? Was he Henry Blanchflower?

Without warning, her brother's face came in to her head. He always seemed to be there when she questioned her own rationale. Back when Matthew had been murdered, things had been different. Policing had been different. The tools they had now weren't available back then, investigations were hampered and slow. Police officers were different in the seventies and the way they worked wasn't as constricted by red tape, too many rules and the Police and Criminal Evidence Act of 1984. Coppers were allowed to be coppers, gathering intelligence by having a quiet word with thieves and mobsters over a cup of tea. Often, nothing was written down and there was an unspoken respect between the law men and women and the lawbreakers. The rules that were broken back then could lose you the case these days. And probably your job.

Sheridan opened her eyes and started the engine. She couldn't let it go. Fuck the rules.

CHAPTER 82

Sheridan was walking up the path ready to knock on the door when Gabriel opened it, pulling a jacket over his broad shoulders. He jumped slightly when he saw her. 'Detective Holler.'

'Hello, Gabriel.' She stood with her hands in her pockets. 'You off out?'

Gabriel closed the door behind him. 'Sorry, you'll have to speak up, my hearing's still a bit knackered.'

'It doesn't matter.' She took a small pad out of her pocket and wrote a note: *I WANT TO TALK TO YOU.*

He read the note and nodded. 'Okay. You want to come in?'

She wrote: *WHERE ARE YOU GOING?*

He replied, 'Just out for a walk, not quite back to my running days, but I like to keep mobile.'

Sheridan wrote down: *YES OR NO. HAVE YOU REALLY SEEN ADRIAN CROW CLIMBING OUT OF HIS WINDOW MORE THAN ONCE?*

Gabriel replied, 'Are you trying to get me in trouble?'

Sheridan shook her head. 'No.' She held the note up to his face.

He looked skyward, hesitating before he answered. 'Yes.'

Sheridan wrote another note: *DO YOU KNOW WHERE HE GOES?*

Gabriel looked at her. 'No. I tried following him, but I always lost him.'

Sheridan replied: *TAKE ME TO THE LAST PLACE YOU SAW HIM.*

◆ ◆ ◆

As Sheridan drove, Gabriel felt his mobile vibrating in his pocket. He took it out to check the message, ensuring that Sheridan couldn't see the screen.

As he'd expected, it was a message from Oliver: *Did you get it ok?*

Gabriel replied: *Yes. I've got it with me. Just sorting something. Don't text back. Will be in touch soon.*

He placed the mobile in his pocket and turned to Sheridan. 'Keep going down this road, about another mile and then pull over.'

As he spoke, he slid his hand into his jacket and felt the knife, pushing it deeper into the lining.

She nodded. 'Okay.'

Nearing a bend in the road, he indicated for her to pull over. 'Just here.'

Sheridan parked the car in a narrow layby and switched off the engine. Turning in her seat to face him, she spoke loudly and slowly, enunciating her words. 'This is the last place you saw him?'

Gabriel shook his head. 'No. We'll have to get out and walk for a bit.'

He opened the door and stepped out of the car, stretching his back. Sheridan joined him as he stood looking out across the field. Long grass swayed gently to and fro before them as the sun dipped behind clouds scurrying across the sky. Gabriel led the way, with Sheridan following a step behind him.

‘Be careful, it’s a bit tricky,’ he said, offering his hand, which she immediately pushed away.

She could feel the uneven ground beneath her feet and looked down, trying to avoid the myriad muddy potholes. As they neared a large tree standing proud on its own, Gabriel stopped. ‘Here.’ He turned to see Sheridan behind him.

He pointed. ‘That’s the last place I saw him, heading that way.’

Sheridan took in the scene. Acres of long grass leading to a row of trees further ahead. Taking out the map he’d drawn on two weeks earlier, she found their location. ‘There’s nothing here,’ she said under her breath, folding the map and shoving it back into her pocket. ‘He could have gone anywhere.’

Gabriel inhaled the evening breeze. Reaching inside his jacket, he tried to grip the knife handle, his hand slipping down it on to the blade, just as Sheridan turned around.

CHAPTER 83

Sam was visiting Sheridan's parents. As she sat at their kitchen table, Rosie Holler was making a third pot of tea, while Brian was flicking through photo albums, showing Sam pictures of Sheridan when she was a little girl.

Sam had asked to see them as part of her planning for Sheridan's birthday. Her idea was to bake a cake and decorate the top with icing in the design of Sheridan's face as a child. But when she called Rosie and Brian to let them in on her little secret, Rosie had pointed out a rather important fact: Sam couldn't cook for shit. She hadn't used these exact words, but her message was pretty much the same.

Sam burst out laughing at a photograph of Sheridan as a little girl, wearing a bright yellow dress and her hair in ringlets. 'She looks like Shirley Temple.'

Rosie turned around. 'That was the first and last time Sheridan ever wore that dress.'

'Why? Because she hated it?' Sam asked, still grinning at the picture, unable to imagine the Sheridan she knew ever putting up with such a garment.

'No. Because that was the day she got into a fight with a little boy down the road. They were playing with plastic swords, and he hit her on the head a bit too hard. She got a nasty cut.' Rosie put a cup of tea in front of Sam. 'So, Sheridan grabbed his sword, threw her own down, and proceeded to lay into him. They ended up rolling around in the street. By the time she got home, the dress was ruined.'

'Who won the fight?' Sam asked.

Rosie smiled. 'Who do you think?'

'That's my girl,' Sam replied, focusing back on the photo album. Just then, Brian turned the next page and smiling back at him was Sheridan with her arms wrapped around her little brother, Matthew. Brian hesitated before turning the page and Sam put her arm around his shoulders.

The kitchen suddenly filled with the smell of the freshly baked cake as Rosie opened the oven door and lifted it out. 'Right, Sam, here you go. You'll have to let it cool before you ice it.' She grinned at the look of horror on Sam's face. 'You'll be fine, I showed you what to do.'

'Do you really think Sheridan will believe me when I tell her that *I* made it?' Sam asked, pursing her lips.

Rosie tapped her own nose. 'Absolutely. I put far too much sugar and salt in it. Not enough to completely ruin it, but enough for it to taste a little bit odd.'

'Perfect. Then I might actually get away with this.' Sam stood up and kissed Rosie on the cheek. 'You're an angel.'

'And you'll need this.' Rosie handed her a piece of paper. 'It's all the ingredients and how to make it. Because we all know Sheridan will interrogate you, if she doesn't believe that *you* made it.'

Sam kissed her on the cheek again.

Brian slipped out a photo and held it up. 'Here you go, Sam, how about this one?'

Sam took the photo from him. It was Sheridan aged seven, her face coated in thick blue eyeshadow and red lipstick. 'What's with the make-up?' Sam laughed.

'Oh, just one of Sheridan's phases,' Rosie explained, peering at the picture. 'She soon grew out of it.'

'It's perfect. I'm going to use that one.' Sam beamed. 'She'll be well impressed.'

Rosie and Brian flicked a look at each other, both imagining what the cake was going to look like after Sam had slapped icing all over it. They held their laughter in as long as they could. Brian broke first.

'What?' Sam asked. 'Oh, you don't think I can do it, do you?' She slapped Brian's arm. 'Well, you just wait.'

They sat chatting while the cake cooled down and as they reminisced through the photo album, the subject of Matthew came up. Sheridan had told her parents about the update on Stephen Tubby and the fact that he'd lied to police about not being near Birkenhead Park at the time of Matthew's murder. Their reaction had been just as tentative as Sheridan's when she'd shared the news with them. She had gently warned them not to get their hopes up. But it was a way forward for the cold-case team. Sam would always listen intently when Sheridan's parents talked of Matthew; they openly shared their thoughts about him with her. She felt their sadness but also recognised the moments when they tried to keep the conversation light, often swapping stories of happier days. Sam adored Rosie and Brian and worried for them. She worried for Sheridan, for the effect Matthew's death had had on her. But Sam *got* Sheridan, she knew how her mind worked and how she would never give up trying to find his killer.

As she left, Sam hugged them both. 'See you soon. Love you.'

'We love you too,' Rosie replied, holding Sam's face in her hands. 'You really are the best thing that ever happened to Sheridan. Give her our love and tell her we'll see her soon.'

CHAPTER 84

Gabriel quickly wiped the blood from his hand and secured the knife deep into his jacket. Emerging from behind the tree, and picking up his pace, he looked up, feeling drops of rain on his face as he headed back to the car.

'Sorry about that,' he said as he climbed in. 'Couldn't hold it any longer.'

'It's fine. Just don't touch anything,' Sheridan said loudly, leaning into the glove compartment and handing him a wet wipe. 'Here, wipe your hands.'

Gabriel grinned. 'Us boys are gross, aren't we?'

Sheridan noticed a fresh cut on his finger. 'How did you do that?'

'Nicked it on something sharp sticking out of that tree.' He tilted his head. 'It's nothing. So, has something happened with Adrian Crow? Do you suspect him now?' Gabriel asked.

Sheridan ignored the question, instead making a note on the pad, tired of having to shout at him so that he could hear her.

WHEN I SAW YOU IN THE HOSPITAL, YOU SAID YOU'D HELP ME BUT DIDN'T WANT DENISE GETTING INTO TROUBLE. WHAT DID YOU MEAN? WHY WOULD SHE BE IN TROUBLE?

AND DON'T SCREW ABOUT, GABRIEL, JUST TELL ME.

Gabriel read the message and replied, looking out of the window. 'I was on painkillers in the hospital, and they just made my head fuzzy. I don't remember much of what I said or why I said it.' He turned to her. 'But whatever I do in my life, I will always protect Denise.'

For a moment, neither of them spoke. The clouds that had obscured the falling sun now turned black. And then came the rain.

Sheridan wrote a note: *DENISE TOLD ME ABOUT YOUR PARENTS. I'M SORRY.*

Gabriel swallowed and bit on his bottom lip. Sheridan turned to study his face. She could see how upset this had suddenly made him.

'My dad tried to save my mum, but he'd never been a strong swimmer. When we were told what happened to them, part of me was glad that they'd died together. Dad wouldn't have survived without Mum. They were inseparable.' Resting his head back, he continued, 'They were fantastic parents, they brought us up right, taught us to be good kids.' He flicked a look at Sheridan. 'I know I've done some wrong things in my life, but I can honestly say – hand on heart – that they'd still be proud of me. Not for what I've done, but for the reasons I did them. Men don't respect women like they should. They don't look after them or treat them right. Maybe I'm old-fashioned, like my dad, but I agree with his principles. Be a good man, do good things or at least try to do the right thing.'

Sheridan wrote a note and raised an eyebrow as she showed it to him: *YOU KNOCKED OUT A GUY'S TEETH AND BROKE ANOTHER ONE'S JAW.*

Gabriel smiled. 'They deserved it. I thought it was the right thing to do after what they did to the two women.'

Sheridan scribbled another note: *WHAT ABOUT EDITH ELLIOT?*

Gabriel read the question and turned his head away. 'That was a mistake. I made a mistake.' His voice was soft and low.

Sheridan hesitated before she wrote the next question. After seeing Oliver Elliot at Gabriel's bedside, she'd been desperate to find the link between them. If she could pretend to Gabriel that she suspected Oliver for running him over, then maybe his reaction would give something away.

She wrote: *I'M WONDERING IF IT WAS OLIVER ELLIOT WHO RAN YOU OVER. MAYBE HE'S ANGRY AT YOU FOR WHAT HAPPENED TO HIS MOTHER?*

Gabriel's eyes were fixed on the notepad. 'No. I don't think so.'

Sheridan wrote quickly: *WHY NOT? IT MAKES SENSE.*

Gabriel shook his head. 'I think it was just an accident.'

Sheridan pushed further, bursting to get a reaction from him: *I THINK WE'LL LOOK AT OLIVER ANYWAY, JUST TO MAKE SURE. YOU COULD HAVE BEEN KILLED.*

Gabriel shifted position. He could feel the knife handle pressing against his back. 'I don't care about the hit-and-run. You need to concentrate on Adrian Crow.' He turned his face towards her. '*Please* listen to me. He leaves his house most nights – he climbs out of the window and walks across this field. I've followed him a few times but each time, I've lost him. If you find out where he goes, I think you'll find his wife.'

Sheridan wrote one more note: *SHOW ME WHERE YOU GOT HIT BY THE CAR.*

Gabriel jokingly pointed to his ribs, leg and arm. Sheridan did everything she could not to find it funny.

Finally, she started the engine and pulled away. Gabriel directed her two miles up the road. He showed her where he'd parked Denise's car and then the route he'd walked before the car had hit him.

Ignoring the rain, Sheridan got out and stood in the road, taking in the area, placing herself where Gabriel had been when he was hit, the curve of the bend up ahead. Few cars had passed them on the way to this point and none were around now. Gabriel joined her.

'I need to take you home,' she said loudly. They headed back to his house in virtual silence.

As he got out of the car, he leaned back in. 'You need to find out where he goes.'

Sheridan pointed at him. 'Leave well alone now, Gabriel. *Don't* follow him any more. I mean it.'

He smiled, tapped his hand on the roof of the car and Sheridan watched as he walked up the path before letting himself into the house.

Five minutes later, he called Oliver.

'Hi. You okay?' Oliver asked.

'Yeah, all good. You need to speak up, my hearing's still muffled.'

'Anything from the police yet about who hit you?'

'No.'

'I take it we don't think it was one of *them*?'

'Sheridan Holler thinks it might have been *you*.'

Oliver replied, 'Really? Well, there's no worries there, then.'

'Whoever it was could have killed me. I could see the vehicle – it looked like a truck – and it started reversing like they were coming back to finish the job.'

'Who would want you dead if it wasn't one of *them*?'

'Trust me, they have no idea that it's me doing this to them. And if they've been looking for me all this time, which is unlikely, then they won't find me. They'd be searching for me under a different name, remember?'

'Just watch your back, though, eh?'

'I will.'

'Did you manage to plant everything?'

Gabriel replied, 'I'm going to do it tonight. I'm all set.'

'And then what?'

'Well, then I sit back and see what happens.'

'Is DI Holler going to want to speak to me about the hit-and-run, if she thinks I was responsible?'

Gabriel checked his watch. 'I think Detective Holler has got bigger fish to fry at the moment. Look, I'd better go. We'll speak soon.'

'Okay. Well, keep me posted and stay in touch.'

'I will. I'll let you know if I find out he's been nicked.' And with that, Gabriel headed out. To plant the evidence that would move his plan forward to the next stage.

CHAPTER 85

Monday 11 May

Everyone cheered as Sheridan walked into CID. A birthday banner was strewn across the window, and an enormous cake sat on Rob's desk.

The whole team sang 'Happy Birthday' as she made a beeline for the cake, grinning from ear to ear. 'Thanks, guys.' She picked up the cake and made to walk out with it, much to everyone's amusement. As she set it back down, Anna called out for her to make a speech.

'Oh, okay. Well, thank you, but you can all get back to work now, you lazy buggers.' She smiled, turning to see Hill walk in. She was carrying an envelope, which she presented to Sheridan.

'We weren't sure what you wanted for your birthday, so we thought we'd give you this.' Hill stepped back, crossing her arms, a rare smile lighting up her face.

Sheridan eyed the envelope suspiciously before carefully opening it. 'Is it plane tickets to the Maldives?' she joked, peering inside before pulling out the sheet of paper.

'Yes!' she exclaimed, re-reading the DNA results that showed Jacqueline Blackstone's DNA matched that of the items found in

Caroline Crow's house. She turned to Hill. '*Please* can we go and nick Adrian Crow, now?'

'Yes, you can. Uniform and CSI are waiting downstairs for you. Happy birthday.'

Rob Wills piped up, 'Can we have some cake first?' he asked, pouting.

'Arrest first, cake later.' Sheridan stepped over to him, picked up the knife that lay on top of a pile of paper plates and cut herself a massive slice. 'I can have some though, because it's my birthday,' she said, shovelling it into her mouth.

Ten minutes later she was in the car with Anna and Rob, following the uniformed officers in their marked cars as they headed to Adrian Crow's house. Anna and Rob had both sneaked a lump of birthday cake out of the office and were devouring it while Sheridan drove.

As they neared Adrian's house, Sheridan felt a mixture of apprehension blended with a generous dose of adrenaline, and she took an exaggerated breath.

'You okay?' Anna asked, finishing the last of her cake and sucking cream off her fingers.

'Yeah. I just hope that he tells us where Caroline is.'

'Do you think she's dead?'

'No.'

'Me neither,' said Rob, trying to wipe jam off the seat. Anna surreptitiously handed him a tissue.

Sheridan noticed this, but let them think she hadn't. 'If CSI get an actual DNA sample of hers from the house and it matches the burnt hands that were sent to Simon and Adrian, *then* we'll know she's dead.'

The marked police car in front of them turned on to Adrian's drive and parked up. Sheridan pulled in next to it. 'His car's here.'

Two officers went around the side of the house while Sheridan rang the doorbell. No answer. She rang several more times, but there was still no response. She walked around to the window that Adrian had previously climbed out of. It was slightly open.

Uniformed officers entered the property and once they had established it was empty, Sheridan and Anna went inside. As they walked into the kitchen, they immediately stopped in their tracks. The dining room table was upside down and two of the dining chairs lay broken. Smashed crockery was scattered all over the floor and the cooker's glass hob was cracked down the middle.

Sheridan took in the scene before making her way through the house. All the other rooms appeared normal, if a little untidy, but nothing like the carnage in the kitchen.

'What do you think?' Anna asked.

'I think we need to get another seal on the house and find Adrian.' She turned to Anna. 'And we need to find Gabriel, too. I think he's been here.'

'What makes you think that?'

'Gabriel's seen Adrian climb out of that window before. What if Gabriel's used that same window to get in and they've had a fight? Gabriel knows there're cameras outside – and he also knows the window isn't covered by them.' She turned to Rob. 'Can you get back to the nick and find out where Gabriel's sister's car is and ping his and Adrian's phones.'

Anna crouched down, spotting something on the floor, and bent to pick it up. 'Adrian's phone's here.'

Sheridan put her hands on her hips. 'Shit. I think Gabriel's got him.'

CHAPTER 86

It was gone 4 p.m. Sheridan's team had established that Gabriel's sister's car was parked outside the florist's shop. Denise had been spoken to and she told the officers that she had no idea where Gabriel was. His phone was likely switched off as it wasn't pinging off any masts. The last mast was a mile away from where he'd told Sheridan that he'd last seen Adrian Crow. Uniformed officers were searching the area. But with the maze of housing estates that lay to the back of the land, locating Gabriel and Adrian was proving almost impossible.

Sheridan and Anna drove to the last place that Gabriel said he'd seen Adrian, and after parking their car, they started walking. Acres of wasteland spread out before them, as they manoeuvred their way through the tall grass.

Anna stopped and held her radio up to her ear. She listened to the updates from the uniformed officers, while Sheridan forged ahead, disappearing behind a dense row of trees. As Anna caught her up, she stopped, looking at the building that Sheridan was staring at.

Anna caught her breath. 'Jesus Christ. It looks like the Bates Motel.'

'Doesn't it just. Come on.' Sheridan started walking towards what appeared to be an abandoned farmhouse. Broken wood pallets were stacked in a pile to one side, and rusting machinery lay on the other. Two outbuildings – equally in disrepair – were situated to the right of the house. Reaching the front of the property, Sheridan peered through the window, wiping her finger in a line on the blackened glass. She realised that the windows were partially blacked out from the inside. Standing on tiptoes, she squinted, letting her eyes try to focus.

She suddenly ducked down. 'Fuck.'

'What is it?'

'Caroline Crow's in there.'

CHAPTER 87

Anna stepped back, quickly relayed their location over the airwaves and instructed all officers to make a silent approach to the property. As she ended the message to the control room, she followed Sheridan along the side of the building.

Anna grabbed her arm. 'We need to wait for uniform,' she whispered.

'She's tied to a chair. I need to get to her. She looks a mess.'

Anna took a deep breath. 'I'm coming with you.'

As they reached the back of the property, they noticed a large wooden door, ajar. Sheridan peered inside before entering, with Anna glued to her side.

The first thing to hit them was the smell. The second thing to hit them was the scene.

Covering her nose and mouth with her hand, Sheridan stood deathly still. In front of them was Caroline Crow, strapped to an old wooden chair. A table, neatly set for dinner, was in front of her. At her setting was a knife, fork and spoon. The other side of the table was also set, along with two plates and two glasses filled with red wine. A half-empty bottle of wine stood in the middle of the table and another empty bottle had been used as a candle holder. A hardened river of wax had dripped down it and on to the wooden table.

On the floor at Caroline's feet was a pool of water.

Caroline's head was tilted back. Her mouth was slightly open and her face was glistening wet. Her eyes were wide open in terror and her once delicate features were now slightly distorted.

With her senses heightened, Sheridan stepped closer, taking in the macabre scene before her. Caroline was fully dressed. Blue jeans, boots, a grey cardigan and black coat. Her arms dropped by her side. Sheridan arched her head to look closer. And then she stepped back.

Shaking her head, she whispered to Anna. 'Her hands are missing.'

Anna screwed up her face as she followed Sheridan's eye line, keeping her voice low. 'Well, she hasn't been dead for two months. The body's too well preserved.'

They stood in the silence of the house. Listening for any movement from within.

Sheridan slowly looked around and noticed a large upright freezer. There were scrape marks on the floor and a small metal ramp leading up to the freezer door. Tentatively gripping the handle, she pulled it open. And then she looked back at the chair legs. 'She's been in the freezer. Whoever did this has dragged her out on the chair.'

Anna whispered, 'It's like a fucking horror film.'

Sheridan whispered back, 'Get on to the control room again, we need *everybody* here.'

Anna put her hand over her mouth as she quietly radioed the control room. Sheridan peered around one of the two doors leading into the room, breathing as quietly as she could. As she took a step into the hallway, she could see inside the room opposite and noticed a pile of black bags in the corner.

At that moment, she heard a creak of floorboards behind her, where Anna stood with the radio pressed to her ear.

And then she saw Gabriel Howard suddenly appear behind Anna.

With a knife raised above his head.

'Gabriel!' Sheridan shouted, as Anna turned and let out a cry. Raising her hands in the air, instinctively trying to protect herself, she dropped the radio.

And then she fell to the floor.

CHAPTER 88

As Gabriel loomed over Anna, Sheridan launched herself at him, jumping on to his back and using all her strength to wrap her arms around his throat, but he was too strong for her. He managed to grab one of her arms, unravelling it from around his neck before pushing her off him. With the knife still in his hand, he now held it in front of him and took two steps forward, just as Adrian Crow stepped out of the darkness and flew towards him.

Out of the corner of her eye, Sheridan spotted Anna trying to get up and reach the radio, but it had slid across the floor, out of reach.

And then Adrian Crow screamed, 'Get away from her!'

Sheridan looked up to see Gabriel and Adrian standing two feet apart, brandishing their knives at each other. It was a stand-off. For a moment, no one moved.

Anna slowly tried to stand up, but Sheridan signalled for her to stay put. She stepped in front of Anna, ready to protect her if Gabriel turned the knife on them.

The heavy sound of laboured breathing from Gabriel and Adrian filled the room. Sheridan was desperately thinking what to do. She knew she couldn't get the knife from Gabriel, and she'd have to get past him to push Adrian out of harm's way.

Adrian was the first to speak. 'Have you seen what he's done to her? He's a fucking monster.' His voice broke as he ignored the tears that fell down his face, choking on sobs as he spoke. 'That's my Caroline.'

Sheridan didn't take her eye off the knife in Gabriel's hand as she tried to inch towards him, the floorboards under her feet betraying her every movement. She watched for any sign that Gabriel was going to lunge forward and stab Adrian, who was holding his own knife, his hand shaking uncontrollably. Sheridan noticed that the knife Gabriel was holding was at least four inches in length, while Adrian's matched the cutlery that was laid out on the table. And that was when Sheridan realised that Gabriel had come armed and prepared. Adrian, however, had grabbed anything he could to protect himself.

She stole a look back at the table where Caroline Crow was displayed. A silent witness to what was unravelling here.

And it was at that very moment that it fell into place for Sheridan.

Everything fell into place.

And then Sheridan said, as calmly as she could, 'Adrian, are you sure that's Caroline?'

Adrian gave an exaggerated nod. 'Yes.' He sobbed. 'Of course I'm sure.'

Gabriel flicked his head to look at her and then back to Adrian, the knife gripped tightly in his fist.

Sheridan continued, 'Adrian, is she wearing the same clothes that you last saw her in?'

He nodded again. 'Yes. That's my Caroline.' His legs began to shake. He placed one hand on the wall.

'Are you positive about the clothes?' Sheridan pressed.

'Yes.' Adrian's face burned red. Tears dripped off his chin.

Anna didn't speak or move. Totally confused about where Sheridan was going with this.

Sheridan flinched as Gabriel made a slight move, keeping himself focused on Adrian, but turning his head a fraction, towards Sheridan. Gabriel shouted, 'Does anyone else know you're here?' He stepped back half a pace and tried to reach down for the radio. But his tall frame, and the pain in his side from where his ribs had been broken, made it impossible for him to do so.

Sheridan didn't answer, her eyes still fixed on the knife.

And then taking a deep breath, she said, 'I know you are Henry Blanchflower.'

Gabriel snapped a look at her, stepping slightly to one side. His back was against the wall, where he could see Adrian to his right and Sheridan to his left. Sheridan watched as the look on Adrian's face turned to disbelief as he fixated on Gabriel.

Sheridan continued, 'I want you to put the knife down, Henry. It's over. I've got officers on their way. Just put the knife down. No one needs to get hurt here, Henry.'

She watched as the knife dropped to the floor and landed at Gabriel's feet.

It was over.

CHAPTER 89

Sheridan walked towards the police car, where Gabriel was sitting looking out of the back window.

Anna joined her. 'That was a bit mental.'

Sheridan agreed. 'Wasn't it just. Are you okay?' She put her hand on Anna's arm.

'Yeah, I'm fine. Just so glad we got him. I can't believe it's finally over.' She glanced at the police car. 'What a monster.'

Sheridan sighed, spotting Rob and Hill driving up the dirt track leading to the property. Hill was out of the car before Rob had even turned the engine off.

'Are you both okay?' she asked, marching towards them, obvious concern on her face.

Sheridan answered, 'We're fine, Hill.' She tilted her head back towards the property. 'It's a fucking horror scene in there though.'

'Is it Caroline Crow?' Hill asked.

'Yeah,' Anna replied.

Sheridan looked towards the police car. 'I'm going to speak to Gabriel.'

She walked over to the car and opened the back door.

Gabriel lowered his head. 'Well, I expect you really *do* hate me now?'

Sheridan didn't reply as she held on to the car door and eased herself down into a crouching position so she could look at him properly.

Gabriel raised his head to look at her. 'I'm sorry. I'm *so* sorry.'

'What are you sorry for?' she asked.

Gabriel said, 'Can you speak up? My hearing's still not quite right.'

'I said, what are you sorry for?' Sheridan raised her voice.

'For pushing Anna to the floor like that. For chucking you off my back.'

Sheridan shook her head, smiling at him. 'What you did in there was really bloody brave. So don't you say sorry.'

'Did I hurt either of you?'

'No. We're made of tough stuff. I'll get you taken to the nick. Are you okay to give a statement?'

'Yeah, of course.' He stretched his legs out. 'What did you say in there to make him drop the knife? I was trying to hear what you were saying, but . . .'

'It doesn't matter.'

As Sheridan stood up, Gabriel looked up at her. 'I was right though, wasn't I?'

'About what?' she asked.

'It's always the husband.'

Sheridan nodded, her eyes now drawn to the second police car, where Adrian Crow was sitting – handcuffed and flanked by two uniformed officers. She carried on watching as they slowly pulled away.

Sheridan made her way back over to Anna and Hill. The place was swarming with police officers and crime scene investigators. They had all witnessed horror in their time, but today was different. Today, they all shared the same look on their faces. This was the job they would talk about for years to come and reflect upon in disbelief.

Anna turned to her. 'How did you know?'

'How did I know what?'

'That Adrian was Henry Blanchflower.'

'I realised that the knife Adrian was holding was taken from where Caroline was sitting.' She crossed her arms. 'The CCTV from the hotel in Llandudno showed Caroline signing for something at reception and I spotted she was left-handed. Caroline's cutlery is set for her, the knife was on the left, not on the right. So, I figured that Gabriel wouldn't know that, but Adrian would. Being her husband, it would have been the natural thing for him to do. And even if Gabriel knew she was left-handed, he wouldn't instinctively set the table correctly.'

'So, at that point you knew he was Henry?'

'No. I knew he was Henry when he said that Caroline was wearing the same clothes as the last time he saw her.'

Hill frowned. 'Sorry, am I missing something?'

Sheridan continued, 'On the CCTV from the hotel in Llandudno, Caroline is seen in reception when they checked out. She was wearing blue jeans, a grey cardigan, boots and a black coat – exactly what she's wearing now. So I asked Adrian if Caroline was wearing the same clothes as she was when he last saw her. When he said yes, I knew he'd killed her. When Adrian first reported Caroline missing, he told Jack Staples that Caroline was in bed when he was about to leave the house, the morning he left to go to Norfolk. He said that him and Caroline always kiss before he goes to work. So, just before he left, he went into the bedroom to kiss her goodbye, but she insisted on getting up and waving him off.'

Hill smiled. 'So, she wouldn't have got dressed, back into the same clothes that she'd had on the day before. She'd have been in her night clothes.'

Sheridan smiled. 'Exactly. So, we know that Adrian killed her because she's still wearing the very same clothes that she had on when they left the hotel.'

Anna interjected, 'So, he probably killed her soon after they left the hotel.'

'Well, we'll find out soon.' Sheridan bit her lip. 'I can't wait to interview him.'

Anna frowned. 'I still don't get the Henry Blanchflower thing.'

Sheridan replied, 'It's a name Adrian made up. There never was a Henry Blanchflower. He doesn't exist.'

CHAPTER 90

It was almost midnight by the time Sheridan pulled on to her drive and felt the tension in her shoulders ease at the sight of Maud in the window.

Adrian Crow had been booked into custody. After a mental health assessment deemed him fit to be detained and interviewed, he was bedded down for the night, ready to be questioned the next day. CSI were working at the property where Caroline Crow had been found. Her body had been removed and was awaiting a post-mortem examination. Once she had thawed out enough for the procedure to take place. The property had been searched and discovered in a dozen black bags were Caroline's clothes, along with most of her personal belongings, including her bank card, and tucked inside a small grey cloth bag was a brand-new man's watch.

Parked in a garage behind the property was an old Land Rover. Closer inspection showed that it had front damage and a broken headlight. The unregistered vehicle was seized for forensic examination to establish if it was the same vehicle that had hit Gabriel Howard.

At the back of the building was a small warehouse, which was searched, revealing several rolls of plastic sheeting, packaging, rolls of brown tape. And a saw. Covered in dried blood.

Rob Wills had taken a statement from Gabriel Howard. Sheridan read it with interest. According to Gabriel's account, he just happened to be out for a walk in the field that led to the property where Caroline was found. He stated that he often went running there, but due to being injured in the hit-and-run, he was slowly building up to his old fitness regime.

He had seen a man walking across the field towards the house on a couple of occasions and felt there was something suspicious. This evening, his curiosity had got the better of him. He decided to go over to the property and see what was going on. The back door was open, so he stepped inside and walked down the hallway. And that was when he saw the woman sitting at the table. He knew that she was dead. He also realised the man was somewhere in or around the property, so he went to look for him. He hadn't heard DI Holler's car pull up, due to his hearing still being dodgy. It wasn't until he went back to the room where the woman's body had been placed that he saw DI Holler and DS Markinson.

That was also when he saw Adrian Crow appear, holding a knife. Gabriel had found a knife on the floor as he'd walked around the house and had picked it up in case he needed to defend himself. At some point during the incident, the man dropped the knife he was holding and it landed at Gabriel's feet. He stood on it to ensure the man couldn't pick it up, then Gabriel grabbed him and brought him to the floor. He and DI Holler then held the man there until uniformed police arrived a few minutes later.

After reading Gabriel's statement, Sheridan shook her head and turned to Rob. 'He certainly knows how to cover himself, I'll give him that. Found a knife on the floor? Yeah, right.' Sheridan grinned. 'I have to hand it to him though, he did put himself in danger to protect me and Anna.'

'He kept asking if you were both okay,' Rob replied. 'Said he felt terrible when he pushed Anna over and threw you off his back.'

'He's got a thing about violence towards women.' Sheridan handed the statement back to Rob. 'Can you do me a favour if and when you get some down time?'

'Go for it.'

'I want to know the link between Gabriel and Oliver Elliot. Apart from the fact that Gabriel broke into his house, they know each other somehow. Can you do some digging?'

'Absolutely. Now, get yourself off home, it's still your birthday, just.' Rob squeezed Sheridan's hand. 'Happy birthday, boss.'

◆ ◆ ◆

As Sheridan approached her front door, Sam opened it. She was wearing a paper party hat and holding a glass of champagne, which she handed to Sheridan. After giving Sheridan a big kiss, Sam said, 'I know you've had a really shit day, but we've only got six minutes until it's not your birthday, so come with me.' She took an amused Sheridan by the hand and led her to the kitchen. On the table was a cake and a card.

As Sheridan opened her card, she couldn't take her eyes off the cake.

'Darling, why is there a creepy clown face on my cake?'

Sam closed her eyes and shook her head. 'It's not a clown. It's you as a little girl. I got the photograph from your mum and dad . . .'

Sheridan kissed her. 'I was kidding. I know it's me, it's brilliant,' she lied. It looked absolutely nothing like her, but Sam had clearly gone to a lot of effort and that was what mattered. Sort of.

'Really? You can tell it's you?' Sam said eagerly.

'Of course I can. I can't wait to taste it.'

Sam launched into her rehearsed description of the ingredients that Rosie had given her, and Sheridan listened as she sipped her champagne. As Sam cut her a piece, Sheridan noticed a sweet but strange taste. *Yeah, Sam definitely cooked this,* she thought as she put her thumb up. 'It's delicious.'

◆ ◆ ◆

Later, as they climbed into bed, Sheridan knew that sleep wouldn't come easily. Sam put her arm behind Sheridan's neck and pulled her close, resting her head on her chest. 'You okay?'

'Yeah. Sorry, my mind's on this job. You get some sleep.'

'We can talk about it if you want. You know I love it when you tell me policey stuff.'

'Yeah, but we never talk about *your* job, it's always mine.'

'My job is what it is; I love talking about yours. Chopped-off hands and toothbrushes, what's not to love?' She gently placed her hand on Sheridan's head. 'Sorry. That sounds like I'm making light of what happened to Caroline Crow.' She sighed. 'I'll never really know the horrors of what you see and deal with every day, or the horrors of what people do to each other.'

CHAPTER 91

Tuesday 12 May

Sheridan was gathering her interview notes when Rob peered around her door.

'The duty solicitor's here for Adrian Crow.'

'Who is it?'

'Lindsey Brabner.'

Sheridan frowned. 'The Bionic Woman?'

Rob burst out laughing. 'No. That was Lindsay Wagner.'

'Oh yeah.' Sheridan grinned.

'If you haven't met her before, watch out. She's ruthless. It's a shame she's not a prosecutor, we could do with her on our side.'

'Thanks for that, Rob.' She stood up. 'Sheridan Holler versus The Bionic Woman. Bring it on.'

Sheridan made her way down to the cells and she and Anna went through the disclosure with Lindsey Brabner. Afterwards, Adrian was brought out for a private consultation with her.

Ten minutes later, Lindsey Brabner appeared. 'DI Holler, can I have a word?'

Adrian Crow was taken back to his cell and Sheridan joined Lindsey. 'Are you ready for interview?' Sheridan asked.

'I won't be representing him.' She raised an eyebrow.

‘Why?’ said Sheridan.

‘Because he says he doesn’t need legal representation. That I am incompetent, and he’d rather represent himself than have, and I quote, “a fucking buffoon” representing him.’

‘Oh,’ Sheridan replied, grimacing.

‘I’ve been a solicitor for a long time, but I can honestly say I have never met such a pretentious prick in all that time. And I’ve met a lot of pretentious pricks.’ She noticed the grin on Sheridan’s face and reciprocated. ‘You appear to have a great deal of evidence against him.’

‘We do.’

‘Good.’

Sheridan bit her bottom lip. ‘Sorry, I know I’m smiling, but it’s just that I’ve never heard a defence solicitor talk like that about a client.’

‘He’s not my client. Thank Christ.’ She snapped her briefcase shut. ‘Oh, and you and I will be working together soon.’

Sheridan frowned. ‘We will?’

‘Yes. I’m switching sides in a few weeks.’ She smiled broadly. ‘I’m joining the Crown Prosecution Service.’ She put out her hand and Sheridan shook it.

‘I look forward to working with you.’ Sheridan smiled.

As Lindsey Brabner walked to the door, she turned around. ‘I hope you fucking nail him.’

Having declined alternative legal representation, Adrian Crow was now sitting in the interview room. Sheridan led the interview, while Anna took notes.

Sheridan asked him to go back to the day that he'd first met Caroline, but Adrian insisted he wanted to go back further than that.

And they had no idea what was coming.

Adrian sat back and, putting his hands behind his head, he told them how back in 1988 he'd picked up a young prostitute. It had been late at night, and she'd been loitering alone on a dark corner of a street in Liverpool, near the Albert Dock. He had beckoned her over to his car and she got in. He told her he didn't want sex, but just to get to know her – he'd still pay her for her time. He had picked her up several times after that, eventually taking her home to the farmhouse that he'd inherited from his parents. He cooked dinner for her. This went on for several months until one night Adrian asked her to marry him, and she laughed in his face. In the time they'd spent together, he'd learned enough about her to know that she was estranged from her family and had been working the streets for four years, earning enough to pay for her drug habit. He thought she loved him, he bought her gifts, promising to look after her if she moved in with him.

The night she laughed in his face was the night he put his hands around her throat and squeezed until she stopped breathing.

Sheridan tried not to react to this stone-cold admission of murder, calmly asking, 'What did you do with her body?'

'Oh, I'm sure you'll find her. I'm happy to talk, but I have to leave you a little bit of detective work to do.' Adrian grinned.

You piece of shit, Sheridan thought. 'What was her name?'

'Mary Lee. She was nineteen, from Manchester. You'll probably want to find her family and let them know that she died on the twenty-second of May 1988.'

'How do you remember the exact date?'

Adrian smiled. 'It was my fortieth birthday.'

The room fell silent for a moment. Without prompting, Adrian went on to tell them how ten years later, he went back to the spot where he'd picked up Mary Lee and that was when he saw Caroline for the first time. He'd watched from a distance as she talked to the young prostitutes, handing them what he thought were drugs. Assuming Caroline herself was a sex worker, he decided he liked the look of her and followed her to the bus stop one night. He pulled his car over and offered her a lift as it was raining. She had politely declined, saying she'd wait for the bus to come along. So he got out of the car, leaving the keys in the ignition, and told her that he would wait in the rain – she could sit in his car until the bus came. She could even take the keys. So she did. Then, half an hour later, with no sign of the bus, Caroline opened the car door and told a drenched Adrian to get in.

He drove her to her little flat in Dingle. They sat outside in his car talking for a long time. She didn't invite him up.

She gave him her number and agreed to meet him for a drink the following weekend, in the pub on the corner of her road.

He smiled as he recalled, 'It turned out she wasn't a prostitute like the girls she was talking to. She was actually handing them leaflets, not drugs. She was trying to help them get off the streets. Just doing the Good Samaritan thing.'

A year later, he proposed. Caroline accepted. They had a quiet registry office wedding before heading off to France for their honeymoon.

'Everything was wonderful up until about a year or so ago. She started acting strangely – became distant. I knew something was wrong. That was when I hid a camera in the bird box on the tree at the front of the house. I could see whoever turned up. It also showed part of the kitchen and the door leading into the downstairs spare room. I used to sit up the road and watch on my laptop. As soon as I was out of the house, *he'd* turn up. I watched them go into the spare bedroom downstairs, he'd follow her in there and then she'd appear a while later, putting her clothes back on. Little slag.'

'Who's "he"?' Sheridan asked.

'Simon Banks.' Adrian frowned. 'I actually didn't know his name until you told me. I knew where he lived because I followed him there. I thought she was just having an affair with *him*, but then when she had them flowers delivered, I knew she was fucking *that* guy as well.'

'Which guy?' Sheridan asked, already knowing the answer to the question. She'd known all along that Gabriel Howard had delivered the bouquet and Adrian Crow was about to confirm that for her.

'The guy who delivered the flowers. The one who was at the house yesterday with the knife. Little prick. I thought I'd sorted him out. He followed me one night when I left my house to go to the farmhouse, to spend some time with Caroline. So, I waited for him and drove the Land Rover into him. I wanted to finish him off, but another car came along so I had to drive off.'

'Did you reverse the Land Rover with the intention of killing him?'

'Well, I wasn't going back to introduce myself.' Adrian shook his head. 'Of course I was going to kill him.'

'His name is Gabriel Howard. Was he the guy that you saw deliver the flowers to Caroline?'

'Yes. I didn't know she'd ordered them. I still don't know why, or who they were for, but I was watching on the camera when he turned up. She opened the door in her dressing gown, took the flowers and he waited outside. A minute or so later, she'd got dressed and let him in. He was there long enough to fuck her and when he came back out, he was putting his coat back on.' Adrian yawned and rubbed his face, clearly trying to show how bored he was. 'When he turned up with the flowers, I thought he was yet another lover, so when he left, I followed him and banged into the back of his car. I tried to get him to exchange details, but he wasn't having any of it. When he drove away, I tried to follow him, but the traffic was shit, and I lost him. That's when I drove home and caught Simon Banks driving away from the house in his big fucking Mercedes.'

'So, at that time, you assumed Caroline was sleeping with Gabriel?'

'Yes, but then you told me that Caroline had ordered the flowers herself, so I figured he was just a delivery guy. But her being the slag she was, she probably invited him in for a shag. Why else would he have gone inside?'

That's a question I'm going to ask him, thought Sheridan.

'Is there still a camera in the bird box?' she asked, knowing that the technical support team had been through Adrian's laptop, and he'd wiped it clean.

'No. I got rid of it just after I killed Caroline,' he said bluntly. No emotion. No more fake tears.

'When did you plan to kill Caroline?'

Adrian stretched his legs out. 'A few months ago. I would have done it sooner, but it's trickier than you think, getting into someone else's hotel room. I tried a few times when I was away on business, but I got lucky when we were in Llandudno.'

'Why did you need to get into someone's hotel room?' Sheridan asked. *Go on, say it – to get their hairbrush and toothbrush*, Sheridan thought.

'To take their hairbrush and toothbrush, so that after I killed Caroline and sent her hands to her lovers, you wouldn't match them with her DNA when I reported her missing. I saw a great programme on it once, really informative.' He smiled. 'Do you watch cop programmes? You really should, you might learn something.'

Sheridan ignored the comment. 'You were asked by Jack Staples if Caroline used an electric toothbrush. You told him that she didn't. Do you not think that looked a little bit suspicious on your part?'

Adrian considered. 'I had no choice but to say that. When he asked me, I thought you might be on to something. So, I said what I said because it might put suspicion back on her. You might think that it was her who planted it.' He smiled smugly. 'Clever, eh?'

So clever that you're in custody. Prick, thought Sheridan. 'How did you kill Caroline?' she asked.

'The same humane way I killed Mary Lee. I strangled her.' He put his head down momentarily. 'You see, I loved Caroline, I adored her and that's what hurt me so much. Knowing she was being unfaithful. I wanted her to die, but I didn't want her to suffer. I'm not an animal. I'm a fair man.'

'Why did you keep her in the freezer?'

Adrian sighed. 'Because even after all she'd done, I still loved her in a strange way. I wanted to keep her for a while, you know, spend time with her and talk about what she'd done to me.'

'How often did you go to the farmhouse and sit her at the table?' Sheridan asked. *You fucking freak*, she thought.

'A couple of times a week. I liked to have dinner with her.' Adrian crossed his arms. 'I expect you're thinking that I'm some kind of freak, but I'm really not.'

'Tell me what happened between the time you went to Llandudno, to when you killed Caroline.'

CHAPTER 92

Adrian went on to describe how, when they arrived at the hotel on Sunday 8 March, Caroline had been delighted with the surprise of a bottle of champagne Adrian had ordered for their room. They opened it as soon as they arrived and toasted her upcoming birthday. After a walk along the promenade, they headed back to the hotel for dinner. That was the first time Adrian spotted the woman eating alone. She was small-framed, like Caroline. Casually dressed in a pair of jeans and a top, like Caroline. With shoulder-length brown hair. Just like Caroline. She was perfect. As she left the restaurant that night, Adrian knocked over his wine glass, making the excuse to Caroline that he was going up to their room to change. Instead, he followed the woman and discovered that she was staying just along the corridor from them.

The following morning, they went down for breakfast and the woman turned up a few minutes later. Adrian watched her and noted what time she left.

The next day – Tuesday – Adrian and Caroline were leaving their room to go down to breakfast, when he spotted the woman coming out of her room. As they passed, Caroline didn't notice that he stopped and bent down to adjust his shoelaces, flipping the woman's 'Do Not Disturb' sign over as he did so the other side was visible. As he reached the lift, Caroline said she'd forgotten her cardigan and would meet him downstairs. Adrian got into the lift with the woman, and Caroline rejoined him for breakfast a few minutes later.

As breakfast was served, Adrian told Caroline that he had a surprise for her birthday, and that he had to go and pick it up. He told her to take her time and he'd meet her back in the room in an hour or so.

Instead, he headed to their room. On seeing the housekeeper's trolley outside the woman's room, he took a quick look inside. The housekeeper was busily wiping the window ledge. That was when he grabbed the trolley and pushed it over, before stepping around the corner and hiding, while she came out and proceeded to start sorting out the mess all over the floor. While she was occupied, Adrian walked into the woman's room and grabbed the hairbrush and toothbrush from the bathroom. Noticing a lipstick, he took that too. He also spotted a top laid out on the bed and a bottle of water on the bedside table, so he took these as well. With the housekeeper still scrabbling around outside, he left, unnoticed. Once back in his room, he wrapped the items in a hand towel, hid them inside his jacket and made his way downstairs. After driving into town, he parked up away from any CCTV cameras and hid the items under the spare wheel in the boot. He then went to buy Caroline's card which he wrote out, before returning to the hotel.

As he got out of the lift, he passed the woman's room and could hear her shouting at the manager, complaining about the staff being thieves and how she was going to sue them.

Anna wrote a note for Sheridan's eyes only. *Remind me to tell you that you're a genius.*

Sheridan flicked a look at the message, and then focused back on Adrian, who was explaining what had happened on the day he killed Caroline. Her birthday.

◆ ◆ ◆

Two months earlier
Wednesday 11 March

Adrian pulled up on the drive outside the house. 'I'll grab the bags, sweetheart. You go on inside.'

Caroline leant over and kissed him on the cheek. 'Thank you. And thank you for a wonderful few days. Best birthday ever.' She gently touched his face before getting out of the car.

As she opened the front door and stepped inside, Adrian appeared behind her and she turned around. 'I thought you were getting the bags.'

'I need to do something first.' He closed the front door and wrapped his arms around her, pulling her in closely. They stood in the middle of the kitchen for a moment. He kissed her forehead and slid his hands down to her neck. And then he started squeezing.

'Adrian . . .' Caroline's eyes began to bulge. A strange sound escaped her lips as she grabbed his wrists, desperately trying to release his grip. He closed his eyes and pushed his thumbs against her windpipe, feeling her body sink down as her legs buckled under her. With his hands still clamped around her throat, he slowly dropped to the floor with her.

Even though he knew she was dead, he lay there on top of her for a few moments longer, his hands aching with the force he was using. Eventually, he let go.

Leaving her there, he went into the bedroom and removed the duvet, which he used to wrap her body in. After taking the suitcases, and the items he'd taken from the woman's hotel room out of the car, he laid Caroline in the boot. Returning to the house, he packed all her clothes into black bags and removed anything from her bedside table and en-suite bathroom that could have her DNA on it. He removed the sheets and pillowcases from the bed, replacing them with a clean set from the airing cupboard. When he'd travelled to Norfolk, he'd purchased new toiletries, which he had planted in Caroline's bathroom on his return, before he'd reported her missing.

After loading everything into the car, he drove to the farmhouse. Carrying Caroline's body into the small derelict warehouse alongside it, he laid her out on a large wooden table.

And then he sawed her hands off.

The process made him retch. He vomited twice, but the anger he felt towards her at that moment consumed him. Her hands that had held him for eleven years – that had touched his skin so many times – were the same ones she had touched other men with. Other men who would now receive those hands on their doorsteps. If they wanted his wife's hands so much, they were welcome to them.

Outside, he threw paper and wood into a disused metal drum and watched the flames grow higher and higher, the heat burning his face. He waited for them to die down until all that was left were red-hot burning embers. And then he threw her hands in, watching as the skin crackled and turned black, removing any trace of the lovers she had touched. And her fingerprints.

He went back into the house and strapped Caroline's body to a small wooden chair, lifting her head slightly so he could look at her. 'It could have been so different, Caroline. We could have been so happy. But you ruined it. Why did you do that? Why have you done this to me?' Heavy tears fell down his face as he pulled the chair over to the upright freezer and dragged her inside. Closing the door, he heard her voice. He could hear her singing, so he reopened the freezer. Her lifeless body still and her eyes slightly open. He put his face up to hers. 'Don't you fucking speak. You only speak when I tell you to. Have you got that?'

Nothing.

'Have you got that?!' The scream was so loud, it tore at his throat. Closing his eyes, he heard her reply.

'Yes.'

'Good.' He slammed the door shut.

Moments later he was back in the warehouse, packaging up her hands. Ready to deliver them. He knew where the Mercedes guy lived, so he'd be first. The one who had taken Caroline flowers, now he'd be a bit trickier, but Adrian would watch the camera and if he turned up again, then he'd follow him. And this time, he'd make sure he didn't lose him.

◆ ◆ ◆

Sheridan had let Adrian talk, without interruption. But as Adrian paused, she asked, 'So, you planned it all? The packaging that you wrapped her hands in – did you buy that beforehand, knowing what you were going to do?'

'Luckily for me, that was already in the house. You see, my parents owned the pet food company I now work for as a rep. The farmhouse is where I grew up, and the business was originally run from there. My mother was never a particularly well woman and she died in 1985. My father succumbed to cancer and died two years later. He knew he was dying so he sold the business, with the agreement that the new owners would keep me on. The business moved location, but we stayed in the farmhouse until my father died. Then, eventually I inherited his money and the house.' He took a sip of water. 'I was going to stay there, but then I met Mary Lee.' His jaw clenched. 'After I buried her body, the place didn't seem the same, so I moved out and used my inheritance to buy the house I live in now.'

'So, once you put Caroline in the freezer and packaged up her hands, what happened next?'

'I went home, cleaned the house, hoovered it, wiped everything down that I could think of. Then I put the hairbrush, toothbrush, lipstick and the bottle of water in place. Put some hairs from the woman's hairbrush on the pillow and in the bed. And I left her top in the wardrobe.' He smiled.

'What are you smiling about?' Sheridan asked.

'I'm smiling because it's just dawned on me how smart I am.'

Not that smart – we caught you, thought Sheridan. 'Then what?' she asked.

'Then I got Caroline's secret little phone out of her wardrobe and rang myself.'

'The call from Henry Blanchflower?'

'Exactly.'

'How did you know about Caroline's secret phone?'

'I found it months ago when I was going through her things. She was at swimming club, and I knew she was being unfaithful. I saw the same number that she'd called. The *only* number she'd ever called. I rang it myself a couple of times from a payphone, but no one ever answered.'

'So, you then booked the hotel in Norfolk for your pretend appointment with Henry Blanchflower?'

'Yes. Then, I drove to Simon Banks' house and left a little present on his doorstep.' Adrian grinned. 'I would have paid good money to see his face when he opened it.'

'How did you manage to leave it on his doorstep without being seen?'

'I walked across the field behind his house. When I got to his front door, I saw a light come on inside and thought he'd heard me. I didn't want him to open the door and see the package straight away, he might have seen me leaving, so, I left the package under the ivy, just sticking out a bit.'

'What did you do with the other hand?' Sheridan asked.

'I put it in my freezer at home until I was ready to deliver it to the flower guy. Luckily Jack Staples didn't look in there when he came to the house.' Adrian laughed. 'That would have been tricky. Might have had to kill him, which would be a shame because he's a good fella.'

Sheridan resisted the urge to punch him in the face. 'Why did you leave the other hand on your own doorstep?'

'Well, I wanted the flower guy to have it, but I didn't know where he lived. I thought it was a clever idea to take any suspicion off me, leaving the parcel on my own doorstep. I waited until the postman arrived, so that he could be a witness when I opened the package. Poor fella, I thought he was going to faint.' Adrian smirked.

'Why did you put Caroline's suitcase in the river behind Simon Banks' house?'

'Oh, come on Detective, surely you can work that one out.' Adrian put his hands out, palms up.

Why don't you just fuck off? 'Why don't you just tell me?' Sheridan sat back.

'Because you told me he'd taken money out of Caroline's account and then he'd left the country, so I realised I could pin suspicion on him that he was involved in Caroline's disappearance.'

'Why did you leave her passport in there?'

Adrian cracked his knuckles and sat back. 'To make it look like she'd planned to go abroad with Simon Banks.'

'Did you know Caroline had applied for a new passport?'

'No.' He ran a hand through his hair. 'I also didn't know she'd stopped going to swimming classes, or that she used to take drugs or that she had children.' He shook his head. 'People shouldn't keep secrets, eh? Caroline would still be alive if she hadn't fucked around behind my back. She kept her lovers a secret from me. And those fucking love letters.'

Sheridan looked up from her notes. 'Love letters?' She opened a file on the table and took out the random notes that Caroline had written, the ones found hidden in her wardrobe. She slid them across the table to Adrian. 'These love letters?' Sheridan asked.

Adrian scanned the notes:

My darling, I know we can't be together and that breaks both our hearts. I lie in bed and think of you

I love you so much it hurts.

I just want to be with you

I've kept the earrings you gave me, I feel so bad that I can't wear them, but I look at them every now and then and know they were given to me with love, with your love

I bought you this watch so that every time you look at it, you'll remember the wonderful times we spent together. If it's too difficult to wear it, then put it away somewhere and maybe just take it out when you can. Maybe you can say you bought it yourself rather than me if that makes it easier. I'd love you to wear it but understand if you can't

I long to hold you

I'm so sorry that I kept so many secrets from you, please don't be angry with me. I love you. I hated going behind your back. But I did it because of love

You have been the one but I can't hide this love any more

I hated all the lies I've told. You deserved a better wife than me

I've lied and lied and lied to you

After reading them, he turned away. 'Yes.'

'So you'd already seen them before we showed them to you?'

'Of course. And that's when I knew for sure that she had been going behind my back. The watch she refers to, that's the one Simon Banks bought with the money he took out of her account, the one he left in the coal shed.'

'We searched the coal shed, there was nothing there.'

'Of course there wasn't. I saw Simon Banks on the camera the day I went to Norfolk. I watched on my laptop, and I saw him go to the coal shed and put something inside. So, when I came home on the Friday, I found Caroline's bank card and the watch.' He licked his lip. 'I knew the watch was for him. She probably wanted to wrap it up in some fancy fucking box before she gave it back to him.'

Sheridan wrote herself a note. *Simon Banks said that Caroline asked him to take £400 out of her account to buy a train ticket. Speak to him.*

Adrian cracked his knuckles again. 'Can I get something to eat? I'm starving.'

Sheridan stopped the interview and Adrian was taken back to his cell.

As they made their way upstairs, Hill was coming out of her office. 'Update me in a minute – but they've found something in the coat that Caroline was wearing when you found her.'

CHAPTER 93

Sheridan and Anna stood in Hill's office. 'What did they find?' Sheridan asked.

Hill read from her computer screen. 'Zomorph. Morphine to you and me. It's a slow-release capsule. And it wasn't prescribed by her GP.'

Sheridan nodded. 'Simon Banks told us that she knew people who could get drugs for her, but he said she was trying to get clean.'

Hill removed her glasses and chewed on the arm of them. 'There's also a strip of Prochlorperazine, anti-sickness tablets, which you can get over the counter.'

'I need to speak to Simon and Gabriel. Can we get an extension on Adrian's custody time? I think this is going to take a while,' Sheridan replied.

Sheridan updated Hill with the interview so far and Hill agreed to getting them more time.

Then Sheridan called Simon Banks and arranged to meet him at his office within the hour. She decided it was best not to tell him over the phone that Caroline was dead.

Simon Banks burst into tears when she broke the news. 'Oh God, poor, poor Caroline.' He wept, repeating his words over and over. His anguish genuine.

'I'm sorry, Simon. I know this must come as a huge shock to you,' Sheridan said gently.

They were in his office. She told Simon how Adrian had concluded that Simon was sleeping with Caroline, and how he had sent him the hand before planting her suitcase and passport in the river behind his house.

Simon sat, his hand over his mouth, taking it all in.

'Were you and Caroline in a relationship?' Sheridan asked.

Simon shook his head. 'No. We were just friends.'

'Adrian said he saw you go into the house on numerous occasions and said you went into the downstairs spare bedroom, is that true?'

'I did visit her at the house when Adrian was at work, but there was nothing in it. I only went into the bedroom once.' He sighed. 'The bedroom's at the back of the house. Outside the window was a bush, and there was a family of thrushes living in it. I remember Caroline showing me them, she used to love having wildlife in the garden. Adrian put a bird box up in the tree at the front of the house for her, so she could sit in the kitchen and watch it.'

Sheridan cleared her throat. 'Adrian put the box up so he could fit a camera in there – that's how he knew you were visiting her.'

Simon's eyes widened. 'Christ. So he thought I was having an affair? That's why he tried to set me up?'

'Yes,' Sheridan replied. 'You told us that Caroline knew people who could get drugs for her. We found morphine in her pocket.'

Simon sat back, placing his hands on the desk. 'Morphine?'

'Yes. And anti-sickness tablets.'

'Well, that makes sense. Morphine can make you feel quite sick and disorientated, so she must have been taking them to stop the side-effects.'

'But she told you she was going away to get clean?'

'Yes. But I think we've learned by now that Caroline had a lot of secrets.'

There was a knock on the door and Simon's secretary appeared. 'I'm sorry, Dr Banks, but you're needed urgently.'

Simon stood up. 'I'm sorry, I have to go.'

Sheridan looked down at her notes. 'I need to ask you some more questions. Can you let me know when you've got time? It'll have to be today or tomorrow.'

'I'll call you,' Simon Banks replied, before heading out of the office.

◆ ◆ ◆

Sheridan left the hospital and updated Hill and Anna that she was going to see Gabriel Howard.

He opened the door as soon as she knocked. 'DI Holler, what a pleasant—'

'Can I come in?' Sheridan cut him short before following him through to the living room. He sat in the armchair while Sheridan plonked herself on the sofa.

'So, what can I do for you?' Gabriel smiled. A smile that quickly disappeared when he saw Sheridan's jaw tighten.

'You lied to me.' She told him how Adrian Crow had a recording that proved that he had been the one who delivered the flowers to Caroline Crow. Not his sister, Denise.

'So, cut the shit, Gabriel, and tell me the truth. Why did you go inside?'

Gabriel now looked very uncomfortable. 'Because she asked me to.'

'Tell me exactly what happened.'

'I did the delivery because Denise was desperate. I knew the address was inside my exclusion zone, but I went anyway because I didn't want to let her down.' He swallowed. 'When I got to the house, Caroline opened the door and took the flowers, then she asked me to wait while she made herself look respectable because she was in her dressing gown. Then when she came back to the door, she said she was having a spring clean and asked me to help her move a sideboard.'

'Where was the sideboard?'

'In the kitchen. She said she'd moved it to one side to clean under it, but couldn't get it back in place, so I moved it for her, we chatted for a bit and then I left.' He ran a hand through his hair.

'Did something happen when you drove away from the house?'

'Like what?'

'Did anything happen to your car?'

'Oh, yeah – some bloke drove into the back of me. He wanted to exchange details, but I knew I couldn't do that because I was inside my exclusion zone, so I managed to blag that I didn't want to take it any further.'

'That was Adrian Crow. He thought you were sleeping with Caroline. He wanted to follow you home.' Sheridan watched as Gabriel processed this information.

'Really? He looked different. He had these thick glasses on and a stupid hat. I didn't recognise him when we were at the farmhouse.'

'How come you left your gloves there?'

'I took my coat and gloves off when I went inside, because it was boiling hot in there. I left my gloves on the chair and just forgot them. Caroline called Denise and told her that she'd post them back to me, and that I wasn't to go back to the house because she was leaving that day to go away.'

'Did she say anything to you when you went inside?'

'Not really. She just thanked me for helping her.'

'So, that's what you meant when you were in hospital and told me you'd help me, but only if Denise didn't get into trouble.'

Gabriel's silence answered the question for her.

Sheridan continued, 'You went back to that house though, didn't you?'

Gabriel searched her face, seeming to weigh up how much he wanted to tell her. But he was trapped. He couldn't deny that he'd been back there because if Adrian had cameras set up, then he'd have caught him. Gabriel knew about the police cameras and had managed to avoid them, but he hadn't banked on there being others. He had no choice now. He had to come clean.

'Yes. I went back there. After I found out that Caroline was missing, I knew I had to remove my fingerprints from the sideboard in case she ended up dead and there was a murder enquiry. But the first few nights the police were there and so I couldn't get in, and I had to keep going back until I saw an opportunity. And that's the first night I saw Adrian Crow climb out of his window.'

'So, that's how you got in. He left it unlocked and you climbed in?'

'Yeah. I did think that maybe I was too late, and the police had already got my prints off the sideboard. But when you didn't say anything, I assumed you hadn't found them, so I wiped it clean anyway.' He shook his head. 'It took me two seconds to wipe the sideboard down and about half an hour to clean up the water.'

'Water?'

'Yeah, it was raining so hard that I got soaked and had to use one of his towels from the airing cupboard to dry the floor with. I had to take it with me when I left.'

Sheridan sat back, a puzzled look on her face. And then realisation kicked in. 'That was the night I saw you running in the rain. The night you got into my car.' She shook her head. 'The towel you were carrying was the one you took from his house?'

'Yeah.' He put his head down. 'I tried to tell you that night about Adrian Crow. I'd just seen him climb out of that window and I desperately wanted to tell you that I had proof he was dodgy, without telling you how I knew.'

Sheridan crossed one leg over the other. 'I read your statement about how you found a knife on the floor at the farmhouse. That's a load of bullshit, isn't it? So, you carry knives around?'

'No. I found it on the floor,' he lied.

Sheridan didn't answer but noted the wry look on his face and knew she had no proof to throw at him. They sat in silence for a moment before Gabriel said, 'So, I guess I'm going back to prison?'

Sheridan stood up. 'What for?'

'Well, you've got me on camera going into Adrian's house . . .'

'Have I?' Sheridan took her car keys out of her pocket. 'I said Adrian set up cameras and watched the house. I never said we've got any of the recordings.' She stepped towards the door. 'Thanks for your time, Gabriel. I'll be in touch.' Without another word, she let herself out.

CHAPTER 94

Wednesday 13 May

Sheridan and Anna pulled up at the farmhouse, which was swarming with forensic officers. Sheridan stepped inside and the smell that had hit her two days before still lingered, like it had soaked into the walls. The smell of death. She stared at the table where Caroline had been sitting.

Anna came up behind her. 'It's a weird smell, isn't it?' she said, placing her sleeve over her nose.

'Yeah. You never get used to it,' Sheridan replied.

'Rob just called; he's tracked down Mary Lee's mother. She still lives in Manchester. Dipesh is heading out there now with an FLO to talk to her,' Anna said.

Sheridan nodded, her mind distracted.

Anna continued, oblivious. 'Her mother hadn't had any contact with her for a few years before Adrian says he killed her. She said Mary was wayward, and assumed she'd made a life for herself somewhere. Or was dead.' She turned to Sheridan. 'Are you alright?'

'Yeah.' Her phone rang, it was Hill.

'Hi, Sheridan, just to let you know we should be getting the post-mortem results today on Caroline. Then you need to crack on with Adrian's interview.'

'Okay, cheers, Hill.'

Anna followed Sheridan through the house, the floorboards creaking eerily under their feet. The wallpaper in the hallway was drab and old-fashioned, a spiral pattern that belonged in the 1970s.

Suddenly, Sheridan stopped.

'What's wrong?' Anna asked.

Sheridan spun around. 'We need to get to Adrian's house.'

Snapping on a pair of latex gloves, Sheridan walked into Adrian's open-plan kitchen. The smell that had wafted in this room when she and Anna had visited before was still present. And stronger. Walking over to the window, she placed her hand on the sideboard that Gabriel had put back in place for Caroline after she had tried to push it, its weight too much for her.

'Grab that end.' She nodded to Anna, and together they pushed as hard as they could, eventually shifting it a few inches. And then a few more, until eventually they'd moved it a few feet.

That was when Sheridan saw the floorboard, sticking up very slightly.

As she knelt down, the smell became stronger. She looked at Anna, before levering the floorboard up. It came away easily and she placed it to one side before peering into the space.

They both saw it at the same time.

Anna's eyes widened. 'So, *that*'s what the smell is.'

At that moment, Sheridan's phone rang – it was Hill.

'We've got the post-mortem results back on Caroline Crow.'

'And?' Sheridan was still staring down at the gap in the floorboards.

'And it's not what we were expecting.'

CHAPTER 95

Sheridan waited for Adrian Crow to sit down, making himself comfortable in the interview room. Anna placed a cup of water in front of him and he took a sip.

Sheridan began. 'Adrian, you told us that you believed that Caroline was being unfaithful to you.'

He scratched his chin and sighed. 'She was.'

'You also told us that you don't know why she ordered the bouquet of flowers.'

'Correct.'

'And you told us that you didn't know she had two children.'

'Correct.'

'You believed that she asked Simon Banks to buy a watch for himself, so that Caroline could wrap it up nicely for him, as a gift.'

'Correct.' He yawned, resting his head back and looking at the ceiling.

'You got it all wrong, Adrian. You misread *everything.*'

'I don't think so,' he replied, arrogantly.

Sheridan took a breath before she hit him with it. 'Caroline bought the bouquet of flowers for *you,* Adrian.'

He stared at her.

'I'll come back to that.' Sheridan glanced down at her notes. 'Adrian. We have the post-mortem results back. Did you know that Caroline was ill?'

Adrian frowned. 'Ill?'

'Yes. You see, the reason she was behaving oddly was because she was ill. *Very* ill. Everything makes sense now – the reason she stopped going to swimming classes, the reason she told everyone she was going away. She was making plans, but you killed her before she managed to carry them out. Caroline wasn't being unfaithful to you. And you didn't have to kill her.'

'What do you mean?'

'Caroline was dying, Adrian. She had stage-four lung cancer. She probably only had a few weeks to live.'

Sheridan didn't pause before continuing: 'The notes you found that you believed were to a lover, were nothing of the sort.' Sheridan pulled out the piece of paper from the file in front of her. The notes Caroline had written, the ones Adrian had found and read before. She had highlighted some of them, which she now pointed out to him.

> *I lay in bed and think of you*
>
> *I've kept the earrings you gave me, I feel so bad that I can't wear them, but I look at them every now and then and know they were given to me with love, with your love*
>
> *I bought you this watch so that every time you look at it, you'll remember the wonderful times we spent together. If it's too difficult to wear it, then put it away somewhere and maybe just take it out when you can. Maybe you can say you bought it yourself rather than me if that makes it easier. I'd love you to wear it but understand if you can't*

I long to hold you

I hated all the lies I've told. You deserved a better wife than me

I've lied and lied and lied to you

Adrian glanced down at them, before crossing his arms.

Sheridan carried on. 'You see, she wrote these notes in preparation for the *actual* letters she wrote later. The *actual* letters that we found under the floorboards, along with the earrings, Caroline's new passport and the bouquet of flowers. This is the letter she wrote to *you*.' Sheridan cleared her throat and began to read.

'"My darling Adrian. Before I start, I want you to know that I love you, I have always loved you, you have been the one for me – the most wonderful husband a woman could ever have. But I have been keeping a secret from you, in fact, so many secrets and I've lied and lied and lied to you. I'm sorry. There are so many things I haven't told you about me. I have two children, Scott and Phoebe. I let them down and was never the mother they deserved, but with what's happening to me now, I have to go to them. I have to see my children before I die. You see, my darling, I have cancer and I know I don't have long left, so I have been planning this for a while. I'm going to see my children and then I'm going to find somewhere quiet and peaceful to end my life *my* way. I don't want the cancer to be the thing that kills me. And I don't want you to see me in my final hours, I want you to remember me as I was. Do you remember the first bouquet of flowers you ever bought me? I do. I remember every flower – the sweet pea, the white roses, the dahlia and the beautiful lilies and their wonderful smell. It was the most beautiful bouquet and I wanted you to remember me, so I bought an identical bouquet and I'm going to dry the flowers out, ready for you to press and maybe keep in a book, when I'm gone. Treasure them as I treasured you. I love you, Adrian. My beautiful husband. Please don't come looking for me, if you adore me the way you always said you did, then allow me this. Allow me to do this my way."'

Sheridan put the letter down on the table, then looked up at Adrian. 'We couldn't figure out what the smell was in your kitchen, but now we know it was coming from the bouquet of flowers she'd hidden under the floorboards. She put them there ready to dry them out for you. For you to treasure. But she never got the chance and so they just lay there, rotting. She knew she was ill, and she was just making plans to see her children before she died. You read it *all* wrong, Adrian.'

Adrian didn't reply. He'd listened. His eyes were closed tight.

Sheridan pulled out the next letter. 'This is the letter she wrote to her daughter, Phoebe. Obviously, Caroline didn't know that Phoebe had died.' Sheridan took a sip of water and then continued, '"My darling Phoebe. As I write this letter, I am making plans to come and see you. I hope that when I do see you, you will allow me to hold you. I love you. Even though I was a terrible mother, I never stopped loving you. Do you remember when you were a little girl, and you gave me a pair of earrings for Christmas? Well, I kept them, I treasured them and felt so bad that I couldn't wear them. I tried to but the metal they're made of made my skin react, but I look at them every now and then and I know they were given to me with love, with your love. I want you to have them now. I love you, Phoebe. I hope that your life, up until now, has been wonderful and I hope you've found love and a good job – you were always so smart, so I know you'll have done well. I'm proud of you, my darling."'

Adrian's eyes were still closed and his jaw tightly clenched. But he still didn't speak.

Sheridan took out the last letter – the one addressed to Caroline's son, Scott. And she began to read.

'"My beautiful son, Scott. I'm sure you've grown into a strong and handsome young man. You were such a beautiful little boy and I'm sorry I wasn't there to see what you've become. I let you down so many times and I can never make up for that. I bought you this watch, you always wanted one when you were little. If it's too difficult to wear it, then put it away somewhere and maybe just take it out when you can. I'm not sure if your father will want to know that I've bought it for you, so maybe you can say you bought it yourself, rather than me, if that makes it easier. I'd love you to wear it, but understand if you can't. As I write this, I long to hold you, I know we can't be together and that breaks my heart. I have spent years, lying in bed thinking of you, and it hurts so much. I just wanted to be with you and Phoebe. Look after her for me, and look after yourself my beautiful boy. I love you."'

Tears fell down Adrian's face and he put his head in his hands. 'Please can I go back to my cell now?'

'We have more questions for you. But if you need a break—'

'I don't want to hear any more.'

Sheridan put the letters back in the file. 'Caroline just wanted to see her children before she died, and you took that from her. She loved you, Adrian, and you killed her. You killed her because you misread the notes she'd written. She wasn't being unfaithful. Simon Banks wasn't sleeping with her. He was just a friend. The watch was for her son, not for Simon. And Gabriel Howard? Well, he just happened to be the guy who delivered the flowers. You got it *all* wrong. You looked. But you didn't *see*.'

Adrian stood up. 'I want to go back to my cell.'

Sheridan raised her voice. 'Where's Mary Lee's body?'

Adrian placed his hands flat on the table and leaned towards Sheridan. 'Fuck you.'

CHAPTER 96

Sheridan and Anna were sitting in Hill's office.

'So, what's the plan?' Hill asked, directing her question at Sheridan.

'Dipesh is at the Cranmire Hospital now, checking the drug logs. If there's morphine missing, then we know Simon Banks was supplying Caroline with it. There's nothing in Caroline's medical records to show she'd been treated for cancer. I think it was Simon that diagnosed her, off the record, at the Cranmire Hospital. My theory is that Simon Banks lied when he told us that Caroline was taking herself off to get clean, and that she knew people who could get drugs for her. He was covering himself. Caroline was getting morphine from *him*. She gave him her bank card to buy the watch for her son and he knew she was going to see her kids.'

'Okay, well, let's see what Dipesh comes back with.'

Sheridan was in CID when her phone rang.

'It's Dipesh. You were right. There's entries in the drug delivery log going back over the last few months. They've been amended, although unfortunately you can't tell who's amended them.'

'What kind of drugs?'

'Morphine.'

Sheridan smiled. 'Okay. Cheers, Dipesh. Can you get Simon Banks here as a voluntary attender? Let's see what he's got to say.'

An hour later, Simon Banks was sitting in an interview room, the colour draining from his face as Sheridan asked him if he was aware that Caroline was terminally ill. Anna had offered to sit in on the interview, but Sheridan wanted to speak to him alone.

'No. I had no idea.' His voice was broken, and his shoulders dropped. 'I can't believe it. How did she keep this a secret?'

'Who has access to the drugs logs at the Cranmire Hospital?'

'Loads of people, why?'

'Were *you* supplying Caroline with morphine?'

'Jesus Christ, no, of course not. Why would I?'

'There're several discrepancies in the drug log, and morphine has gone missing. How do you explain that?'

'It happens. It's a busy hospital and sometimes the records don't get filled out properly.'

'Did you diagnose Caroline with cancer? At the hospital, but off the record?'

'This is ridiculous. Am I being accused of something here?'

'I'm just trying to find the truth.' Sheridan paused. 'When Caroline gave you her bank card, you told us that she asked you to take out four hundred pounds from her bank account to buy a train ticket. What did you do with the money?'

'I told you – I left it in the coal shed with her bank card.'

'You didn't buy a watch with the money?'

'Why would I buy a watch? I'm sorry, I don't know where this is all coming from.'

'Did you buy a watch with the four hundred pounds?'

'No.'

'Did you help Caroline find her children?'

'How could I have done? I didn't know she *had* children.'

Sheridan crossed her arms and left his answer hanging in the air. He didn't flinch and his expression didn't change. Eventually, Sheridan stood up. 'Thanks for your time, Simon. I'll show you out.'

As they reached the front desk, Sheridan held the door open, before saying under her breath, 'Did you love her?'

Simon Banks looked to the floor. 'I loved her as a friend, nothing more. She was a beautiful person, and she didn't deserve this.'

Sheridan put her hand out and Simon took it. As she shook his hand, she placed her other one on his wrist.

And then she pulled his sleeve back. He immediately pulled away, but Sheridan had already seen what she needed to see.

'Goodbye, Simon.' And with that, she turned and walked away.

CHAPTER 97

Simon Banks just made it through his front door before falling to his knees. Letting out a cry, he sobbed unashamedly and curled himself into a ball on the floor.

Eventually, he pulled himself up and went into the kitchen, pouring a large whisky, downing it in one and then pouring another. As he stood at his kitchen window, Caroline's face came into his head.

A sudden rush of guilt consumed him. Guilt for all the lies he had told the police. The lie that Caroline had taken herself off to get clean from the drugs that had ruined her. The lie he'd told Sheridan Holler about how Caroline still had contacts who could get her any drugs that she wanted. He had said it all to cover himself after Caroline was found. The last time he saw her, he'd given her enough morphine to stave off the pain of her cancer. And enough for her to end her own life. His mind went back to the day, almost a year before, when she'd called him and told him that she'd been feeling unwell and knew something was wrong. After she had refused to go to her doctor or A & E, he'd arranged to meet her outside the Cranmire Hospital, where, as darkness fell, he smuggled her inside and X-rayed her. Knowing immediately what he was looking at, he carried out a lung biopsy and created her as a patient on the hospital system, using false details. When the results came back, he carefully and gently told her that she had cancer. And it was bad. He begged her to seek treatment, but she was adamant that she didn't want to go through that. He begged her to get a formal, second opinion, which she also refused. She, in turn, had begged him to keep it their secret. And he had agreed.

He agreed because he'd do anything for her, his love for her was that strong. Simon Banks had fallen for Caroline from the moment he'd laid eyes on her – when she was first brought into A & E all those years ago. But he was married and ever faithful to his wife. After Caroline's diagnosis, she had told him about her children – the children she'd abandoned – and begged him to find them for her. Caroline didn't use computers and had no idea where to start. She also had no idea where her children might live now. The last letter she'd received from her ex-partner, William, had mentioned that they were no longer in the country. Had they moved abroad?

Caroline wanted to be prepared for everything. She wanted to be ready to leave at a moment's notice if Simon discovered her children were indeed living abroad. That was when she applied for a new passport. Simon Banks made sure nothing could be traced back to him and so he spent hours on the computer in the library, searching for her children. And he discovered that William and her son, Scott, ran pubs in Scotland. A little more digging and he found their home address in Scotland.

And that was when Caroline started finalising her plans.

By Saturday 7 March she almost had everything in place.

CHAPTER 98

Two months earlier
Saturday 7 March

Caroline Crow waited for Adrian to drive away, before retrieving her secret phone from the wardrobe and dialling Simon's number.

'Hi.' He sounded out of breath.

'Hi, are you okay to speak?'

'Yes, I'm fine, just out for a run.'

'Are you free to come round? It's safe – Adrian's at work all day.'

'I'll be there shortly. Do you need me to bring the usual?'

'Yes, please. I'll see you soon.' Caroline ended the call.

Thirty minutes later, he arrived at the house.

'How long have you got?' Caroline asked.

He checked his watch. 'Couple of hours.' He lifted his stethoscope out of his pocket and followed Caroline into the downstairs bedroom, where he respectfully turned away while she removed her top. As she faced the window, he listened to her lungs. He noticed that she'd lost weight – her sallow skin was stretched across protruding ribs.

He left her to get dressed while he returned to the kitchen.

'Come and look at this,' she called from the bedroom. Simon joined her as she pointed to the window, smiling. 'There's a song thrush family in the bush outside.'

Simon turned to her. 'I love how you still see the beauty in things. You are quite remarkable, you know.'

Without looking at him, she replied, 'I'm constantly tired and I have no energy. I can't even go to swimming club any more. I can hardly breathe most of the time.'

'Is there no way you'd think about going to your GP, tell him you haven't been feeling well? He'll send you for an—'

'I don't want to. And I don't regret never getting treatment, it was just meant to be that this has happened to me.'

He placed a hand gently on her shoulder. 'Is there *anything* I can do?'

'There is something.'

Caroline told Simon of her plans to travel to Scotland and see her children. He waited while she wrote a letter to her ex-partner, explaining her plans to travel there, and asked Simon to post the letter that day. Adrian had mentioned that he was taking her away for her birthday, but she had no idea where they were going or the exact date they were leaving. Or when she'd be back.

'Adrian still doesn't suspect anything, does he?' Simon asked.

'No. Definitely not. I've been super-careful. He can't find out what we're doing. I can't tell him – it would destroy him. I do need you to do something for me though, if you've got some time spare today.'

Handing him her bank card, she asked him if he could go into Liverpool and buy a watch for her son.

'Any particular type of watch?' he asked.

'Like the one you're wearing. I've always admired it.'

Simon told her he knew where to purchase the exact same one and that it would cost around £400.

'Take the four hundred out of my account and pay cash. If you can get it back to me today, that would be perfect. I'll have everything ready then for whenever Adrian and I get back from my birthday trip. That's when I'm going to go and see my children.' She smiled.

'What if I can't get the watch today?'

'Just get it when you can and leave it in the coal shed, with my card. Adrian never goes in there. He'll never find it.'

Simon put his head down and Caroline stepped forward, lifting his chin gently. 'What's wrong?'

'I've got to go to a conference in Oxford on Thursday and I'm back on Monday. Then I'm off to Australia to see my son for a couple of weeks.'

Caroline touched his cheek with the back of her hand. 'And you're worried that by the time you get back, I'll be gone.'

Simon placed his hand on top of hers. 'I love you, Caroline. I've always loved you.'

'I know. And I've always loved *you.* Hey, maybe in another life we'll find each other and—'

He put a finger over her lips. 'You have a good man in Adrian. He's a good husband.'

'I have no guilt, Simon. Even though you and I have always felt love for each other, I've remained faithful. I can rest easy knowing I never betrayed him.'

Simon nodded slowly, reached into his pocket and handed her a full box of Zomorph – slow-release morphine capsules. 'These will be enough.' His eyes stung with tears as she took them from him.

'You won't get caught over these, will you?' she asked.

'I haven't got caught yet, have I?'

She kissed him on the cheek and watched as he got back into his car.

His stomach heaved. He thought for a moment that he was going to be sick. Reaching for a bottle of water in the door, his hands trembling as he unscrewed the lid, he took a sip. His heart was breaking. He knew he might never see her again. It would all be over soon – she'd be gone, and he'd have to carry on. Carry on with the knowledge that he was the one who had been supplying her the morphine to ease the pain she was in. The same morphine she would take enough of to end it all, after she'd visited her children. He thought about getting caught but he knew he'd covered his tracks. He had been careful so far. Careful not to leave any evidence.

Anything that could link him to her.

As he drove away, he was unaware that sitting up the road, out of sight, was Adrian Crow. Watching the feed from the camera hidden in the bird box via the screen on his laptop.

CHAPTER 99

Simon made his way into Liverpool and withdrew the £400 from Caroline's account. Before he got the chance to purchase the watch, he received an urgent phone call from the hospital and had to make his way there. By the time he'd finished with his patient, it was too late to go back into the city, so he made his way to Caroline's house, knowing he had to at least give her back the bank card. As he pulled on to the drive, he looked up at the house and could see Caroline in the upstairs window. He was about to get out when he saw Adrian's car turn off the main road.

'Shit,' he said to himself, quickly starting the engine and turning the car around, before driving off, looking straight ahead as Adrian passed by.

◆ ◆ ◆

Caroline's heart was thundering in her chest as she watched Simon pull away. Quickly making her way downstairs, she tried to catch her breath. Glancing at the sideboard, she was satisfied it was back in its right place.

She had contacted the florist earlier to order the bouquet of flowers, asking the florist if they could deliver them within the hour. She needed to hide them under the floorboards before Adrian came home. When Simon had left the house that morning, she'd showered, before making the call, giving the name Julie Jones. She'd felt ridiculous giving a false name, but she'd thought it through. If Adrian came home early and the florist called back, or arrived with the delivery, she could say there had been a mistake, and she hadn't ordered any flowers. It was only after she'd put the phone down to the florist that she realised all she had to say to Adrian – if he came home early – was that she was treating herself to some flowers. But she'd said it now.

She'd eventually managed to move the sideboard enough to reveal the loose floorboard, but it had taken it out of her and left her exhausted. So when the young man arrived with the bouquet, she'd taken it from him and asked him to wait for a moment while she made herself respectable, telling him she needed a small favour. Once she'd closed the front door, she quickly hid the bouquet under the floorboard and put it back in place, before dressing and letting the delivery guy inside the house.

'I'm sorry to ask, but I've been having a spring clean and can't get this sideboard back where it was. I was hoping a strapping young man like you could push it back for me.'

Gabriel Howard had smiled as he stepped inside, feeling the heat from the place flush his cheeks. He slipped off his coat and Caroline took it from him, folding it over her arm while Gabriel tried to push the sideboard back in place. His hands slipped twice and after removing his gloves and placing them on the chair next to him, he tried again.

'It's stuck on that floorboard,' he said, using all his strength to try to tilt the sideboard enough to get it over the floorboard. 'There, done it,' he said, tapping the top of it and putting his hand out as Caroline handed him back his coat.

'Thank you so much. You're an angel. What's your name?'

'Gabriel.'

'The angel Gabriel.' Caroline smiled.

When he left, she went into the bedroom, mentally picking out what she was going to take with her the day she left. The day she'd leave forever. She went back into the kitchen and feeling the sudden, familiar pain in her back, she took one of the morphine capsules, and an anti-sickness pill.

Then, she spotted Gabriel's gloves.

Checking the time, she realised that Adrian could arrive home at any moment and quickly called the florist back, telling the woman that Gabriel was not to return to collect them as she was leaving immediately to go on a trip. She told the florist that she would post the gloves back to the shop. Taking them upstairs, she thought about where to hide them, but as she glanced out of the window, she saw Simon's car pulling on to the drive. Followed by Adrian's.

In her panic, she opened the bedroom window and threw the gloves out, peering out quickly to see them landing in the bush below. She made a mental note to remove them when she got the chance.

What she didn't know was that from the moment Adrian walked through the door, after his day at work, she was never going to get the chance.

Except Adrian Crow hadn't actually been at work. He'd sat up the road all day in his car, watching the cameras on his laptop. When he'd seen the guy delivering a bouquet of flowers to Caroline, he knew that she had not one lover, but two. He'd watched the flower guy go inside and emerge some minutes later. Long enough to fuck his wife. It was when the guy reappeared at the front door, putting his coat back on, that Adrian felt the rage inside of him. That was when he followed the guy's car and banged into it. All he needed was his name and address. But when the guy had refused to play ball, Adrian tried to follow him. Unsuccessfully.

So, Adrian drove home instead – and caught Mr Mercedes pulling away from his drive.

He walked through the front door, to find Caroline extremely flushed and out of breath. *Two men in one day,* thought Adrian, his eyes scanning the place for the bouquet. *You've got rid of the evidence, you little slut*, he thought, as he cheerfully waved the piece of paper in front of her. Their reservation for the Hampshire Hotel in Llandudno.

CHAPTER 100

Wednesday 13 May

Back in the interview room, Adrian Crow sat with his arms crossed, looking very defiant. Anna pressed the 'Record' button while Sheridan scanned her notes. After the usual formal introductions and caution, she began.

'Why did you use the name Henry Blanchflower?'

Adrian closed his eyes before answering, 'Because he was a prick.'

Sheridan stole a look at Anna. She wasn't expecting *that* answer. The theory was that Adrian had used a random false name, when he set up the imaginary phone call.

'He's a real person?' Sheridan asked.

'He was a kid I knew when I was growing up. He was taller than most of us and he played on it. He was a fucking bully.'

'In what way?'

'He made me and the other kids do stupid things.'

'Like what?' Sheridan wrote a quick note to Anna: *Get the details of the Henry Blanchflower who was killed in a hit-and-run in 2001.*

Anna stood up. 'DS Anna Markinson is leaving the interview. The time is 16.12.'

Adrian continued, 'He threatened us that if we didn't do things for him, he'd burn our houses down. He threatened to kill my dog once if I didn't chuck a rock off a bridge on to a car passing underneath.'

'And did you?'

'Throw the rock? Yeah, of course I did. I loved my dog and Henry *would* have killed her. He was a mental case.'

Adrian went on to describe how Henry Blanchflower thrived on his size and power over the local children. He got them to shoplift for him, always with the threat that if they didn't, then bad things would happen. Adrian was terrified of him and it wasn't until Henry and his parents moved to Southport, an hour up the coast, that Adrian and the other children were finally free of him.

Anna came back into the interview room. 'DS Markinson has entered the room, the time is 16.16.' She handed Sheridan a slip of paper. *Henry Blanchflower, born 1948 in Bootle. Died 2001 in a motorcycle accident, Formby, Merseyside, hit-and-run. Found in a ditch, partial decapitation, no arrests made.*

'So, you didn't see Henry after he moved to Southport?' Sheridan continued.

Adrian grinned and then started laughing. 'Only the once.'

Sheridan didn't take her eyes off him as she pushed on with her questioning. 'When was that?'

'2001 out at Formby. Let's just say, I *bumped* into him.'

'Why don't you elaborate on that for me?' Sheridan said, a little impatiently.

Adrian crossed his arms, still smirking, happy to boast. 'Henry Blanchflower was getting on his motorbike in a car park. As soon as I saw him, I recognised him, and he recognised me. He saw me going back to my car and pulled up alongside. He was laughing about all the stupid things I did for him as a kid and asked if I'd managed to grow a pair of balls.' Adrian cracked his knuckles. 'I followed him out of the car park and when we both reached the coastal road, I smashed into the back of his bike and left him in a ditch. So, I suppose that answered his question. Yes, I *had* grown a pair of balls.'

'Did you know he was dead?'

'Well, his head was hanging off, so that kind of gave it away,' Adrian said bluntly.

'You were married to Caroline at the time. Did you tell her what had happened?'

'No. Of course not. I told her someone had damaged my car in a car park and driven off.'

'You killed Henry because of what he made you do as a kid?'

'Yes. He's to blame for all of this. You see, he's still making me do bad things. It's not me – I'm not a bad person. Henry gets into my head, and he tells me to do bad things. It's all Henry's fault.'

Sheridan tapped her pen on the table. She was weighing up the possibility that Adrian was building his case for an insanity plea. Did he really believe Henry Blanchflower was making him do these things? Or was he playing a game, pretending that Henry was in his head?

'When we were at the farmhouse, you shouted to Gabriel "Get away from her". Who were you referring to?' Sheridan had assumed, at the time, that Adrian was referring to *her* – telling Gabriel to step away from the police officer. Now, she realised he had meant for Gabriel to step back from Caroline.

Adrian licked his bottom lip. 'I was referring to Caroline. I didn't want any of you near her, especially that prick.'

Sheridan continued, 'And you said something like, "Look what he's done to her, he's a fucking monster"; who were you referring to then?'

'Henry Blanchflower, of course.' Adrian licked his lip again. 'I'm very parched with all this talking. Can I have a cup of tea?'

'One last question. The day you were arrested, we went to your house first. The kitchen was smashed up. What happened there?'

Adrian shook his head. 'Dear me. You don't get it, do you? *That* was Henry. He was in my head and I got angry. You see? All the bad things that happen are because of him.' Adrian stood up. 'Now, how about that cup of tea?'

The interview was terminated and after briefing Hill, Sheridan began preparing the case for the CPS to consider the evidence. It was late by the time she switched off her computer and headed home. Home to sanity, sanctuary and Sam.

CHAPTER 101

Sheridan opened her front door and excitedly scooped Maud into her arms. Maud yawned in her face.

Sam appeared from the kitchen, holding a large glass of wine.

Sheridan took a sip and told Sam about Adrian's interview and how she had wanted to punch him in the face.

Adrian Crow had been charged with the murder of Caroline Crow, Henry Blanchflower, and Mary Lee, along with the attempted murder of Gabriel Howard and perverting the course of justice. By the end of his interview, he had admitted that Mary Lee was buried in the grounds of the farmhouse and gave an exact location of where she would be found. Forensic officers had started the process of recovering her remains. Adrian had been further assessed by the psychiatric team. Their findings were detailed in a report that they shared with Sheridan. Adrian Crow was not psychotic. He was a liar. Adrian was remanded for court the following morning, before being bedded down for the night.

'So, he told you everything?' Sam raised her eyebrows. 'Why didn't he just keep his mouth shut?'

'Because some people love to talk about their crimes. They think they're clever and can't wait to boast about what they've done.'

Sheridan went on to tell Sam about her conversation with Simon Banks. Sam was riveted, as always.

'So, you think Simon was stealing morphine for Caroline?' Sam asked.

'Absolutely. But it'll be pretty much impossible to prove.'

'Would he go to prison if he was found out though?'

'Yeah, and he'd be struck off. He'd never work as a doctor again.'

Sam studied Sheridan's face as they sat top and tail on the sofa, with Maud in her happy place, lying across Sheridan's legs, purring like a train.

'So, how are you going to prove that Simon lied to you?'

'I'm probably not.' Sheridan raised an eyebrow.

'You think he shouldn't be punished, don't you?'

'I think he did what he did because he knew Caroline was in pain.' Sheridan rested her head back. 'At the end of the day, apart from stealing the morphine and supplying it to Caroline, he didn't do anything wrong. He was trying to help out a friend, a friend he really loved.'

'But he told you that he knew nothing about her illness, he didn't know she had kids, and he took the money out of her account because she told him she was buying a train ticket.'

'He didn't take the cash out for that. He took the cash out to buy her son a watch.'

'How do you know that?'

'Because when he left the nick today, I shook his hand and pulled his sleeve back.' Sheridan looked Sam in the eye. 'And he was wearing the exact same style of watch that we found in the farmhouse. The one Caroline got Simon to buy for her son.'

Sam smiled. 'You're not going to investigate him, are you?'

'Oh, I am. It's my job.'

'How thoroughly?'

'Not very.'

CHAPTER 102

Gabriel Howard answered his mobile. 'Hey. How you doing?' He felt a twinge of pain in his side as he eased himself down on to the sofa.

Oliver Elliot replied, 'All good. Any news?'

'Well, he's been arrested.' Gabriel breathed in slowly, holding his side. His injuries had healed well, but he was still in some pain. He was starting to feel normal again and was grateful that there was no permanent loss to his hearing.

'Arrested? That's great news.'

'Yeah, it is. That's both of them now.'

'So, what's next?'

'I need to let the dust settle for a while, see what happens and then carry on with the plan.'

'Is there anything I can do?'

'I don't think so, not for now anyway.'

'I take it you don't need any more stuff then?'

'No. That part of the plan's done now.'

'Okay. Well, just let me know if there's anything you need.'

'I will.' Gabriel ended the call and rested his head on the back of the sofa. The tears came too easily and wiping them away, he whispered to himself, 'I'm coming for you. And you have no idea how bad it's going to be.'

CHAPTER 103

Anna sat by the window of the pub and checked her phone. A moment later, she looked up to see Steve walking in, a handsome grin on his face as he made his way over. He bent down and kissed her on the cheek. 'You look lovely.'

'I look knackered.'

'Well, I always liked that look. Can I get you a drink?' Steve asked cheerfully.

'Dry white wine, thanks.' While he was at the bar, she studied him as he ordered her wine and a tonic water for himself.

She'd been apprehensive when he'd called her that morning, asking if they could meet up, somewhere public, just for a drink and a chat. She'd made it clear that although they'd recently slept together, it didn't mean for one second that the relationship was back on. She would never be able to forgive him for the times he'd hit her. Her trust in him had been battered. But she did agree to meet him.

'There you go.' Steve smiled as he passed her wine over and sat down.

'You still not drinking, then?' Anna nodded towards the tonic water.

‘Nope. Not touched a drop. I learned my lesson.’ He picked up a beer mat and began folding the edges. ‘We’d still be together if I hadn’t let alcohol rule me.’

Anna didn’t answer.

‘I was a different person back then, Anna. I’ve changed now.’ He sighed. ‘I know I’ve lost you, but I want you to know that I did love you. And I still do.’

‘Steve . . .’

‘I know, I know, we’ll never get back together. But can we at least be friends? We were so good together until I fucked it up.’ He wiped a frustrated hand across his face. ‘I’ll never be able to make up for what I did, but I’d like it if we could just meet up every now and then, like this, just for a drink.’

He was clearly welling up and Anna instinctively reached her hand across the table. He gently placed his own over it, linking his little finger around hers.

‘I’d like that,’ she replied. ‘I really would.’

Steve smiled. ‘Nothing serious, just friends.’

‘Just friends.’

CHAPTER 104

Thursday 14 May

Sheridan was at the back of the court as Adrian Crow was remanded in custody, with a date fixed to appear at the Crown Court a month later. Looking small and dishevelled, nothing like the killer he really was, he was led back down to the cells.

As Sheridan left court, her mobile rang. 'DI Holler.'

'It's Anna. They've found Mary Lee's remains.'

'Okay. I'm heading back to the nick now.'

Sheridan walked into CID. The place was buzzing after the result on the Adrian Crow case. But the workloads had piled up and her team didn't have time to take a breath as they knuckled down to concentrate on their other cases.

Sheridan plonked herself next to Rob Wills and cheekily stole a sip of his coffee.

'That's weird,' Dipesh suddenly piped up from across the desk. 'Rob, what was the name of that guy you dealt with a couple of months ago? The one who called in a burglary and then uniform found a load of drugs in his house?'

'Kenneth Blake. Why?' Rob answered, snatching his coffee back from Sheridan.

Dipesh continued, 'Because I've just been handed a job that uniform picked up the other day. This guy, Patrick Ryan, gets home from the pub and finds his house trashed, calls it in as a burglary and when uniform arrive, they find a shitload of knives, two guns and a hand grenade at the address. Ryan gets nicked, denies any of the stuff is his and they bail him out, pending further enquiries.'

'Any point of entry?' Rob asked.

'Nope, no POE, no sign of a break-in at all – it's almost identical to *your* job.'

Sheridan joined in. 'What's the update on the Kenneth Blake case? Has he been charged?'

Rob shook his head. 'No. I've had to keep bailing him – the Adrian Crow case kind of took over. I should be able to move forward on it now though.'

'Have either of these guys got previous?' Sheridan asked.

'No,' Rob and Dipesh replied at the same time.

Dipesh sat back in his chair. 'Talk about a weird coincidence, eh?'

Sheridan thoughtfully drummed her fingers on the desk. 'That's not a coincidence. That's a set-up.'

CHAPTER 105

Friday 15 May

Anna walked into Sheridan's office. 'I thought you were off today?'

'I am, just came in to tidy up a few jobs before my weekend off.' Sheridan smiled.

Her mobile rang. 'DI Holler.'

'Sheridan, it's Rob. Sorry I know it's your day off but—'

'I'm in my office,' she cut in.

'Oh. Okay, I'm on my way. I need to speak to you.'

Anna left to return to CID and clear up some case files. A minute later, Rob appeared at Sheridan's door.

'What's up?' she asked.

Rob sat down. 'You asked me to dig around and see if I could find a link between Gabriel Howard and Oliver Elliot.'

'And have you?' Her eyes widened, expectantly, hopefully.

'Well, not exactly. But I have found out something *very* interesting about Oliver. He's no trace on PNC, but there is *this*.' Rob handed her a sheet of paper and sat back, watching in silence as she read the notes typed on it.

Sheridan glanced up at him. 'How did you find this out?'

'I was talking to my dad last night and he recognised the names. He was one of the detectives at Hale Street who dealt with it.'

'And no one was ever arrested?'

'No. The police couldn't prove anything.'

Sheridan stood up. 'Okay. Thanks, Rob.'

'So, do you want me to keep digging and try to find the link between Gabriel and Oliver?'

'No. It's okay. You can leave it now.' She put her jacket on and switched off her computer.

Rob frowned. 'I know you, Sheridan. You've figured something out, haven't you?'

She smiled. 'I need to go.'

'Do you need me to come with you?' Rob stood up.

'No. I need to do this by myself.'

CHAPTER 106

Gabriel Howard opened the front door and smiled. 'Detective Holler, this is a nice—'

'Are you on your own?' Sheridan butted in.

'Yeah, Denise is at the shop.'

Sheridan didn't ask to be let in. Instead, she pushed straight past him and into the living room. Gabriel followed her, bemused.

'I know what you've been doing, Gabriel. I know everything. And I know who you *really* are. Let's start with the fact that your name's not Gabriel Howard. Your name is, or was, Joseph Sinclair.'

Gabriel stared, stunned. And then he sat down. Sheridan sat opposite him.

'I'm going to say three names. Patrick Ryan, Kenneth Blake, and Oliver Elliot.' She waited for Gabriel's reaction and noticed how uncomfortable he suddenly looked.

Sheridan continued, 'Patrick Ryan and Kenneth Blake were both arrested recently. Someone, somehow, got into their houses and planted drugs and weapons.' She paused momentarily. 'Whoever this person was, is the same person who broke into Oliver Elliot's house. *You,* Gabriel, *you* broke in and planted those things. You're setting them up and I know you've only just begun.'

'How do you know that?' Gabriel's voice was at a whisper.

'Because when police searched Patrick Ryan's house, they found a note under his pillow which read "*This is just the beginning*" and I'm assuming you left the same note for Kenneth Blake, so I'll be calling Kenneth later to ask him.'

She readjusted herself on the sofa. 'I know who Patrick Ryan and Kenneth Blake are. And I know what they did.'

Gabriel didn't respond. Instead, he sat with his hands clasped together.

'And I know that Oliver Elliot was involved, but now you're working *with* him to get the other two. So, I asked myself, why are you going after *them* and not Oliver?'

Gabriel remained silent.

'You see, I found out that Patrick, Kenneth and Oliver were all part of a drugs gang back in the seventies, calling themselves "The Seven" and unsurprisingly, there were seven of them. Their rivals were called "The Merseys" – they got their name from the rumour that if you crossed them, you'd end up at the bottom of the Mersey wearing a pair of concrete boots. The Seven and The Merseys hated each other.'

Gabriel looked at the floor.

'So, I'm going to ask you some questions and you *are* going to answer them.'

Sheridan noticed a subtle nod of Gabriel's head.

'Why are you working with Oliver Elliot? He was part of The Seven. Who is he to you?'

Gabriel bit down hard on his lip.

Sheridan raised her voice. 'Gabriel, *who* is he?'

'He's my father.' He looked up. 'And Edith Elliot was my grandmother.'

CHAPTER 107

Sheridan digested Gabriel's words before responding. 'You need to start from the beginning. Because I'm not moving from this house until you tell me the whole story.'

Gabriel sat forward and in resignation, he went back to where it had all begun.

Saturday 3 August 1974

Melissa Sinclair tucked her eight-month-old son, Joseph, into his cot before turning to kiss her five-year-old daughter, April, who was already asleep and clutching her favourite doll, Molly. As Melissa quietly closed the bedroom door, the doorbell rang and she opened it, lighting a cigarette.

'Hi, come in. The kettle's just boiled. You want a coffee?'

Oliver Elliot put his arms around her. 'We need to talk. Are the kids asleep?'

'Yeah.'

'Can I quickly see Joseph?' He kissed her on the cheek. 'I mean, I want to see them both, sorry.' He walked into the hallway and pushed the bedroom door open, the light shining gently across his son's face. He crept over to the cot and touched his hair, feeling its warmth and softness. Then, turning to April, he moved her doll away from her face and kissed her. Although Joseph was his son, and April was another man's daughter, Oliver didn't care. He loved them equally.

As he rejoined Melissa in the kitchen, he watched as she put her cigarette out and immediately lit another.

'We have to talk about you leaving The Seven. Patrick's fucking furious. No one leaves, Melissa, it's not an option.'

Melissa flicked her ash. 'I've already spoken to him, he's fine about it. He understands that I've got to think of my kids now. He's asked me to do one more job and then he'll let me go. He's paying me two hundred quid.'

'What's the job?' Oliver asked.

'He wants me to give a warning to The Merseys. All I have to do is walk into The Mason's Arms with a pram and leave it there, then walk out.'

'That's it? That's all you have to do? That doesn't make sense. What kind of a warning is *that*?'

'He said there's going to be a clock inside the pram with a message underneath that says "Tick tock". The message being that time's running out. Soon The Seven will be taking over and The Merseys will no longer exist. It'll give them a good scare.'

'So, you'll have to buy a new pram for Joseph if you've got to leave his at the pub?'

'No. Patrick's bringing me the pram with the clock and note inside, I'll just take Joseph out of it before I leave the pub. Don't worry, he's got it all planned.'

'When have you got to do this?'

'Next Saturday.'

'Okay. Well, that's crackin' news. Then you'll be free from all of this shit, and you can concentrate on the kids, eh?'

'Yeah. And I'll be two hundred quid better off. I'm going to buy April a new dress. I've seen one in Woolworths and I think she'll love it.' She smiled, stubbing out her cigarette. 'Easiest money I've ever made.'

CHAPTER 108

Saturday 10 August 1974

As Oliver Elliot knocked on Melissa's front door, he could hear Joseph screaming. Melissa had called earlier asking him to come over as Joseph had a temperature.

She opened the door with Joseph in her arms. 'I don't know what's wrong with him, he won't stop crying.'

Oliver took Joseph from her and kissed his forehead before gently rocking him back and forth.

'I've got to go. Patrick will be waiting for me.'

'I'll take Joseph, he'll be fine. I'll get my mum to take a look at him, she's great with babies.' He kissed Melissa on the cheek and went to leave, before turning around. 'I hope it all goes okay today. I'll come round tonight, maybe bring us some fish and chips?'

'That would be lovely. I'll pop into Woolies and get April's dress. Then I'll head straight home.'

'Take your time, just enjoy the day. Treat yourself. Joseph will be fine with me.' And with that he left, cradling Joseph in his arms.

Ten minutes later, Melissa was walking down Parker Street, hand in hand with April who was clutching her beloved doll, Molly. Patrick Ryan was waiting around the corner with the pram.

'Where's Joseph?' he asked as Melissa approached him.

'He's not well. I've got a friend looking after him.'

'Right. Well, just push the pram into the pub, get yourself a drink and before you leave, press the little button on the front of the clock and that will start it ticking.'

'Why do I have to do that?'

'Because the clock will tick for five minutes and then the alarm will go off. When they look inside, they'll see the note and they'll know we're sending a message.'

Melissa gave a nervous laugh as she whispered, 'It's not a bomb, is it?'

Patrick smiled broadly. 'No, it's not a bomb. Look, I'll show you.' He leant inside the pram, pulled the blanket back slightly and pressed the button. The clock started ticking. He pressed the button again and it stopped. 'See? It's just an alarm.' He reached into his pocket and pulled out a wad of notes. 'Here's your two hundred quid. Enjoy.' He smiled again.

Melissa took the money and squeezed it into her purse. 'Thanks, Patrick. So, then we're done, right?'

'Then we're done.' He placed a hand on her arm. 'No hard feelings. You've done a grand job, and you've never let us down, so I don't mind that you want out, honestly. You're a young woman with your whole life ahead of you. You don't need to be caught up in our wars, Mel.'

'Thanks, Patrick.' She looked down as April reached up and dropped her doll into the pram.

Patrick Ryan put his hand on April's head. 'There's a good girl.' And then he turned and walked away.

◆ ◆ ◆

The pub was thick with smoke that hung in the air like London smog. As Melissa walked in she spotted them all in the corner, The

Merseys, deep in conversation. None of them looked up as they shared a bottle of Scotch, huddling together like scheming rats.

Melissa pushed the pram towards the bar, holding April's hand as she looked around the place.

After ordering a Coke, she took a sip before holding the glass to April's lips. Setting the glass down on the bar, Melissa reached into the pram and pulled the blanket back. Revealing the clock face. She leaned forward and took Molly out, handing her to April.

And then she pressed the button.

CHAPTER 109

Sheridan could see the sadness on Gabriel's face as he spoke. 'Eleven people died that day. My mum, my sister, the barmaid, two men who'd been sitting at the bar and the six members of The Merseys gang. They were wiped out. Just like that. At the press of a button.' Gabriel continued, 'Oliver took me back to my mum's flat and put me in my cot. Then he called the police and said he could hear a baby crying, and that's when I was found. When it was discovered that my mum and sister had been killed, I was put up for adoption. Oliver couldn't keep me, not with the life he was living. Plus, none of The Seven gang knew that he was my father.'

'How come?'

'Because there were often tensions between members of The Seven. Patrick was the boss and Oliver didn't always agree with his methods of how he got things done. Oliver was worried that if Patrick knew that him and my mum were seeing each other and had a kid together, that Patrick would use it to get to Oliver if they ever fell out. So, he kept it a secret to protect us.' Gabriel cleared his throat. 'My mum had a small role with The Seven, making the odd drug run here and there. She was the perfect front for that kind of thing – no one suspected a woman with children.' He sighed. 'She was just a young woman trying to make the best of her life.'

'So, who was April's father?'

'I don't know. Oliver tried to find out from my mum, but she said she didn't know and April's birth certificate just said "father unknown".'

Sheridan had been listening intently before she spoke. 'The bomb had been rigged not to go off the first time the button was pressed. So, when Patrick pressed the button the first time, it started the countdown, but as soon as he pressed it again, it stopped. But when your mum pressed the button in the pub, it set the bomb to go off straight away.'

Gabriel nodded slightly, and a note of sadness crept into his voice as he replied. 'I know. She was set up. Patrick told Oliver afterwards that no one leaves The Seven.'

'Did Oliver stay a member of The Seven?'

'Yeah. Only Patrick and Kenneth knew about the bomb and Oliver wanted to kill them, but he's not like that, he hasn't got it in him. So, he decided to keep them close, pretend everything was cool – he would make as much money as he could and then leave. He made a *lot* of money and invested it all. He's a wealthy man now. By the early eighties, the police were getting closer to The Seven, they were following the members and it all got too heavy. None of them had ever been nicked for anything and so they folded. They all walked away and set up new lives for themselves. Kenneth and Patrick spent most of their money on drugs and booze, but Oliver was savvy. He always wanted to find me, but once I was adopted, he had no way of knowing where I was.'

'Does Denise know who you really are?'

'No. She knows I'm adopted but she doesn't know the truth about why.' Gabriel looked up. 'Are you going to tell her?'

Sheridan didn't answer. For a moment, silence hung in the room until she asked, 'So, you've been planning revenge on Patrick and Kenneth all this time?'

'Yeah. When I was twenty-one, my adopted dad told me what happened to my mum and sister, and I knew even back then I was going to get them for what they did. I just didn't know how. It took me years to learn and perfect how to get into people's houses, without actually breaking in. Once I found out where they all lived, I started watching them, whenever I could. I spent years watching and learning things about them, working out their routines. I wasn't in any particular hurry. I knew I had to get it just right.' He sighed. 'I had no idea that Oliver was my father.'

'So, what happened the night you broke into his house?'

CHAPTER 110

Wednesday 22 October 2008

Gabriel Howard stood deathly still. He'd checked his watch a thousand times and knew that any second now, Oliver Elliot would open the back door and pull his wheelie bin from the back garden to the front of the house, ready for it to be collected the following morning. Oliver Elliot would then go back inside, and a few minutes later, he'd emerge and get into his car. Gabriel knew that every Wednesday he visited a woman who lived in a flat by the Albert Dock. He knew he'd be out all night and not return until early the following morning. Like most people, Oliver was a creature of habit. All Gabriel had to do was learn those habits. And that took time. But time was on Gabriel's side and tonight was the night.

With his eyes fixed on the back door, he saw it open. Oliver appeared, grabbing the handle of the wheelie bin and disappearing round the side of the house. And that was when Gabriel walked through the back door, straight upstairs and into the spare room, where he hid inside the wardrobe. And that was where he was when Oliver Elliot left the house a few minutes later.

'So, that's how you got in? You just walked through the door?' Sheridan asked.

'Yeah.' Gabriel's head dropped. 'Except I didn't know Edith was staying there.'

◆ ◆ ◆

When Gabriel heard the front door closing, he climbed out of the wardrobe. Peering out of the window, he saw Oliver's car backing out of the drive. Taking the note out of his pocket, he read the words '*This is just the beginning*'. Stepping out of the spare room, he made his way across the landing into Oliver's bedroom, where, as he was about to leave the note, he spotted a photograph on Oliver's bedside table. A photograph of a woman, holding a little girl's hand. In her arm was a baby. Gabriel leaned in closer and suddenly stepped back. The picture was of his mother, his sister and himself.

His mind began to race, and he shoved the note back into his pocket. Now he was going to search the house. As he opened the bedroom door opposite Oliver's, he stopped dead. Lying in the bed was an elderly woman who looked up as the door opened.

'Who are you?' she asked, her raspy voice sounded surprisingly calm.

'I'm sorry. I'm sorry I . . .'

'Are you a burglar?' she asked, her eyes wide.

'No. No I'm not.' Gabriel put his hands out, palms up.

'Oh. Well, that's good. Not that I've got anything worth stealing.'

'I'm so sorry if I frightened you.'

'Well, as long as you leave now, then no harm done.'

Gabriel spotted the telephone next to her bed. 'I'm going right now, but . . . can I ask you a question? I know this sounds really weird, but there's a photograph next to Oliver's bed and it's of my mum . . .'

The old woman squinted at him. 'You're Joseph, aren't you? You're Ollie's son.' She patted the bedclothes. 'Come closer, I want to see your face.'

Gabriel stepped towards her slowly and she reached up to touch his cheek. 'Yes, I can see it now. You're my boy's boy. My grandson.'

Gabriel sat on the edge of Edith's bed, and they talked like two old friends. And that was when Edith told Gabriel the story of how his mother and Oliver had kept their relationship a secret, and how Oliver had protected him the only way he knew how. To give him up.

'So, you see . . .' Edith stopped talking for a moment and started coughing; lifting her head from the pillow, she started gasping for breath.

'Edith? Are you alright?' Gabriel jumped up.

She grabbed her chest as her face twisted in pain. A pitiful sound escaped her mouth. And then, the sound stopped.

'Shit.' Gabriel put his hands on top of his head. He quickly picked up the phone and dialled 999. Before the call was answered he whispered, 'I'm so sorry. I'm so sorry.'

He then placed the receiver into her hand, standing there for a moment, panic washing over his body. He had no choice, he had to leave her there. Her chest was still. He couldn't hear her breathing. Was she dead? He couldn't be sure.

He raced back downstairs and, opening a window, he climbed out, just as a police car pulled up.

He didn't bother running, his head was too full of what had just happened. The revelation of who Oliver Elliot really was. As the officers climbed out of the police car, Gabriel remembered the note in his pocket and quickly grabbed it and shoved it in his mouth.

'Spit that out!' shouted the first officer to reach him.

Gabriel put his hands out, furiously chewing the piece of paper, before swallowing it.

And then he felt the handcuffs being snapped tightly around his wrists.

◆ ◆ ◆

Sheridan nodded slowly. 'So, that was what you swallowed when you were arrested. The officers thought it was drugs.'

'I know. I spent the first night in the police station in a drug cell. They were hoping I'd shit out whatever I'd swallowed. But it was just a piece of paper.'

'So, when you planted the stuff in Patrick and Kenneth's houses, that's why there was no sign of forced entry. But how did you get out of their houses?'

'The same way I got in. You see, people have a habit of not locking their doors when they get home. All I had to do was wait inside the house until they were due back, then position myself in a room where I could easily walk out the door. I'd been watching long enough to know that when Patrick gets home, he goes into the kitchen and gets a beer out of the fridge, then walks out to his back garden and lights a cigarette, so I just waited in the living room, which is next to the front door and when he went past into the kitchen, and then into the garden, I walked out the front door.'

'And Kenneth?'

'When he gets home, he almost always goes straight up to the toilet. He then makes himself a coffee, lights a cigarette and sits in the living room. So, I waited in the kitchen and as soon as he was upstairs, same thing, straight out the front door.'

'How did you get in touch with Oliver after your arrest?'

'I wrote to him from prison and told him I was his son, Joseph. We met properly when I got out. It was then that I learned that it was only Kenneth and Patrick who knew about the bomb, the other members of The Seven had no idea. So I changed my plan to just go after them two.'

'Where did you get the drugs and weapons that you planted?'

Gabriel shook his head slightly. 'I can't tell you that. I'll never tell you, I'm sorry.'

'So, it was Oliver.' Sheridan nodded.

'No. It wasn't him,' Gabriel lied.

'I could have you followed wherever you go, and I'll find out where you're getting the stuff from.'

Gabriel shook his head slightly. 'I don't need any more stuff. That was just one part of the plan.'

'What's the next part?'

Gabriel didn't reply.

Sheridan rubbed her forehead. 'This ends now, Gabriel. I can't unknow what I know. Whatever you're planning for Patrick and Kenneth *cannot* go ahead.'

'I know.'

Sheridan pushed, knowing he would never tell her, but she asked anyway. 'What *was* the plan?'

'It doesn't matter.'

'Were you going to kill them?'

Gabriel rubbed his knee. 'No. I was going to make them suffer, but I wasn't going to hurt them.' He sighed heavily. 'So, what happens now?'

Sheridan looked at him. 'Well, for starters, there won't be any action taken against Patrick or Kenneth for the things found in their houses.'

Gabriel nodded in resignation.

'And I'm going to tell you this once. If anything happens to either of them on my patch, I'll have you arrested so fast you'll think your arse is on fire.'

'What if something happens to them and it's not on your patch?' He smiled wryly.

'Don't push me, Gabriel.' Sheridan stood up, taking her car keys out of her pocket. 'Look, I get it. I get that you hate them both for what they did, but you can't carry on with this one-man vigilante thing. You have to leave it now. And I know that won't sit right with you – but leave them alone. Like I said, if anything suspicious happens to them, I'll find out – I know everything that happens on my patch – and I'll know it's *you*.'

'I promise you. I won't do anything on your patch. I respect you too much for that.' He lowered his head, his voice almost at a whisper. 'You always thought that Edith Elliot's last moments were spent in fear. That I frightened her that night.' He raised his eyes and for a moment, they were locked with Sheridan's. 'She wasn't frightened, I can promise you that.'

Sheridan didn't reply. Instead, she made her way to the front door and Gabriel followed her. Before she opened it, she turned around to face him. 'Oh – you're getting a bravery award, by the way, for what you did at the farmhouse. I'll let you know when you're being invited up to headquarters to receive it.' She looked him up and down. 'Wear a suit.'

And with that, she left.

As Sheridan arrived back at the nick, Rob Wills was coming out of the gents' toilet. He looked around, checking no one was in earshot before whispering, 'How did it go with Gabriel?'

Sheridan frowned. 'What makes you think I went to see *him*?'

'I figured it out. My dad told me about the little boy, Melissa's son. He wasn't there the day she set off the bomb. So, I guessed that

Gabriel is him and . . .' Rob noticed the look on Sheridan's face. 'And I'm going to stop talking now.'

'That's a great idea.' She smiled.

'One question.' Rob whispered, 'Is it all sorted?'

'Yes,' Sheridan whispered back.

'And I take it you need us to take no further action against Kenneth Blake and Patrick Ryan through lack of evidence.'

'Yes.' She nodded.

'And we never talk about this again?'

'And we never talk about this again.'

CHAPTER 111

Scott Collins walked into the pub and made his way straight to the back office, where his father William was sitting behind his desk.

'This better be important.' Scott stood with his arms crossed.

'Please sit down, I've got something to tell you.'

Scott remained standing. 'Like the last time you had something to tell me? I told you then that I wanted nothing more to do with you, and I fucking meant it. We're business partners now, nothing more.' He dropped his arms to his sides. 'You lied to me. You told me my mother was dead and I spent my whole life thinking it was true. Just because you thought she was a danger to me and Phoebe, you made the decision to deprive us of the choice of having contact with her. She wasn't a fucking danger to us. Yes, she made mistakes in her life and probably regretted them. But you—'

'Stop it. Please just stop.' William burst into tears. 'She *is* dead.'

Scott sat down. 'What do you mean?'

'Your mum – Caroline – she's dead. For real, this time.'

William went on to tell Scott that he'd received a phone call from the police, explaining the circumstances around Caroline's murder, that she'd left letters and gifts for her children and had been planning to visit them before she died. William knew that when he called Scott that afternoon, he was about to lose him forever. Scott had hardly spoken to him since the police had visited them almost two months before. Scott couldn't believe that his father had pretended that his mother was dead all these years. And now she really was gone, in the most horrific of circumstances. And in that moment, William knew that any chance of reconciliation was gone.

When William had finished, Scott stood up. 'I want nothing more to do with you. I don't want the pub. I don't want to see you again. And I don't want you to contact me. Ever.'

And with that, he left.

CHAPTER 112

Gabriel dialled his father.

'Hey. How's it going?'

Gabriel took a deep breath. 'I have to change the plan.'

He told Oliver about his visit from Sheridan Holler. How she knew everything, except that it was Oliver who had supplied the drugs and weapons that Gabriel had planted. Although Gabriel knew that she probably did know. Nothing got past DI Holler.

'How come she didn't nick you?'

'She doesn't have any actual evidence that it was me.'

'So, what happens now?'

'Well, she said that if anything happens to either of them on her patch, then she'll come for me.'

'So . . .'

'So, I need to fix that.'

CHAPTER 113

As Sheridan drove out of the Kingsway tunnel, she called Kenneth Blake.

'Hello?'

'Oh hello – is that Kenneth Blake?'

'Yeah, who's this?'

'It's DI Sheridan Holler from Hale Street CID.'

'Oh, right. Your colleague DC Wills just called me and said I won't be charged with anything after that cock-up. Bloody right I won't be charged,' he snapped.

'That's correct, you won't be charged. The matter's closed.'

'What about the person who broke into my house? Are you going to find them? They totally trashed the place and fuck knows why they left all that shit in there. I told the spotty little officer that turned up that none of it was mine. I'm not into any of that sort of thing, I'm a working man, never been in trouble with the police. I want whoever did this to be arrested and charged. I pay my taxes and *your* wages, so I want you to put every officer you have on this and find that fucker and get them sent down.'

'We'll do our best.' Sheridan paused, raising her eyes. 'I just have one question. Did you find any sort of note in your house? Maybe something that was left by whoever broke in?'

'Note?' He hesitated. 'No. No note.'

'Okay, well, thanks . . .'

'So, am I going to get some kind of apology? Because if I'm not, then I'm going to make a formal complaint. I'm going to write to my local MP and tell them I was arrested for nothing and that spotty little prick who arrested me will lose his fucking job. You mark my words. I've been traumatised by what happened, and I don't know if I'll ever get over it. I want compensation and trust me, I'll get it. You lot should be out there arresting real criminals, not innocent blokes like me. It's a fucking joke.'

'Like I said, we'll be looking into it and believe me . . .' *We won't find a fucking thing, because we won't be looking.* 'We won't stop until the person's found.'

'Too right you won't.'

Kenneth Blake terminated the call.

Sheridan rolled her shoulders and whispered to herself, 'Fill your boots, Gabriel. Fill your fucking boots.'

CHAPTER 114

Saturday 16 May

Patrick Ryan squinted at the bedside clock as his phone rang and he reached to answer it.

'Hello?' He put his head back on the pillow and rubbed his eyes.

'Hello, Patrick.'

'Who is this?'

'Oh, that's not important. What's important is that you don't speak. You just listen.'

'Who the fuck is this?'

'Naughty. I said don't speak. I'm looking at your mum, right now. Nancy Ryan. She's just left her address – 16 Chapel Road – and she's on her way to the community centre on Haversham Drive, where she goes every Saturday between 10 a.m. and midday. She'll leave her scooter outside, and when she comes out, she'll make her way to the little Tesco's on Maple Street, where she'll get herself a pint of milk and a bag of sweets – the mint ones that she likes. She'll pay on her card – PIN number 2475 – and then head home. She's got a lovely little bungalow, but she really ought to fix that dripping tap in her bathroom. It's been like that for months now and she can easily afford to get it fixed, with her having six thousand pounds in her bank account. She really shouldn't leave her statements in that little box in her wardrobe. Maybe she's planning to leave the money to your daughter Debbie and your little grandson, Callum, so that Debbie can keep him at the day care centre he goes to three days a week on Satchell Road. Debbie could do with the money, what with that nasty little bald patch in her front nearside tyre, that looks very dangerous, and it would be a tragedy if something happened when she was driving home from her part-time job at Hornby Garden Centre. Yeah, Debbie definitely needs the money, that damp patch in the back bedroom is getting bigger and I'm sure that's not good for little Callum's lungs. Especially now that he has to use that inhaler for his asthma.'

'Who the fuck are you?'

'I'm your worst nightmare, Patrick.'

'What do you want?'

'I want you to do something for me. You have one month from today and if you don't do it then I will do unspeakable things to everyone you love. Tick tock, Patrick. Tick tock.'

◆ ◆ ◆

Kenneth Blake answered his phone as he lit a cigarette. 'Hello?'

'Hello, Kenneth.'

'Who's this?'

'That's not important. What's important is that you listen extremely carefully and don't interrupt me.'

'Who *is* this?'

'Last chance, Kenneth, you be quiet now. I've just been to your girlfriend Jackie's house at 63 Marlen Road. She was out, and I was going to have a cup of coffee, but she drinks that cheap powdered make and I like granules. The metal biscuit tin she keeps in the cupboard above the kettle was empty too. I was really looking forward to one of those orange chocolate ones she buys every week at the big Asda on Janer Road. You need to tell her that next time she goes shopping, she needs toilet rolls, she's down to her last two. Maybe she could pick some up when she collects Lucas from his football training in Sefton Park this afternoon. And tell her not to park her car so close to those trees. There's no CCTV there and someone could grab her so easily and drag her into the bushes. I was there the other week, and I could smell her perfume, I was *that* close. It was that Tom Ford, Grey Vetiver, the one she keeps in the en-suite bathroom. I guess she wears it because it reminds her of you. Did you buy it for her birthday last month, or did her dad get it for her? He seems like a nice fella does Eric, volunteering with his wife Angela at the children's play centre on Thursdays and Fridays. Now, *they* know how to keep their biscuit tin stocked up. I really enjoyed those fig rolls, haven't had them since I was a kid. I must say though, their bedspread, a bit old-fashioned, and the colour scheme? Purple and brown? Really?'

'Who the fuck are you? And what the fuck are you—'

'Now, now, Kenneth. Be nice.'

'I'm going to ask you one more time, *who* are you?'

'This is like déjà vu . . . Me, Kenneth? . . . I'm your worst nightmare.'

'What do you want?'

'Ahh, now that's better. Okay, I want you to do something for me. You have one month from today and if you don't do it, I will do unspeakable things to everyone you love. Tick tock, Kenneth. Tick tock.'

At the end of the call, Kenneth Blake opened the drawer in his kitchen and took out the note. The note that was left under his pillow the day he called the police to report the burglary. He read the words. *This is just the beginning.*

CHAPTER 115

Hill Knowles got out of her car and glanced across the road at her neighbour's house.

Parked on Gloria's drive was a brand-new sporty-looking Honda. After Hill's recent encounter with 'Elvis the will guy', she thought it best to check out this new visitor, so she headed over to Gloria's.

Letting herself in, she immediately heard raucous laughter. So loud that even Barney, Gloria's dog, hadn't heard her coming in and only barked when she pushed the living-room door open.

Gloria was sat in her usual armchair. On the sofa opposite was her friend, Doreen.

'Hello, Hill,' they both said in unison as Barney got up to welcome her and started sniffing her shoes.

'What's so funny?' Hill asked, watching Doreen wiping away tears of laughter.

'We're writing our obituaries,' Gloria replied, as if it was a perfectly normal and everyday kind of thing to be chatting about. 'Do you want a cuppa?'

'No, thanks. I just wanted to see who your visitor was. New car, Doreen?'

'Yep. I thought I'd treat myself. I'm loaded and my family have told me they want me to spend it all. So, I am. I'm off to Florida in a couple of weeks, so I thought, just in case the plane crashes, that I must write my obituary, and then Gloria thought she'd do the same, what with her dodgy ticker and all that. I mean, she could drop dead any time now, so she really needs to be prepared.' Doreen ducked as Gloria threw a coaster at her.

'There's more chance of your plane crashing than my ticker packing up.' Gloria looked up at Hill. 'Do you want to hear them?'

'Your obituaries?' Hill sighed. 'Yeah, why not, I could do with a laugh.' She perched herself on the arm of the sofa and crossed her arms.

Gloria popped on her glasses and read her notes out loud. 'Dearly beloved, we are gathered here today to celebrate the life of Gloria Mavis Wright. A woman of strength, courage, intelligence and who bravely fought many illnesses during her long but tragic life—'

'What illnesses?' Hill interrupted. 'You've never had anything wrong with you apart from a mild heart condition and that's only a recent thing.'

'I'll have you know I've got skin cancer.'

Doreen spat her tea out. 'No you haven't.' She turned to Hill. 'She's got a hairy mole on her left bum cheek. I've told her that cancerous growths don't have hairs growing out of them. I took a picture and showed my friend's neighbour's daughter, she's a dermatologist and she said—'

Hill put her hand up. 'You took a picture of Gloria's bum?'

'Yes, on my new mobile phone, it's got a camera on it.' Doreen smiled broadly. 'And a video. I used it the other day when my neighbour's cat did a poo on my back patio. I mean, I love cats, but this one goes like an elephant. I told her that I'm going to send the video to the papers – and if she can't control Floppy then I'm going to get a conjunction out on her.'

'You mean an injunction?' Hill replied.

'That's the one.'

'Who's Floppy?' Hill asked, mildly confused.

'The cat,' Gloria replied. 'Keep up, Hill. Floppy's the cat that shits like an elephant. Are you sure you don't want a cuppa?'

Hill stood up. 'No. I think I need something a little bit stronger.' She stroked the top of Barney's head. 'I'll leave you to it.'

'But you haven't heard the rest of my obituary,' Gloria said disappointedly. 'I talk about the time I was a lap dancer . . .'

Hill sat back down.

Doreen started laughing so hard that her cheeks turned a worrying shade of red. 'You weren't a lap dancer. You were drunk on port and lemon, slipped on a napkin at The Grafton ballroom in Liverpool in 1954, and landed on some poor fella who was sitting there minding his own business.'

Hill stood back up.

'You off, Hill?'

'Yes. Because if I stay here a minute longer, I think I'll actually go completely insane.' She made her way to the front door.

'Hill?' Gloria called after her.

'Yes?'

'Thanks for popping in.'

'You're welcome.'

'Do you want to see my hairy mole?'

Hill opened the front door, grinning at the sound of the two women cackling loudly as she closed it behind her.

CHAPTER 116

Sheridan was sitting at her desk when the phone rang. It was Hill.

'Yes, Hill?'

'My office *now*,' Hill replied before slamming the phone down.

Sheridan shook her head and, easing herself up slowly, she wandered off to Hill's office. The door was open and sitting there was the assistant chief constable. Two chairs had been strategically placed, facing him. One was already occupied by Anna, who sat bolt upright and looked extremely sheepish.

Sheridan's pulse began to drum in the side of her neck. *Oh shit*, she thought.

'Sit down, Sheridan.' Hill pointed to the vacant chair.

Sheridan sat.

The frown on the ACC's face was so deeply furrowed, it made his eyes look squinty.

Sheridan cleared her throat. 'Nice to see you again, sir.' *I'm in the shit*, she thought. Images of being back in uniform, directing traffic around Liverpool city centre flashed through her mind.

The ACC leaned back in his chair, his enormous arms folded across his even more enormous chest. 'Detective Inspector Holler, are you familiar with section 90 of the Police Act 1996, more specifically sub-section 56.2 and 65.3 paragraph 8?'

Sheridan tilted her head to one side. 'Er. Section 90 refers to the offences of impersonating a police officer, but—'

The ACC put his hand up to shush her. 'Sub-section 56.2 and 65.3 paragraph 8 specifically refers to the offence of a police officer of lower rank impersonating a police officer of a higher rank. It's a relatively new but very serious offence and one which you committed recently, where you impersonated DCI Knowles. DCI Knowles being of a more senior rank than yourself. Now, DCI Knowles has spoken to me privately, and – in your defence – she's told me that she holds you in high regard, and has asked that I take a lenient stance on this situation. However, *Detective Inspector* Holler, my position is this. I am the new ACC and I *cannot* and *will not* tolerate any breach of the Police Act. If I allow this breach to go unpunished, then it will open the floodgates for every officer in the whole of Merseyside police to go around flouting the rules and I have no intention of having a reputation as a soft touch. You are facing a very serious disciplinary.' He leaned down and lifted his briefcase on to his lap, flicked it open and took out a brown envelope, which he handed to Sheridan.

'I'm serving you with this. It's formal notice of my intended action against you.' The ACC turned to Anna. 'DS Markinson, I have decided that although you did not impersonate an officer above your rank, you were fully aware that DI Holler did, and therefore I shall be taking action against you as well.'

Sheridan jumped in. 'Sir, with all due respect, DS Markinson was acting on my orders and would never have gone along with it if I hadn't—'

'That's no defence, Detective.' The ACC stood up. 'I'm bitterly disappointed in you, DI Holler. I'd heard such good things about you and yet here we are.' He turned to Hill. 'I'll see myself out.' And with that, he left, closing the door behind him.

'Fucking hell.' Sheridan shook her head and opened the envelope. 'This is bullshit, it was a joke.' She flicked a look at Hill.

Hill shook her head. 'I'm sorry, Sheridan. I honestly tried to persuade him to be lenient, but he's a bloody rottweiler. He just wouldn't let it go.'

Sheridan pulled out the sheet of paper from the envelope and read it. One word. Just one word.

GOTCHA

She closed her eyes. 'You fuckers.' She balled up the sheet of paper and flicked it at Hill. And Hill did something she hadn't done for a very, very long time.

She burst out laughing.

And so did Anna.

Sheridan turned to her. 'You knew about this?'

Anna nodded frantically, unable to speak.

'Section 90 of the Police Act, sub-section 56.2 and 65.3, paragraph 8?' Hill was still laughing. 'I don't know how I kept a straight face.'

'Those sections don't exist, do they?' Sheridan was still shaking her head.

'No.'

Hill's door suddenly flew open, and they all looked up to see the ACC standing there, a huge grin on his face. 'I may be the ACC, but I do have a sense of humour.' He winked and left.

EPILOGUE

Adrian Crow pleaded guilty to all charges and was handed a whole life sentence. His claims of diminished responsibility were rejected. During a fight in the prison canteen, he stabbed another inmate in the face, causing him to lose an eye. Adrian denied the offence, stating it wasn't him. It was Henry Blanchflower.

Mary Lee's remains were laid to rest. Her mother visits her grave every day to be close to the daughter she lost. Twice.

An investigation was carried out into the missing morphine at the Cranmire private hospital. Due to lack of evidence, no one was arrested. The hospital have since tightened their procedures for the recording of drug delivery and dispensing.

Before Caroline's funeral, her body lay in the chapel of rest. And Simon Banks sat with her every day. Tucked inside her pocket were the earrings her daughter had bought for her as a child. And copies of the letters she had written to her children. Simon also placed one more item in her coffin. A one-way train ticket to Scotland, to send her on her final journey to the place she had planned to end her life.

Scott Collins gave up on the pub that he ran for his father, William. He moved to the Isle of Mull, where he lives with his girlfriend. He never spoke to William again. He still wears the watch his mother, Caroline, bought for him.

Anna and Steve meet up occasionally. Having promised he'd abstain from the alcohol that he blamed for his violence towards her, he doesn't touch a drop when they meet up. He saves that for when he goes home. Where he sits alone, plotting his next move to crowbar his way back into her life.

The investigation into Sheridan's brother's murder continues. Stephen Tubby denied that he was working on a building site near to Birkenhead Park at the time Matthew was murdered. The cold-case team are currently trying to locate witnesses who worked at the site, in the hope of placing Stephen Tubby there.

Gabriel Howard kept his promise to Sheridan, that he wouldn't seek revenge on Patrick Ryan and Kenneth Blake. Not on her patch.

After telling his family that he wanted to make a fresh start elsewhere, Patrick Ryan gave up his tenancy on his house in Liverpool and moved to Cardiff. Two months later, he was found by a neighbour after falling down the stairs. Having broken his neck, he was permanently paralysed and unable to speak. He now receives twenty-four-hour care in a nursing home where he is fed by a tube. Although it appeared that his injuries were not entirely consistent with falling down a flight of stairs, there were no suspicious circumstances surrounding his fall.

Kenneth Blake did not make a complaint to Merseyside police. Instead, he put his house on the market and moved to Birmingham. After returning home drunk from the pub one night, he fell asleep in his armchair with a cigarette in his hand. After being pulled from the fire that engulfed the property, he suffered fourth-degree burns to most of his body and face. After emergency surgery, his left hand and left leg were amputated. He continues to suffer with impaired eyesight and is in constant pain. There were no suspicious circumstances surrounding the fire.

Gabriel Howard received a bravery award from the chief constable of Merseyside police. Sheridan and Anna were there to witness his presentation. He wore a suit.

Doreen went on her trip to Florida. The plane didn't crash. She and Gloria are still working on their obituaries.

ACKNOWLEDGEMENTS

I love this bit. The acknowledgments. Why? Because it means the book is finished (phew) and I can now thank everyone who has helped me along the way. Of which there are many. Because at the end of the day, I'm just the storyteller.

First, as always, is you, the reader. Without you, there would be no books or certainly no reason to write them. Thank you to each and every one of you who has bought this novel, hopefully enjoyed it and if so, please leave a review. I do read every single one, sometimes behind a cushion in case it wasn't to your taste. But I read them because you took the time to write them, as you take the time to read my novels. Now, I know there are those who have fallen in love with Maud, the cat. So, I would like to put your minds at ease. Even though I kill off characters in my novels (being crime fiction and all that) I will never kill off Maud. Even if the series goes on and you astute lot realise she must be about thirty years old. Artistic licence will come into play in this instance. Or CATistic licence . . . See what I did there? . . . Anyway, moving on.

So, as in the first two books in the series, I also dedicate this one to Susie. You are incredible and I hope I tell you enough. You work as hard as I do and take so little credit. I'm utterly blessed to have you in my life and by my side. I promise one day I'll learn how to do all that fancy stuff you do on my computer. Just not today though, I'm busy. You are my strength, my muse and you believed in me from day one and that has never faltered. But we are a team, and a great one. Now, pop the kettle on, all this soppy talk is making me parched.

Next, my gatekeepers: Michael Doherty, Breda Byrne, Lorraine Burns, Jane Edwards and Katharine Robinson. You are the ones who, after Susie, read my manuscripts before I even send them to my agent. I love your honesty (most of the time), your passion for Sheridan Holler (all of the time). I listen to you because you are all older than me . . . (even though Jane Edwards swears she's younger. Trust me, she's not). Thank you again for your time, suggestions, feedback and excitement. And most of all for your love and patience. Oh, that's enough of all that. You're all brilliant but as always, remember your services are free of charge, so please don't send me bills for your time. I mean it. I won't pay.

Supt Sonia Humphreys: as always, thank you, my lovely, for your knowledge and advice on police procedures. Is there anything you don't know?! You help make these books authentic and I will forever be indebted to you. Not financially though. You're not getting paid either. And not only are you a brilliant and all-round wonderful human being . . . you gave me 'swamp toad'.

Fraser Ritchie: my ever-reliable CSI expert. Fraz, thank you. You are always there when I need you (time difference permitting). You're the one who makes sure that I get the forensic side of the novels right. Without you I'd probably look stupid. You don't need to respond to that comment by the way, even though you're probably tempted to. You're a star, cheers.

Paul Sturman: my firearms 'go to' expert. Paul, I can't believe we're on book three and I still haven't caught up with you for that beer. Shame on me. I shall darken your door one of these days and we shall drink. A lot. Thank you for your help as always. You top banana.

Joanne Farrelly: senior probation officer. Cheers, Jo, for all your advice. It was always a pleasure to work with you back in the day and you have been gold dust with your advice. Now, don't think you're going to get away with helping me just on this book. I've got your number on speed dial for the next one . . . and the next.

Mark Mosey: pharmacist. Mark, thank you for taking the time out of your crazy-busy day to advise me on the pharmaceutical stuff. You might regret it because you are now officially my 'go to' for all things drug related. You're a star and I'm so grateful for your help.

The Doherty clan (aka The Doh-Nuts): for all your incredible support, what an amazing family I have been adopted by. I can't name all of you here, because let's be fair, there are a LOT of you and it would take up too many pages. But know that I love you.

Broo Doherty: my amazing agent. (No relation to the other Dohertys I am surrounded by.) I'll never forget the phone call when you first read *Play With Fire*. I wish I could have bottled your excitement, so if I ever have an off day, I could re-play it. (Okay, I don't have off days but you know what I mean.) You are the most wonderful person and we adore our time spent with you, which isn't enough. I love your belief in Sheridan . . . oh and me. 'Thank you' doesn't cut it, so I'll just raise a glass and say 'cheers' . . . for everything.

Helen Edwards: translation rights genius. The woman who looks like the woman . . . you know where I'm going with this. You are a legend, and the lovely thing is, you don't even know it. Thank you for all you do (which I still don't quite understand). Hope to see you soon, even if it might confuse Susie as to who you are. Bless her.

Everyone at DHH Literary Agency: what a family you are. You are all very special and I am genuinely blessed to be a part of it all.

Vic Haslam: my editor. Your unerring belief in me is humbling. Thank you for everything you have done to make these books a success. I just cannot thank you enough for all your hard work, enthusiasm for Sheridan (and Maud, obvs) and this series. I know I email you at stupid times and ask stupid questions, but I only do it because I'm stupid. Did you not know that? You are wonderful and a total joy to work with.

To everyone at Thomas & Mercer: what a fantastic team. Thank you for everything.

Russel Mclean: my very picky dev editor. I won't go on about how picky you are. Joking aside, I love working with you and adore how excited you get when Maud makes her appearances. Thank you as always for all your hard work and for putting up with me when I type expletives into the comment boxes. Even when I threaten to throw something at you when you pull me up on POVs and stuff. I wouldn't actually do it. You live too far away. You're safe.

To my copy editor, proofreader and cold reader: you work so hard to get my books in tip-top condition and point out the mistakes that I've missed. You work behind the scenes, quietly and calmly, fixing stuff and I appreciate every one of you. Thank you.

Heather Bleasdale: audio book narrator. Heather, when I first heard your voice as Sheridan Holler, I knew you'd nailed it. You bring her and all the other characters to life and you make it sound effortless. I'm absolutely delighted that you were chosen to narrate the Sheridan Holler series. Thank you.

Lynn Parsons: thank you for your incredible support and friendship. And to think we got to know each other because I created a giraffe out of a parsnip (those who know, know). At the end of my long days writing, we always love listening to your show. Thank you, my friend.

Zillah Bell: I wanted this to be a surprise. You *had* to make it into the acknowledgements because you are my number-one fan! Thank you for your total enthusiasm for this series, your love of

Sheridan and her team . . . and, of course, Maud. Cheers, lovely! (You're smiling, aren't you.)

To the authors who have supported me. For taking the time out of your incredibly busy schedules to read my novels and give endorsements, share tweets about my books and all the other things you do.

To the bloggers, Instagrammers, tweeters and podcasters. I have had a blast with all of you and hope you are recognised for all you do for us authors. Let's do it again . . . I'll bring Jaffa Cakes.

To my wonderful Twitter follower friends. Some of you have been there from day one and you've stuck around. Thank you for every 'like', retweet and comment – I love interacting with you. What a great bunch.

A final note from me. I just want to say that there are times in my novels that I make up a road name or place. I only do this because it fits the scene I'm writing. I only ever want to do Liverpool and the Wirral justice. I hope I do. It's an incredible place and I truly feel like an adopted Scouser. Your warmth and your humour is infectious. So, thank you.

Oh . . . sorry . . . *this* is actually my final note. As you can see from the acknowledgements, I turn to a lot of people for their expert advice because I want to make sure I get the procedural side of my books right. There are occasions, however, that I may decide to bend the rules, just a little bit. So, any mistakes are mine.

Right, that's it. I hope I haven't missed anything or anyone. Catch you later. x

ABOUT THE AUTHOR

Photo © 2023 John McCulloch @ Studio 900 Photography

T. M. Payne was born in Lee-on-Solent, Hampshire and now lives on the Wirral with her wonderful partner. Having worked in the criminal justice system for eighteen years, the last fourteen of which as a police case investigator within the Domestic Violence Unit, she has now taken a break to concentrate on her passion for writing crime novels.

T. M. Payne is crazy about animals and if you walk past her with your dog, she will probably ask if she can pat it on the head. Or take it home with her. Or both.

She loves laughing, Christmas, playing golf (badly), walking along New Brighton beach (not walking her dog because she hasn't got one), snow, sunshine, sunsets, family and friends.

She dislikes beetroot.

Follow the Author on Amazon

If you enjoyed this book, follow T. M. Payne on Amazon to be notified when the author releases a new book!
To do this, please follow these instructions:

Desktop:

1) Search for the author's name on Amazon or in the Amazon App.
2) Click on the author's name to arrive on their Amazon page.
3) Click the 'Follow' button.

Mobile and Tablet:

1) Search for the author's name on Amazon or in the Amazon App.
2) Click on one of the author's books.
3) Click on the author's name to arrive on their Amazon page.
4) Click the 'Follow' button.

Kindle eReader and Kindle App:

If you enjoyed this book on a Kindle eReader or in the Kindle App, you will find the author 'Follow' button after the last page.